INNOCENT SEDUCTION

His back was to the door, blocking her way out. He was gazing down at her in that strangely intent way.

"Juliet." His voice was no more than a sigh as he gathered her into his arms. He bent his head, unable to resist the tempting lips. He kissed her, and she didn't pull away.

Surprise held her quiescent for the first few seconds, then her mouth softened under his kisses. Her senses seemed to leave her suspended and melting in the heat that sparked through her body. His strong arms and the close contact from shoulder to thigh burned like fire and was just as dangerous.

His hands locked behind her waist and his head bent to the neckline of her gown. She leaned back against his grip, struggling with her own desire. Palms flat on his chest, she strained backwards, forcing his eyes to meet hers.

"Captain! Is this your due for a paltry hair ribbon?" She heard her own voice, gasping and harsh.

Ross stiffened, the fire dying out of him. He stared into the gray, indignant eyes.

"Due?" He frowned. "No, dammit! That was a gift."

"Then why . . . ?"

"Haven't you ever looked into a glass? You're tempting enough to make any man lose his senses. Good heavens, girl, don't you know anyth'_____tion.

Reluctant Rapture

Marjorie Shoebridge

LEISURE BOOKS   NEW YORK CITY

**For my daughter,
Jill.**

A LEISURE BOOK

Published by

Dorchester Publishing Co., Inc.
6 East 39th Street
New York, NY 10016

Printed in the United States of America

Reluctant Rapture

I

For as long as she could remember, Juliet Westover had been awakened in the early hours of the morning by the heavy footsteps passing her bedroom door. During her childhood they had been firm and determined but in latter years the steps had become heavier, more stumbling. But always they turned into the room next to hers. Perhaps they were not as frequent as they used to be, but even so, Juliet buried her head in her pillow and drew the blankets about her ears, leaving only her small shaggy dark head visible.

She could foretell the outcome with accuracy—her father's growling oaths, the sound of a blow, the soft moaning, then the stamping away of those same footsteps, the creak of stairs and the slam of a door. All that was left was a muffled whimper, holding all the desolation of the world in its tone. Only then could Juliet relax and hope her mother would find peace in sleep from whatever nightmare visited her.

She knew her father was a violent man and many times had felt the sting of his hands on her ears when she had chanced upon him. With his massive girth and heavily-bearded jowls, he had seemed to her young eyes like some great bear. But unlike an animal parent, he seemed to have no affection for his young. 'Damned little hellcat' he called her, and his eyes always glowed malevolently when they fell upon her. Why did her father hate her so? Why did he seem to hate her mother too, although he visited her room so often?

During the daytime, Lady Westover moved about the house like some frail grey shadow and what little animation she possessed fled when she heard her husband's voice in the hall. Juliet watched the fading of her mother, and in spite of her sympathy, a tiny corner of her mind was exasperated by this lack of spirit. To be a docile wife was a woman's lot, her mother had said. A wife belonged to her husband and must obey his every wish and suffer patiently whatever treatment she received. Every man wanted children, especially sons to continue the line. Then why, wondered Juliet, did she throw him into such rage that he beat her to get them? Why not do as she was bidden? But despite the beatings, no sons came. Juliet would have liked a brother.

At ten years old she was enough the country girl to comprehend nature's procedure of procreation, but contrary to the litters and calves dropped with regularity by the animals, her mother had not foaled more than the once and consequently suffered for her shortcomings. It was all very puzzling.

As no one in the county ever called at Westover House and the family, it seemed, was not favored by invitations elsewhere, Juliet had grown up in the company of Farmer Shepheard's children. She was always welcomed by Mrs. Shepheard who had a soft spot for the small dark-haired girl with the soft grey eyes.

"Poor little thing," she had often commented to her husband. "You'd never know her for Sir George's child, she's that plainly dressed. A village girl is a sight better turned out. You'd think her mother would be ashamed to have her seen in those drab ill-made dresses."

Her husband nodded agreement. "Maybe the lady's no hand with a needle like you, my love, but it's my belief Sir George is as tightfisted as they come, save for his own concerns."

Mrs. Shepheard sniffed in disdain. "And we all know what those concerns are, don't we? 'Tis a wonder there's a penny left in that ramshackle place, what with his gambling and visits to low places."

" 'Tis none of our business, m'dear," he warned. "Now watch your tongue for the little lass is heading this way with the children and she do look as if a piece of your pie wouldn't do her any harm."

Diverted, Mrs. Shepheard ran an experienced eye over her healthy brood approaching the open kitchen door. Two strapping boys and a plump little girl were hers and in their midst was Juliet, slender as a blade of grass between three saplings.

They surged into the kitchen, only Juliet hesitating on the doorstep. She was well-versed in manners and awaited Mrs. Shepheard's invitation to step inside. It was never withheld and Juliet happily joined the children round the kitchen table.

"You all right, Ma?" asked the elder boy glancing at his mother.

"Of course I am, lovey. Don't fuss. It's not as if it'll be the first." She chuckled and patted her stomach.

"Ma's expecting," said the little girl proudly.

"Expecting what?" asked Juliet blankly.

The boys choked over their bread and jam. "A baby, silly. What did you think?"

Juliet reddened. "I'm sorry."

"We're not," said the girl. "I hope it's a sister then we'll be even."

Juliet gazed in astonishment at Mrs. Shepheard's cheerful countenance. She looked happy and there was no sign of bruises on her face—and this was her fourth!

Without thinking she said, "Mr. Shepheard must have beaten you a lot."

The children stopped eating to stare at her but Juliet was smiling sympathetically at their mother. "Papa believes it's the only way to make sons but he must be getting tired for Mama had only me." She dropped her gaze to the pie and missed the warning look Mrs. Shepheard gave her children. "And Papa really wanted a son so that makes him cross with me and Mama all the time. But you have two sons already. I suppose that makes a difference," she finished in a matter of fact tone.

Mrs. Shepheard turned quickly to the stove to hide the rush of tears to her eyes. Her ready sympathy now encompassed the mother of this child too. What she had taken for haughty avoidance of the lower orders by Lady Westover might just as easily have been a disinclination to reveal the scars of her husband's ill-treatment. And this poor child would grow into womanhood believing that beatings and not tender passions were a necessity for childbearing.

As she reported later to her husband, "I was hard put to hold my tongue, I can tell you! It would never do for me to criticize Sir George to his daughter." Her bosom swelled with indignation. "But that poor lady!"

"It's as well you held your tongue, my girl," said her man. "Sir George could throw us off this place if he'd a mind to, and

it'd set him in a real fury if the child had
gone back with any words of yours on her
lips."

But Juliet rarely saw her father and took
steps to avoid him by using the back stairs
in her comings and goings. Mostly she was
away at first light, racing into the woods to
stand in wonder as the drowsy world came
alive and the sun made lacework in the high
trees. Birds chirped and fluffed out their
feathers, greeting a new day, while the wild
ponies of Exmoor flung up their heads and
stampeded over the heathland in a wave of
joyous abandon. She loved to watch the sun
gild their rough coats as they nudged and
buffeted each other in play. Sometimes
they allowed her to come close, watching
bright-eyed, but a sudden noise in the
distance had them flying headlong in
packed formation across the moors.

Juliet was quite at home with horses. Although their own stable housed only her
father's old horse, she had learned to ride at
the farm. Whether bareback or saddled, it
was all one to her and she was the equal of
either of the Shepheard boys.

The first time Mrs. Shepheard had seen
Juliet riding her husband's big roan, she
had stood aghast with horror. Head laid low
to the horse's neck, black hair streaming,
skirts billowing thigh-high, the girl had
thundered that big brute like some
avenging fury over the fields and into the
spinney beyond the farm. She was not

using a saddle and her bare feet were clamped to the horse's sides.

Mrs. Shepheard almost swooned with horror. Visions of delivering the lifeless body of their daughter to Sir George and Lady Westover crowded her mind. Sir George was a magistrate. He would hang her man for allowing his horse to be used—they would be evicted—her children would starve.... She waited agonizingly for the scream and the crash of falling bodies. There was a thud of hooves coming nearer. They were bringing her the news of the tragedy! They paused before Mrs. Shepheard whose eyes had been tight shut to blot out the dreadful future.

"Good morning, ma'am. What a lovely day."

Mrs. Shepheard's eyes sprang open and she stared unbelievingly at the flushed face under the cloud of tangled curls.

"Never..." she gasped. "Never ever do that again!"

"Do what, ma'am?"

"Ride that—that brute of a horse." Mrs. Shepheard gestured with a trembling hand.

"I'm sorry, ma'am, but Billy said I might. I haven't done him any damage. He answers most beautifully."

"It was not the horse I was thinking of, young lady. What if you'd come off? How would I explain that to your father?"

Juliet shrugged, her expression suddenly remote. "I doubt he would have cared." She

looked down at Mrs. Shepheard's white
face and her conscience smote her. She
slipped easily from the horse's back and put
her arms round the woman's shoulders.
"Forgive me. I didn't mean to worry you. I
promise I'll never ride him again if you dislike it."

"I'm not against you riding, my dear, but
a young lady should be dressed properly
and ride a saddle horse. It isn't seemly
to . . . to show so much of yourself and ride
so furiously."

Juliet smiled with a hint of bitterness. "I
have no riding habit and there are times
when I must go headlong or burst into
flames. I am so sick of being poor and having nothing to wear that I feel like screaming with the sheer frustration of it all."

Her eyes looked so dark and stormy that
Mrs. Shepheard was suddenly afraid. There
was a look of her father as he had been in
his young days when Mrs. Shepheard was a
girl. The stories of the wild and reckless
behavior of young Sir George were history
in the village. Even after his marriage there
was little improvement in him. And this was
his daughter! Please God let her mother's
nature be dominant, prayed Mrs. Shepheard silently. But even as she prayed she
knew her plea was doomed to go unheeded
on this earth. The girl was the female image
of the man she remembered and the blood
of the Westovers ran too strongly through

her veins. The grey eyes set in the flowerlike face were those of a wild wood creature, aware of life yet innocent of its effect. How long would that inborn knowledge remain latent? Juliet might be ruled by her instincts but she was her mother's daughter too, and Mrs. Shepheard comforted herself with that thought. Sir George might drink himself into an early grave before the inherited evil showed its face. If he should be so obliging, Lady Westover could easily become again the woman she was and her influence on Juliet hold greater effect.

In the matter of needlework, Mrs. Shepheard had misjudged Lady Westover. It was her one accomplishment and this skill she had passed on to Juliet. Lack of clothes and the inadvisability of approaching Sir George had taught them both the virtues of mending and reshaping their attire.

As her sixteenth birthday approached, it became a matter of envy to Juliet to see the Shepheard girls—the second daughter now a bonny five year old—pass by in new prints and summer muslins and the boys show off in their homemade but well-cut jackets. Her own few dresses were dark and serviceable but no matter how many times the seams were unpicked and gussets inserted, there came a point when her growth outran the material.

"It's no use, Mama," she complained, wriggling out of a dress that was too tight under the arms and strained painfully across her young breasts. "I'll have to ask Papa for money. He surely cannot refuse when he sees me bursting indecently out of everything."

She stood in her cotton underwear, eyeing the dress with distaste. Lady Westover gazed at her as if seeing her for the first time and realizing, with a jolt of the heart, that her daughter was no longer the tiny twig she had been for so long.

In the tight and threadbare shift she glimpsed the blossoming of a woman's figure—the small breasts upthrust against the cotton, the tiny waist and long slender legs outlined by the pantalettes. Below the knees stretched slim brown calves and neat ankles. Juliet's dark curls, disarranged by taking on and off the dress, fell about her face, framing its delicate oval and darkening the grey eyes now frowning in exasperation.

Lady Westover made an inarticulate sound and her hand flew to her throat. She could almost see the ugly bruises forming on that flawless skin. If Sir George should marry her to one of his rich friends! It was not beyond him to use her for his own benefit.

"Dear God," she murmured. "It must not be."

Juliet glanced at her. "What did you say, Mama?"

"Nothing, child. "But she glanced at the door nervously although she knew the house was empty.

Of late, her husband had begun to entertain more but Lady Westover was never present at these functions. They were hardly the kind that a lady of refinement was expected to attend. But thankfully they kept Sir George from her bedroom. He always had been a gambler and a lusty man, and their arranged marriage had disappointed them both. For a man who had bedded most girls in the county and no doubt sired a few bastards, he never could understand why his frail and timid wife had not produced a brood of children. One child only and that a mewling girl. It was an unforgiveable insult to his virility and she had felt the weight of his hand in consequence. For herself she had long ceased to hope for a gentle word. Fear had been her companion for too long.

Over the years the house had become more barren and ill-kept as Sir George expended his wealth and possessions on his gambling passions, and she doubted that any of the land was unencumbered by mortgages. Her own jewelry was long gone and empty spaces on the mildewed walls pointed out the absence of miniatures and paintings. It was many months since a servant had been employed and Lady Westover was reduced to taking on each role that fell vacant for want of money to pay wages.

But all that was of no consequence in the light of her sudden realization of this moment. Juliet was almost a grown woman, and should any of her husband's cronies discover the presence in the house of a fresh young virgin, might they not come to persuade her into their revels?

It was not her imagination that had conjured up the sound of coarse female voices from below on the nights her husband entertained. In complete disregard of the respect due to her position, she knew beyond doubt that trollops were being brought into the house to satisfy the lusts of these dissipated idlers. These were men of good family from her own sort of background—men of wealth but of little character, ne'er do wells, blacksheep, younger sons and those who felt that life was for living, however much hurt they brought on their families.

As an innocent young bride she had thought herself lucky to be affianced to Sir George Westover. He was tall and romantically handsome with his black hair and steel gray eyes, but no novel she had read had prepared her for the harsh and casual deflowering she had undergone. He had used her arrogantly and without tenderness, freezing her emotions into an icy state of permanent fear. Her generous dowry had paid his gambling debts and that passion surpassed the fleeting attraction of his wife.

Lady Westover now gazed on their daughter with mingled feelings. On the one hand she was a biddable girl, well-schooled in the realms of ladylike behavior and taught by a governess until the money ran out—yet she was also her father's daughter. The dark hair and grey eyes were his, as was the proud tilt of her chin. Her eyes would flash in the same way when she was impatient to be done with a task but her temperament was not vicious. Pray God she would never become as reckless and uncaring as her sire, her ladyship pleaded silently, unaware that she echoed the prayer of the farmer's wife.

Juliet gazed down at her mother with laughter in her eyes. "No wonder I never get invited downstairs when Papa entertains. I would be ashamed to appear in the rags I wear."

Lady Westover started violently. "My dear child—don't ever think of walking in on them! They are your father's friends and even I am not invited. They . . . they play cards and such and must be left entirely alone. Promise me, Juliet, that you will never even attempt to catch a glimpse of them."

Juliet was puzzled by the vehemence in her mother's tone. "Of course I will not if you forbid me, but somehow I feel that I have heard ladies' voices. I assumed it was mixed company."

"No, my dear. You must have imagined

it. There have never been any ladies
present." She spoke so firmly that Juliet
accepted her words with a shrug of
indifference.

With her new insight Lady Westover
pondered deeply on the question of Juliet's
protection. The child was rapidly develop-
ing into a beautiful woman. Her father
might not be aware of the fact but if his
guests should catch a glimpse of her, there
was no knowing what might happen—for
George was usually too drunk when he
staggered upstairs to pay any heed to his
family. It lay with her mother to provide
that protection.

Since the advent of evening parties, Sir
George had ceased to visit his wife's bed-
chamber and she felt safe enough to
suggest to Juliet that they share the same
bedroom. Only one fire need be lit and the
spare blankets from two beds would give
them both a cozier night in the large double
bed.

Juliet was agreeable. Her mother had
recently seemed much happier, her eyes
less fearful. It was quite a time since she
had appeared with bruises on her face and
an equally long time since those heavy footsteps had stumbled into the room next
door. Sir George, it seemed, had at last
accepted that his wife would bear no sons
and Juliet now understood much that had
puzzled her in the past.

For so many years Lady Westover had

been a silent self-effacing creature in the house that it came as a surprise to Juliet to hear her mother's soft laugh. From her own blossoming womanhood she envisaged more clearly the girl who had come as a bride to the Westover house some eighteen years ago. The years with Sir George had not been kind but there remained traces of her fair fragile beauty. Juliet was shocked to realize that her mother was not yet forty years old, and it hardened her own resolve to allow no man enough dominance to create of herself a fearful shadow. She had too much pride for that.

She sighed. What was there to be proud about? A moldering old house, a drunken father too sunk in dissipation to care that his only child went in rags, and the sure knowledge that society had closed its ranks against the Westovers. It was humiliating but not the end of the world. She could shape her own future, perhaps in another place. To become drab and faded like her mother, pitied by the villagers and be-friended only by a farmer's family, was not to be tolerated.

Dear as the Shepheards were to her, the life of a village wife was not in keeping with her spirit. She smiled to herself. It would not be in keeping either with Mrs. Shep-heard's ideas for her sons. That good lady had kept a sharp but not quite unobtrusive watch on her sons' attitudes toward Juliet. Thank heaven neither of them had viewed

her in a romantic light for instinct told
Juliet that a mingling of Westover blood
with good Shepheard stock would be disastrous to the sensibilities of Mrs. Shepheard.

That evening was spent the same as any
other. Juliet was reasonably pleased with
the dress she had fashioned from an old red
curtain. The color was faded and the cotton
was old but there had been just enough
material to give the garment tiny cap
sleeves. It was not the height of fashion—
she knew nothing of that—but it covered
her adequately and a frail piece of lace
hemmed to the neckline gave it a hint of
faded elegance.

As she smoothed out the lace she wondered for a moment what it would be like to
be rich enough to have gowns fashioned for
her by expensive modistes—gowns of satin
and lace, stitched about with pearls and
silver tissue—while she, a glittering figure
in diamonds, was the cynosure of all eyes.
The gentlemen, elegantly attired in knee
breeches, silk stockings and brocaded
coats, would be drawn like bees to the
honey of Miss Juliet Westover, that most
delectable of creatures.

She smiled, mocking her thoughts. It was
her birthday eve but with no disturbance of
their routine. She imagined even her
mother had forgotten.

But here she misjudged Lady Westover.
When they retired for the night, her mother

went to the old bureau that had come to the house with her.

"Even your father does not know of the secret drawer," whispered Lady Westover as she beckoned Juliet near. "All my jewels are gone but I was determined he should never know of the ring my mother gave me when I was sixteen. It belonged to her mother too, and I could not bear the thought of it being sold to pay gambling debts." She stared into Juliet's face sadly. "You cannot help but know your father's nature and his passion for gaming which has brought us to this ruinous position. He never seems to win and borrows only to lose again. There will be no dowry for you, my dear. Your looks will commend you . . . but then, I suppose a man prefers the more enduring things of life."

Her look was so desolate that Juliet gripped her hands fiercely. "Dowry?" she demanded. "I need no dowry! I shall never marry and put myself at the mercy of a man."

"But it is usual. . ."

"Then I shall be unusual! No man shall break my spirit and use me as you have been used. No man will ever take what I do not freely give. I am sorry, Mama, but I know what your life has been like and I do not intend to endure the same way of living."

"You are under age, my dear, and can only obey your father in the matter of your future."

Juliet laughed harshly. "My father is barely aware of my existence. Our dislike is mutual. If he should come to realize that I am now a woman and seek to capitalize on that fact, it will not be to my advantage but his. I belong to myself until I choose differently and it will be my choice."

Lady Westover gazed at her daughter for a heart-turning moment. With Juliet's grey eyes sparkling, her black curls almost alive by themselves and her heart-shaped face animated by passion, Lady Westover realized too well that Sir George might belatedly come to the conclusion that this girl was a valuable asset in his constant search of money. One glimpse of her in this mood and he would seek to line his pockets at her expense. Lady Westover had no illusions about the man she married. As long as he was able to indulge his gambling fever, any means in his power would be used to further that indulgence.

She reached into the secret drawer and turned, forcing her stiff lips to smile. "Here is my present to you, Juliet. It is the last thing I own but you must always keep it, with my love."

Juliet stared down at the ring, her face softening. "Oh, Mama, it is beautiful. How can you bear to part with it?"

"I dare not wear it so what use is it to me? See, the ruby glows so wonderfully and the tiny diamonds framing it are like stars round a blood-red moon. Wear it tonight so

I may see it adorn your finger but from tomorrow you must hide it away."

Juliet kissed her mother's sunken cheek gently. "Thank you, Mama. I shall never part with it and tomorrow it shall hang inside my dress on a ribbon. It will go with me always."

She helped her mother into bed and sat for several minutes on the edge, turning her hand about so that the ruby and diamond ring glittered and flashed in the light of the candle set in the tarnished brass candlestick on the chest.

"Come to bed, child. You will catch a chill in that old shift. It barely covers you."

Juliet smiled and slid into bed, taking a last look at the ring before snuffing the candle. The moon was full and its light streamed through the uncurtained window. Juliet moved her fingers to catch a moonbeam on her ring. Its glow was deep and mysterious, a blood-red moondrop, and Juliet fell asleep pondering on other hands that had worn this same ring.

An outbreak of distant laughter brought her half-awake. She turned her head into the pillow to shut out the noise from below. There was a crack and tinkle as of shattered glass and she realized hazily that her mother's body had grown taut and still.

Sleep tried to draw her down into its restful pool but a rising sense of alarm made her fight to reach the surface of consciousness. Was the noise louder than usual? Whose were those footsteps, now pausing, now stumbling?

The moonlight seemed to cast an eerie green radiance over the room as sleep fled from Juliet. Lady Westover was sitting bolt upright in the bed, her thin arms hugging her slight frame. From eyes that were dark pools of terror, her gaze suddenly scorched Juliet.

"Get out! Go and hide! He must not find you here!"

Infected by her mother's fear, Juliet half-fell from the bed, terror searing through her body, making her movements jerky, her mind disordered. Hide? There was nowhere to hide! The window? She fled to the chest that stood under it, overturning the brass candlestick in her panic.

The catch was stiff. She climbed onto the chest. Her cold fingers fumbled frantically as she tried to pull up the lower half of the window. It gave with a protesting shriek. So rapidly did it rise that Juliet had to cling to the upper frame to avoid falling headlong into the garden.

But her efforts at escape were too late. The bedroom door was flung open. Swaying on the threshold was Sir George Westover. From bloodshot eyes he surveyed his wife, sitting wide-eyed and hypnotized like a rabbit facing a snake. The sheets were drawn up to her shoulders and her fingers grasped the cotton nervously.

Sir George wiped the sweat from his face, and the aroma of the tavern pervaded the room. His grey hair was damp, his face red and blotched. Wine and food stains marred the waistcoat bulging over self-indulgent corpulence. He held a candle as he swayed.

Juliet repressed a shudder of revulsion. He had not yet noticed her, the light from the candle falling only on the bed. She dare not move and draw his attention but her up-raised arms gripping the window were growing chilled, as were her legs, fully in the path of the night breeze. The old shift barely reached her thighs.

Sir George peered down blearily at his silent wife. "You think I don't know you've still got it, don't you? I had your father make a list when I took you. I know—knew —to the penny what you were worth and I've been waiting, counting them off."

His wife remained silent.

"Don't pretend you don't know what I'm talking about, you milk and water bag of old bones! Every diamond, every emerald, every damn stone you had I knew about. Now I want the ruby ring."

Lady Westover stared at him piteously. "It was my mother's and my grandmother's. Can't you leave me just that?"

"They're dead, aren't they? And what good is it to you? I need it to settle a debt. I know there's a secret drawer in that bureau but I'm damned if I could ever find it. Get up and open it."

"I haven't got the ring anymore."

"You're lying, woman. Get out of that bed," Sir George growled, coming closer.

Lady Westover threw back the sheet and went to the bureau. She opened the drawer and stood back. "You can see it's empty." Her voice trembled but she held still, keeping her gaze fixed on his face, afraid but defiant.

The gross face purpled and the blow he dealt his wife sent her staggering back toward the bed.

Juliet could stand no more. "Leave her alone!" she shouted fiercely. "She's telling the truth."

Sir George's head came up sharply and he tried to focus on the area from where the cry issued. A shaft of moonlight edging from behind a cloud illuminated a slender, shift-clad figure, seemingly poised in midair and surrounded by a nimbus of light.

He blinked, his gaze taking in the length of bare leg, the young body outlined against the light, then rising to the breasts held high by the upraised arms. The glitter of a ruby caught his eye.

"What's this?" he snarled at his wife. "Has your brain turned with age? Who is this slut that shares your bed and wears my ring? How dare you bring up a kitchen wench and let her flaunt my property? What right have you to do as you please, woman? It seems I must teach you who is master here!" He slammed down the candlestick on the bureau and the naked lust glittered in his eyes. "By God, I'll take both the wench and the ring before the night is out."

Juliet jumped off the chest, her heart beating painfully. Through swollen lips her mother uttered a strangled cry of despair and reached out.

"George, you can't . . . you don't understand. . ."

He thrust her aside, struggling out of his coat and waistcoat. "Out of my way! I'm not too old that I can't handle a wench without your advice."

Juliet felt sickness rise in her and her hand went to the chest for support. Her fingers brushed the brass candlestick. She gripped the stem and her strength revived. Her eyes darkened, and hatred of this man grew from a spark to a deadly flame. Let him come close and he would read murder in her eyes. Let him be snuffed out like a candle, she thought wildly, for all the suffering her mother had endured at his hands. He was no father to her but an evil lecherous enemy, a man who should be put down like a vicious animal.

Lady Westover flung herself upon her husband with a despairing shriek.

"For the love of God, George! She's your daughter!"

In a blind rage, Sir George took her by the throat and hurled her away.

"Dammit, woman, leave me be!"

For a long moment he stared stupidly at Juliet, shaking his head like a dog flinging away water. He swayed, staggering a little, his gaze full of uncertainty, the words of his wife slowly filtering through to his consciousness.

Juliet brought the candlestick into view. Suddenly she felt supremely confident. She crouched a little, baring her teeth. "You should have listened. Mama was telling the truth. A father who would carry out what you had in mind is too evil to live. The world will be cleaner without you."

"I didn't know . . . I wouldn't have. . ." he said, his eyes uneasy. "Put down that candlestick and we'll say no more about it. But give me that ring."

"I shall do neither, dear Father," she said mockingly. "I intend that you suffer tonight as my mother has suffered for years. I shall kill you and glory in it."

He backed away. "You're mad . . . unhinged! Keep the ring if you must but put down that damned candlestick."

"Oh, no, dear Father." She advanced on him. Perhaps she was a little mad at that moment but her mind seemed to turn and spin with clarity and his death became part of a glorious crusade. He was the infidel, she the bearer of the cross that was to strike him down into hellfire.

"Juliet . . ." he began, and the candlestick flashed down. He staggered back, cursing, a hand to his head. Blood trickled slowly from a deep cut. "Hell and damnation—you savage bitch! A taste of the whip you'll get for this! A hell-cat if ever I saw one! But would you bare your claws at me? I am your father, do you hear?"

Juliet's face contorted with disgust. "Since when did you give any thought of that?" she spat at him. "Or consider the woman who bore me? We've lived in rags like gypsies, shunned by even the commonest people, head over heels in debt throughout the village, and all because you must grub up every penny for your accursed vice."

With the candlestick raised aloft she bore down on him, her mind ablaze with hatred. He should learn the nature of the child he had sired and know that here was no pale imitation of the woman he had dealt with so cruelly. No thought of consequences crossed her mind. She had made a vow like some knight to his king and it was sacred vengeance she sought—the destruction of evil in the name of honour.

Her second blow took him painfully on the shoulder and brought him from his stupor. With a roar of anger his hands reached out but she twisted away, teeth bared, hair flying. Sir George eyed her balefully, his eyes narrowed and watchful. She was mad—no doubt of it. But her madness was dangerous. She must be caught and put away before she could do him more damage. He couldn't have such a savage creature in the house. It was beyond all supporting. There was an insane glitter in her eyes that warned him of her intent to carry out that wild threat if she could.

He laughed swiftly, his heavy body propelling him forward. Juliet moved but too late. Sir George's hand reached the candlestick. They fought for possession like wild animals.

Juliet's vision of a glorious crusade faded and she struggled with all her strength to retain her weapon and retreat from this massive embrace of wine-drenched flesh. But the sheer weight of the heavy body prevailed and the candlestick was torn from her grasp. As his grip relaxed, she pulled free and backed away, her breath coming jerkily, her spirit plummeting in despair. She had lost. He was still alive to torment her mother and deal out further punishment to them both.

"Now, by God!" Sir George growled, shooting her a venomous glance. "We'll see who's master here. A bedlamite if ever I saw one. I'd not believe a child could strike her own father—and in front of her mother, too!"

Juliet's head jerked up and she flung herself forward. "Mama!" she screamed. "Where are you? Are you all right?"

Heedless of her torn outfit and the amount of bare leg she showed, she was across the room in a flash, her eyes searching. Beside the bureau, where she had been flung, lay her mother. Juliet dropped to her knees, her fingers reaching gently towards the livid face discolored by bruising. Her fingers froze before they touched. Lady Westover's head lay at an impossible angle. The cold came swiftly, freezing Juliet into a rigid statue of a crouching girl.

Lady Westover's neck was broken. There was no doubt of it. The room was very silent, Juliet completely unaware that her father had gone white with fear as he gazed down over her shoulder.

A violent shudder ran through her and she covered her mouth with her hands. Through a blurring of sudden tears, the ruby on her finger grew and shimmered like a spreading blood-red pool. Blood on her hands—the blood of her mother! She gasped, holding the ringed hand away from her face. It was evil—she hated it for destroying her mother. And yet Lady Westover had hidden it away, waiting for the right moment to present it to her daughter. She had treasured it more than any other piece of jewelry, defied her husband's demand and suffered his blows in its defense. And at the last she had died defending her daughter's innocence and her right to own the ring.

"Oh, Mama," she whispered. "I never meant this to happen. I would have given up the ring. Forgive me . . . I'm sorry. . ."

A wave of stale wine assailed her nostrils. Sir George held her shoulder in a fierce grip. She stared up, wide-eyed, dismayed by the cunning and vindictive expression on his bloated face.

"Sorry, are you? So you will be, you insane murderess! You'll hang for this! As your father I can't preside on the bench myself, though I am a magistrate, but by God, I'll bear witness to this foul deed when you're committed to the Crown Court."

"What are you saying . . . you know I am innocent of this!" She stared at him aghast. Was her father calling her murderess?

"And I suppose you're innocent of this, too?" he growled, pointing a thick finger at his forehead.

"No, but. . ."

"What jury will believe your word when they see the injuries I sustained in trying to protect your mother? I would hardly have inflicted them on myself!"

"I will admit to striking you but never to the murder of my mother. How dare you accuse me of it when it was you who threw her down?"

"By God, don't play the innocent with me. You wanted her ring on your finger and she wouldn't give it up. I always respected its sentimental value and let her keep it though she offered it many a time. Had I known the viciousness of your nature earlier, I would have taken it and removed the temptation from your path. Now you have robbed me of a loving and devoted wife! Do you expect forgiveness?''

Juliet stared at him for a long moment. "It seems I need expect nothing from you," she said slowly. "You would send your own daughter to the gallows to save yourself. But don't think I'll stand mute in the dock. The world shall hear of the life we led and know you for the monster you are.''

"The ravings of a lunatic girl," he scoffed. "Who will believe the stories you invent? If you escape the rope, they'll clap you into the madhouse and I'll make sure it's one or the other. You're too dangerous to be let loose on civilized society. You leave here as soon as I can get the constable." He gave her a long brooding look and his small eyes showed no mercy. "You think I want a hell-cat about the place any longer? The sooner you keep an appointment with the hangman the better, and there's nothing you can say that will make me change my mind.''

He left the room. She heard the key turn in the lock and she was alone. But not quite alone. Her mother's body still lay on the floor. Juliet moved swiftly to the poor broken creature, her heart full of grief. She was not afraid to look on the dead face of the woman she had not really known.

"I never loved you enough," she whispered. "I never understood or tried to help. We could have fought him together. . ." She was still murmuring brokenly as she lifted

the frail body gently and laid it on the bed.
She straightened the lolling head and
placed her hand on the cold brow. "Look
down on me, Mama, and say that you
forgive my part in your death." A violent
shudder racked her. We shall meet soon and
I need your help to face what is to come. Let
me go as bravely as you did."

She put the covers in place but left the
face exposed. Lady Westover was at peace.
For her there was no more suffering.

Slowly Juliet began to dress. The red
cotton gown she slipped over her shift, then
donned the mended pantalettes and stockings. She slipped her feet into scuffed
slippers and stared round a little helplessly. What did one take to prison? There
was so little she possessed but cleanli-
ness must be a first consideration, she
supposed, visualizing a dank, mouse-
infested dungeon. Into a small tapestry bag
of her mother's she placed her hairbrush
and comb, a small wedge of soap and a
rough towel. Another pair of mended
stockings, an equally threadbare shift and
an old shawl followed. With an apologetic
glance at her mother, she drew out from the
wardrobe a plain cloak of Lady Westover's.

There seemed nothing else to do so she
sat by the window watching the sky slowly
lighten. Would she see another sunrise?
Through the bars of a prison cell, she supposed, and not many of those if her father
had his way.

She stared down at the ring. Yesterday she had been a child, expecting nothing, but her mother had not forgotten her sixteenth birthday—the day when, for most purposes, she officially became a woman. All these years she had kept the ring for this special occasion. But what had her determination achieved? Only the sacrifice of her own life and the recipient of the gift destined for the gallows. Surely one ring was not worth the destruction of two lives?

Juliet rose and began to pace the room. The shock of what had happened was wearing off. Was she to sit waiting patiently until they came for her? Did her father expect her to be so spiritless that she would accept a guilty verdict and go meekly to the hangman?

She crossed to the window and looked out. The stone walls were bare of creepers—there was nothing to facilitate a descent. This room was two flights of stairs high and to jump from the window would have the same result as falling through the hangman's trap. Even a rope would need to be some thirty or so feet long and it was not the sort of thing one usually kept in a bedroom. There was no escape, it seemed, but the court should hear her version of this night's work and judge for themselves. But underneath her bravado, she realized that her father's status was superior to her own. He was a magistrate himself, a man pledged to uphold truth and justice. Would they not believe him without question? And to save his own life he must accuse her of the crime he himself had committed.

She raised her head. The sound of hooves and the creaking of a carriage came to her clearly. Sir George had not wasted any time. She rose and approached the bed for the last time, bending over her mother in a gesture of farewell. Then she turned and faced the door, waiting.

It was over. The jury had returned the verdict expected of them. Juliet had known her fate the instant they filed back, eyes carefully averted from the prisoner in the dock. A sigh ran through the public gallery and the onlookers stared down at the small erect figure gripping the rail. The Quarter Sessions at Exeter was one of the highlights of the year and those lucky enough to gain entrance were sure of a rapt audience when they related the details of this particular case.

She was a cool one all right, they muttered to each other. No creature guilty of such a fearsome crime should be so composed. It offended their sense of what was right and proper. An exhibition of remorseful tears, an hysterical plea for mercy would have been more fitting—and a great deal more exciting—but this girl seemed lost to all decency, daring to accuse her poor heartbroken father of the crime. She, not he, ought to be the one to hide her face beneath her hands.

Juliet knew that between the fingers of his hands her father's eyes never left her.

"This most heinous of crimes . . ." the red-robed judge was intoning. Sir George leaned forward suddenly, his hands on the prosecutor's gown.

"Matricide—no more despicable act in the history of. . ." The prosecutor's brow rose and he gave a little shake of the head.

"Do you have anything to say before I pronounce sentence?"

"No, your lordship." Juliet's eyes returned to her father. He was suffering some agitation, his words to the Crown counsel insistent.

The judge became aware of the subdued altercation. He turned a frowning bewigged face towards them.

"Is there something you wish to put before this court, sir? A plea of mitigation, perhaps? Speak up, please. I am about to pass sentence."

"The ring, my lord," her father blurted out. "Make her tell where it is."

"The ring?" The judge looked bewildered.

"The one she killed her mother for. I can't find it."

"Really, Sir George! In view of the seriousness of this crime, I wonder that your thoughts are on such minor matters as a mere trinket."

"Forgive me, my lord, but it has a deep sentimental value for me."

"Very well. I will put the question to the prisoner if you insist."

In answer to the judge's question Juliet turned and faced her father squarely. For the first time during the trial she allowed a slight smile to show.

"I returned it to Mama. Didn't you notice when you made your last farewell? When you held her dear hands in yours as you said?" She allowed a touch of irony to enter her voice. "I was sure it would have been your wish, dear Papa, to have her take it with her."

Sir George Westover's mouth went slack and his shoulders sagged as he understood the meaning of her words. The ring was lost to him forever.

The judge took his silence for acceptance of the point and turned his gaze back to Juliet.

"It is the sentence of this court that you be transported to the penal colony in the settlement of New South Wales on the continent of Australia. There you will remain in servitude for the rest of your natural life."

II

The months Juliet spent in a Bristol jail were merely a foretaste of greater horrors to come. Most of the women prisoners were prostitutes, petty thieves or poverty-stricken wretches taken for stealing food for their children. Some nights there were fights which the jailor broke up with heavy-handed violence, striking out at everyone within reach of their clubs. They answered the obscene language with as much foulness of tongue, and Juliet cringed against the walls with the less belligerent inhabitants.

Prison fare was supplemented by what the women could bribe the guards with for extra rations. The prostitutes had no problems but Juliet was determined to retain her self-respect and declined to offer her body, despite the open invitations of the jailors.

For one so small, the prisoners were surprised at her ferocity in guarding her possessions and gave her a rough respect, knowing the nature of her crime. She didn't enlighten them on any point. A murderess was someone to be cautious of, they decided, and for that reason she was able to barter her spare clothing without fearing it would be stolen from her first. She kept only the towel and soap. It was rather pointless as the toilet facilities were primitive, but she endeavoured to wash as best she could. It was not to be supposed that a convict transport had better conditions. From what she learned, things were even more barbarous.

It was late summer before an East Indiaman put into Bristol harbor with orders to convey a number of convicts to Australia. The accommodations were small for the ship was primarily a trading vessel, but His Majesty's Commissioners were a little concerned about the overcrowding in the jails. Any ship bound for the East could serve His Majesty by transporting a number of felons and so reduce the necessity of housing them any longer in England.

The three-masted barquentine, the 'Grace,' stayed in Bristol harbor for three weeks, unloading tea and spices from Ceylon and a quantity of wool from Sydney. They were due to take on a variety of farming implements and an assortment of furniture requested by the new settlers.

Captain Ross Jamieson was not overly pleased to learn that fifteen convicts had been assigned to his ship. There was more profit in goods for the Company; livestock of this sort needed more attention than a hold full of cabinets and shovels. But as a servant of the Company he must obey his superiors who needed the goodwill of the Crown Commissioners.

Long before dawn on the morning they were due to sail, an open wagon drew up on the quayside. In the flickering light of the lamp swinging from the driver's seat, a bedraggled bunch of men and women were handed down, all heavily shackled. Ross Jamieson stared from the poop deck, an expression of distaste twisting his lips. With his tanned skin, black hair and, at this moment, a look of unconscious hauteur on his face beneath the tricorne, he might have been one of his own Scottish ancestors, hawk-eyed and granite-jawed, facing the encroaching redcoats of Hanover. And a miserable bunch they were too, he thought. Filthy rags, unwashed bodies, their smell reached him though they huddled far below, shivering uncontrollably in the chill dawn.

The guards were coming aboard. He went to meet them and was given a sheaf of papers.

"For the Governor, sir, when you put into Botany Bay. Names, crimes and terms of imprisonment. Don't expect you'll have much trouble with them, sir, they're mostly pickpockets and housebreakers. Nine men and half a dozen women."

"And what are the womens' crimes?"

"Thievery and prostitution mostly, sir, and a-robbing of their clients. That is, save one, and she did her ma in."

Ross Jamieson's brows shot up. "Killed her mother? That's a capital crime. Why wasn't she hanged?"

"Don't rightly know, sir. A soft judge, I'd reckon, and her being so young."

"She sounds a vicious piece of goods," Ross said, shocked to the core of his Presbyterian soul. "Is she violent?"

The guard rubbed his bristly chin. "Meek as you like most of the time, sir, but fights like a cat if the older ones try to take advantage."

"I'll have no fighting on my ship! A rope's end will teach her not to be troublesome if she starts a melee."

"Aye, sir." The guard looked into the dark face, half-shadowed in the lamplight. The hard eyes and the set of the mouth convinced him that this man would be as good as his word. "Will you have them on board now, sir?"

"Yes. My second officer will show you the aft hold we've set aside."

Ross retreated to the poop deck and leaned his elbows on the rail, watching the convicts come aboard. The women were indistinguishable from each other, all with lank hair and filthy clothes. They staggered slightly as the deck heaved on the swelling tide, then they were led aft by the officer and the guards.

Ten minutes later the young officer reported. "All holds battened, sir, and all cargo aboard."

Ross nodded and issued his orders to the crew. "Stand by all stations, ship anchor and cast off."

The 'Grace' slid down the estuary on the tide, and once out to sea all canvas was flown and she set a spanking pace out from the Bristol Channel, heading towards the French coast. The winds were fresh and the 'Grace' flew along as dawn pearled the heavens and faint rose-pink fingers crept steadily up from the horizon.

The Scilly Isles were skirted and left astern during the first week without a break in the weather, but the sky lowered its brows as they approached Northern France to head into the notorious Bay of Biscay.

The helmsman glanced at Captain Jamieson who stood, hands clasped behind him, frowning down at the compass.

"Bad weather ahead, Cap'n," he ventured and the dark face turned towards him.

"Aye, curse it. Alter course to bring us nearer the mainland." He peered forward. "Can't outrun it, more's the pity. It'll add days to our time if we must creep along the French coast. Damn this Bay. The waters here are as capricious as a female." He nodded to his helmsman and went below to check that all cargo was lashed securely.

The winds freshened and the ship was trimmed to ride the storm fast approaching. Jamieson passed the aft hold with barely a thought for his human cargo. The agricultural implements he carried were worth more to the settlers in New South Wales than a handful of convicts. As long as they had food and water, a thin mattress apiece and the services of the ship's doctor if needed, they were of less account than the goats he was to embark in Capetown.

The rain came and Captain Jamieson changed into oilskins before battling his way to the bridge, impeded by the gale that shrieked through the riggings. The sea grew wilder, waves breaking over the prow and tossing the small ship up and down like a child tossed a ball.

Cursing fluently, the Captain fell into the wheelhouse and grinned at the helmsman. There was enjoyment on both faces. A battle with the sea was the worthiest battle of all to a seaman. No matter what terrible traps were laid for the unwary, the foiling of them was a triumph indeed. The wheel was lashed and the two men rested their hands upon it, staring forward, silently defying the sea to alter their course by the slightest degree.

For more than a week, the sea and the

barquentine were locked in combat. The French Coast was seen at times but the 'Grace' clung steadily to her course though the timbers creaked and shivered with the battering. Slowly, as the Bay was crossed, the sea's hold slackened and the sky raised her lowered brows as if to concede defeat. The sun peered anxiously through the clouds, then smiled on the small ship in congratulatory fashion.

Captain Jamieson rubbed his unshaven chin and smiled up into the sky. "Lisbon, it is, Jake, and no damage that I can tell."

"Aye, aye, Cap'n. On course for Lisbon."

Down below in the aft hold, Juliet Westover opened her eyes to see a blue sky through the grating of the hatch cover. For so long the heavens had been black, the spray from the waves breaking over the decks hurling icy cold water down the ladder, it seemed incredible to view the sun. She glanced round the hold with its vile smell of sickness and saw the inmates sprawled on their mattresses, faces slack and pale from the weeks of seasickness. She had been ill, too, but more from the atmosphere than the motion of the ship. Had she been allowed on deck, the wind tearing at her hair and the fresh salt spray driving into her face, she felt she would not have suffered this stomach cramping discomfort and the constant nausea. What bliss to lie steady on the mattress, gazing up into a blue sky after the tossing turmoil of so

long. How long, she wondered? Weeks,
probably. One lost all sense of time
confined in the darkness. Now, perhaps,
they might be allowed the usual exercise
period on deck. Apart from the Goanese
galley boy, who had slung down a barrel of
water and food in a wicker basket at the end
of a rope, they had had no human contact,
save with each other—and that was a
contact not at all to Juliet's taste.

In the calm waters off the Portuguese
coast they were ordered to clean out the
hold. Brushes and mops were thrown down
and the hatch remained open. No one descended the ladder but the galley boy hauled
up the canvas buckets of filthy water and
let down fresh ones. All this was under the
supercilious eye of a junior officer who
stood with a loaded carbine at the ready.
Only when the hold seemed reasonably
clean were they allowed on deck.

Juliet drew in a deep breath of fresh sea
air. The breeze tossed her hair as she held
on to the rail. How different winds were,
she thought—all from the same heaven, yet
catching the atmosphere of the space it
swept through. The winds of her childhood
were those of the woods, damp hedges and
overall the scent of wild ponies. This wind
held a salty tang and invigorated both body
and mind. Later, she knew, the wind would
grow hot and maybe fail altogether when
they reached Africa. What of the winds in
New South Wales? Was the climate hot or

cold? No one in the hold knew and such information was unlikely to be offered by the man with the carbine.

It seemed no time at all before they were ordered back into the hold. The ship was to cross the Straits of Gibraltar before beating down the coast of West Africa. A large continent, she knew, and how many more weeks were to pass before they reached their destination? Even a life of bondage in the fresh air was beginning to have its attractions compared with the sordid, airless occupancy of this hold by fifteen none too clean persons. How callous righteous people were! To throw them all together in one hold, irrespective of sex or age. Did they imagine a convict had no feelings or any vestige of sensibility?

Captain Jamieson stood on the bridge. The weather was heating up. They were due to call at Rabat in Morocco—flies and tropical heat at this time of the year. He glanced down towards the stern of his ship. The junior officer who was responsible for guarding the prisoners was passing below to return the carbine to the gun cabinet. That sighting reminded him of the distasteful presence of the felons.

Up to now there had been no trouble, but as they ran down the coast of West Africa and the temperature rose, Ross wondered if he should transfer the women to the gundeck. The aft hold was an airless place and tropical heat tended to put tempers on edge. It wouldn't take much to spark off an explosion down there and the carbine might be emptied in panic by an officer unused to carrying convict cargo. Apart from his orders to hand over fifteen persons to the Governor, he wanted no deaths on his ship—nor did he desire six pregnant females!

As to that, it might already be too late, he realized with grim humor, and the women reluctant to be parted from their companions. On the other hand, if the trollops played one man against another, his action would put a stop to any violent scenes of jealousy. He had little sympathy for any of them, but the stench rising from the hold when the battens were removed twice a day was enough to turn the strongest stomach and common decency required some kind of action to be taken in this climate.

Had he but known it, his musings were being echoed in the foul confines of the hold. Juliet Westover, with perspiration dripping down her face, was striving to keep her sanity by concentrating on thoughts of Spring rain—fresh cool rain sweeping over the moor, the wind in her hair as she rode Mr. Shepheard's horse and the intoxicating scent of cut grass and early violets. If she willed herself to think only of those things, the present discomfort could be overlooked. The captain, she reflected resentfully, might at least have allowed the hatch to be opened to the sky, permitting entry of whatever air was to be obtained. How could they escape in the middle of the ocean under the eyes of armed men? It was inhuman to treat even convicts this way.

She closed her eyes, imagining the cool spring water of a pool caressing her sticky body. It was dreadful to smell so badly! All her attempts to stay clean had to be done under the speculative stares of the male convicts. She longed to strip off and stand naked in the bucket of sea water, soaping her body and toweling it briskly with the rough towel she still hung onto. But that would be like giving an open invitation to the first man whose hands grabbed her. Up to now they had left her alone after the initial pawings and lewd invitations. She had used her feet, elbows and fists to great effect, receiving unexpected encouragement from the other women who had no wish to give up the trifles paid to them by the men for their services.

She thought of the long weeks, even months, ahead before they reached their destination. The intense heat was already having an effect on them. Petty squabbles broke out; food and water was commandeered by the stronger men and fists were used to emphasize points of view. She wondered desolately how long she could hold out in the face of any combined attack, either on the meager rations she guarded or, for that matter, her body. There was no privacy here and she was becoming increasingly conscious of the lustful stares that were directed on her every movement.

In such a small hold, it was difficult to remain unobtrusive when one's attire consisted of a cotton dress and ragged undergarments, both having suffered from the scuffles endured during her days in Bristol jail. Shoes and stockings had had to be bartered for food and her bare legs and feet seemed to hold an attraction for the male convicts whose eyes roamed up and over her slight body with increasing boldness. Her five female companions were accommodating enough, heaven knows, but the time would come, she knew, when the men would try their luck with the only one to scorn their overtures.

She was perched on the lowest rung of the ladder, her mind fixed on recapturing the cool fresh smell of Mrs. Shepheard's dairy with the heavy scent of summer roses drifting through the open door, when she felt a hand on her ankle. She started violently, her daydream shattered.

She looked down into the black-jowled face of a convict. His grin, showing stained teeth, was meant to be ingratiating and his grimy fingers moved slowly up the calf of her leg.

"Get your filthy hands off me," she gritted, pulling away her leg.

"Still the uppity little spitfire, aren't you?" he leered. "Why can't you be nice to

Jeb White like the other doxies? They never say no to a bit of fun, 'specially when I give 'em a bite of my rations. Tom Cooper down there, he don't eat much, so he gives me what's left.''

"Or you take it, which is more to the point," said Juliet angrily.

"Well, Tom don't mind. He's not much of a one for the ladies but I'll give you a fair share if you'll toss up your skirts for me in the corner. I can't speak fairer than that, can I?"

"Then give it to someone else who'll appreciate your generosity, Jeb White. I want none of you and you'd better understand that now and save your breath."

"You're talking high and mighty, girl, but before we make Botany Bay you'll be crawling to me for a bite of food."

"Why should I? I can survive on the regular rations."

"But not if I take 'em off you when the officer goes away."

Juliet pushed down the feeling of panic his words brought. He was strong enough to do just that and she'd get no help from the others.

"I'll complain to the officer if you try it," she said, injecting fierceness into her voice.

"That young fellow with the carbine?" Jeb White sneered. "He's as nervous as a cat as it is. You'd not get him down here to argue the toss with me."

"Then the captain. I'd call for the captain. He wouldn't be afraid of you."

Jeb White laughed and his foul breath
fanned Juliet's cheeks. "You've maybe not
seen the captain. I doubt he's given us a
thought since we left Bristol. High-nosed
fellow. Stared at us coming aboard as if we
was a bunch of lepers. Not used to having
his ship stenched out with gutter rubbish, I
reckon, and none too pleased about it. His
sort'll keep well away from contact with
vermin like us. Only to be supposed the job
goes to the lowest officer in line. You'd best
be sensible, m'dear, and let me be your protector. Joe Bates has his eye on you too and
not only him. Better not turn me down, for
I'm giving you a chance like a proper gent
to come nice and quiet. I'd have you
anyway, first or last, so don't make any
trouble."

"And who says you would?" a voice
grunted from behind Jeb White. "We
decided to toss for who takes her first,
didn't we? And here you are a-crawling up
to her as if you already won."

"Oh, it's you, Joe Bates," growled Jeb.
"Well, it's like this. I reckoned she'd rather
have a city man who knew how to give a girl
a good time than a fellow who got took for
stealing a penny loaf. A real country bump-
kin you are, getting took for a penny."

"And I suppose filching a gent's wallet
has more class, eh? If you're so clever, what
are you doing on the same transport as
me?"

Jeb White removed his sweating hand from Juliet's knee and rose to face Joe Bates. They eyed each other like dogs bristling over a bone. A feeling of sickness that she should be the object of their disagreement rose violently in Juliet and she squirmed higher up the ladder. God in heaven, death by drowning would be preferable to suffering the embraces of either of these men! Let the hatch be opened soon, she prayed. If the officer shot her as she made for the rail, it would be less degrading than having her body fought over.

The two men were shouting insults at each other, then as their tempers snapped, they were locked in kicking thumping combat. The prisoners gathered round shouting encouragement, the women screaming with excitement. The noise bounced and reverberated round the confines of the hold, and Juliet huddled halfway up the ladder, her hands clapped over her ears in terror. Whoever won would claim victory by dragging her off to a corner and demonstrating his success in the most basic fashion.

She scrambled up the ladder and beat her fists on the battens. Let someone come, for pity's sake, her mind screamed. Not only were the two men fighting, it seemed the whole area was one mass of struggling people, tempers exploding into blows between all the convicts over previous arguments or imagined slights. She saw the women clawing and tearing at each other

and using their knees to good effect as the
unbearable heat set sparks to tinder dry
passions.

The battens came off with a scream of
creaking wood. The shouts and shrieks
funneled up to burst into the face of the
junior officer who stared down with a
glazed look of horror on his face. The floor
of the hold was revealed as a stinking,
heaving mass of struggling bodies. His lips
moved but the sound was too intense for his
words to be heard.

Juliet stared up, clinging to the ladder.
More faces appeared but she caught no
words. A tall, hawk-faced man gazed
stonily down and jerked his head in an
order to someone. Juliet began to drag
herself upwards.

Something was flung over the edge of the
hatch, then a great rush of water hit her
squarely in the midriff, lifting her bodily off
the ladder and casting her below into the
midst of the bodies. A boot thumped her
forehead and she hit the deck with a re-
sounding crash. The hold spun dizzily and
pain stabbed as she went down into the
blackness of oblivion.

Men and women tumbled over each other,
shrieking with shock, and above the noise
the clanking of a hand-operated pump
ground out, sending drenching jets of salt-
water into every corner. Slowly the furor
died away. Dripping convicts stared up,
open-mouthed.

One of the women gave a scream of laughter. "Thank-ee, cap'n, for the bath but you forgot to add the essence of lavender. Will you be coming now with soft towels and powder to dry our bodies? You'll be right welcome to mine."

"Silence!" roared an infuriated Captain Jamieson. "I've a mind to flog the lot of you." His gaze roamed the hold and alighted on the crumpled figure of Juliet.

The force of the water had swept her skirts wide and her long bare legs were revealed. Her sopping dress clung to her young body following every line from breast to hip. He frowned, noticing her stillness.

"What's wrong with that one?"

Jeb White crawled swiftly to Juliet's side and cradled her in his arms.

"A bump on the head, that's all. I'll take care of her. Don't you be worrying about that. My woman she is, and a bit of a cuddle from me'll put her right and tight again."

"You're a liar, Jeb White!" yelled Joe Bates. "She's as much mine as yours. We haven't finished the fight yet."

Ross Jamieson looked at the girl again. Her black hair was drying into curls about her white face and the sea water shower had removed some of the grime from her dress. Her limp form hung with unconscious grace in the convict's arms. She appeared young— no more than a child—and he wondered if that slightly superior quality over the other

sluts had given her bargaining power in her
fight for survival. He looked into the convict's black-stubbled face and noted the
coarse hands creeping over her breasts.
Was the man staking a claim without
foundation in fact? The other convict
obviously thought so by the glare he was
directing on his fellow. If the hatch was
closed again, it was certain to be the signal
for the fight to continue.

The girl's eyelids flickered, then enormous
pain-filled grey eyes settled on him. She
looked dazed and there was no awareness in
her face.

"Forgive me, ma'am. I cannot comprehend how I came to be thrown—such a
gentle mount. . ." The eyelids drooped and
her pallor became ghastly.

In the silence of the hold a woman's voice
cackled with mirth. "A gentle mount indeed! Not Jeb White nor Joe Bates—as I
can vouch if you count my bruises. 'Tis like
being dropped on by a sack of coal!"

"Hold your lip, trollop," snarled Jeb
White, "or I'll add to your bruises. My
woman's a cut above the lot of you and I
mean to take good care of her."

"Then you'd best make haste while she's
out of her senses for she'll rake your face
when she comes to." There was a burst of
coarse laughter.

"And what about me? growled Joe Bates.
"I've a fancy for the piece, myself." He
towered over the crouching man, his hands
balled into fists.

Jeb White's small greedy eyes leered up at Ross. "Pay no heed to him, sir. He's had all the women here and now he wants mine. He's a jealous swine but I'll not let him near my woman. She's too good for the likes of him."

Ross was near the end of his patience. He needed a bath and a change of clothes after the heat of the day. A cold drink wouldn't come amiss, either. But he had a strange feeling of presentiment. To withdraw now would leave that inert body at the mercy of the two contenders, and she was in no state to receive embraces from either party.

He cursed himself for this feeling of pity. She was a felon, just as they all were. Why should he concern himself over a trollop, however tiny and defenseless she appeared at this moment? And yet those words, that whispered remark, had not been delivered in the coarse tones he expected. There was in addition an almost tangible air of excitement, a curious feeling of waiting, like the expectancy of pleasure before a theatre curtain is raised.

He fixed his stare on Jeb White. "Does the wench acknowledge she's your woman?" he asked, wondering at himself for giving in to this absurd feeling of unease.

"I told her, sir, just before the hatches went off."

"And what did she say?"

"She whispered all sweet in my ear that I was the man for her. We was sitting all quiet and making plans for when we land, sir. Talking all soft and loving she was. On my life, sir, it's the Gospel truth."

"With all that noise going on behind you, I suppose? Or didn't you notice it?" Jeb White's eyes shifted uneasily and Ross went on, "How come then, she was at the top of the ladder when I put the sea hose in? Where were you? Not on the ladder or I'd have seen you."

Jeb rallied. "It was a game, cap'n. She was a bit of a tease, pretending to run away so I'd chase her."

"So you were not sitting as quietly as you claim. You are a liar and most certainly a troublemaker. I'll have no fighting on board my ship."

Jeb shrugged. "I has to fight to keep my property, don't I, cap'n? Joe Bates started it, the sniveling thief."

"Then you'll both be given ten lashes at sunset. And I warn you, if I have any more trouble down here, it'll be twenty lashes apiece. Now hand up that girl."

"What for, captain, sir? She'll be all right in a trice."

"Do as you're told or I'll make that twenty lashes tonight. She needs medical attention, that's obvious. Put your carbine on this man, Foster, and shoot him if he still wants to argue."

Jeb White obeyed, not caring for the merciless glint in the captain's eye. Juliet was taken off him by two seamen and laid on the deck. She felt the fresh air on her face as she floated up from darkness and her eyes flickered and opened again.

She was staring up into a brilliant blue sky and all she could smell was the sea. Licking her dry lips she tasted salt. Her mind was coming to life. There had been a great wave breaking over her, a wave so strong that it took her breath away and hurled her from its path. No, not a wave but a wide open-mouthed canvas hose that had been thrust in the hold and directed on the convicts.

"You'll let me have her back, cap'n?" She heard the sly ingratiating tones of Jeb White. "I'll be right lonely without my woman in my arms."

"You'll be too busy tonight to think of aught but your stripes," said Ross callously. "But she'll be back as soon as she's recovered. Give it a rest tonight, man. Neither of you will be in a state for romping."

Juliet thrust herself painfully up on one elbow. Her dazed eyes took in the scene, then her glance traveled up the tall figure looking down on her dispassionately. She saw the hard eyes and haughty face of a man obviously in authority.

"Captain?" she quavered.

"Yes?" The response was curt and unhelpful.

"Please . . . please don't send me down there again!"

"Why not?"

"They . . . they're animals. Those men. . ."

"They're convicts like you."

"I . . . I know, but they frighten me."

"You've got a protector. The man, Jeb White, says you're his woman. He'll look after you."

"He's lying! I'm not his woman." She spoke with such vehemence her head throbbed anew.

"Then who is?"

"What? What do you mean?"

"Who have you been lying with on the voyage?"

"No one. I swear it!"

"Come now, girl, don't play the innocent with me. We've been at sea for weeks. Don't pretend you haven't been tumbled already. Why, there are nine men down there. You must have declared your availability for a fight to start over you. Did you tire of your lover and seek the excitement of playing off two violent men against each other?"

"No, no! I had no lover! I didn't want them to fight. I couldn't stop them. They had no right to think. . ."

"What did you expect them to do when you flaunt yourself half-naked?" Ross said savagely. "This is no Bristol drawing room, though I doubt you've ever seen one!"

Juliet came to her knees, shaking with rage. Had she not felt sick with pain and half out of her mind with terror, she might not have spoken as she did.

"What would a gentleman such as yourself know of prison life? To stay alive one
must eat, and without money one has to sell
everything that has the smallest value. A
ribbon, an old pair of stockings or shoes,
even my hairbrush! That is why I am half-
naked as you call it. And as to my morals,
sir, they are my own business as yours are!
If there was any decency in the system of
justice, men and women would be housed
separately. And you, so quick to condemn,
perpetuate that indecency by herding convicts of both sexes together in one hold!
And you have the effrontery to hold up
your nose in horror at what happens!"

Stunned for a moment by this verbal on-
slaught, Ross found his voice at last.
"Silence, woman!" he thundered. "I am not
here to bandy words with you."

But Juliet was past bandying words with
anyone. Her eyes glazed over and she
swayed, then crumpled into a small heap on
the deck.

Ross was nonplussed. His anger had
risen to towering heights but now the
object of his disgust had collapsed into
unconsciousness, unable to suffer the lash
of his contemptuous tongue. He stared
down at the huddled form, noting the
bruising on the forehead. He frowned
angrily.

"Put her in a passenger cabin," he
ordered, "And have the surgeon take a look
at her. And batten that hatch again. I've
had enough of this scum for one day."

He settled his tricorne firmly on his head and strode away, his mind seething with impotent fury that a female convict should address him in such a way. Later, with a glass of wine in his hand and his feet on the chest in his cabin, he recalled her words. Insolent bitch that she was, her diatribe had been articulate and delivered in educated tones. That in itself was not remarkable—she might have worked in some respectable house and picked up the elements of good speech—but what she had said about segregating the prisoners was reasonable. Supposing, purely hypothetically of course, that a girl of decent moral standards had fallen into crime. It would prove almost impossible for her to uphold those standards if pitched into rough company and locked away for weeks on end with a bunch of determined ruffians whose only entertainment was the slaking of their desires.

He had the uncomfortable feeling, and one he didn't like, that he should have used the gundeck for females as he had once considered. But the majority of his female prisoners seemed not averse to the company of their fellows. Why pander to the odd one? He shrugged. In any case it was too late now. The girl was frightened by the violence she had engineered and sought only to elicit his sympathy. Not for a moment did he believe her an innocent victim. She was young, but then girls went early to prostitution and soon learned the art of survival. Whatever her crime, she was judged guilty and justice must take its course. She wasn't worthy of any more thought, he decided, draining his wine glass. When the surgeon pronounced her fit, she would be returned to the hold. Let them settle their own squabbles, but in a quieter manner.

Captain Ross Jamieson was a professional sailor and had served the East India Company for ten years. The 'Grace' was his first command and had fulfilled the ambition that had been his since his fifteenth year when he had joined the Company as a cabin boy. His father, the younger son of an old Scottish family, had gone South with his wife and child after a bitter quarrel with the old laird. His heart was in learning and he wanted no part of the farming that went with the land, content to leave that duty to his elder brother who was heir to the estate. Why should he act bailiff to this indolent brother who cared little for his inheritance? He wanted to be a schoolmaster and bury his head in books, not his boots in ploughed earth. But for all his love of learning, success eluded him, for he was unable to communicate with the young. As a scholar he might have made his mark but financial needs forced him into tutoring a succession of disinterested young boys. Pride forbade a return to Scotland, so his wife and son existed in cramped dwellings on inadequate resources. Ross never knew the land of his fathers as the old laird's pride equaled that of his younger son and all contact was lost.

On the death of his parents, both lacking resistance in their fight against a pneumonic infection, Ross left the little house in London and applied to the dock office of the East India Company. Like his father, he had a fierce pride and nothing would have made him appeal to his grandfather for aid. Luckily a ship that stood in harbor had but lately lost the cabin boy to a broken leg. Unlucky for him, but lucky for Ross. The ship was due out and the captain's normal irascibility was inflamed by what he considered the gross impertinence of the unfortunate cabin boy—to leave him without prior notice.

That first voyage from Tilbury to Bombay in one of the smaller Company ships gave Ross an enduring love of the sea. Because he was quick-witted and educated, it amused the officers to instruct him in chart-reading, the use of the sextant and the value of star-gazing. All this was in gratitude for the inexplicable calmness of the captain's temperament, due it seemed to this lad who was so apt in his duties that the captain was rarely out of temper.

With the captain's recommendation, Ross was appointed two years later as a junior officer, and in the ten years with the Company, his rank increased. Although the 'Grace' was a small ship, barely three hundred tons, he accepted the command eagerly when it was offered. An officer's first ship was a landmark in his career. One day he hoped to command the flagship of the East India Company but for that he would need another ten years of unblemished seamanship. For the moment he was content to be, at twenty-five, the youngest captain in the Company.

He gave a start as his own cabin boy hammered on the door and stumbled in.

"What the devil's amiss," he snapped.

"Nothing, Captain. Just coming to make ready for the night and set out your dress clothes."

Ross eyed the boy in an unfriendly fashion. "Did you sew on that button that was missing last night? And I trust you've polished my boots better this time."

"Yes, sir." He placed the boots beside Ross's chair and the greasy thumbprints stood out all over them.

Ross glanced at his white-faced blue jacket. The button was on but stitched in so inexpert a fashion that it lay unevenly spaced. There was a dark fingermark on one lapel.

"God in heaven, boy! Do you expect me to appear for dinner with your thumbprints over everything? Let me see your hands."

The boy stretched out grimy palms, his nails black-edged. "I washed 'em, sir."

"Before or after you cleaned my boots?" Ross inquired wearily.

"Before, sir," the lad answered with an air of pride. "Just like you told me."

"And stitched the button on afterwards, I suppose?"

"Yes, sir. Is something wrong, sir?"

Ross shook his head. "No, nothing I haven't brought on myself. Tell me, boy. Have you ever had a fancy to be a powder monkey?" It was an idle remark but the boy's face lit up.

"Oh, yes, sir!" His sudden grin died. "But I couldn't be one."

"Why not?"

"Who'd look after you, sir, and take care of your clothes?" the boy inquired with earnest innocence.

Ross kept his expression blank. "There is that, but I rather think I'd manage," he said mildly. "Now cut along while I change."

After the boy had gone, Ross sponged the fingermark off his jacket lapel and gave his boots a rub with an old cloth. It was customary for the captain to have a servant, but if the truth be told, he would rather dispense with the lad's noisy and clumsy attempts to act the valet and care for himself. He was not a gentleman officer as was to be found in the Royal Navy, but a working seaman, used to being self-sufficient.

He tied the crisp white stock beneath his chin, bending his tall lithe figure slightly to avoid the bulkhead, and settled his bro-

caded waistcoast in place before easing on
the dark blue jacket with its long white
lapels.

Two silver-backed hairbrushes lay on the
bolted-down chest of drawers. He smoothed
back his springy black hair, gazing into the
glass from under thick dark brows. His
eyes were blue and tiny creases fanned out
from the corners, due to the constant
scanning of the horizon in wind and sun.
But his scrutiny was impersonal and
automatic. His thoughts were on the
landfall they were expecting to make in
three days time.

Capetown, the Dutch settlement off the
coast of Africa, was where they normally
took on fresh provisions and water. It
boasted a bleak coastline but the Dutch
farmers were quite willing to sell them fuel,
fresh fruit and even animals for the Aus-
tralian settlers. After Capetown it was a
long routine haul to the South and then to
the new continent.

He crossed the corridor to the large
dining cabin where his officers awaited him.

Farther down the corridor in one of the
two passenger cabins, Juliet Westover lay
in a drugged sleep. A blanket covered her
from shoulders to feet and an ointment-
smeared bandage was wrapped round her
head. The surgeon, an elderly man, had not
thought it good policy to remove her dress
while she was unconscious. He was too ex-

perienced to lay himself open to allegations
of misconduct, but he had examined her
head with thoroughness, deciding that she
suffered only bruising. To allay any after-
effects, he had, during a brief return to
dazed consciousness, dosed her with laud-
anum, a sure way of resting the brain in
head injuries.

She woke to the daylight next day and
apart from a soreness in her forehead was
none the worse. Her experience as a
prisoner had taught her to come alert at the
sound of movement. Those who slept on
were apt to lose out when the rations were
distributed. But this day she woke to find
the noises came from outside, and for a
moment she stared in bewilderment at her
strange surroundings. But memory
returned swiftly. The soft bed, the clean
blanket, and the lack of companions were
the height of luxury despite the sparse
furnishings. She turned her face into the
pillow, determined to wring the last ounce
of pleasure out of the situation before she
was returned to the hold.

A tap on the door, then the entry of an
elderly man caught her unaware. He stared
at her and smiled, seeing her awake. Her
hazy half-formed plan of pretending to be
still unconscious was gone when he spoke.

"Good morning. You look much better.
Sleep well?"

"Yes, sir."

"I am the surgeon." He sat on the edge of

the bed and removed the bandage. "Very good. You were lucky to escape with only bruising."

"Lucky?" she echoed. "I could wish I had broken my neck."

"Nonsense! You'll feel better presently."

"When I am returned to my rightful place, you mean?"

"I am only the doctor, child. My duty is to care for the sick wherever they are—not pass judgment on anyone."

"I'm sorry. I'm truly grateful for your kindness." Tears of weakness stood in her eyes. "It is so wonderful to be in a real bed again—almost like a dream. Forgive my stupid remark."

She blinked away the tears and looked round the cabin. In a small dressing room off, she glimpsed the high back of a hip-bath. She stared in longing, then dragged her gaze back to the doctor.

He glanced over his shoulder to see what had brought on that strange look. He turned back to her with a smile.

"Are you wondering what that is?" he asked.

"I know what it is. A hipbath." She looked again.

"Have you ever used one?"

"Frequently."

She saw his brows rise in tolerant amusement.

"I did come from a respectable home, sir. Such refinements are not unknown to me. I have not suffered imprisonment for so very long." She looked into the kind face. "Would it be possible ... I know I shouldn't ask ... but I would dearly love ... could there be any harm in it?"

"You are asking if you could use the hip-bath?" he queried in surprise.

"Yes, sir. I know I have to go back, but just once on this voyage I would like to take off my clothes and wash properly. It isn't possible down there, not with the men watching."

"I should report to the captain that you are recovered."

"Please, sir. Will half an hour make so much difference?"

He stared into the grey eyes so full of appeal and was reminded of his own daughters. Whatever her crime she was a female and a nicely spoken one at that. It was not, after all, such a great thing she was asking.

"All right, but only half an hour, mind. You'll find a towel and soap on the stand. There is a tank of sea water by the bath. We thought to have a passenger but he was delayed. You understand that I shall have to lock this cabin door behind me? Don't abuse my trust by trying to escape."

"No, sir, I promise," she said with a glowing look. "Thank you, thank you!"

He shook his head gently at her excitement and left the cabin. The key grated in the lock. Juliet threw off the blanket and moved swiftly into the dressing room. The tank he had spoken of stood by the foot of the bath and a tap had been fitted to a hole in the side. The water that cascaded as she manipulated the tap was lukewarm through standing in the sun's glare.

She hurriedly stripped off her soiled dress and shift, removed the ragged pantalettes and dropped them in a heap before stepping into the unexpected luxury of an overall soak. The cake of soap in its dish on the stool was unscented but of reasonable quality, and she soaped her body with delight. There was no lather to be had with sea water but it was enough to rinse off the accumulated grime of the voyage.

Her hair underwent the same treatment and by the time she had finished, the water was grey. But her body and spirit were refreshed and a hard rub down with the towel gave her skin a rosy glow. She looked with distaste at her filthy clothes. How could she bear to put them on again? Impulsively she dropped them into the water, then draped the towel about her body, knotting it under her arms. On her knees beside the bath she soaked and rubbed the dirt from her garments.

She had just finished twisting out the water from her dress when she heard the key turn in the lock. Half an hour already? Well, her clothes would soon dry on her body once she was back in the heat-laden hold.

"What the devil do you think you are up to?" came a harsh voice.

Her head shot round, damp curls flying, and her eyes widened in dismay. It was not the doctor framed in the doorway but the tall angry man who had towered over her as she lay on the deck yesterday. The man, she recalled, to whom she had been appallingly insolent in her distress! Her heart quailed under the captain's dark stare.

"I'm . . . I'm taking a bath," she stammered.

"That is quite apparent," he snapped, his eyes raking her from the top of her wild tangle of curls to the slender legs and feet. The damp towel covered only her breasts and hips and was molded to her body like a second skin. Even in his anger his mind acknowledged the perfection of her shape. His gaze rose from the ivory-white shoulders, up the slender column of her neck to the heart-shaped face with its trembling lips and wide dove-grey eyes. It was not hard to guess how she had earned her living! What man of means and lustful temperament could fail to be tempted by those ripe lips and the promise of paradise in that exquisite body.

Ross Jamieson realized he was staring and pulled himself together, frowning at his own brief contemplation of her attributes. She was a convicted felon and her past had caught up with her and now she was facing the consequences.

"And who gave you permission to indulge in this liberty, may I ask?" he said, more harshly than he intended.

"I . . . I begged the doctor to grant me this favor, sir, and he was kind enough to say I might use the hipbath. I see it was wrong of me and I'm sorry, but please vent your anger on me, not him. He . . . he is a good compassionate man."

"Allow me to be the best judge of that," Ross said coldly. "Now get dressed. I'm sure your friends are eager for your return."

Juliet's face went bleak and white. Her lashes swept down but not before Ross had glimpsed a naked terror in her eyes. He frowned.

"Are you not looking forward to being re-united with your lover—or lovers?"

The eyes that were raised briefly held a haunted look. "Lovers? The scum down there are intent on who shall rape me first."

"Rape? That's a strong word for one of your sort."

"One of my sort?" She gave a bitter smile. "How typical of your sort to suppose that every female convict must, without doubt, be a slut, corrupt in mind and morals."

"Are you trying to tell me that your mind and morals are above corruption?"

"Would you believe me if I did?"

"No."

"Then why should I try?" She shrugged.

"A conviction in the courts carries its own stamp of evil and that is sufficient for most people." She rose to her feet. "Would you now allow me the courtesy of being alone while I dress?"

He looked at the dripping garments she had picked up. "Did you think to spin out your time of freedom by washing your clothes?"

"No." Her voice was dull and unemotional. "I have a distaste for donning filthy clothes when I have bathed. At least I will go clean."

"Devil take you, girl! Hang your rags by the porthole and I'll give you time to get them dry. But don't presume on my generosity too far by thinking up some further shift to delay your return!"

"No, sir. Thank you, sir," she said as calmly as she could though her heart sang at this additional respite.

Nodding curtly, he made for the door. There he paused and looked back, struck by an idea. "Can you sew?"

"Yes, sir." She gazed at him in surprise.

"Then come with me."

She followed him to his own cabin and he closed the door behind them. Her head was at the level of his shoulder and he could smell the fast-drying, freshly-washed hair with its tang of sea water. The face that was upturned in query had a flawless, rose-tinted look about it and the luminous grey eyes were clear under well-defined brows. It was the face of an innocent child. No doubt she had found it a great asset, he thought cynically.

"Over here," he said, and she followed obediently as he threw open his clothes press and drew out the white-faced evening jacket. "See if you can position that button correctly. Needles and thread in this box. And when you've done that, you might see what you can do with the rent in this waistcoat. As you can see, the repair is a poor effort."

"Yours, sir?"

There was some faint hint of amusement in her tone and he stared at her closely.

"My cabin boy," he said coldly. "You find that ludicrous?"

"Not at all, sir, but I thought sailors were quite apt with the needle."

He held back a sudden urge to grin. "Not when they have ambitions to be powder monkeys."

She gave an involuntary gurgle of laughter. "That explains it."

It was such an infectious sound that Ross almost laughed with her but he quickly restrained himself, remembering his position. He was not to be charmed into any indiscretion or favor by any unexpected moment of shared amusement.

"I will leave you to your task then," he said, injecting authority into his voice.

As he opened his cabin door, the crosscurrent between that and the open porthole

lifted the edge of Juliet's towel and flung it
away from her leg. He glimpsed the shapely
rounded thigh and a bare buttock before
Juliet blushingly wrenched the towel back
into place. But in doing so she loosened the
knot and the upper part of the towel fell
away, revealing her breasts. She turned
sharply, dragging the towel together as it
threatened to abandon her completely.

Could a girl blush at will, wondered Ross
as he saw the crimson flame in her cheeks?
Had this been a clever piece of mani-
pulation designed to ensnare him? If so, he
knew how to counter the move. He strode
to his sea chest and pulled out a striped
cotton nightshirt. He dropped it onto his
bunk.

"Put that on and hide your maidenly
blushes. They're wasted on me, so don't try
any more tricks like that."

He was gone, slamming the door before
Juliet could do more than give him a
flashing outraged stare. With trembling
hands she donned the long nightshirt. By
turning up the sleeves and hitching up its
length with a piece of twine she found in a
corner, she felt a great deal more comfortable. What a thoroughly unpleasant
man he was, she decided, and how conceited
to imagine she had the faintest wish to offer
her body to him as he had implied.

It didn't take her long to resew the
button on his jacket and she mended the
waistcoat rent expertly until the original

damage was barely discernable.

She sat still for a moment, then with nervous daring went through the contents of the clothes press, checking for tears and hanging buttons. Several items came to light and she sewed and snipped happily, willing her thoughts away from the inevitable outcome of this brief respite from misery.

A clatter at the door startled her and her heart pounded painfully at the thought of being banished once more. But it was a large boy who entered, his bare feet slapping as heavily as if he wore farm boots. He shouldered open the door and set a large bowl of broth beside her.

"Cap'n thought you'd like something, seeing as how you missed the rations this morning," he said, staring at her curiously and eyeing the bruise on her forehead.

"Oh, thank you!" said Juliet warmly, the fragrant smell of the broth almost making her head swim. She laid aside the last item of mending.

"What are you doing here, miss?"

"I had a fall yesterday and the doctor put me in the spare passenger cabin, then your captain asked me to do some mending for him. I hope you don't mind."

The boy gave her a beaming look. "Mind? I can't abide sewing but a cabin boy has to do it, see?"

"Don't you like being a cabin boy?"

"Not much, miss. Not now I've seen the

guns. Sewing and cleaning is for females but the captain needs me so I've got to stay. You're a convict, aren't you, miss?"

Juliet nodded as she ate the soup.

"You don't look like one," said the boy. "You look a nice respectable girl, miss, like my sister."

"I am," said Juliet, smiling. "But nobody will believe it."

"It's a real shame you being down there in the hold with all those bad ones."

"I agree with you there, but there's no cure for it. Did the captain say when he was coming for me?"

"Soon, he said, miss. He's had his food and the watch has been changed."

"Then I'd better get my own clothes on."

The boy took away the bowl and Juliet tidied the threads and needles, then made her way to the passenger cabin. Her clothes, hung in the hot sun, were dry.

She slipped the nightshirt off and laid it on the bunk. Her shift went over her head and she smoothed it down, wishing it was of soft silk, not rough threadbare cotton. She sighed and gazed for a moment out of the porthole. There was only sea but a fresh breeze blew in, so welcome after the airlessness of the hold. And she had to go back there again! To become once more the object of rivalry between two equally revolting men!

The scene blurred before her eyes and tears of despair trickled down her cheeks. It was so unfair to be convicted of something she hadn't done and then looked upon as an object of scorn or lust, depending on the status of the onlooker. She raised her hand and brushed away the tears with the back of her wrist.

"Still trying to tempt me with your half-clad body, girl?" a voice asked.

She spun round, not having heard anyone enter, and saw the captain dimly through her tears. The sun's rays outlined her figure and she stayed immobile for a moment, then her shoulders sagged.

"I didn't know you were here," she said dully.

"Didn't the boy tell you to expect me?"

"Yes. That's why I am changing into my own clothes."

"And making a pretty long job of it, I gather, so that you may blush prettily again when I find you half-naked," he said with scorn.

"What makes you consider yourself so irresistible to women? You are merely a man with authority and power," Juliet said, stung into retort. "I know that you hold my fate in your hands but that gives you no right to insult me. I have no wish to tempt you and will not be subject to your taunts. . ."

He was across the cabin in two strides, catching both her wrists in a fierce grip.

"You are subject to whatever I choose for you. You have no rights on this ship. I can flog you for insolence if I please."

"Then do so, if it upholds your pride," she
spat at him. "I would as soon be flogged as
forced to listen to your abuse any longer. I
find you intolerable and far too high in your
own conceit!"

The dark face stared down. "Indeed?" he
said in a steely voice. "And if I offered you
a choice between my bed and the hold, what
would you answer to that?"

Juliet gasped. Such a thought had never
occurred to her. Could there be a way of
escape from the horrors of the hold? She
tried to sort out her suddenly disordered
mind. It had become very obvious that her
resistance to the two convicts who lusted
after her could not be maintained much
longer. It was still a long voyage to
Australia. One of them must succeed in his
pursuit, whether by force or trickery, and
when he tired of her she would be tossed to
the other as carelessly as a child discards a
toy once the novelty has worn off. She
would still be a prisoner of the dirt, the
stench and the fought-over rations, as
steeped in corruption as those she despised.

But this man was a gentleman. Whatever
his demands she would be clean and well-
fed, free to breathe in the untainted air
above decks, and free from the sly hands
and lewd tongues of the other convicts. All
she could lose would be her innocence—but
wasn't it better to lose it to him, rather
than a sweating, unshaven, foul-mouthed

man like Jeb White? She would use this man as he thought to use her.

Ross waited, his expression impassive. Was this long pause contrived to inflame his passions and give him the chance to view her scantily-clad body more fully? The cynic in him argued that her ultimate response would be acceptance. What harlot would not seek to better her position? For all her proud talk of insults and taunts, when it came to the comforts of life, what woman would turn down the prospect though it involved a retreat from those hotly-voiced sentiments?

He released her hands and stepped back a pace, watching her from narrowed eyes. She was pretty, a beauty one might say, and had she been a respectable girl of good birth, her suitors must certainly have been legion.

"Well?" he said in a quiet voice.

Juliet smiled a little tremulously and stretched out a hand to touch his face. Ross stood very still and she came closer, laying both hands on his chest. The warmth of her palms seemed to burn through his uniform and he stared into soft grey eyes that held—what? Relief, satisfaction—a hint of triumph that she had enslaved yet another man with her young body and tempting ways?

"I would answer yes," she whispered in a husky little voice.

Ross smiled and removed the hands from

his chest. He stepped back and let his gaze wander deliberately over her breasts and down her thighs to the narrow bare feet.

"Of course you would say yes. What strumpet would not?" His voice answered silkily but it held a steely quality. "I merely asked how you would answer such a proposition. I was not making you an offer!"

III

Juliet felt her body grow cold and stiff as if the life blood had drained away. There was a strange emptiness in her head. She stared into the hawk-like face that held a supercilious look. The half-smile he showed was nothing more than a cruel twist of the lips. He had merely been making game of her, she realized, and had every intention of returning her to the hold. Had her hot words made him wonder how long she could hold to them if a chance to stay above decks was offered? To be called intolerable and conceited had, no doubt, wounded his pride, especially coming from a female convict, and this was his way of paying her back. But how cruel a revenge! Offering her hope then snatching it away in a gesture of petty spite to punish her for daring to defend herself.

A wave of intense heat swept through her and filled her head with a blinding light. His face wavered in a mist and exploded into a violently colored kaleidoscope. Through it all she heard her own voice speaking.

"How very small-minded and vindictive you are..." and then there was nothing but a long spiraling drop that turned and twisted her body, flinging her down into endless darkness.

Ross saw the ghastly pallor and the slow, almost boneless collapse of the rigid little figure, and his arms reached out automatically as she fell forward. He caught her round the waist and she hung limply against him. This was no trick! He knew by the upturning of the eyeballs and the terrible stillness of the sagging body. She was out cold and he was responsible! What devil had forced him into such a despicable act? He had been fully prepared for a stream of abuse to be hurled at him. It had been the whole object of his scheme, to watch her reactions and attempts to retrieve her position by flattering wiles until his final remarks. Then should have come the abuse and oaths.

But she had done neither thing. Just stared at him dully from shocked eyes, like a small animal acknowledging the swooping falcon and realizing escape was impossible.

A noise behind brought him out of his own shock. The doctor stood in the doorway, his grey brows drawn together.

"May I ask, Captain Jamieson, what your intentions are towards my patient? I expected to find her resting and to ensure her privacy I locked the door."

Ross saw the suspicion in Doctor Fernley's eyes and felt himself grow hot.

"Dammit, Doctor, I have no intentions. The girl fainted."

"Lay her on the bunk, please."

Ross did as he was told.

"What happened, Captain? I left the girl on the point of taking a bath—after locking the door." he repeated. "I would have been back sooner but the carpenter cut his hand and I had to attend to it." He looked at Ross, his brow heavy with question.

"It's very simple, Doctor," Ross explained, trying not to feel like a midshipman in front of the commander. "I looked in to see how she was and found her washing her clothes. I allowed her extra time to get them dry and was on the pont of returning her to the hold when you came."

"In her shift?"

"Of course not!"

"Then why is she not wearing her clothes?"

"She was taking too damned long about it," Ross said irritably. "I came to tell her to hurry it up."

"I imagine she would find that task rather difficult, clasped in your arms" the doctor said dryly.

"Confound it, Doctor, the girl just fainted."

"I wonder why?"

"Would you mind leaving me alone with her, Captain? There must be some reason for this collapse. Perhaps the head injury was more severe than I supposed. I will examine her thoroughly and let you have my report in due course. But until then, Captain . . ." He fixed his gaze on Ross. "I assume charge of this prisoner. She will not be returned to the hold without my permission. Is that understood?"

"Naturally. I had no intention of overriding your authority in this department."

"Then I wonder why you didn't wait for my final report?" murmured Doctor Fernley, and held open the door for him.

Ross strode down the corridor, his brow thunderous. A young officer on his way to make a request of the captain veered off course rapidly after one look at his superior. It wasn't that important after all, he decided, and could just as well be discussed with the second in command.

It wasn't until Ross was dressing for dinner that he noticed the perfectly stitched button on his jacket and the neatly repaired rent in his waistcoat. He surveyed his clothes press, keenly and a trifle suspiciously. Someone had been through it carefully. The sagging hem of a jacket he had meant to bring to the attention of his cabin boy was no longer sagging. Tiny stitches, certainly not the boy's, held the hem to its original position. She'd certainly been busy but had it been just an excuse to cover up her curiosity of his possessions? Was anything missing? He'd best make sure.

His silver-backed brushes were still in place, so were the guineas in his chest of drawers. Only the clothes press had been opened. She was not a thief, that was evident, but she was still a puzzle to him. Well-spoken, obviously unhappy to reside in dirty conditions, and terrified of being returned to the hold. Why else would her proud defiance collapse? Rape? The word she had used came back to him. It was a violent, unspeakable word. A bid for sympathy? Very likely. After months in jail and weeks on a transport, it was inconceivable to suppose that her favors had not been already distributed. He put her out of his mind and went in to dinner. He deliberately refrained from mentioning her to Doctor Fernley who joined them and the doctor also kept silent on the subject.

Juliet had wakened once more in the bunk of the passenger cabin. A man was bending over her, and at the touch of his fingers on her ankle she gave an involuntary scream and kicked the hand away.

"I beg your pardon, my dear," came a calm reassuring voice. "I wondered at this slight bruise. Perhaps you knocked your ankle somewhere."

Juliet found herself staring into the con-

cerned face of the elderly surgeon. Her eyes
searched the cabin, but the captain was
gone.

"I . . . I'm sorry, Doctor. For a moment I
thought it was Jeb White grabbing my
ankle again." She shuddered, and he murmured soothingly, pulling the sheet up to
her shoulders.

"Jeb White? Is he one of the convicts?"
She nodded.

"Has he been cruel to you?"

"It's not cruelty he has in mind," she
said, wearily, "but I would die rather than
let him touch me. I know we are judged all
the same, Doctor, but to be herded together
like animals makes people act like animals.
We're human beings, not cattle. No wonder
convicts die, or kill each other, on a voyage.
The conditions make it inevitable."

"I entirely agree but have not been able
to convince the authorities of that. Most
law-abiding citizens would say it is only
what you deserve for daring to break the
law of the land. But justice is not always as
merciful as she would have you believe."

"I know that too well."

"Well, let us dwell on happier things. My
report to the captain will state that after a
thorough examination I find that you are
suffering from exhaustion and the after-
effects of a head injury. A slight fever and
nervous condition will necessitate—shall
we say—rest and quiet for a period of time
that could easily bring us within sight of
Capetown."

"Thank you, Doctor." Juliet could barely hold back her tears of relief. "Will he . . . will he accept that? He seems a very autocratic man."

"He must accept it. My authority in matters of health on this ship is final. Now try to rest, and this time I shall take the key with me."

He patted her shoulder and left the cabin. It had been so long since anyone had been kind to her that Juliet lay shaking and crying for some time before falling into an exhausted sleep that lasted into the night. She awoke several times, starting up in alarm, but all was quiet and the motion of the ship with a glimpse of stars through the porthole lulled her back to sleep.

By morning reaction had set in and she tossed feverishly, her head on fire. She was barely aware of the gentle hands that soothed her hot body with damp cloths and spooned some milky concoction into her mouth. Day and night merged into one as her tightly-held control over the months crumbled, and she was as helpless as a sick child.

And that, thought Doctor Fernley, as he gazed down into the pale face and restless body, was all she was. God knew what her crime was but there was no viciousness in it, he'd guess. She was as clean and fresh as one of his own daughters, no hint of disease or sores as one might find in a prostitute. He had removed her sweat-soaked shift to carry out his examination and he would

swear that her misfortune had come about
through some youthful folly. Illegal, obviously, or she would not otherwise be on
this transport, but he doubted that she was
of the criminal classes. He would have liked
to have known her crime but in the face of
Captain Jamieson's bland civility, he would
not ask. The convict's papers were locked
away, he assumed, in the strongbox and
only the captain had access.

A slight constraint still lingered between
the two men, and as the captain had made
no inquiry as to the health of the patient,
Doctor Fernley refrained from comment.

But Ross's apparent lack of interest was
not as complete as the doctor supposed. His
stubborn nature held back any question
and his pride had not recovered from the
astonishing interpretation Doctor Fernley
had put on his actions when the girl
collapsed. Force his attention on an unwilling convict girl? It was unthinkable!
And yet, to the good doctor, it appeared
very much the situation as he found it. And
the girl, confound her, had swooned as
typically as a shy young virgin after an im-
proper suggestion from the local squire.
Why did that stunned, sick look disturb
him so much? He felt as he had when he put
a bullet into the brain of a palamino pony
whose forelegs had snapped in a sudden
flurry of fear at being embarked—the same
soft trusting look that made him feel like a
murderer when he fired.

It was ridiculous to compare them, he

argued, in the privacy of his cabin. It was necessary for the pony to die. No blame attached to that. But it wasn't necessary to taunt the girl in so cruel a manner, his other self accused, and there was blame in that. It ill became an officer, and supposedly a gentleman, to subject a female, albeit a felon, to such a crude display of ridicule.

He turned, hands behind his back, from an unseeing contemplation of the unbroken expanse of sea. Yes. Blame and shame both, he acknowledged, and it was his duty to set things right.

After dinner that night he invited a somewhat surprised Doctor Fernley to take a nightcap in his cabin. He poured two measures of whisky into cut glass tumblers and with his profile only towards his guest, he inquired in a careful flat voice, "And how is your patient faring, Doctor?"

In an equally noncommital voice Doctor Fernley answered.

"Improving, Captain."

"What precisely did you find wrong with her?" asked Ross, handing the doctor a glass and seating himself, crossing one long leg over the other.

"Apart from the obvious head wound, a great deal of nervous tension. In the conditions she lived under, her emotions were held taut as violin strings. A release, however temporary, from those conditions brought the inevitable breakdown and loss of control she had built up." He leaned forward, addressing Ross earnestly. "I would request in all humanity that you do not return her to the hold. Confine her if you wish in some other place."

"On what grounds do you make this request, Doctor?"

"On my own observations and reading of her character. I would fear for her mental state, quite apart from the demands she would be subject to physically. That girl is a child, Captain—an innocent child!"

"Innocent?" queried Ross, raising a sardonic eyebrow. "She is a convicted felon."

"I was speaking in medical terms, Captain, not legal terminology."

Ross thought of the exquisitely shaped body, the dark curls and dove grey eyes. Could the doctor have been swayed by the air of virginity about the girl? It would not be hard to play on the sympathies of such a compassionate man. But the doctor was no fool. Even a malingering seaman was likely to be shown the door under that cool scrutiny.

"Have you ever dealt amongst convicts before, Doctor?" he asked gently.

Doctor Fernley smiled, answering the implied query. "No, Captain, but on shore I have dealt with imaginitive ladies who dearly love to suffer from ill health!"

Ross laughed. "Forgive me. I was not doubting your competence. But you think this girl is truly as you find her and not feigning weakness?"

"I would stake my reputation on it. And I don't do that lightly, I assure you."

Ross nodded. "Very well, Doctor. But where do you suggest I confine her? The gun deck is rather too near the crew's quarters for a lone girl."

"Why not leave her in the cabin? The crew are not allowed on the passenger or officer deck. I will guarantee her security."

"Then you have my permission to inform your patient of her new status, and I hope your trust in her character is justified."

"Thank you, Captain."

There was a long pause and the doctor drank his whisky thoughfully. Finally he raised his eyes to Ross.

"I rather think the information would come better from you, Captain."

The dark brows rose in surprise. "From me? Why do you say that?"

"I gather," said Doctor Fernley carefully, "that the girl goes in some fear of being summarily returned to the hold. She expects nothing else, but the prolonged tension of waiting for that moment to arrive is taking its toll of her health. Coming from you, the ultimate authority, it would go far to improving her mental state. My words make little impression."

Ross frowned, wondering at his own reluctance to face her again. Would she accept his reassurance or believe it another sadistic trick?

This ridiculous notion of the ship's captain being looked upon as untrustworthy by a female convict brought a flush to his cheeks. He stiffened and said,

curtly, "I will speak with her in the
morning."

Doctor Fernley nodded, setting down his
glass. He left the cabin quietly without
another word.

Juliet had been warned to expect the
captain but even so, the first sight of that
hard-eyed stranger who entered after one
sharp rap on the door drove the blood from
her face. For a long moment they stared at
each other in silence.

She was dressed in her own clothes, the
faded red cotton of her dress accentuating
her pallor, and her small thin hands were
clasped tightly in her lap as she sat on the
hard wooden cabin chair.

Ross stared into the darkened grey eyes
that held a barely restrained terror and
found himself unable to utter the few cold
words he had intended.

"What is your name?" he amazed himself
by asking instead.

She took a gulping breath. "Juliet . . .
Juliet Westover, sir."

He locked his hands behind him and
stood leaning forward a little, his eyes surveying her from under dark brows.

"You know why I am here? Has Doctor
Fernley told you?"

"Yes, sir."

That painfully vulnerable look was still
there and for some strange reason Ross
found himself searching for the right
words.

"You don't appear to have much confidence in him." he said.

"I have every confidence in Doctor Fernley," Juliet said quietly, with the faintest lift of her chin.

Ross stiffened then relaxed. He deserved that cut. "In that case, perhaps you will accept my corroboration and believe that I have no intention of returning you to the hold."

"At the moment?"

"At any time. You may occupy this cabin until we reach New South Wales. Doctor Fernley has argued your case and you have my word on it."

"And your conditions?"

"Conditions? Only that you hold faith with him and keep yourself out of the way of my officers and the running of this ship."

A little color had returned to her face. "You may be assured of that, Captain. I have learnt the value of privacy. You will not regret your indulgence to Doctor Fernley."

A strange creature, mused Ross, watching her closely. She sat as quietly as a young lady in her own drawing room making polite conversation. She had not overwhelmed him with thanks, and her attitude was far from coquettish. She spoke of indulgence to the doctor, not to herself.

Subconsciously he had been prepared for an inviting move, a subtle offer of her charms which he could have countered icily. Instead she had accepted his word with the dignity of a well brought-up girl. Which was the act? The lady or the hussy who had been willing to share his bed to keep her from the hold? He preferred the former but the latter stayed in his mind. It said little for his personal charm! She had thought to use him but her present relief implied that it had not been a course of her own choosing!

He suddenly realized that her gaze was as watchful as his. Was she still unconvinced of his motive? Did she imagine he would impose some personal conditions later?

"You are in Doctor Fernley's charge, Miss Westover, and our paths are unlikely to cross again. Good morning to you!"

He bowed briefly and was gone, leaving Juliet glowing with relief and intense gratitude to Doctor Fernley. She could hardly believe that she need never see Jeb White or her companions of the hold again. To be knocked unconcious was a small price to pay for this marvelous unexpected freedom. And Captain Jamieson had been quite civil too! That dreadful scene in this very cabin two days ago might never have happened, to judge from his attitude!

Doctor Fernley marveled at the change in his patient when he called later. She was completely transformed and no longer wore the haunted look of a girl suffering mental torment. Her eyes sparkled and her curls, brought under control by the gift of a spare hairbrush from the doctor, gleamed with dancing lights.

As Capetown was sighted the mood of the crew and officers became buoyant. A chance to stretch their legs on firm ground, an opportunity to purchase gifts of native craft for wives and sweethearts, and the attraction of stocking up with Cape fruits and fresh water. Juliet was as excited as the rest of them, gazing out over the Dutch-ruled coastline. Obviously she wasn't allowed ashore and had no money to spend anyway, but the sheer joy of seeing people and activity in the harbor entranced her.

As the 'Grace' docked she watched eagerly from the porthole. Doctor Fernley had told her they were to stay a week, taking on board some cattle in addition to provisions. She glimpsed Captain Jamieson going ashore, resplendant in white buck-skins and russet jacket, his gold-edged tricorne clapped firmly on his dark head. She saw the sudden smile on his lean tanned face as he greeted the Company representative. Had she met him under different circumstances she might have considered him an attractive man, but their dealings had been marred by mutual distrust. She thought him a tyrant and he thought her a whore. There was no common ground to meet upon.

IV

While in harbor the convicts were not allowed their daily exercise. The hatch was opened but no one was permitted above decks in case of escape. Juliet was light-headed with relief that she was no longer confined below in the stench and fear of the past long months. In gratitude to Doctor Fernley she insisted on caring for his clothes, finding a sad case of sheer inability to hold together a full set of buttons on any of his jackets. He had laughed ruefully, declaring himself a complete incompetent with a needle, but complimented Juliet on her skill, finding her eagerness to repay him touching.

In the cool of the evening he took her on deck to enjoy a leisurely stroll fore and aft. In the face of her doubts he assured her that he had the captain's permission. Even so, Juliet's eyes were watchful and she

101

shrank close to him at the sound of a male
voice, pulling back from any meeting.

"Surely, my dear," he said laughingly,
"you have mixed in company before."

"You are mistaken, sir," she answered in
a small voice. "I have never been in
company other than that of the farm
children on my father's ..." She caught
back the rest of the sentence.

"Your father's—what, child?"

"They lived near us, that's all. They were
my only friends."

"And what of your family?"

"My ... my mother is dead. I was an only
child."

"Ah—an orphan?"

She gave him an upward slanting look,
compressing her lips, and he was chilled by
the bleakness of it. She made no reply.

"So you had no one to guide you," he said
softly. "Poor child."

"Don't pity me, sir," she said in a small
hard voice. "Pity if you can, for I cannot,
the one who will answer to a higher court
for bearing false witness."

Doctor Fernley sighed, was there ever a
felon who did not cry innocence?

Juliet heard the sigh and divined its
meaning. She gave a mental shrug. Sufficient that she was free of the hold by the
good offices of this man. She must not sour
their relationship by involving him in her
bitterness.

They paused at the rail, gazing over the

quiet glittering sea towards the township. Smoke from fires spiraled lazily into the night sky, and she could hear the beat of drums and the chanting of natives from somewhere along the coast.

"What strange smells emanate from the docks" she said, lifting her face to the breeze. "Spices, fruit, sawdust and the scent of the farmyard."

As if to answer her, a sheep bleated loudly. She laughed. "Do you take them to New South Wales?"

Doctor Fernley leaned over the rail. "Yes, indeed. Pigs, too. The settlers are hungry for animals to populate their new pastures. There's much grazing, they say, and the Government only too happy to allot thousands of acres to those willing to farm them."

"And you, Doctor? Would you become a settler?"

"Not me, my dear. They need young strong men with the vision to build a new world. I am a doctor not a pioneer. My roots are in England."

Juliet was silent. Her own future was in that raw pioneering country. What was it to be, she wondered? Sold to some farmer for field work or taken as scullery maid? Whatever it was, her freedom would never be hers again. Whoever paid the price took her body and soul for the rest of her life. She pushed away the thought of that black future.

"Do you go ashore, Doctor?"

"Yes. I had thought to buy some trinkets for my wife and daughters. There might be letters, too. And I must write my own to be taken on board a homebound ship." He glanced at her. "If there is anyone you wish to communicate with I should be only too happy to include your letter with my packet. . ." He stopped in sudden confusion as if struck by some ineptness in his words.

Juliet gazed at him in puzzlement for a moment, then smiled. "Yes, I can read and write, doctor, but as my roots will be henceforth in this new land I see no reason to maintain any contact with England. I thank you for the thought, however."

Doctor Fernley's face in the lamplight was a study of relief, then he glanced over her shoulder in surprise. "Good evening, Captain, I thought you still ashore."

Juliet gasped and swung round, her pulses thudding. But the captain's eyes were on a paper he carried.

"Damned if I can read the fellow's scribble" he said. His gaze fell on Juliet and there was something in his eyes that challenged her. "You claim to be a reader, Miss Westover. See if you can make sense of this settler's request. I can't believe he expects me to carry a sow in pig! What the hell happens if she gives birth?"

Juliet held the much creased and thumbed paper to the lamp. She was conscious of Captain Jamieson's closeness and the long brown finger pointing over her shoulder. Her eyes quickly ran down the ill-spelled column, stopping by the finger. She held back an involuntary gurgle of laughter.

"I rather think he requests a fowling-piece, although his spelling leaves a lot to be desired. A gentleman of few words, I'd guess," she went on solemnly, "and even fewer on paper."

Ross grinned down at her. "And by the smell of the letter he'd had a few tots of rum before laboring his brain." He stared at the letter again. "And half of it split over on the relevant parts. Well done, Miss Westover. You've relieved my mind." He leaned on the rail beside her. "Tell me, what do you think of Capetown?"

"If you'll excuse me," murmured the doctor, "I have to write a letter."

Juliet looked at him for a panic-stricken moment but he bowed and smiled, turning away.

"See the Table Mountain? Magnificent isn't it?" Ross was saying, and Juliet realized she could not avoid being left alone with him. To scuttle after the doctor would declare a sad lack of dignity.

Ross, for his part, had been cudgeling his brains for a simple way to make his peace with her and this chance encounter had given him the opportunity. Might as well let his long suffering cabin boy achieve his heart's desire. It was a long way to Aus-

tralia, and this girl's aptness with a needle
and sponge had made all the difference to
his wardrobe. Give her something to do as
well, as long as she kept out of the way of
his crew. One flutter of her long eyelashes
at his officers and she'd find herself tossed
willy-nilly back into the hold, he told himself sternly.

Meanwhile she was feminine company,
and according to Doctor Fernley, an in-
telligent female. Perhaps he had been
wrong to treat her in so cavalier a fashion but
his experience with convict shipping was
limited. There was crime and crime, he
acknowledged, and hers was possibly less
serious, but the courts were hard even on
minor wrongdoers.

Juliet watched him warily, then moved
her gaze to the shadowed outline of the
mountain looming over the small settlement. She had seen it in daylight with the
brazen sun beating down and considered it
rather a menacing sight.

"I'm afraid I cannot pass an opinion on
Capetown," she said coolly, "as I have seen
it only from this ship. As to the Table
Mountain, I find it quite uninspiring."

She leaned her arms on the rail, looking
straight ahead. He should not have the
satisfaction of seeing her struck dumb by
his condescension or find her echoing his
sentiments with nauseous servility.

Ross turned a little, leaning one elbow
only on the rail so that he could study the

girl. In profile she had a delicate, even aristocratic look, and her dark curls were massed behind her head, secured by a rough length of twine. Her arms lay slim and bare, the small shoulder edges darned. The tears in the faded red dress were neatly mended and he remembered the shift of rough cotton that had chafed his hands when he held her limp body.

He removed his gaze abruptly as he also recalled the feel of that body and the glimpses he had had of the silken thigh and rose-tipped breasts. Perhaps that revealing moment had been truly accidental. But her scornful attack later had not survived his offer to bed her as an act of favor. He faced the truth. What girl would not, given the choice, opt for sharing any man's bed above decks rather than rejoin that herd of illiterate ruffians crammed in the hold. Who could blame her? And yet he had scorched her with the heat of his tongue, reducing her to an ashen creature, shattered and disintegrated before his eyes.

The clean smell of her floated to his nostrils. He felt an uncharacteristic lick of desire start at his feet and travel like a wind-driven flame to his brain. Had her scent been heavy with perfume he would have turned as from a painted harlot, but somehow the very freshness of this creature enmeshed his senses and played havoc with his orderly mind.

"Juliet Westover," he said, musingly and

she glanced sharply at him. "What was your crime?" he asked in a conversational tone. "You borrowed your mistress's jewels and were accused of theft, perhaps?"

Her smile was thin. "You are the captain. Surely you are aware of the reason for my conviction?"

"I haven't looked at those papers since we left Bristol."

"Then I suggest you do. It might deter you from indulging in such democratic behavior as this."

"My behavior is directed by purpose or inclination, not by the judgment of others."

"And what is your purpose in holding this conversation?"

"I have no purpose, just the inclination."

"Am I meant to be flattered, I wonder?" She gazed at him with a mocking glint in her eye. "Please excuse me from reciprocation. I might be accused of seeking to ravish your Scottish sensibilities."

Ross grinned wryly. "An apology seems to be in order. Would you accept one?"

"If you will accept that a female of very limited wardrobe needs a moment of warning before receiving unexpected visitors."

Ross extended his hand. Juliet hesitated, then laid her hand against the brown palm. His grasp was firm and her fingers were locked in his for a brief moment of intimacy. Just before his grasp loosened, Juliet gazed into his eyes and surprised a strangely intent look. She stiffened, drawing back, and his hand dropped, his face expressing nothing. For a giddy moment she thought he intended drawing her to him and her body had almost swayed forward before her wits came to her aid. If this was another attempt to brand her a willing whore, she must not play into his hands by allowing her senses to overcome her caution. He was, she realized, a very attractive man—dangerously so at close quarters. How easy it would be to melt against that hard masculine body, to feel caressing hands such as she had never known. To a girl whose only emotions had been of fear and grief, it would be fatally easy to succumb to a few kind words and the warm clasp of a hand. Had she done so, his previous estimation of her character would have been reinforced. It was something she must guard against and take his friendship as lightly as it was offered. No wonder his look had been intent! Calculating her response to a show of amiability, she surmised. The experience in the cabin was not one she cared to repeat.

"Would you excuse me now, Captain Jamieson, I am rather tired."

Her voice was steady and casual.

After she had gone, Ross stared out over the Bay, trying to make sense of his feelings. She was a damned attractive creature. The touch of her tiny hand in his had seemed to fan the spark of his desire.

What the devil was he at, mooning over a convict wench who must have known men whatever the doctor believed. She had been lucky, that's all, to avoid disease. Her youth and the short time she had had to ply her trade was the answer. And yet it was a puzzle. She had seemed to read some danger in his face and had drawn back like a nervous fawn. Had he intended an embrace, caught unknowingly by that moment of desire? He was damned if he knew! But the more he thought of her, the clearer her shape became in that revealing towel. She had been there for the taking, willing to accept his offer. But some fastidious facet of his character had despised that willingness, deeming it a self-seeking attempt to escape the hold.

He turned from the rail, irritated by the clamminess of his stock and tight-fitting jacket. Down in his cabin he stripped and stepped into a bath of lukewarm water. He squeezed the sponge over his head and shoulders, feeling relief as the water coursed down his body and around his strong thighs and legs, taking the heat from his loins. He grinned a trifle mockingly at his thoughts. If he was to make the wary Miss Westover his mistress, he'd have to court the wench first and allay her suspicions. He'd a notion it wouldn't be easy. She was too sharp to accept a straightforward offer. He'd find himself the one scorched and cindered. She'd take the hold first, just for the hell of it, and whatever his threats, he knew he could not send her back there.

The next morning Captain Jamieson and Doctor Fernley went ashore together. Their first call was to the offices of the East India Company to pick up the mail held there for them. There was nothing personal for Ross but the doctor was gratified to find letters from his wife and daughters.

Before leaving they were both summoned to the office by the manager. He spread out a map on the table and beckoned the two men to his side.

"I regret, Captain, that something has just cropped up and means a diversion of the 'Grace's' course to Mozambique. It will unfortunately add a few weeks to your voyage but you are the only British ship in harbor. The plea for medical supplies comes from the Portuguese governor and I have been ordered to accede to it."

"Mozambique?" asked Doctor Fernley "What's wrong there?"

"They have an outbreak of some kind of fever in the shanty area of the harbor, probably through lice, and the governor has put the place in quarantine. He is desperately afraid of it spreading. His own doctor is down with it and he seems to be in some panic that he, himself, will succumb."

"Does he know what kind of fever?"

"He mentions rashes and spotting, and in

some cases a swelling about the neck."

"Maybe chicken pox or a variety of typhoidal infection. But the sooner we get supplies there, the sooner I'll know. The doctor is an old friend of mine. I'll go ashore and help them organize the relief. How soon will the medicines be ready?"

"The Dutch are aiding us in this. Two days should suffice to collect what is needed. Can you sail in that time, Captain?"

Ross nodded. "If we can speed up the provisioning we should be ready."

"Thank you, gentlemen. This action will commend us to the government of Portugal and our own, of course. My clerk will take you to the warehouse, Doctor, and you can advise on the supplies you consider necessary to cover any eventuality."

Ross and Doctor Fernley parted outside the office and Ross strolled through the street of small shops and stalls. He had some vague idea of searching out a gift for Juliet Westover as the first step in his campaign, but would the girl accept anything from him? A bracelet perhaps? Then his eye was caught by a discreet little shop whose window displayed an oriental shawl and a pair of satin slippers. The sign above declared it to be a high class modiste.

On an impulse he entered and before his nerve failed he addressed a smartly attired female.

"A shift, monsieur? A pure silk shift? But, of course."

There was no surprise on the smooth French countenance. One might almost have been requesting a coil of rope. And that reminded him. A hair ribbon.

"Dark red, monsieur? Certainly. The exact color, if I might bring it to your notice, of the elegant negligee you see on the display figure."

Unwittingly, Ross glanced at the model. The sheer diaphanous nature of the material showed every voluptuous curve of the blank-faced mannequin. He had a sudden vision of other curves and a touch of color tinged his cheekbones.

"You have considered pantalettes, monsieur?"

"I beg your pardon?" Ross said bemusedly, dragging his gaze from the model.

"To match the shift." The girl put her head on one side. "Or perhaps not. It is a matter of the lady's preference in a hot climate."

"Yes, of course—to match the shift."

"Your lady is petite, monsieur? The sizes, you understand?"

"Yes ... she is petite ... like yourself, mademoiselle."

"The satin shoes in the window are especially for the petite."

"No, no, not those." Ross struggled for common sense. "Not on a ship."

"Eh, bien, monsieur, the very thing. A sandal with low heel. The kid is fine but strong. Ah, how very delighted this lucky lady will be with your choice. She has, of course, the lightweight robes for daytime wear?''

Ross left the persuasive presence of the modiste with his arms full of boxes and his wallet a great deal lighter. His mind was still in a whirl, his eyes dazzled by the glowing colors of satin and chiffon. He grinned weakly. Trust a Frenchwoman to empty your pockets in the course of business. But what the hell business was he doing, buying negligees and shifts for a convict girl? Not to mention the fine embroidered cotton dress with the lace flounces. What possible explanation could he make to the confounded girl that wouldn't seem like bribing his way into favor? As he went up the gangplank, he toyed with the idea of tossing the whole lot into the sea but his Scottish blood revolted at the waste of a considerable amount of money. No! The resolution of this madness would take a great deal of finesse if he was to view the negligee on a living breathing body.

He dumped the boxes on his bunk and stood with his back to them as his cabin boy lunged in. The forbidding scowl on Ross's face went unheeded.

"Cap'n, he gasped. "Young Lukey's gone and broke his leg. We'll have to leave him behind." He grinned delightedly.

"Who the hell is Lukey and what's so joy-making about breaking a leg?"

"He's the powder monkey, Captain." The

boy seemed as if that explained everything.

Ross gazed at him for a long moment and a reluctant half-smile appeared.

"I can see you're overcome with sorrow! If I didn't know you better I'd think you had a hand in it, you damned young popinjay! What happened?"

"He were gaping at a bunch of native girls, Cap'n. Singing they were and near naked as babes. Then he fell over a barrel of fish. The bloke selling 'em was real narked, all over the place they were. But Lukey was screaming louder than him and the Dutch fellows came and carted Lukey off to hospital."

Ross sighed. "Then I'd better go ashore again and sort it out. Is the doctor on board?"

"Yes, sir."

"Fetch him for me."

"Yes, sir." The boy moved slowly to the door, his steps lagging.

"Damned inconvenient, sailing without a powder monkey." Ross mused, his eyes on the slumped shoulders. "Where do I get another at such short notice, I wonder?"

The boy turned, his earnest freckled face hopeful. "I've been learned a bit by the gunner, sir, and that young miss done your mending a lot better than I did." He waited, his ambitious dream transparent on his young face.

The captain appeared much struck by his words. "Do you know, young fellow, I think you've come up with the very notion."

The boy waited, holding his breath, while the captain pondered, frowning.

The brow cleared. "Fetch the doctor then cut along to the passenger cabin and tell that girl she's to have your duties in future."

The lad gulped. "Aye, aye, Captain!" He snapped to attention, then clattered off at a fast trot in case the captain changed his mind.

Ross grinned to himself. He could leave the persuasion to the lad and remain aloof from argument. Fate, in the shape of a gaping powder monkey falling over a barrel, had solved the problem of getting the girl into his cabin. If he couldn't achieve the rest for himself, he was not the man who had bedded a number of willing and wellborn females in his naval career!

While the lad was gone, he unpacked the parcels, laying the clothes in his seachest and crushing the boxes to obscure the name of the modiste. What arguments the boy used he never knew but when he and Doctor Fernley returned from arranging Lukey's stay in hospital and subsequent passage on the next ship to England, he found his bedclothes turned back smoothly, the hanging lamp alight and his shaving gear laid neatly alongside a can of hot water.

It became evident during the following day that Juliet had discovered his approximate timetable from his ex-cabin boy as the duties were performed without him catching a glimpse of her.

On the day they set sail for Mozambique, he varied his routine. Once the 'Grace' was safely en route and instructions given to the helmsman, he went down to his cabin.

Juliet looked up in surprise from the shirt hem she was mending. She rose, color mantling her cheeks.

"I'm sorry, I should have taken this to my cabin but there seemed more breeze here."

"No need for apology. It is my place to thank you for stepping in and agreeing to take over the cabin boy's duties." He gazed around. "I can see the difference already. A willing lad but hamfisted. He'll be happier in his new role."

"There seems little more I can do in regard to your mending. The contents of your clothes press appear to be in good order."

"Try the seachest." Ross said, frowning over a map. He rolled it up and tucked it under his arm, raising his head to smile at her. "It's time I sorted out my tropical clothes. It'll get hotter than this."

Juliet eyed the small brass-bound seachest standing by the bulkhead. Now that she had been given permission to open it, there could be many more garments requiring her attention and giving her something with which to occupy her mind. She had dreaded having nothing to do in case the unpredictable captain regretted his words and found her a nuisance above

decks. She laid aside her completed task
and approached the chest.

Beneath a lightweight jacket of linen she
found a froth of chiffon. She sank back on
her heels regarding the wine-red, ruffle-
edged negligee with astonishment. She
drew it gently through her fingers, mar-
veling at the featherlight softness of it. A
gift, no doubt, for his wife or fiancee, but a
lovely thing that brought a sigh to her lips.
She laid it carefully on the bunk and
explored deeper. Sheer silk shift and pantalettes came to hand. A wife most certainly.
A single man did not buy such things for a
girl—unless, of course, their relationship
was of the most intimate kind! A man
might buy them to delight a mistress. The
cotton dress of palest blue with the delicate
flounces of crisp white lace made her gasp
with delight. How wonderful to own and
wear such things. And the elegant kid
sandals! He must have bought them in
Capetown, either for a girl in Australia or to
take back to England as a homecoming gift.

She roused herself sternly and laid them
together on the bunk. No use dreaming
over such things. Her future wardrobe
would be of the coarsest cloth, ornamented
only by apron and mobcap, she thought
wryly.

Beneath these feminine things she found
drill uniforms and thinner shirts. Removing
all the masculine attire, she replaced the
female garments, wrapping them in tissue

paper to protect them from contact with the metal studs.

The uniforms and shirts required no attention at all. She shook them out and hung them in the clothes press, then sank onto the bunk staring at the now closed sea-chest. She imagined a girl in the blue dress, her hair piled shiningly on top of her head, her fingers resting on the strong arm of a lover. She must be a small girl, rather like herself, the tucked waist was narrow and the full skirts would emphasize that tiny waist. She visualized her gazing into the dark handsome face of Captain Jamieson and the captain smiling down, his face full of love.

She didn't hear him come in. Suddenly he was there and he was smiling. Her heart turned over and she couldn't tear away her gaze. Ross stared into the dreaming face. He had never seen such beautiful dove-grey eyes. He couldn't take his eyes from that soft, heart-shaped face with the full red kissable lips.

"Juliet," he said huskily, unable to move for the sudden pounding in his temples.

She came to her feet slowly, the dreamy look fading. Soon she would be gone, he thought in panic. He stepped back and his gaze fell on the dark red ribbon that had fallen from the chest. He scooped it up and held it out.

She looked once and her brows arched in question.

"Instead of that piece of twine, I ... I bought you a ribbon." He was stammering like a schoolboy. "A present. Nothing really."

She reached out a finger and smoothed the satin. "You bought me a present?" Her tone as incredulous.

"Instead of that piece of twine" he repeated idiotically, trying to delay the moment of her going. "Take it. Please."

Like a sleepwalker, her hand came out and touched his, drawing the ribbon away. The color washed over her skin and he saw her eyes soft and glowing.

"Nobody ever bought me a present before. Why should you?"

He spread his hands and shrugged. "No reason. I was buying something else at the time and thought your hair would look prettier with a ribbon in it."

"Thank you." She glanced at the sea-chest. "They're very beautiful. For your wife?"

"I'm not married."

"Oh!" Her color deepened a little. She looked at him rather helplessly. His back was to the door, blocking her way out. He was gazing down at her in that strangely intent way.

"Captain?" She tried to pass him but the entrance was narrow. He caught her shoulders as she stumbled.

"Juliet." His voice was no more than a sigh as he gathered her into his arms. He bent his head, unable to resist the tempting lips. He kissed her and she didn't pull away.

Surprise held her quiescent for the first few seconds, then her mouth softened under his kisses. Her senses seemed to leave her suspended and melting in the heat that sparked through her body. She tried to pull her thoughts into some kind of order but with his lips caressing her mouth, her cheeks and the curve of her neck, it was almost impossible. His strong arms and the close contact from shoulder to thigh burned like fire and was just as dangerous.

His hands locked behind her waist and his head bent to the neckline of her gown. She leaned back against his grip, struggling with her own desire. Palms flat on his chest, she strained backwards, forcing his eyes to meet hers.

"Captain! Is this your due for a paltry hair ribbon?" She heard her own voice, gasping and harsh.

Ross stiffened, the fire dying out of him. He stared into the grey, indignant eyes.

"Due?" He frowned. "No, dammit! That was a gift."

"Then why . . . ?"

"Haven't you ever looked into a glass, girl? You're tempting enough to make any man lose his senses, especially one who has been at sea for months on end. Can you wonder men want you? Why do you think the convicts were fighting over you? Not for your sweet conversation, that's for sure.

Good heavens, girl, don't you know anything?" he finished in exasperation.

Juliet was bewildered by his change of mood. "But you don't even like me!" she protested.

"What has that to do with anything?" he snapped. "Does a man have to declare undying passion before he can make love to a woman?"

Juliet flushed deeply. "So I am still a whore to be bedded. Is that it?" Her temper began to rise and her eyes flashed with a cold brilliance. She stared into his face. "May I ask if Captain Jamieson's previous whores were content then with hair ribbons?" she inquired scornfully. "Was your virility so magnificent they were glad to offer their services practically free? I may know little of gentlemen, Captain, but I do know that even they must pay the girls they bed!"

Ross was stunned for a moment, then his anger rose to equal hers. "Very well, Miss Juliet Westover!" He crossed to the seachest and flung open the lid. "I see you've been through these contents. Will what you found be sufficient due for your services? I doubt the convicts can offer you a better deal but you are quite free to consider their proposals."

Juliet flinched at his tone, her anger evaporating rapidly. She might have known her freedom was conditional, if she'd had an ounce of sense in her head. He was a man.

She should have known better than to trust his word. Now what choice did she have?

Ross strode to the door. "Consider this cabin as your own now. You will not object, I trust, if I lock the door? Tonight we dine here alone and you will wear the dress I bought. Later, you will put on the negligee and endeavour to arouse my, as you call it, magnificent virility! Tonight your performance will have a rapt but critical audience of one." He looked back coldly over his shoulder. "Your future may depend on how I view that performance, Miss Juliet Westover!"

V

Ross strode blindly down the deck corridor, his face dark with anger. Had he met anyone on the way he would have walked right past them without noticing. Luckily the deck and companionway were empty as he went up the steps two at a time. The breeze caught him in its grip and he ducked his head to avoid his hat being swept away. He was furiously angry, not only at the impertinence of the girl below but with his own inept performance. He should have given her time to appreciate her new position and consider the gift as a forerunner of other possible favors. But no, confound it! The urge to kiss her had overthrown his cool calculation and she had linked the two together. How could he now hold to his plan of spacing out the gifts to draw her gradually into his debt until she offered as a token of her gratitude all that

was left for her to give? She had nothing
but her body, and instead of coming
gratefully into his arms, his instincts told
him she would fight all the way!

He had given her an ultimatum. He
hadn't meant to—not after assuring her
that she would not be returned to the hold
at any time. To back down now was not in
his nature but neither was breaking his
word. How would she respond? He stared
towards the coastline, watching the sun
lose its spendor, and his lips curved
cynically. Soon he would know whether self-
preservation had ousted the pose of refined
outrage.

Juliet, left alone so suddenly, sank onto
the bunk in an agony of self-recrimination.
Why had she let her temper flare and lead
her into this trap? If anything was needed
to confirm his belief that she was a whore,
she had given it by her words. She cupped
her chin in her hands staring down at the
carpet. Talking so wildly of payment for
services had played right into his hands. A
lady would not talk so. But then, a lady who
had not experienced the lifestyle of a felon
would not have gained the knowledge she
had. And after all, she was no longer a lady,
just a female felon en route for a life of
slavery. Very well, he should have a
mistress if it kept her from the hold, but he
would not find her a willing partner.

In the hour before dinner, Juliet took a
bath and used the captain's soap liberally

before drying herself on his large soft towels. The shift slid over her head, its silky folds clinging to her body as satisfyingly as she had imagined. The pantalettes and sandals followed and she shook out the blue flounced dress. It fitted her perfectly. Who had he bought it for, she wondered, gazing into the glass, eyeing herself in her very first professionally-made gown. The lace ruffles gave her forearms and hands a slender elegance and the darted waistline might have been made to her own measurements.

With deliberation she used the captain's own silver backed hairbrushes until her curls lay black and gleaming on her shoulders. Glancing curiously at his toilet things, she fingered a bottle of eau de cologne, then poured a drop into her hand, patting it onto her face and neck.

She was considering investigating the contents of the top drawer of the chest, perhaps for a small handkerchief she might appropriate, when a tap on the door sent her pulses racing. She turned, leaning her back against the chest, aware of the need for support. Another soft tap. Surely he would walk straight in!

"Come . . . come in," she managed huskily, and the door was unlocked and opened.

A dark face glanced at her briefly from under a small turban. "Permit me, memsahib, to make ready the table." A

dark-skinned, slightly built man bowed and
waited, his eyes downcast.

"Yes . . . yes, of course." Juliet watched
him set a small table in the middle of the
carpet. From a trolley in the corridor he
took a white damask tablecloth and
proceeded to lay on it an assortment of
silver cutlery and wine glasses. Soup plates
and lidded tureen followed.

"Captain sahib, he come one moment. I
wait outside door, memsahib."

"Thank you. What is your name?"

"Joseph, memsahib. Joseph Garcia."

"Are you from India, Joseph?"

"West Coast, memsahib. From Portuguese Goa. Lots of Goanese boys liking to
work on English ships."

They both heard the footsteps. Joseph
backed from the cabin and Juliet's fingers
clung to the chest. She stared at the doorway then drew herself erect, schooling her
expression to indifference.

Ross paused in the doorway and his eyes
moved slowly over the enchanting picture
she made. The dress could not have been
more fetching, he decided, the tight waistline defining the gentle swell of the breasts
above. The ruffled lace neckline was low
enough to give a glimpse of the shadowed
cleft between the ivory breasts. He raised
his eyes to her face and caught the half-
smile of amused contempt with which she
was regarding him.

"The first course is ready, Captain."

Juliet murmured and Ross's glance sharpened as he heard the underlying mockery in her voice.

"So I see. But we mustn't let the soup get cold," he answered pleasantly and saw her lashes veil the leaping spark in her eyes.

He threw his hat and jacket on the bunk and held out a chair for her. As she sat down the aroma of eau de cologne came to him.

"A refreshing scent, is it not?" he said.

"Yes, indeed. And I already had your permission to treat this cabin as my own so I used your hairbrushes too. I'm afraid your towels are rather damp." There was no hint of regret in her voice.

He seated himself opposite. "Joseph will bring more. We shall eat first, then I shall take a bath."

Juliet shrugged. "An unusual way about it but then one can only be thankful that you have not just come from the stables."

"Had I done that, I might well have needed someone to scrub my back." His dark gaze rested on her in interested speculation.

Juliet met his gaze blandly. "I would not care to risk these lace ruffles in your tub, Captain, apart from lacking the aptitude of a gentleman's gentleman."

Ross smiled. "One of those gentlemen will be distinctly superfluous tonight. I am quite capable of managing without any help."

"I am glad to hear it."

"A little show of enthusiasm for what lies before you would not come amiss at this moment."

Juliet's brows rose to their full height. "Enthusiasm?" she choked.

Ross looked concerned. "Joseph would be most distressed if he thought you disliked his soup. He is a very good cook."

For a full minute Juliet stared at him speechlessly then looked down at her plate onto which Ross had ladled some soup.

"Do try it," he said politely, as if he were nothing more than a genial host tempting the appetite of a guest.

Juliet picked up her soup spoon, unaware that Ross had not done the same. His wait had been deliberate, a desire to see if she recognized the correct spoon.

Fish in cream sauce followed, then a shoulder of mutton. Juliet accepted one glass of wine but refused more. She was glad to see her host replenish his glass several times. With a bit of luck, she thought savagely, he might drink himself into a stupor. Unfortunately, he showed no signs of obliging her.

"Did you purchase the wine in Capetown?" she asked at last, as Ross seemed unnervingly content for the meal to proceed in silence.

"Yes, I did. It's rather good, don't you think? I believe their vineyards will prosper in the climate."

Juliet twisted the stem of her glass between her fingers. "I can see that you find it very palatable. You laid in a good stock, I conjecture?"

Ross caught the derisory note in her voice. "Indeed yes," he said blandly. "A most pleasant aid to digestion. Not potent enough to inflame the mind nor render one incapable. Perhaps you would have preferred gin yourself, for one reason or another?"

"I have never tasted gin, nor any other spirit, so I have no idea of its effect. And this is my first glass of wine."

"Really? I find that hard to believe."

"You will believe what you want to believe," Juliet said on a bored note. "I am indifferent to your opinion."

He leaned forward, looking into her eyes. "You are a strange girl, Juliet Westover. You eat like a lady and have no hesitation in picking up the correct knife or spoon. You could have learned etiquette in service—or had an educated protector. Which was it?"

"Neither."

"How did you earn your living?"

"I had no need to."

He leaned back, surveying her slightly flushed face from blue eyes that held a hint of bafflement.

"You would have me believe you were born a lady? Your own clothes give the lie to that. Where are the silks and fine cambrics?''

"I never had any. There is such a thing as genteel poverty, Captain. One soon becomes accustomed to making the best of it.''

"Your father is dead?'' he asked, abruptly.

The small face closed and the eyes were like blank shutters sealing off all expression. It warned Ross that he was on delicate ground with his curiosity still unsatisfied. He could look at the papers given to him by the prisoner's guard but he was loathe to do that. He had hoped she would tell of her own accord but he found he knew little more than when she first collapsed on the deck after the riot in the hold. Most felons by this time would have poured out their grievances, declaring themselves innocent as babes unborn, but not this one. She accused no one and made no attempt to excuse whatever she had been convicted of. He had to admit she intrigued him and her mind was as sharp as her body was beautiful.

Joseph was removing the fruit and coffee, folding the damask cloth when Juliet looked up and smiled at him.

"Thank you, Joseph. A most delicious meal." Her smile was warm and friendly.

The Goanese bowed. "It was a pleasure to serve you, memsahib.''

He was gone, soft-footed, and there was silence in the cabin. Juliet drew a deep breath and gazed calmly at Ross.

"Do you take your bath now, Captain, while I follow your orders?"

She leaned back and he could not see the hands clasped tightly in her lap. All he saw was the uplifted brow and what he judged to be a mocking expression on her face.

"Why not?" He rose and moved first to lock the door and then to the dressing room with the key in his pocket. "I bathe very quickly" he added.

"I was sure you would." The calm voice followed as he dropped the curtain behind him.

Out of sight, Juliet's expression changed. She was desperately afraid but saw no way out of her predicament, short of screaming the place down! And that, she decided wryly, would certainly earn her a speedy return to the hold. The role of harlot was not in her repertoire so she must allow him to do as he wished while preserving a ladylike indifference to the proceedings, praying for a quick release.

The beautiful blue dress she hung carefully in the clothes press. As she lifted the negligee from the bed, she could clearly see the lamplight through it. Her cheeks flamed. Her body would just as clearly be revealed, but of course, that was exactly the reason for its purchase! She gave a quick scared glance at the dressing room curtain then slid out of her shift and pantalettes, kicking off the sandals as she

hurriedly donned the negligee. It really was
a beautiful shade of deep red, curiously an
exact match of the hair ribbon he had given
her. At any other time she would have been
enchanted to feel the cool, flowing lines of
silky chiffon caressing her body but now
she clutched the folds over her breasts in
near panic.

Ross came suddenly and softly out of the
dressing room, a towel knotted about his
waist. One strong hand held back the curtain as he paused to look at the girl by the
bed.

The knuckles of her clenched hands
gleamed whitely and the grey eyes staring
at him were enormous pools of apprehension. He frowned. What trick was this?

"What the devil's wrong with you, girl?
It's not a hanging I've invited you to!" he
said harshly—and Juliet flinched, remembering.

Her fingers uncurled their grip and her
arms sank slowly to her sides. In spite of
the warmth of the cabin an icy chill stroked
her back. No, it wasn't a hanging. That, she
had escaped, and a further escape had been
achieved from the hold. Surely she could
ask for no more than that? Repayment was
due and the man standing here before her
had been chosen to collect that debt.

Through the revealing chiffon, her body
was as exquisite as Ross remembered.
Small high breasts, a narrow waist, then
the gentle swell of the hips. A flat stomach,

and slender, rounded thighs tapering down to slim legs. His eyes moved up again, resting on the shadowed triangle of her loins. The skin of his back prickled and he laid a hand on the knot of the towel, loosening it slowly whilst his gaze strayed over the taut pink nipples and came to rest on the pale face.

The towel crumpled to the floor and Ross stood naked. Juliet's eyes had followed its fall automatically and her hypnotized gaze took in the black-haired maleness of him, the strong thighs and length of well-muscled leg before he stepped towards her. With a hand on the ruffles at each side of her throat he looked down, smiling.

"A beautiful thing, this," he murmured. "But even more beauty lies beneath." His hands moved over her shoulders holding the negligee, then it rippled down and away from her body, curling into a soft heap on the floor.

Juliet tried not to gasp as she felt Ross's hands leave her shoulders and slide over her breasts. He caressed the taut nipples for a moment, then his hands moved across her stomach and round her waist, drawing her to him by firm hands laid on her buttocks.

Juliet was incapable of resisting the strong grip but as her naked body met his, she felt the heat of him flare through her in a shockwave of emotion, denying her mind any coherent thought. His lips were on hers, then on her throat and cheeks. She was hardly aware that he had lifted her and laid her on the bed. The glow of lamplight dazzled her and the experienced hands and lips were drawing her to some strange sensual place beyond her imagining. It was impossible to resist, even had she wanted to, the insidious pull of her senses and the drowning of reality in waves of mind-numbing delight.

Sensitive fingers touched and caressed, awakening in her a throbbing response. His lips on her breasts, the warmth of his tongue gentling the nipple, the gliding hands swept her aloft into heights of soaring emotion. Her lips clung to his and her fingers moved through his tousled black hair, holding him close. Her body was liquid fire bending to his every move. She welcomed his weight, easing her thighs as he slid them apart with his own.

The entry into her soft body was achieved in an explosion of pain and she writhed in agony for a moment, her shocked mind whirling. The pain stopped suddenly and a deeper pleasure took its place as their bodies united in the act of physical love. She moved with him, her arms locked behind the long smooth back, her lips buried in the softness of his throat and cheek. She was enmeshed in a rising tide of fiery heat that strung out every nerve end into an all consuming urge to continue this moment for all eternity.

But all fires must die and flames weaken.

With a gasping sigh she lay still, her arms relaxing their hold as Ross moved. She had never realized that love of the body could be so sweet. Her mother had not known it—but how would she, with a husband who had cared for nothing but his own gratification? Her mother had not felt the gentle hands soothing her body and the lips drawing the sweetness slowly into the beginnings of passion. Had the captain forced her into submission, coldly and brutally as she imagined Sir George had taken her mother, only hatred and despair would have been left.

Juliet turned her head and looked at the man lying silently beside her. His eyes were on her, his strong face grave. She raised a hand and touched the damp dark hair on his brow, her lips trembling in a smile.

Ross caught the hand, holding it steady against his cheek. He knew, even without the telltale signs on the sheet, that he had been her first lover.

"Why?" he asked. "Why, for God's sake, didn't you tell me?" He had known many women before but had made it his policy to steer clear of virgins. Too many problems attached to figuring as a romantic young girl's first beau. They fancied their hearts were broken if a mild flirtation did not culminate in a visit to Papa. A woman who knew the rules and expected no more than an evening's joint pleasure was more to his taste.

"I did," Juliet said, mildly. "But you chose not to believe me."

"But those men in the hold?" he exclaimed, puzzled. "Didn't they try?"

"Of course. I told you that, too."

"Yes" he said slowly. "I remember you spoke of rape."

"A strong word from one of your sort," she quoted. "Isn't that what you said?"

Color touched his cheekbones and he bit his lip, nodding. "I was wrong. Crass and stupid. I assumed all women felons were the same. But you were untouched and I have used you as a harlot against your will."

"My will to resist disappeared when you touched me." She smiled into his eyes. "Did anyone so determined have so feeble a will?" she finished with a wry look.

Ross gathered her in his arms, kissing her lips and throat. "What's done is done, and for my part, I have no regrets save on your account."

"You have used me kindly, without the brutality I expected, so for this introduction I am grateful. No need for regrets. I am still a convict and you will hand me over in Sydney and go your way. We know what the future holds. No power on earth can prevent it. But until then, I shall be happy if you look on me in friendship and we can part with no ill feeling on either side, God willing."

Her arms slid round his neck and she

drew his lips down to hers. They were both lost in timeless passion again and again until at last they drifted into sleep, their bodies entwined.

Ross woke first. It was half-light and the horizon was hiding the brilliance that would burst on them suddenly from the Eastern sky. He gazed down at the naked sleeping girl. Her skin had the silken glow of a child and the tangled black curls fell disordered. Her breasts were pink, the nipples rosy, and he bent to kiss them lightly. He slid off the bed, resisting the urge to run his fingers down the insides of her thighs. If he touched her now he would never get himself on deck.

He walked barefooted into the dressing room and used the cool water from his previous night's tub to splash down his body. He dressed as quietly as he could and, placing the cabin door key on her pillow, left the cabin.

Joseph was hovering in the corridor. "Breakfast ready, sahib."

"Thank you, Joseph. Would you prepare a tray for the memsahib and take it into my cabin when she wakes?"

"Yes, sahib."

Juliet woke sometime later. She seemed possessed of a strange lethargy, even her bones felt weak. Then her eyes sprang open and she was gazing at another pillow, the indent of the head still visible. She came bolt upright, staring about the captain's cabin, her mind fully alert. He was gone but the crumpled towel on the floor and the scarlet heap of chiffon were still there, evidence of something not imagined. There was a key on the pillow beside her. Was that a hint to vacate his cabin before he returned?

She leapt from the bed gathering her own clothes and made for the dressing room. Washing quickly in water from the hipbath she struggled into her old shift and pantalettes and slid her red dress over her head.

The negligee she folded neatly along with the silk underwear and placed them in his chest along with the sandals. Her gaze fell on the bed. Bright spots of color, as bright as the stains on the bed, flew into her cheeks. She dragged off the sheet, bundling it up, ready to take it with her to the passenger cabin to wash.

A tap on the door had her whirling about. An officer come to see the captain? If she remained quiet he would go away. A voice spoke.

"Memsahib?"

Relief flowed through her. Joseph! He knew she was here. She opened the door a crack. His dark face smiled over a tray.

"I hear you moving, memsahib. Captain, he tell me to bring coffee and breakfast when you wake."

"Not in here, Joseph, surely?"

"But yes, memsahib. You are captain's lady now. You stay in cabin."

Juliet stood back, not entirely convinced that Joseph had understood the situation.

He laid the tray on the table. The fragrant smell of coffee, the crisp toast and dish of fresh fruit dispelled any indecision. She was ravenously hungry. Joseph bowed himself out on her thanks.

Did love-making usually make people so hungry, she wondered in amusement, then found herself blushing fiercely as she recalled her own wanton behavior of the night, her eagerness for his kisses and her own hands guiding him into the sweetness of fulfillment.

She finished her breakfast in a rush, collected the sheet, and hurried down the corridor to her own cabin. Whatever Joseph said she mustn't take it for granted that Ross wanted her in his cabin. He had intended to prove his mastery and bed her for one night only in revenge for her insolence over the hair ribbon. As he had said, a man at sea has little opportunity. Who could blame him for taking a convict woman to his bed? And who could blame him for tasting the sweetness again and again when the woman was as willing as any harlot? The only shock he had received was to find her a virgin. But why should that matter now?

By the time Juliet had brushed her hair and devised a line on which to hang the

sheet, she had argued herself into a
fatalistic frame of mind. He was the captain
of a trading vessel. He had more to do than
entertain females for dinner. Only when he
felt the hunger for a woman would he seek
her out. Meanwhile she must continue with
the duties she had taken over from the
cabin boy.

VI

It was true that Captain Jamieson had little time that day to muse on the previous night's activities. The seas had grown choppy and visibility was not good as they headed towards Mozambique. All eyes and hands were needed as the ship beat up the coast. But by midafternoon he descended to his cabin to take a belated lunch.

He stared round. The cabin was tidy with the bed freshly made with clean linen, but of Juliet there was no sign.

"Has Miss Westover eaten?" he asked Joseph.

"Yes, sahib, I took a tray to her cabin."

Ross made no comment but later he glanced in his seachest to find the new clothes carefully laid away. He frowned in thought. Hadn't he made it clear that from now on she was to share his cabin? Did she have scruples about that after last night?

Or was last night just meant to show him that she could bow to superior force if necessary but her will was her own?

Damn the girl, he thought wrathfully. She should be grateful he had taken her from the hold and freed her from the constant fear of sexual attack by the convicts. He caught sight of his angry face in the mirror. He grinned suddenly. What was he proposing to put in place of that but his own use of her body? Even thinking of last night made his stomach tighten but he would stand no nonsense from her. She was in no position to play games with him.

He strode down the corridor and walked straight into her cabin. Juliet looked up warily into the dark frowning face.

"Why are you here?" he said, curtly.

Juliet flushed. "Where else should I be?"

"In my cabin. Did I not tell you to consider it your own?"

Juliet came to her feet, her eyes glinting. "You spoke those words in anger. I obeyed your orders last night. Do they extend past that?"

Ross glared at her. "You were not so independent in bed!"

The color left her face and Ross cursed his unruly tongue. "Juliet, I'm sorry. I didn't mean that. I want us to talk and laugh together and share our meals. Does the thought distress you so much?"

"No," she said slowly. "I had hoped to earn your friendship and respect, but it is rather too late for that, isn't it?''

Ross frowned. "Why do you say that?"

"From your anger at finding me here. Now that I have shared your bed, you think I should be permanently on hand and casually taken like dessert at the end of a meal? Close enough to reach with one hand while you study a chart with the other? I may now be what they call a fallen woman, Captain, but I am still not a harlot!''

Ross took a deep breath and clasped his hands behind him. "My apologies, Miss Westover. You will, of course, continue to occupy this cabin if that is what you wish. Forgive my intrusion." He eyed her impassively, his dark brows meeting to make a straight line across his forehead. He bowed and moved to the door, his back rigid.

Juliet watched him, hiding her dismay at his coldness. Could she really blame him for thinking she would jump at the chance of living in his cabin? Was it just her Westover stubborness that held her back, the inborn pride that disliked the idea of becoming a mere plaything? Because he had taken her once, he was not to imagine her body was his to do with as he pleased. Yet, deep in her heart, she knew that was exactly what she wanted too.

Later that day Joseph came to her. In his arms was the blue dress with the lace flounces. Folded inside were the silk underwear and sandals.

"Captain's compliments, memsahib. He ask for honor of your company at dinner." His dark eyes smiled into hers. "I serving very nice dinner, memsahib. Captain most anxious you come. Doctor sahib there too."

"Thank you, Joseph," Juliet said, returning his smile. "I will come."

As she changed into the new clothes her heart grew lighter. Doctor Fernley's presence would ease any constraint between them. Ross was obviously intent on refuting her accusation.

Her reception might have taken place in the best drawing room of the county. Both men rose as she entered and Doctor Fernley's compliments on her appearance added to her ease of mind. The conversation flowed as smoothly as in any drawing room and Juliet's past interest in the mildewed books that rotted in the Westover House library afforded her knowledge on a variety of subjects.

All the time she was aware of Captain Jamieson's smooth, tanned, impersonal gaze across the table. The blue eyes were unreadable, showing nothing but the natural courtesy of a host to his guests. He made no move to prevent her leaving after the coffee had been cleared away, but thanked her politely for her company and allowed Doctor Fernley to escort her to her cabin.

They met for dinner each night and Juliet

returned to her solitary cabin, at first with satisfaction that she had avoided being alone with him, but as the days passed, with a growing feeling of desolation. She lay in her bunk, staring at the bulkheads, knowing that her body craved the touch of his hands. Like a drug, once experienced, she wanted more. Did he feel the same or had he achieved his objective that first time? Only a man of experience could have drawn such response from a girl of no experience. To be shown paradise then expelled from the garden was a pain too exquisite to be borne. But had she not expelled herself?

On the night before they entered the port of Mozambique, Doctor Fernley excused himself after one cup of coffee. There were arrangements to be made for the morning, he said.

Ross didn't look at Juliet. "Would you be good enough to escort Miss Westover to her cabin on your way, Doctor?"

Doctor Fernley glanced at Juliet. "There is no need for Miss Westover to leave early as well. Unless you have urgent business elsewhere, Captain?"

"No," said Ross, "I have no business elsewhere. But the decision must be Miss Westover's. I should be happy for her to stay but will not press her against her will."

Juliet felt her stomach curl into a small knot of fire. "Thank you," she managed to say. "I will stay."

Doctor Fernley smiled and bade them goodnight. Juliet caught the twinkle of amusement in his eye as he glanced down at her. He knows, she thought in amazement—he knows and approves. Had he followed her stand for independence and now deemed it time she struck her colors? She thought for a moment. Tomorrow he would go ashore and the protection he afforded be withdrawn. Had his words meant to urge her to safeguard herself and now accept the captain's protection and goodwill? She turned her head and looked into Ross's eyes.

"Coffee, Miss Westover?" His words were as bland as his face.

"Thank you."

They said little as she sipped her coffee, Ross seemingly lost in some thoughts of his own. Finally she put down her cup and rose. Ross came to his feet too and looked at her, a question in his eyes.

"Will you lock the door?" she asked.

He raised a black eyebrow. "Before or behind you?"

"Whichever you wish. I shall not press you."

A light sprang into his eyes. "Then it shall be before you."

Juliet remained motionless until he came back from the door. They stared at each other for a long moment then Ross reached to unbutton the blue dress. It fell to her feet. The shift slid over her head and she stood naked.

"Do you want the negligee?" he asked huskily.

She shook her head. "Only you."

Her voice was so faint and trembling that Ross held her gently to him as if she were a child in need of comfort.

"Juliet, my darling," he said with a half-groan, "you've no idea how difficult I found it to let you leave every night with Doctor Fernley."

She raised her face. "And I to go, when I wanted you so much."

He kissed her gently. "Then we must make up for the time that pride and stubbornness kept us apart."

His clothes followed hers onto the floor and she was whisked to the wide bed. The hands and lips that explored her body lifted her to the heights once more, and there was no pain this time. She gave herself gladly into the power of her senses, delighting in the touch of his lips on her breasts and thighs. Time ceased to exist as again and again they joined as one, the throbbing maleness of him sending an ecstasy of sweetness coursing through her body. She learned his body as well as her own, running her fingers through the dark hairs of his stomach and caressing his thighs and the warm strength that lay between.

The sky was lightening as they fell asleep, clasped together, Ross's cheek on her breast. Only the insistent tapping on the door woke them. Ross slid from the bed and strode to the door. Juliet regarded his straight lean back and long legs dreamily. He was beautiful. Joseph entered with a tray of breakfast and placed it on the table without glancing at the bed. It had not occurred to Juliet to hide herself under the bedclothes until he had gone. Then she sat up and Ross looked at her, smiling.

"Brazen baggage!" he teased, eyeing her exposed breasts.

Juliet laughed. "And who opened the door naked as a babe?"

Her eyes moved over him and she felt no shame in her gaze. "I will now," she said frankly, "subscribe to your magnificent virility, Captain. If your seamanship equals your expertise as a lover, then you should be, at least, an admiral of the fleet."

"We're not in the Royal Navy, my girl," he said, pouring out the coffee. "Will you join me here for breakfast or shall I join you? I warn you, it will be safer here—in view of my magnificence!"

He grinned as she slid out of bed. He tossed her the long striped cotton nightshirt she had worn when she had taken her first bath. "Put that on for the sake of my reason. I have to take the 'Grace' into harbor this morning."

"Aye, aye, Captain," she murmured, demurely sliding the shirt over her head.

Dressed in his lightweight uniform, his hat under his arm, Ross paused in the doorway. "Will you be here when I come back?"

Juliet smiled. "I will be here."

The few days they spent anchored in Mozambique harbor, unloading the medical supplies, were the happiest of Juliet's life. She and Ross ate together, strolled the decks as the sun went down, and made love every night in the wide bed. For Juliet there was no future, only the present. She asked for no more.

The storm came suddenly, as tropical storms do. The 'Grace' heaved on the running swell and fretted at anchor. The harbor was crowded with small boats making for cover, and the 'Grace's' bulk, as she thrashed nervously, set their decks awash. Ross ordered the anchor slipped and the 'Grace' made to stand off the coast in the less turbulent Mozambique Channel. It was pure mischance that a fleeing fishing boat, running without lights, crossed their bow and was drawn into the slipstream of their passage, the canvas of its single mast tangling with the anchor cable. Unable to drop anchor, the 'Grace,' towing the fishing boat, was caught by the wind and swept out to sea, the smaller boat heeling wildly behind, unable to free herself.

The crew could do nothing to halt her progress, save steer into the mounting waves. Her canvas had been furled in harbor and the bare masts and spars creaked as torrential rain, lashed by fierce winds, drove her implacably north. At some point the fishing boat disintegrated but the howling fury of the wind masked any human voice raised in terror.

Juliet, clinging in fright to the bed, could only think of Ross up there somewhere on deck. Chairs and small articles were thrown about the cabin; only the bed was bolted to the deck and Juliet in her blue dress clung grimly, praying for an end to the storm ad the return of her lover.

All night the storm raged. There was nothing to see from the portholes but mountainous green waves, lashing the thick glass. Dawn came quickly, a faint lifting of the blackness, but Juliet believed there was a slight easing of the wind's ferocity. The waves seemed not so high and there was a chance of the ship surviving the hammering she had borne.

But where were they? Miles from Mozambique, Juliet surmised. Doctor Fernley had been ashore with a few of the officers. If the ship was capable of it, they must head back and take them on board again. As it grew lighter, she longed to leave the cabin and search for Ross. Was he all right? Were any of them injured or—God forbid—swept away. She clasped her hands tightly, trying to stop them shaking. How could she live if Ross died? She was totally, irrevocably in love with the captain of the 'Grace,' the ship that was bearing her to servitude in the colony of New South Wales. As long as he was unharmed she prayed silently, whatever desolation her future held she would bear gladly.

She rose with the idea of righting the upset chairs. At that moment the 'Grace' struck. Shuddering, heeling, she ground her way with a splintering of timber over a submerged reef. As if to mock and highlight her distress, the sun appeared, enfolding the ship in shades of amber and sparking brass into gold. Juliet was flung back to the bed, dazed, bewildered. The sea calmed, and the wind dropped. Screaming rose above the dragging sound of a wooden ship in mortal pain. The convicts? Locked in the hold, hearing only the storm, then the crashing of bulkhead on rock? What was happening?

Running feet above her head, the crack of a distress rocket, then an eerie silence save for the tortured creaking. Unable to bear it any longer, Juliet flung open the cabin door and ran along the corridor. Joseph was coming, barefooted, the other way.

"Joseph," she called "What happened? Is . . . is . . . ?" Words failed her, but the Goanese understood.

"Captain all right, memsahib. Nobody hurt, but ship bad. Little boats coming from shore. Soon be taken off. I fetch ropes from store. Excuse, please." Juliet smiled her relief and stood aside. She could do nothing until Ross sent for her.

She returned to the cabin and looked through the porthole. Several small boats were skimming the waters towards them, the fresh wind filling their striped sails. At the speed they were coming it should only

be minutes before they reached the 'Grace'
now swaying uneasily in the water.

The men in the boats were brightly
attired and dark-skinned, she noticed.
Turbaned heads bobbed and she caught the
glint of sun on steel. Behind them the
shoreline was clearer; a town of some size
with white buildings and tall thin towers
was visible. Arabs, she decided suddenly,
and tried to remember her geography.
What country lay north of Mozambique?
Tanganyika, she guessed, unless they had
been driven in another direction entirely.

The boats slid from her line of vision and
the 'Grace' gave a lurch. Voices shouted
and there was a great babble of talk in
strange tongues. She stood in the doorway,
listening and waiting for Ross. He must
come, for a captain needed his logbook and
papers of authority before abandoning a
ship.

She was not prepared for the pistol shots
and clash of steel. A scream that rose and
faded, cut off abruptly as if life had fled,
had her clutching the doorpost. A tramp of
feet, stumbling and ragged, more shots and
violent shouts, a hiss of weapons as if men
fought with blades. She stared up and down
the corridor. No sign of Joseph. Then the
companionway was blocked by a jumble of
barefooted, turbaned men, bearded and
grinning. They saw her stunned by shock,
they reached her and threw her, shrieking,
from one to the other, dragging her finally

up the companionway.

On deck, in the clasp of a giant Arab, her heel slipped in a pool of liquid. He dragged her upright but not before her horrified gaze had identified the liquid as blood. She stared round wildly, seeing the deck strewn with bodies, some turbaned and some in uniform. Though her eyes searched she could not find Ross at first.

Then he was there, surrounded by circling Arabs and swinging a boathook around with telling effect, while cursing fluently in a language they seemed to understand.

The Arab holding Juliet was grinning, even as the boathook sent two of his brethren stumbling overboard. A flashing dagger spun through the air and Juliet's scream of warning was choked by the arm round her throat. The dagger buried itself to the hilt in Ross's right arm and the boathook fell from the paralyzed fingers. Then they closed in on him, and he went down under a pile of flowing robes.

They took their time bringing him to the surface and he emerged, bloodstained and bruised. He was very white under his tan and blood was soaking the torn sleeve of his jacket. Juliet longed to rush over to him but the arm round her throat restrained her.

The Arabs were herding the convicts to the middle of the deck. Then they separated the men from the women. Their leader examined each convict in turn, his gaze assessing, as if he were buying cattle. They talked amongst themselves, moving the convicts about until each group was split in two.

Then, with as much feeling as if they were peeling fruit, the older and less healthy looking of the convicts were run through by curved daggers and casually tossed overboard. The sea boiled and erupted for a moment then was calm. Juliet felt her stomach churn as the water turned crimson and a ghastly debris littered its surface. Of course there must be sharks in these waters but how dreadful a death—and so callously performed.

Ross and the remaining six men convicts were directed into a dhow at the bottom of a rope ladder. Juliet, together with four female convicts, was pushed to the rail to await the incoming dhow. Ross looked up once, his face ashen, and their eyes met. He looked away and she was chilled for a moment, wondering. Perhaps he thought it safer that way for some reason. She climbed down the ladder herself with some difficulty and sat huddled to one side with the four younger women from the hold.

No one spoke, but a few minutes later, the Arabs began to laugh and point back at the ship. Juliet glanced over her shoulder and saw the 'Grace' slide steeply into the water, the sea opening to claim her for its own. Ross had lost his ship and his crew. The only free man amongst them, he had now joined their ranks and was in bondage too.

A white sandy beach received them. The dhows were dragged up past the water line and lengths of rope removed. Pulled from the boat, the girls had their hands bound before them, and a neck halter secured each to the other. A jerk on the leading girl and they stumbled up the beach, following each other dumbly. The dhow, with Ross and the male convicts, was not in sight. They were not to be together after all. Would she ever see him again? The thought was like a cold stone in the pit of her stomach. She noticed an Arab eyeing her thoughtfully and her chin rose. She must not shed tears or he would think her afraid. How could he know her anguish was only on account of a man she had loved and lost? Her glance was scornful and he gave a faint smile as if satisfied.

"Where are we going?" she asked boldly, pointing as best she could with bound hands.

He glanced ahead then back at her, nodding. "Bagamayo." He gestured towards a distant point. "Bagamayo."

Juliet shrugged. She was no better off for asking. Perhaps it was the name of the town she had glimpsed through the porthole, but it was obviously much farther than it had looked. There seemed to be nothing but shifting sand and rocky ridges ahead.

The Arabs' endurance far exceeded their

own. Mile after mile they staggered, urged
on by a jerk of the neck rope. The sun was
like a brazen orb with glittering pointed
spears that bored into their skulls and eye
sockets. Perspiration glued their hair to
their heads and molded their garments uncomfortably.

The sand gave way to sharply pebbled
rock over which they skidded. Juliet, who
had been glad of her sandals on the hot
sand, now found her toes pierced by razor-
edged stones working their way through
the decorative sides. When the leading girl
fell to her knees, she brought them all
down, and they collapsed in a panting heap.
The girl, Juliet noted, had a ghastly pallor
and her breath whistled hoarsely in her
throat.

The Arab, gesticulating furiously, was
jerking the rope. Juliet had a moment of
pity for the ill-fed convict girl. It might
have been herself. She turned to the Arab
who had answered her question. Anger and
fear made her voice shrill.

"Are we camels to travel for hours
without stopping?" she demanded. "Let us
rest, for the love of God, and give us
water." She tilted back her head and raised
her hands in a drinking movement. "You
want us dead of the heat before we arrive
wherever we are going? She gestured at the
sun and touched the top of her head,
wincing.

There was an angry interchange of words

between their captors, but the Arab to whom she had spoken appeared to be their leader. He cut through the talk with curt words and the Arab holding the halter rope let go. A goatskin bag was taken from the back of another and a small horn beaker emerged from a voluminous robe.

Incredibly, and without expecting any result from her outburst, they received a beaker of water in turn. Juliet looked at the leader who was now squatting on his heels, regarding the prisoners.

"Thank you" she said, dipping her head to him in gratitude. He had understood her mime if not her words.

While they rested, Juliet took the opportunity of removing her sandals to make for easier going. They were not allowed much respite and were soon on their way. As the day's heat increased, it became one long tortured effort to drag aching limbs forward, one foot in front of the other. It was less exhausting, she had decided earlier, to close one's eyes against the sun and splay the feet so that balance was maintained in a rolling gait. Who was to care if they looked like a file of drunken sailors?

So, with her eyes closed, she was unaware that they had entered the outskirts of the town until children's voices reached her and the blessed relief of tall buildings cut off the red haze under her eyelids. Only then did she open her eyes, squinting dazedly at the peeling whitewashed square tower before them. The barred windows were those of a prison and it seemed their destination had been reached.

Tall, turbaned Negroes guarded the gates as they were herded into a bare stone-floored room. Its coolness was an aching relief and her sun-dimmed eyes took in the flat mats set by the walls. Once inside, the halters were removed and their hands unbound. They stood in a small bewildered group until the Arab leader pointed to the mats.

Only then did Juliet notice a dark young girl reclining on one of the mats. She eyed them with interest and Juliet, in turn, noted that, although brown-skinned, the girl had finer features than one would expect. Her nose and lips were narrow, rather like a mixture of Negro and Arab.

"Welcome," the girl said in a dry, mocking voice. "Your first visit to Dar-es-Salaam, I take it?"

"Dar-es-Salaam?" Juliet repeated. "They said something that sounded like Bagamayo."

"Of course," said the girl. "Bagamayo is the town's slave market."

VII

Juliet's throat went dry with horror. "Slave market? Which country is this and who were those men who brought us?"

The girl shrugged and yawned, stretching her long sinuous body on the mat. "You are in Tanganyika. The Arabs are corsairs—pirates I think you call them in Europe. They captured you at sea?"

Juliet nodded and crossed the stone floor, sinking on to the mat next to the girl's. Her bones and muscles ached intolerably and her wrists and neck had been irritated by the ropes. The support of the cold wall was welcome. She eyed the girl, realizing that their conversation had been in English.

"You speak our language very well," she said.

"Also Portuguese, French and Arabic," answered the girl casually. "My master was a great traveler. He bought me in Ethiopia

161

when I was twelve. I was his favorite concubine and it pleased him to educate me."

Juliet gazed at her uncertainly.
"What . . . what do they call you?"

"Khurrem. My real name I don't remember but my master was an admirer of the
great Suleiman and named me after his
favorite wife."

"That sounds . . ." Juliet went on carefully, "as if your master no longer lives."

Khurrem nodded. "His son rules now and
has no use for the women of his father."

"And that is why you are here."

"Allah be praised—yes." Seeing Juliet's
bemused expression, the girl laughed, her
white teeth flashing. The almond-shaped
eyes mocked her. "You will learn, white girl,
that to be sold again is better than being
put to death. The new pasha has his own
women. He shows mercy by sending us here
and not to the executioner. My sisters have
already been sold. I am held back because I
am young and they say the Sultan's emissary comes tomorrow. Perhaps I may
please him."

"Who is this Sultan?"

"Seyyid Said bin Sultan has the throne of
Oman. He is ruler here but has his capital in
Zanzibar. They say the palace is magnificent." Khurrem's eyes glowed. "I would
not, of course, be chosen for the Sultan but
perhaps I may please one of his lesser
pashas."

Juliet leaned back. "Why not the Sultan?

You are very beautiful."

Khurrem smiled. "But I have lost what can only be offered to the Sultan."

"What is that?"

"I am no longer a virgin. Only the young, untouched girls are taken for his harem." Her gaze moved speculatively over Juliet. "They say he has a taste for well-formed, fair-skinned girls. You may find favor with his emissary and be offered to the Sultan."

Juliet stared at her dumbly, her eyes wide. "But . . . but I don't want to . . . to join a harem!"

Khurrem shrugged. "You have no choice in the matter. You will be sold tomorrow, along with your companions." Her eyes rested contemptuously on the four convict girls sprawled ungracefully on their mats. "They are low-born by their language, but may please the camel traders. You are of a different class, I believe. Were you held in some honor in your own land?"

Juliet smiled at the words. "My father is a baronet and a Justice of the Peace, but held me in little honor. He really wanted a son."

Khurrem nodded with understanding. "And he was denied one. Daughters are of little account here, too. But explain, please, what is this baronet and Justice, you mention. He is close to his king, yes?"

Juliet tried to explain. "A baronet is a king's knight. It is an honor conferred on a brave man and the title passes from father

to son once it has been bestowed. And a
man elected to be a magistrate must keep
the king's peace and administer justice in
the area over which he has authority."

"Ah, yes, I see. He is like a pasha who
rules in the Great One's name," said
Khurrem, and Juliet, whose knowledge of
pashas was limited, did not argue the point.

She was too tired and hungry to brood on
tomorrow. Whatever happened she was
unlikely to be reunited with Ross and when
the 'Grace' failed to return to Mozambique,
it would be assumed she had foundered in
the storm. There might be a search and
they might find wreckage, but in the
absence of life, only one conclusion could be
reached. Doctor Fernley, while mourning
the loss of the captain and crew, might
conceivably spare her a thought but no one
else in the world would grieve over the fate
of Juliet Westover.

Food was brought—some kind of goat's
meat stew and vegetables. Juliet ate thankfully, dipping into the gravy a large flat
cake of rough bread as Khurrem did.

"It is made from manioc" explained
Khurrem. "It is a root vegetable ground
into a sort of grain, then soaked in water
and cooked. If you have to make it be sure
it is well soaked first, otherwise it can be
poisonous. The leaves are good too if mixed
with palm oil." She smiled at Juliet. "But
perhaps you will have no need to make food
for some merchant. You might catch the

eye of the Sultan's man. Far better to live in luxury at the palace."

"And warm the bed of a degenerate ruler and submit my body to his whims?" asked Juliet tartly.

Khurrem shook her head in gentle wonder. "Why do you foreign girls show such horror at the thought of being chosen for so much honor? Are you not trained in all the ways of pleasuring a man so that he will receive you with kindness? To be clumsy and fail to arouse his passion will bring shame on the Mistress of the Harem who is charged with training the concubines. You could be put to death or sold again. Learn well if you are chosen for the Sultan. Your life will be harder with a merchant or camel trader, and your master more demanding."

There was a significance in her words and Juliet looked at her questioningly.

"A rich man like the Sultan," Khurrem went on patiently, "has many women he can summon to his bed, therefore one's presence is infrequent. A poorer man, with fewer concubines, may take them all nightly if he is a lusty master. Be wise and go gladly with the emissary if his eye falls on you."

In spite of her weariness, Juliet took a long time to fall asleep that night. She realized that Khurrem's advice was sound but the girl was taking it for granted that as a well-born European captive, her virginity was intact. Should she keep up a pretense of never having lain with a man or admit it at the onset? Which was the safer course if escape was impossible?

She was no nearer to answering that question when, after a few hours sleep, they were roused by the entrance of a large Negress bearing food and goat's milk. She was followed by several more, carrying pitchers of water and long muslin robes. Their gestures were easily understood, even without Khurrem's helpful words.

"When we have eaten we must strip and wash our bodies, putting on these robes only." She raised a cynical eyebrow at Juliet. "As you can see the robes have a certain transparency."

Juliet answered her in the same wry tone. "In order that our prospective masters may view the merchandise before making their offer?"

Under the impersonal gaze of the Negress, the girls obeyed, then made their own clothes into small bundles to carry with them. Juliet stayed close to Khurrem as they were led from the stone building. The already brilliant sun dazzled her eyes, but across the flat baked earth she saw that men were already assembling in the shade of a tree. Girls of all shades, from pale brown to black, were sitting cross-legged to one side. Their voices, rising and falling like a twittering of birds, held no fear and their expressions were animated.

As Juliet's party approached, there was a

turning of heads and the faces showed surprise as their eyes fell on the five white girls. The twittering voices resumed and they became, it seemed, the subject of curious and excited speculation.

Before long, the square was crowded with men. The balconies of the colonnaded buildings surrounding the square were packed with onlookers. One of the small chambers below was doing keen service as a coffee house, and merchants had set up stalls for trading around the enclosure.

Just like a fair, thought Juliet sourly, but the bargains to be haggled over were live girls, not trinkets and toys. She hugged her bundle to her chest, wondering where she would be that night.

Khurrem had been listening to the surrounding conversation. She turned to Juliet.

"The emissary has not yet arrived but the market must begin for they stop at midday. They will therefore begin with the slaves who are good only for menial tasks."

Those destined for domestic work were paraded by the slave master and Juliet compressed her lips as she saw the thoroughness with which they were examined. Mouths were opened for an inspection of teeth, muscles were felt, and hands gripped thighs and calves to ascertain the strength of the property.

The sun was well risen before their turn came. The only difference in treatment was

the welcome lack of similar inspection. The
buyers of concubines were discouraged
from intimate examination. Juliet stared
bleakly into the distance, avoiding all eyes,
but conscious of the bold posturings of her
fellow convicts. Their giggles of delight as
they were bought by thick-set, darkly handsome men grated on her. If a white-faced
girl in the entourage added to the consequence of an Arab, she had a feeling that
these particular girls would have no ob-
jections, preferring that life to the one
destined for them in New South Wales.

She became aware of some altercation
between the slave master and a merchant.
Her gaze came down cautiously and she
found to her horror that it seemed to center
on herself.

She glanced at Khurrem. "What are they
saying?"

"The man wants you, but the slave
master asks a high price. He is still hoping
the emissary will come. Because you look
proud and show no feeling, he is convinced
you have a quality the Sultan will desire.
His reluctance to sell is making the merchant angry."

Juliet stole a quick glance at her prospective buyer, then averted her eyes
quickly, a wave of revulsion sweeping over
her. He was short and enormously fat, his
bearded face sweat-stained. The small eyes
were glaring at the dealer as his thick
fingers tugged his beard.

He flung up his hands suddenly in a gesture of acceptance and fumbled in his robe. Money changed hands and Juliet found herself pushed towards him. She twisted round desperately and saw a look of pity on Khurrem's face, then the neck strap went into place and she was being pulled away from the place of bargaining. There was no escape. She was now a slave concubine to a man whose very appearance filled her with disgust. Far better to have been taken by the Sultan's man, as Khurrem had said.

She stumbled behind her new owner, clutching her bundle, her eyes darting round desperately. Even had she been unhaltered, the crowded buildings offered no sanctuary. And where could she run to? Ross was gone and so was the 'Grace.'

Their progress was hampered by a crowd of people converging on another area. Her owner was pushing through, jerking the neck strap as his shoulders forced a passage. A man stepped back heavily, his boot-heel fully on Juliet's instep. She screamed in pain and grasped the halter, jerking it back furiously. The heat, smells and sheer indignity of being dragged across the square like a haltered animal set her temper flaring. There was nothing of fear or caution in her tone as she let forth a torrent of hot words.

"How dare you haul me on the end of a rope like some prize exhibit from the cattle market?" she yelled. "Who gave you the right to buy me in the first place, then having done so, to treat me with less regard than you would a she-goat?"

Faces turned towards the outburst and her owner gaped over his shoulder at being addressed in such a fierce manner by a mere female. Her words in English passed him by but her attitude of defiance was plain and could not be overlooked in front of his grinning countrymen. A space cleared round Juliet and men craned to catch a glimpse of her. Her owner's face darkened and swelled under the staccato stream of comments thrown at him. Juliet's heart quailed as she saw his hands bunch into fists. His approach held purpose and she realized that retribution was about to descend on her. The remarks of his fellows, the sly grins, the opinions, no doubt lewdly expressed, on the lack of docility of the merchant's new acquisition had caused a great loss of face that must be countered publicly.

She stared round, horrified, but a sea of robes and turbaned faces hemmed her in. A calloused hand rose to deal her a stunning blow but she ducked, cannoning into a solid body who thrust her back into the merchant's path. Her flying hair was caught and her body dragged roughly forward until her face looked directly into the bloodshot eyes of her owner. His fingers twisted painfully in her hair and she screamed again as his hand clamped on her shoulder, bruising the bones.

A voice roared through the babble of noise. Harsh, but with a definite cutting edge of steel, it rang across the square, the phrasing deliberate and cold. The twittering of women died, men's voices stopped in mid-sentence and even the birds fell silent as if the voice of Allah himself had spoken.

The group of men about Juliet thinned and melted away, leaving her owner and herself exposed to the view of the man who had spoken with such authority. He was tall and thin, she noted, and dressed in a green robe. Short-bearded and turbaned, his dark face was stern, the eyes like black marble above the hooked nose.

The man beside Juliet dropped to one knee, his breath hissing from his lungs. Juliet remained motionless and regarded the stranger curiously. The regard was returned impassively, then his eyes moved over her, assessing and speculative. She hugged her robe round her shoulders, clasping her bundle tightly, and her chin rose defiantly. She was vaguely aware of men grouped behind him but her eyes never left his face.

"My lord," called a voice, "it is the lady I spoke of—the English lady."

Juliet started violently. It was Ross's voice! She stared past the man, her eyes searching. Ross was there, stripped to the

waist, wearing only his breeches and boots,
his wrists bound before him. The slave
master growled and his short whip flicked
Ross's back, but Ross ignored him,
speaking again to the man Juliet supposed
was someone of eminence in the Arab hierarchy.

"My lord Vizier, it is the Lady Juliet
Westover, a noble lady traveling to India.
His Majesty's Government will be greatly
displeased to hear of the lady's detention in
your master's country. The lord, her father,
will demand her release."

The Vizier looked over his shoulder.
"Demand?" he asked, haughtily.

"He will wonder, my lord," said Ross,
eyeing the Vizier steadily, "how it comes
about that a subject of the King of England
is taken prisoner by pirates and delivered to
the slave market to be sold for gain."

"My master, the Sultan, has no
knowledge of these things. How should he
be held to blame for the actions of
corsairs?"

"But are these corsairs not subjects of
your master? And your master, I believe, is
on friendly terms with His Majesty's
Government."

The Vizier's hand came up to stroke his
beard. His black marble eyes rested
thoughtfully on the speaker, noting the
bruised body and rag-bound arm.

"Your ship was lost, I believe, Captain.
How then can any tidings reach your
Government?"

"My ship was standing off Mozambique when the storm broke. Half of my crew were ashore. They will mount a search when the 'Grace' fails to return."

The Vizier nodded slowly. "And they will find a wreck on the reefs of Mafia Island. It will be assumed, therefore, that all have perished."

The eyes of the two men held for a moment, then the Vizier looked at Juliet.

"And you say this girl is nobly born and reared in the strict confines of her class?"

"Indeed, I do."

"And returned undefiled to the bosom of her family would elicit a generous response to my master?"

"If that is his wish, yes."

The Vizier allowed a faint smile to touch his lips. "And would eliminate the possibility of a visit from His Majesty's Royal Navy?"

"I believe so—providing, of course, that I am allowed to resume the charge placed upon me by his lordship and convey the lady to her destination."

"Those are your terms, Captain?"

"Save one, my lord, and that is something we might discuss privately when the matter is settled to our mutual advantage."

The Vizier nodded and Ross gave a silent prayer of thanks. The oriental mind would accept more readily the word of a man whose reason for guarding a woman was not entirely without self-interest. The Vizier had understood the hint that Ross, too, expected to profit from the transaction. It would also eliminate any lingering doubt that his plea on Juliet's behalf stemmed from sentiment. He schooled his expression rigidly and stared into Juliet's bewildered and appealing face with blank disinterest.

The Vizier was speaking to the fat merchant who held Juliet's halter rope. The man attempted to argue, but the curt words of the Vizier covered the heavy face with beads of sweat, and he accepted the money tossed to him and turned away in silence.

Juliet's relief at seeing the back of the man who had bought her was dimmed by Ross's cold look. She had followed the conversation but was not sure that she understood it fully. To be with Ross again was what she wanted but what was this talk of the King and her noble birth? It didn't make sense—but if Ross expected her to play some part of his own devising, then she must follow his lead whatever it meant.

"My lady," the Vizier was saying, "I offer sincere apologies for the mistake made by the corsairs. They were not to know your rank. Would it please you to accept the hospitality of my master until arrangements can be made to secure your release? You will be treated with honor, I assure you, and the task of guarding you will be entrusted to the man appointed by the lord, your father, until you reach the safety of the women's quarters at the palace."

"Thank . . . thank you, sir," faltered

Juliet, not daring to look at Ross.

"There you will find," went on the Vizier, "clothes more suitable to your rank and, of course, a personal servant will be assigned solely to you."

"Thank you, sir," repeated Juliet, her confidence growing a little. "As it happens, there is a girl here who has been of help to me recently. Would I be permitted to take her with me?"

"Of course, my lady. I will have her brought to you, even if she has been sold. Her name, please?"

"Khurrem. She is an Ethiopian girl."

The Vizier spoke to one of his men. In a few moments Khurrem appeared. On seeing Juliet standing with the green-robed Vizier, she sank to her knees, bowing her head, first to the Vizier and then to Juliet.

"My lady," she said, "I feared for you when that camel trader took you away but Allah is good and placed you in the path of his Excellency. The pasha, your father, will be pleased to know that fortune smiles on you."

If the Vizier had any doubts about Ross's story, they were now put to rest by Khurrem's unwitting but mistaken corroboration of her rank. To emphasize the point, Juliet allowed her bundle to unfold and reveal the silken shift and fine lace of the blue gown. The Vizier's eyes flickered briefly over the garments, then he spoke rapidly to Khurrem.

In the privacy of a small chamber, Juliet resumed her own clothes, dropping the muslin robe distastefully on the ground. She emerged to find a horse-drawn litter awaiting her. Ross, the Vizier and a number of uniformed men were already mounted and grouped about the litter. Juliet, without glancing at Ross, climbed in, followed by Khurrem, and the curtains were drawn.

Almost submerged in large cushions of multicolored satin embroidered with silver thread, Juliet and Khurrem were carried swiftly and in great comfort to some unseen destination. Khurrem had dissuaded Juliet from peeping through the curtains.

"For the common people to gaze on ladies of the Sultan's household is an offense punishable by death," she pointed out.

"But I am not one of the Sultan's ladies," Juliet protested.

"You are under his protection, my lady, and it is the same thing. To show yourself in public, unveiled, would bring disgrace on your character and insult to his."

Juliet subsided and gave in to the feeling of drowsiness brought on by the swaying motion of the litter. Hours later, it seemed, they halted. A voice spoke and Khurrem reached through the curtains to draw in two voluminous garments.

"You must put this on, my lady, before being permitted out."

"What is it?"

"The burka, which all Moslem ladies must wear when outside the women's quarters. Let me slip it over your head."

Juliet found herself enveloped from head to toe in a flowing garment. Khurrem positioned the veil across her face so that only her eyes were visible. They climbed from the litter with difficulty after Khurrem had donned the second burka.

For a moment Juliet's eyes were dazzled by the light, then she found herself gazing at the sea. A brilliant sun threw sapphire sparks across the lazy ripples and a few stripe-sailed dhows bobbed and curved in unison. The Arabs in command wore similar uniforms to the escort. In the bows of one sat several strong-looking men, their wrists chained. Their skin color ranged from pale brown to black but most had Negroid features.

The Vizier spoke from beside her. "Slaves to work on the clove plantations, my lady. That was my main mission today. But the Sultan will be gratified by the honor I bring him with your presence. It will soften any disappointment he may feel by my inability to procure Circassians for his pleasure. Those pale-faced beauties from Georgia are especially welcomed by his highness, but alas, the caravan was delayed."

He turned away to issue orders to his men, and Ross spoke softly from behind Juliet.

"It seems we sail for Zanzibar where the

Sultan has raised a palace. An island, unfortunately, which adds somewhat to our difficulty."

Juliet stared up into the dark face and frowning eyes. "It seems we are deeper in difficulty by your own contriving. What possessed you to concoct such a tale? Do you suppose that anyone in England, least of all my father, will pay. . ."

The crack of Ross's palm on her cheek sent her staggering back and she stared at him in shocked surprise.

"I am not your servant, madam!" he exploded harshly. "And I am sick to death of your high-handed patronage. God knows why your father should want you back, for you have been nothing but a nuisance to me. In his place I should leave you to your fate, but that would not be fitting for the daughter of so noble a gentleman, would it? I will write the letter for your deliverance, but don't look to me to dance attendance on you any longer!"

With a hand on her stinging cheek, Juliet's mouth opened to utter a bewildered protest at his action, but a soft voice behind stilled her tongue.

"Have a care, Captain." A silky thread of menace ran through the Vizier's words. "To lay hands on the Sultan's guest is to lay hands on the Great One himself. He would not be pleased by such action. The Lady Juliet must remain unharmed, whatever your personal feelings. Her deliverance—and yours, my friend—rests on a happy outcome. May Allah permit that your words to the lord, her father, are in gentler tone than your speech to his daughter." He stroked his beard and regarded them both from expressionless black eyes. When he spoke again, a musing note had entered his voice. "Should the noble lord not heed the urgency of your plea—why then, the lady stands forfeit to my master. And by your own words she holds no blemish to prevent her finding favor with him. I speak truly, yes?"

Ross bowed his head. "As the Prophet himself, Excellency."

"The alternative is harsh, Captain. Consider it, if you please. The tongue or hand that strays from the path of righteousness may lawfully be struck away, as the deceased branches of the aloe are stripped from the living trunk. The ganching spike may pierce the body without harming the soul, but life may linger in torment, without the deliverance of death, until the sin is cleansed. And only Allah knows the terms of pain to be borne, and only Allah in his wisdom can bring that term to its conclusion and release the soul."

The black marble eyes held the deep blue ones of Captain Jamieson. Both faces were devoid of expression. Juliet held herself very still, understanding at last the reason for Ross's savage action. They had won a reprieve. But for how long?

The thin mouth above the beard moved and the words came softly but with a clarity that drove all color from Juliet's face.

"But for an Unbeliever the term allotted will seem an eternity."

VIII

Beneath the enveloping burka, Juliet's hands were clinging damply together. Her skin prickled with perspiration, but her blood ran cold. The Vizier's words lay on her mind like a coating of ice. Her bones ached with the effort of remaining upright, and though her muscles complained, she held herself rigid, her eyes on the sand. She mustn't faint or show a hint of the terror that his words invoked.

How much had he heard before the sea-hardened palm of Ross's hand had closed her mouth? Enough perhaps to raise a slight doubt in his mind and sufficient to permit the mention of the fate awaiting those who departed from the path of truth. With her limited vision from outside the burka, she had not been aware of the Vizier's return. Only Ross had seen the danger and silenced her in so practical a way. What had he in mind? Once on the island and in the custody of the Mistress of the Harem, what chance of escape was there? As a prize to be ransomed, she would be guarded day and night and allowed no contact with the outside world.

She raised her eyes slowly. And Ross? Would he be confined to the same degree? A measure of freedom perhaps until it became obvious that nothing would come of the ransom demand. But in that time, a man of resource might escape—especially one unhampered by a female!

She felt his eyes on her and turned her head. There was nothing in his gaze of encouragement or warmth—just a cool, appraising look. The Vizier had moved towards the dhow. Nothing prevented Ross from speaking now, but he was silent. Then he turned away and walked, hands clasped behind him, along the beach, studying the coastline.

Juliet stared after the lithe figure in stunned silence, fighting back the urge to call his name. This studied rejection hurt more than the blow he had delivered. Had she been right in her surmise? Why should he care what happened to a convict girl who had entertained him and satisfied his senses on board the 'Grace'? Not once had he said he loved her, she recalled, even in the height of passion. This respite he had gained for them both might prove more beneficial to him than to her.

They traveled in separate dhows to the island of Zanzibar. It took several hours and although the small boats kept pace with each other, darting and wheeling lightly over the sapphire waters, Ross stared straight ahead. He did not, Juliet noted miserably, allow his gaze to wander in her direction. A precaution perhaps? But to Juliet, bruised by his coldness on the beach, it spoke of abandonment.

Beside her, Khurrem was pointing excitedly. Through the hot haze, land was appearing. White sandy beaches, and between tall breeze-swept palms, a view of dazzling white buildings was caught. Onion-domed towers, glittering gold in the sun, stood tall above narrow streets that ran almost to the water's edge. A mosque, precise and balconied, soared upwards and the voice of a priest rang out clearly as they neared the shore. A drone of chanting voices interspersed the harsh cadences, and the name of Allah was invoked again and again.

Juliet found herself clasping Khurrem's hand. The girl smiled.

"It is one of the hours of prayer for the Muslim people. The voice is that of the Mufti. You will recognize the priests by their white robes. The Viziers, as you have seen, wear green. By the color of a man's robe and the shape of his turban, it is possible to tell his position at court. There are many men in the service of the Sultan

but few that we shall see—save the Kislar
Aga and the slave boys."

"Kislar Aga? Who is that?"

"The Head Eunuch and Master of the
Girls. He has control of the harem and is
the only link with the outside world. A most
powerful man and one it is unwise to
anger."

Juliet's brow wrinkled. "I thought no
man but the Sultan was allowed inside the
harem."

Khurrem gave her a swift sideways
glance. "The Kislar Aga is not quite a
man," she said softly. "He is a castrated
African."

Juliet's voice wavered with shock. "The
slave boys, too?"

"Of course, but they are of all races—
some African and some white Christian
boys captured by corsairs."

The dhows were running parallel to the
coast, heading for the landing stage. Juliet
hugged the burka around her as she was
helped from the boat by the uniformed seaman. She risked a glance at Ross but he was
striding up the beach, escorted by the
Vizier and an armed group of soldiers. She
and Khurrem were led by silent Negroes
towards a narrow street that ran up the
gently sloping hillside. Warehouses jostled
with marble-walled villas; cypress groves
concealed pavilions of splendid design and
over all hung the scent of spices. A bakery,
a wood store, a silk warehouse met Juliet's

bemused eye, and merchants of varying skin shades rushed by without a glance.

"The Island of Spices," commented Khurrem. "Nowhere else does the clove tree grow, save in these few islands, so the Sultan needs many slaves to gather the crop from the plantations."

"And labor is cheap when supplied by corsairs," said Juliet dryly.

Khurrem shrugged. "They are fed and kept healthy. There was much famine in the lands my master took me to. Here they will not starve."

"But their freedom has been taken from them!"

"Freedom? We must all belong to someone. Does it matter who owns you if you are treated well? As women, we are servants to men. If Allah gives you a good master, you must be thankful. What else is there for a woman?"

"The right to choose her own life and the man she will share it with."

"And you have the freedom to do this?"

Juliet opened her mouth, then closed it again. Looked at logically, her situation and Khurrem's were not so very different after all. She shrugged. "I appear not to have any freedom at all at this moment so the argument is academic. What do you think will happen to us now?"

They had traversed the packed-earth lane and were standing before a pair of tall iron gates, guarded by blue-uniformed men in yellow boots and white felt turbans. An exchange of words and the two girls were allowed to pass through.

Juliet's eyes opened wide as she saw the stretch of well-tended grass and the cypress trees, arranged like well-drilled soldiers, bordering the numerous paved avenues. They followed their black escort along the center path, coming at length to another gateway. Here they were handed over to yet another Negro. It didn't make Khurrem's indrawn breath and deep obeisance to enlighten Juliet on the man's position. The flowered silk robe under a sable-trimmed cloak and the strange, conical, sugar loaf headdress that rose at least two feet above the heavy black face warned her that here was the Kislar Aga. She almost followed Khurrem's example, then remembered her supposed position and regarded him with cool hauteur.

"I am Lady Juliet Westover," she said. "And this is my maid."

"Come," he said, and swung his enormous bulk around. "Leave the robes."

They obeyed and followed through yet another court past marble fountains, where water jetted up and fell glinting into pools of carp and rainbow colored fish. Another gate, but the final court they entered was a blaze of color. Singing birds of all varieties swooped and fluttered between fruit trees and rose bushes, nestling in climbing vines and flaunting their colors against backdrops of red and purple bougainvillaea.

Equally colorful were the garments of the numerous girls gathered there. Reclining on the ground or scattered over the steps of the mosaic-floored summerhouse, they were like a collection of delicate butterflies. Juliet stared, fascinated, into the tinted faces, the daintily arched brows and the kohl-ringed eyes that turned to the newcomers. Like butterflies they rose, winged with silk and satin, a damask-waistcoated, kaftan-flowing cloud, gleaming tresses threaded through with matching ribbons or twined with pearls. Loose trousers or diaphanous skirts did not conceal the perfectly formed bodies that ended in fine-strapped sandals of dyed kid.

In moments she was surrounded by giggling girls, exclaiming, pointing, fingering the lace of her dress, touching their jeweled bracelets and glittering earrings, brows upraised, as if questioning Juliet's lack of adornment. She bore it with a smile clamped on her face as they twittered and speculated. Her mind pondered vaguely on the red or black hair with no spectrum of color between. The answer came as palms of henna were upturned— dyestuff much favored as decoration. Did they turn blondes into red or black images of themselves, she wondered? The Circassians? Those of the fair Georgian race? Why buy a blonde beauty, then force her into the Arab mould?

She swayed suddenly, overcome by tiredness. A nerve-wracking day! Her thoughts were wandering. What was a Circassian, anyway? She was English and black-haired. Her purchase was not for the same reason. These girls were the Sultan's concubines. Her own freedom was assured. When the ransom came . . . ! Her mind jerked, sending a flash of pain through her temples. What ransom? There would be no ransom! How could there be? It was a tactic of Ross's to delay the end. And when the Vizier realized he had been tricked—not once, but doubly—the slow death he had promised would become a reality.

The floating voices faded, the sun went out, and she recovered her senses to find herself lying on a thin mattress, the coverlet scented with musk and civet. A small brazier was set in the cool, stone-walled room. Aloe wood burned slowly, giving off a pungent aroma. As her gaze moved over the small latticed window, the hangings of silk, the green and blue tiles of the stove base and the painted ceiling, a voice spoke softly.

Juliet's eyes searched the dimness. Seated on cushions, gowned in brocade and heavily jeweled was a lady of infinite grace with smooth, honey-colored skin and amber eyes under perfectly-arched brows. She reclined at ease, her narrow hands with the painted nails clasped loosely in her lap. Like a bird of paradise, she glittered and sparkled with every gentle breath, the slight movement of her breast revealing yet another color in the brocaded gown.

"I am Gabriella, Mistress of the Harem. It is my duty to oversee your well-being for the duration of your stay with us. Your servant has been sent to bring food and khoshab. Rest now and we will talk again later."

Juliet sat up. "You are very kind. I appear to have fainted in your garden."

Gabriella smiled. "It is a hot day. You are not yet used to our climate. In time you will grow accustomed and dress accordingly." Her amber gaze moved over Juliet's slender body. "When you have eaten you will be taken to the baths. I will send your Ethiopian with a selection of clothes. I hope you will approve my choice."

"How could I not?" asked Juliet, her eyes admiring. "When you have such exquisite taste in your own person. But I will be permitted, I hope, to retain my own garments?"

"Of course, if you wish. They will be washed and pressed for your leave-taking, but while you are here, the clothes I send you will be cooler and more suitable—especially if the Great One grants you an audience."

Juliet's heart thumped. "Is that a possibility?"

"As his guest, he may wish to ascertain that you are being treated with the honor

due to your rank. I will dress you myself if
you are summoned to the presence." She
spread her hands revealing rose-stained
palms. "You will, naturally, be ignorant of
the etiquette on such an occasion. I will
teach you how to conduct yourself. There
may be slight differences between our court
and yours."

"Mine?" asked Juliet, unwittingly.

"The court of your English king. There
are rules to observe there, too. Is it not so?"

"Oh yes, of course, indeed there are,"
Juliet came back faintly. "Perhaps it will
not be so different but I shall be grateful for
all the help you can give me."

Gabriella came to her feet in a smooth
practiced movement, her robe settling in
sculptured folds about her golden sandals.
Juliet glimpsed painted toenails as Gabriella glided with stunning elegance to the
doorway.

Her exit was followed shortly by
Khurrem's entrance with cheese, fruit, and
rose-leaf jam to spread on hot, sesame seed-
coated rolls. The khoshab, mentioned by
Gabriella, turned out to be a fruit drink.
Juliet ate hungrily. It seemed a long time
since they had been given food in the slave
quarters of Bagamayo.

"I have eaten," said Khurrem, in answer
to Juliet's question. "Servants do not eat
with ladies of rank." She watched, bright-
eyed, as Juliet wiped her fingers on the
damp cloth she had brought. "I can hardly

believe I am in the palace of the Sultan, and I owe it all to you, my lady."

Juliet smiled. "You are my only friend, Khurrem. How could I leave you behind? The Mistress speaks English but with the others I shall need you to translate their words."

"I shall be sad when the ransom comes and you leave us."

"How did you know of that? You were not present when Captain Jamieson spoke to the Visier."

"Everyone knows of it here, my lady. People gossip. Few secrets can be kept in a palace full of idle women. The Vizier tells his secretary . . ." she shrugged. "Soon everyone knows everything."

"I see," said Juliet, slowly, remembering the moment on the beach with Ross. Had he held his tongue for that very reason? Khurrem had been beside her. His coldness and the calculating look could well have been designed to add strength to the fiction that she was rich and untouched. A hint of the truth in front of a sharp-witted girl like Khurrem could have been their undoing. What did she, in fact, know of the girl? It would be most unwise to confide her secret to anyone. Khurrem might see it as a chance to promote herself into greater favor, owing loyalty to no one in her ambition to find a new master of rank. Even a word dropped unwittingly in gossip, and without malice, would bring the same result. Juliet repressed a shudder as she thought of the Vizier's last words. She forced a smile to her lips.

"By the time I do leave Zanzibar, Khurrem, you will no doubt have attracted the attention of a visiting pasha or some noble sheik."

"If Allah wills it, my lady," Khurrem said. "I pray that he smiles on us equally."

The scented steam rose in clouds above Juliet's prone figure. Stretched out on the marble couch, naked, sweat-soaked, she suffered the women of the baths to knead and scour her body with rough cloths. Pummeled, massaged with flower-scented oils, she lay unresisting as the Mistress of the Baths deftly removed every hair from her body. Completely relaxed under the strong, expert hands, she felt all tension drain away and her whole being drift into a state of euphoria. Her hair was washed and rubbed, anointed with some sort of pomade, then a stream of cold rose water shocked her into awareness and the blood surged through her veins with new vigor.

The young attendants brought her to her feet, wrapping her in large, soft towels and pinning her gleaming curls on the top of her head. From the baths she was led to an outer room and directed to a long low couch onto which she sank gratefully. In moments she was asleep.

When she woke, it was to see the glow of lamps high on the painted walls. A movement beside her revealed Khurrem sitting cross-legged on a cushion.

"The Mistress said you were to be left until you woke. I am now to take you to the apartment allotted." Khurrem rose in one little movement and Juliet saw that her maid's own skin was gleaming coffee-colored, her hair loose and shining. Soft muslin trousers and a thigh length jacket of green satin had replaced the slave market robe.

Juliet rose and donned the loose kaftan presented by Khurrem, letting the towel slip from her body. She followed the girl, her mind still hazy from sleep. Several plump, soft-faced men passed them by, mostly African but occasionally fine featured, pale-skinned men. They took little notice of the girls, moving silently and with a feminine grace that slightly unnerved Juliet. And all of them eunuchs, she supposed, robbed of their manhood but seemingly indifferent, to judge by their expressionless faces.

As if in answer to her thoughts, Khurrem said, "They take them as small children before they know the meaning of life. Some remain content, but others know the torment of desire without the means of fulfillment. They are examined regularly by the Hakin to ensure that their condition remains unchanged." She glanced over her shoulder then lowered her voice. "They say the Kislar Aga is both corrupt and capri-

cious but he has the ear of the Sultan so
beware of him, my lady. He holds life and
death equally in his hands."

Juliet shivered, remembering the small
cold eyes of the Head Eunuch. What man
would not be capricious, stolen from his
family, sold into slavery, and then
mutilated in so appalling a manner—and all
on the orders of a Sultan who possessed,
heavens knows how many, obedient
females to cater to his every sexual whim.

"But you forget," said Juliet, firmly,
"that the Kislar Aga is concerned only with
the royal concubines. I am a hostage and
therefore not in his province. He has no
reason to watch me."

"But he will, my lady. All females come
under his eye. It would be wise not to anger
him for who can foretell the future?"

They had reached the chamber allotted to
Juliet. Inside were two sleeping mats piled
with cushions. A hanging lamp of brass
with enameled panels gave off a soft glow.
A small brazier, cast in bronze and shaped
like a peacock, warmed the night air. A
bowl of fruit, containing some varieties
unknown to Juliet, stood on a low table
beside a carafe of khoshab. Khurrem
poured a measure into a glass goblet and
offered it to Juliet who had stretched out on
the cushions.

"You find the khoshab to your taste, my
lady?"

"Most agreeable," answered Juliet,

thirsty from the baths and her sleep.

Khurrem laughed. "That is what they call it—agreeable water." She glanced at the other mat. "Do you wish me to sleep here, my lady? If you prefer privacy, I can go to the servant's quarters."

"Stay with me, Khurrem. I should be lost without your knowledge." Khurrem's words in the passage came back to her. "What did you mean when you spoke of the future in connection with the Kislar Aga?"

The girl subsided gracefully onto the other bed. Her almond-shaped eyes were soft. "They say our future is determined at the hour of our birth but only Allah knows the direction it will take. What we hope and pray for has no bearing on our destiny. We, ourselves, cannot direct the course of our lives. It is predetermined by events beyond our control."

"That is our belief, too, but what has it to do with the present situation?"

"You hope to be released and you pray that the lord, your father, will hear that plea. It is many months since you left your own country, yes?"

"That is true."

"The Sultan will ask a high price. It is always so with ladies of rank. May your father be in health and prosperity when he receives the demand. Even so, the ransom will, of necessity, travel through many hands of officialdom. It is the custom. Much time will pass which is why I warn you of the Kislar Aga.''

Juliet spoke more bravely than she was feeling. "What you are saying so delicately is that providing my father still lives and is in possession of sufficient funds to line the pockets of dignitaries along the way, leaving enough of worth for the Sultan, I have nothing to worry about, save the time I must spend under the eye of the Head Eunuch?''

Khurrem bowed her head in assent.

"And therefore, should any mischance occur," went on Juliet, "and I fall into the Kislar Aga's power, it would be folly to antagonize the man from the outset? Well, rest assured, my friend," she continued cheerfully, "I will treat him most politely. I might even send him a card for my next At Home!''

Under Khurrem's mystified look she sank back onto the cushions with a gasp of laughter. Could one be light-headed, almost to the point of hysteria, yet be filled with foreboding at the same time? It was too hard to keep her mind steady at this moment. She closed her eyes and tried to evade the tangled thoughts that floated like seaweed, ebbing and flowing with the turning tide. She didn't hear Khurrem rise and dim the lamp. Deep in the depths of the soft satin cushions, her mind let go and she floated weightlessly with the tide.

A solid night's sleep does wonders for the constitution, Juliet told herself on waking.

The fears that beset one in the dark reaches of evening, the claws that hold a tired mind in a state of suspense, seem somehow less menacing in the bright dawn of another day. Not strictly less, but a shade more bearable. It could hardly be said that optimism exuded from every pore, she decided, yawning, but a refreshed body and mind were assets in dealing with seemingly insoluble problems. There were two to tax her mind. How to escape and how to keep her lack of virginity a secret. If the first could be solved, the second would have no value. Therefore, her sole occupation must be to familiarize herself with the palace, discover the strength of the guard on the harem, and find the outer walls. The problem of what she was to do if she succeeded in these aims and found herself wandering lost and penniless through the streets of Zanzibar was an entirely different problem and one she decided not to dwell on at the moment.

But it seemed that the Mistress of the Harem had other plans for the occupation of her time. As soon as she had finished the breakfast brought by Khurrem, a small page, honey-skinned and brown-eyed, in green velvet and a little pearl-edged cap, brought her a summons from Gabriella. Khurrem helped her to dress. As promised, the Mistress had sent a selection of garments from which Juliet chose a blouse with lace-edged collar, wide satin trousers of vivid gold, an embroidered waistcoat, and a kaftan of amber silk. There was not enough time to do much with her hair so she tied it back severely with a ribbon of matching gold satin.

"The page will escort you, my lady," said Khurrem. "He waits outside."

"He is very young," Juliet said. "He can't be more than eight or nine. What do they call him?"

"This one is Hyacinth. They are all given the names of flowers. All possessions of the Sultan must receive new names, including the concubines. No infidel names are allowed."

"A new life, a new name," mused Juliet. "I wonder what I should be called—if I was staying, of course. How do I look?" she went on, hastily, shrugging away the touch of an icy finger on her spine.

"The color suits you, my lady, but you are pale. The Mistress will give you paints, I am sure."

"Paints? We don't paint ourselves in England. At least," she conceded, "respectable females don't. I dare say independent concubines do!" She gave a puzzled Khurrem a laughing glance and went out into the corridor.

"Hyacinth! I don't suppose you speak English, do you?" Under his blank gaze she sighed. "No, I didn't think so. Between Khurrem who doesn't know anything yet, and the Mistress who does but is unlikely to say, I shall have to find out everything for myself."

Outside the door of the Mistress's apartment, Juliet smiled and touched the boy's
soft golden cheek. "Thank you, Hyacinth."

The boy returned the smile of this
strange, pale-faced lady who seemed kind
but talked to herself in a tongue he had
never heard before.

Juliet knocked and was bidden to enter.
She faced once again the supremely elegant
figure reclining on cushions. By daylight
the lady was not quite as young as Juliet
had supposed but the planes of her face,
delicately tinted, and the brows and lashes,
artificially darkened, gave her a look of age-
less beauty.

"You will take coffee?" she asked in a
serene voice. "Please sit." She clapped her
hands and a servant appeared swiftly.

Juliet accepted the strong sweet coffee
served in a tiny cup. She was aware that
Gabriella was studying her closely.

"You are pleased with your clothes?" she
asked.

"Thank you, Lady Gabriella. They are, as
you said, cooler and more comfortable."

"There is an art in the wearing of Eastern
clothes," went on the Mistress. "You have
a certain natural grace, but tuition in
carriage and the art of enhancing your
appearance might appeal to you."

Juliet choked a little over her coffee.
"You mean I should be trained like the concubines."

Gabriella spread her pink-nailed hands.
"It is a thought only—to help you pass the

time of waiting."

Juliet bit her lip, thinking, then met the
Mistress's eye. "You are telling me that
such negotiations are protracted and I may
be here for a long time?"

"It is possible, my dear. One must be
patient in matters of this sort."

Juliet veiled her eyes under the pretext of
sipping the muddy coffee. And if, she
thought, the ransom did not materialize,
she would be already trained to take her
place in the harem. Had the Mistress
thought of that? Was it the reason for this
kind offer? No unseemly haste to prepare
her if the negotiations came to naught?
Had such things happened in the past?

She could refuse, of course, and act the
outraged maiden. Or she could accept on
the grounds the Mistress had suggested,
acknowledging it openly as a way to pass
the time. It might be wiser to take the
second course and keep the Mistress's
goodwill while seeking an escape. If none was
possible, then she would have to throw herself on the lady's mercy, pleading ignorance
of Muslim custom. No one had asked her
directly if she was a virgin, and no one had
given her a choice in the slave market. The
blame must be equally shared.

Innocent grey eyes opened wide and
settled on the classical features of the
Mistress. "It is a kind thought, Lady
Gabriella, and would indeed occupy my
time. I should like also," she went on,

carefully, "to view the town of Zanzibar, which I glimpsed very briefly on my way here. There are many places of note, I am sure, which would be of great interest to the Western eye. . ." She faltered to a halt as she saw the perfect eyebrows rise in horror.

"My dear Lady Juliet! Such a thing would never be allowed! No lady under the protection of the Sultan is ever permitted into the streets of Zanzibar, not even veiled and clad in the burka. The penalty for such unseemly behavior would be most severe!"

"But . . . but with a guard. . ." Juliet struggled valiantly. "And because I am only a guest and not of the harem. . ."

"No!" The Mistress spoke sternly. "I will excuse your words because you are not of our faith but I beg you will not raise the subject again. The Jannissaries have no time to play guardian to a woman's whim, and if news of this request should reach his highness. . ." Her expression was appalled.

Juliet clenched her teeth and forced her back rigidly upright. What dreadful penalty ws the Mistress visualizing? Torture—even death? For doing what every English girl had a perfect right to do as freely and as often as she wished? She drew in a deep, steadying breath and expelled it softly.

"Forgive me, Lady Gabriella. You are right to reprimand me. I would not have you blamed for my thoughtless words. I will not speak of it again but set myself to learn your customs in order to spare you shame over my conduct. As a guest of his highness, it is my duty to behave with the greatest of consideration towards his household.''

The Mistress smiled, her face regaining its composure. She lifted a small handbell and summoned Hyacinth. "You have a visitor, my dear. It is the captain of the ship wrecked off our coast. Hyacinth will direct you to the haremlik—that is the place of meeting for such business. There, you will be allowed to write a letter to the lord, your father, explaining the situation. This man has been acquainted with his highness's terms but requires a note in your own hand to prove your presence here. Please be circumspect for the Vizier who brought you will read your letter before it is dispatched.''

Juliet bowed her head in assent. "Will the Vizier be present at the interview?'' she asked, as calmly as she could, though her heart beat like a forge hammer.

"No. You will be allowed privacy but under the eye of the haremlik aga, naturally. And, of course, you must be veiled and robed as is seemly in the presence of a man, even one of another race.'' She rose gracefully and brought forward a burka of soft russet muslin.

Juliet, once more clad in a hooded floor-length garment, followed Hyacinth, holding the veil up to her eyes as instructed by the

Mistress. The page led her through a court where fountains played, along a corridor, through yet another court, until they reached a guarded gate. Hyacinth spoke to the Negro guard and they were allowed to enter the anteroom beyond the gate.

Hyacinth bowed, then placed himself against the wall, ready to escort her back. For a moment, Juliet could see nothing after the sun-filled garden, then her gaze fell on a richly dressed Negro who smelled overpoweringly of violets. He pointed across the room.

Juliet turned slowly, keeping the soft muslin folds of her veiling tight against her lips. With his back to a window stood a tall, hawk-faced man regarding her without expression. He wore a brocaded tunic over a white shirt. Black trousers were tucked into soft, calf-length boots. For a moment she didn't recognize him, but as he stepped forward and the blue eyes looked into hers, she knew it was Ross.

He bowed. "My lady" he said, formally. "You will find writing materials on the desk. There is a French ship in harbor. Please be brief or we may not be in time before she sails. The sum to be requested is twenty-five thousand English pounds. I leave the wording of the plea to you." He bowed again and walked past the desk to stand with his arm on the stone sill of the window, to stare over the courtyard, his attitude one of complete disinterest.

IX

Juliet stood very still for a long moment, staring at the unmoving figure by the window. Her own bright glance of joy at the reunion had not been mirrored in his eyes. They had remained cool and hard, like blue glass. Her breath came jerkily, fluttering the tiny veil. Her gaze dropped to the table.

Pen and paper lay at hand, together with wafers of varicolored paste. She sank onto the stool with her back to Ross and drew a sheet of paper towards her. Hyacinth and the eunuch made no sound, but without glancing up, she knew their eyes would be upon her. The letter had to be written and addressed to her father in order to satisfy the Vizier. That much was obvious. From her previous reluctance to discuss her father, Ross must have guessed that he was still alive, but why he should suppose that a man whose daughter had been sentenced to

transportation would be interested in
sending money for her ransom was beyond
her. Even had he the means, her release was
the last thing for which Sir George Westover would lay out money.

With a mental shrug she began to write
as she supposed a distraught daughter
might write to a loving father. How
surprised her sire would be to receive such a
moving epistle! The veiling hid the cynical
curve of her lips as she imagined his
bloodshot eyes perusing with mounting joy
the news of her predicament. Whether
received from Zanzibar or New South
Wales, his reaction would be the same.

She folded the sheet and enclosed it in a
wrapper on which she wrote Sir George
Westover, following it with the word
Baronet in large letters. She added his
address then reached for a wafer, noting
absently the variety of colors.

Ross moved from the window, paused
beside her then, with a show of impatience,
turned to the eunuch. His soft voice
lingered. "Insist on red!"

Juliet kept her eyes on the wafers,
resisting the urge to look up. She scanned
them quickly. There was a red! But with a
lift of hope in her heart, she said loudly and
plaintively, "I must have red wax! I always
use red!" She stared then at the eunuch, her
expression demanding.

He frowned, his black eyes puzzled by her
tone. Ross repeated her words but the

eunuch's face stayed blank. Ross shrugged
and spread his hands, rolling his eyes up in
exasperation as he glanced first at her and
then back to the eunuch, his face clearly expressing his opinion of wilful females. He
turned towards Juliet.

"Use whatever you wish. I was merely
testing his knowledge of English." He
stood, hands clasped behind him as Juliet
sealed the wrapper. "Spend all the time you
can in the fourth court. The outside wall
runs beside it." He lifted the letter and
scanned it, nodding as if satisfied. "A
higher title might have been better but this
will probably suffice." He ran his free hand
across his chin. "I shall grow a beard."

"How nice," said Juliet, faintly. "Thank
you for telling me."

For a split second their eyes met and she
saw the old Ross looking down at her. He
took a sharp breath and said in a slightly
unsteady voice, "A warning—to prevent
you screaming when I peer down into the
kiosk."

He turned swiftly to the eunuch and indicated that the meeting was over. Juliet
rose and, without a glance in his direction,
beckoned Hyacinth and swept out of the
haremlik. She forced her limbs to operate at
a sedate pace but it was almost more than
she could bear. The urge to hop, skip, turn
cartwheels across the immaculate lawns
was well nigh irresistible. The veil hid her
wide grin and if Hyacinth noted her

shaking shoulders, he must suppose that
she was overcome by the emotional fact of
writing to her beloved father!

Ross, her heart sang, had not deserted
her after all. As a man, unemployed in the
Seraglio, he could well have been allowed to
move about the island. A strong escort of
Janissaries, always at his heels, was perhaps the only precaution the Vizier had
deemed necessary. A half-prisoner only,
until the matter was resolved one way or
another.

By the time Juliet reached her room, she
had her elation well under control. The
fourth court he had said. She believed that
to be the one in which the girls of the harem
had gathered on her first day.

In the weeks that followed, Juliet set herself to learn everything she could of the life
fate compelled her to live. It was better
than brooding on the inevitable
outcome—or wondering what scheme Ross
was endeavoring to put together. She even
learned a little Arabic at the lectures the
girls were obliged to attend. The subject
matter was far from intellectual—no female
was allowed to acquire an education—but
interminable instruction on the arts to be
used when summoned to the Master's bed.

They were taught how to paint their lips,
to dye lashes and brows, to gloss the finger
and toe nails, and to draw fine lines above
and under the eyelashes with a moleshair

brush dipped in kohl. She learned to make the kohl herself with plumbago and lemon over a brazier. There was face powder to be mixed, a putting together of beanflour, lemon, eggs, ground rice and several other ingredients Juliet did not recognize.

She found out that henna was painted on the palms of the hands and the soles of the feet to prevent perspiration. Each girl was provided with her own brushes and pots, and the Lady Gabriella was a stern critic. A great deal of attention was devoted to the hair. Washed and brushed with great frequency, it was oiled and scented with tonics and essences, until the most ordinary hair glowed with luster.

Juliet, herself, was given a little latitude. Where the concubines were forced to suffer the sting of the eyebrow tweezers, her own dark brows had been deemed quite presentable and well-arched by the Mistress.

Lessons on deportment brought their own hilarious moments. To walk across the room bearing an earthenware jar on the crown of the head and reaching the other side without shedding it was no mean feat. The crash of pottery, combined with a scathing comment from the Mistress, reduced the younger girls to blushing imbeciles. Juliet contributed her own share of breakages but laughed when she did so, ignoring the astonishment she aroused. But it was still a useful exercise, she decided, persevering until she could glide without mishap the length of the room. An elegant, almost arrogant, carriage could only add credibility to her supposed rank when the time came for her to face the Sultan.

She was familiar now with the fourth court. The kiosk, hung with vines of ripening grapes, was cool. Colored tiles lined the walls on three sides, the fourth being open to the lawns. Mosaic steps on which the girls reclined were shaded by palms. Inside the summerhouse were low benches of marble and numerous cushions. Music was considered an essential accomplishment, and they were entertained by the more expert girls on the lute. Juliet formed the habit of seating herself near to the lute player and professing an interest in the music.

The kiosk in the fourth court, Ross had said. How could he hope to show his face anywhere in this female holy of holies without the wrath of heaven, in the shape of scimitar-armed eunuchs descending on him, she could not imagine. Guest or not, they would drop him into little pieces, she thought with a shudder. The more she thought of it, the more impossible it became. Would he really risk his life for her sake?

As the weeks passed, her hopes dimmed and her heart grew a little heavier. There had been no further communication with Ross, and the French ship bearing her letter must surely be nearing its destination. How long would the Sultan wait? A few months, perhaps, but in the absence of the ransom, or an acknowledgement that funds were being sought, there must come a time of suspicion, followed by the realization that both she and the captain had lied.

Lady Gabriella's voice at her elbow made her jump. The girls were playing some kind of ball game across the lawns, the lutist had laid down her instrument to join them, and only Juliet had remained in the kiosk. Reclining on the cushions, her gaze unfocused, she had been sunk too deep in thought to notice the silently gliding figure enter and dispose herself gracefully on the cushions beside her.

"You are pensive, Lady Juliet. Has something distressed you or does your mind dwell on your native land?"

Juliet forced herself to smile. "Neither one nor the other. I cannot fault your hospitality or kindness, and at this time of the year my own country will be in the grip of winter. Rain, snow and cold winds sweep over Exmoor. How should I miss that?"

"But your look held sadness. This life would not content you, I feel."

Without looking into the clever, experienced face, Juliet knew she was being observed closely.

"My companions are happy in the knowledge of their future. Under your tutelage, Lady Gabriella," she said, "they cannot fail to reach the required standards.

They are taught all the sensuous arts and will be a credit to you should they be summoned in honor down the Golden Road and into the presence of the Master."

"And if they acquit themselves well, they can look to further rewards. The date on which the girl is so honored is noted down, and should she have the felicity to bear the Great One's son in the due passage of time, an apartment and her own retinue of servants is hers. To be a kadin is almost equal to being a wife." She paused, then added softly, "There is no deviation from the path Allah had designed for women."

Juliet looked into the shrewd amber eyes. "You teach them the arts of the body but is the mind of no account? Can a man converse only with another man? Is even a kadin mute when her lord visits her?"

"It is ordained that a female is nothing but the servant of man. Her role is to feed his body and pleasure his senses. She is the mother of his children but not the companion of his mind or soul. Mohammed has decreed that women should not be treated as intellectual beings."

"In case they become equal?" Juliet asked dryly.

Lady Gabriella's eyebrows rose, then she frowned. "It is not fitting to speak in such a manner. It denies the word of Allah through his prophet Mohammed."

"I beg your pardon. I meant no disrespect. But our faiths are different and learning is allowed in my country for girls as well as boys." Juliet shrugged, smiling. "Perhaps it is the absence of books that makes me pensive." She gazed round the kiosk and her eyes fell on the discarded lute. "Perhaps I should take up music," she commented idly.

"Skill on a musical instrument is always an asset," said Lady Gabriella.

Juliet stared at the lute, an idea forming in her mind. "May I be taught?"

"Of course." It was plain that this subject of conversation was more to the taste of the Mistress. She smiled warmly. "I will have the best girl instruct you."

Juliet laughed, her eyes dancing. "And as soon as I attempt my first solo this kiosk will erupt like water from a fountain, the girls fleeing as larks before the bird-catcher!"

The Mistress smiled. "Then Fleurette shall instruct you. She has proved the most proficient." She clapped her hands and the girls on the lawn stopped their game to attend, the one she beckoned coming forward.

The lessons began immediately. Juliet was pleased, not only with the occupation but with the fact that it gave her an excuse to linger in the summerhouse. The building was roofed with crossbeams, the vine stems weaving in and out, clusters of ripening grapes hanging through the foliage. Was it strong enough, she wondered, to hold a

man's weight? And how did Ross propose
to reach the roof? The outer wall was not
close enough for it to be reached
easily—and what of the gardeners? Hadn't
Khurrem mentioned idly that the position
of Head Gardener was combined with that
of Chief Executioner?

She saw Fleurette's pained expression as
her fingers jerked on the lute strings. A
chord of great unpleasantness, the grimace
conveyed, and Juliet grinned wryly,
pushing her forebodings to the back of her
mind.

The lessons progressed as Juliet set herself grimly to the task of mastering the instrument. She learned a few simple tunes
and Fleurette was happy to leave her alone
as she repeated and improved on them.
Juliet encouraged the girl to join the others,
professing more interest in the lute than
the games they played.

Juliet's feigned interest in the lute became more real as she gained experience.
Snatches of old Somerset songs from her
childhood came back and she tried them out
experimentally, tuning the lute strings to
emit softer notes. The harsh Arab music
was sharp to her ears. Absorbed in the
music she was making, the days passed
swiftly.

She raised her gaze from the lute one day
to find Lady Gabriella regarding her.
Laying down the lute, she rose, smiling.

"Do I disturb you with my English
songs?" she asked.

"Not at all. What was it you were playing?"

"A very old tune called 'Greensleeves.' They say it was composed by King Henry of England many years ago."

Lady Gabriella nodded. "Then it must be a worthy tune, though strange to my ears, for it to have come from a king. You have made good progress with your music and my ears have not been alone in listening. You have come to the notice of someone of supreme importance." Her gaze moved slowly over Juliet. "I will dress you myself as I promised. A great honor is to be yours, my lady."

Juliet stared into Lady Gabriella's face and her body turned cold. She tried to speak but her throat was dry.

"Not . . . not the Great One?" she managed huskily.

Lady Gabriella looked faintly shocked. "You have not reached that standard where I could send you down the Golden Road with complete serenity of mind. Why should you suppose it when your position here has not yet been defined?" The amber eyes were keen and probing.

Juliet realized her mistake in letting her apprehension take over. She managed a smile, forcing herself to relax.

"Indeed you are right, Lady Gabriella. I would have much to learn if I were in that position. It was merely your mention of this supreme person that made my thoughts fly to the Great One. Who else is of such importance as he?"

"No other, naturally, but in the realm of women there is the one who rules the harem on his behalf. She is the Crown of Veiled Heads, mother of the Great One. All Kadins are subservient to her, as are we all. No one may approach her unless she grants permission. The Great One himself sends her word of his coming."

Juliet waited. What had the Sultan's mother to do with her? Somehow her lute playing had been overheard. A great honor, Lady Gabriella had said. What did that mean?

"You have been granted an audience, Lady Juliet. The Sultana Valideh, that is the Queen Mother, requests that you play your lute tonight in her private apartments. I must instruct you in your behavior and mode of greeting. The greatest formality is essential and you must address her at all times by her full title. Though your position differs from the other girls, courtesy demands that you will only speak when directly addressed and a reply is indicated. Do you understand?"

Juliet bowed her head. "I understand, Lady. I am overwhelmed that my poor playing has reached the ears of so high a lady and I am honored to be summoned to her presence. I will endeavor to remember your teaching so that I may bring no disgrace upon you."

Lady Gabriella seemed pleased by her

assurance but her manner as she dressed
Juliet later hardly conveyed certainty that
all would go well.

"You are a girl from Europe where I am
told they have no such tradition as this.
Girls from the colder climates are much
more difficult to train. Is it true that a man
of your country may take but one woman to
his household?"

"Quite true," Juliet said solemnly. "One
wife is all that the law allows. Should he
seek to introduce a concubine into his
household, he will be looked upon with displeasure and his wife will have the right to
leave him."

"Leave him?" Lady Gabriella's fingers
paused as she pinned the small veil over the
lower half of Juliet's face. "Where would
she go in her disgrace?"

Juliet eyed her mentor with amusement.
"It would not be her disgrace though she
would feel shame for her husband. He
would be shunned by polite society." She
thought briefly of her own parents. Sir
George had not been received anywhere for
years but Lady Westover had not left him.
Although Juliet had condemned her
mother's lack of spirit, she could not deny
her pride. It was pride that had kept her
from allowing her villagers to witness her
suffering. Pride and the protection of her
daughter. Both virtues had caused her
death but Juliet now understood her
mother better in death than she had done in

life. Could she, herself, show such bravery if her deception was discovered? Ah, Ross, she thought, in sudden desolation. Save yourself now and leave me in the bondage I would have entered had the 'Grace' reached the new colony.

She was still a little pensive as, painted and perfumed, she was led along a corridor into a garden of great beauty—a private garden with fountains of marble and perfume laden bushes, where doves and love-birds floated and swooped.

The Lady led her past a high closed gate. Juliet glanced at it.

"Is that the. . . ?"

Lady Gabriella's lips compressed. "It leads to another garden, beyond which is the Gate of Felicity. Through that one takes the Golden Road. Now be silent, if you please. Remember that you are—as yet—a guest, and may count this as a greater honor than is afforded to any other."

The amber glance flicked over Juliet and away again. As yet—a guest? Was the Lady Gabriella beginning to doubt her story? It was true that time was slipping away and weeks had turned into months but it was a long way to England and the Sultan must know that a transaction of this nature took time: bad sailing weather, the difficulty of raising the ransom, the time it took to filter through many hands before finally reaching the ruler of Zanzibar. He

must realize all that and make allowances.
She determined to think no further than
that. Her chin rose, her shoulders squared,
and as they approached the marble-pillared
entrance to the Queen Mother's suite,
Juliet adopted the graceful, swaying walk
she had learned from the Lady Gabriella.

Eunuchs guarded the delicately wrought
iron gates. Black, impassive faces watched
the two women. Juliet eyed the long
curving daggers thrust into their sashes
and sought to forget what might happen if
she displeased the Queen Mother.

Lady Gabriella spoke to them and their
dark eyes turned to Juliet. She raised her
brows slightly and stared back calmly.

"They are satisfied, with my assurance of
course, that you are a woman."

Juliet turned her gaze to Lady Gabriella.
"Do . . . do they doubt it?"

"It is their duty to ensure that no man,
other than the Great One, is ever allowed
this side of the gate you saw in the garden
wall. With my word, it will not be necessary
for them to make sure."

She nodded to the guards and swept
Juliet between them. Make sure, wondered
Juliet in horror? There could only be one
way of doing that and the thought of those
large hands making some kind of investi-
gation of her sex was appalling!

Before she had time to dwell upon the
prospect, Lady Gabriella had stopped
before a pair of marble pillars twisted about

with flowering creepers. Perfume hung
heavily in the room. Large satin cushions of
all hues possible seemed banked into
lounging position in every direction.

Lady Gabriella was bowing low, her arms
crossed over her breasts. Juliet did the
same, seeing no one at all in the shadowed
room. The lute, hanging from a ribbon on
her waist swung gently but she steadied it
as she rose, following Lady Gabriella's lead.

A husky voice spoke in languid tones. A
slight push in the small of her back pro-
pelled Juliet forward. Then she could see
the reclining form of a small plump female
on the far cushions. Juliet lowered her gaze
and became aware of the empty space beside her. Lady Gabriella had gone and she
was alone with the most powerful woman in
Zanzibar.

Remembering Lady Gabriella's words,
she remained mute and still, awaiting some
sign from the Valideh.

"Come."

The English word took Juliet by surprise
and she glanced up. Her eyes met a pair of
bright brown ones, curiously youthful in
the face of a woman of middle age. She advanced a few steps and waited politely.

A jeweled hand waved to a pile of
cushions below the level on which the
Queen Mother lay.

Remember your training, Juliet told herself firmly as a heavy scent of musk
enveloped her, seeming to fill her head and

cloud her wits. Her skirts billowed wide as
she crossed her legs and sank gracefully
into the soft depths of the scarlet satin
cushion. Arching her wrists in elegant
motion after the fashion of Lady Gabriella
she drew the ribbon from the neck of the
lute and positioned the instrument on her
lap. She could only pray that the strings
she had so carefully tuned were still as they
were. Guest she might be but a bad impression on this great lady would auger
disasters for her future in the harem. And
that future was fast approaching! She
swallowed hard and awaited the command.

"Italian?" the soft voice queried.

"English, Sultana Valideh," Juliet murmured, keeping her eyes down.

"Pity. I hoped to speak of my country."

Juliet was so surprised that her gaze
widened and rose to the smooth unlined
face with the youthful eyes. She opened her
mouth, then closed it again, remembering
Lady Gabriella's warning. Italian? It had
never occured to her that the Sultan's
mother could be anything other than Arab.
But considering that girls were abducted,
bought and sold, his mother could have
been of any race and taken the fancy of his
father. Had she too served her time in the
harem, being groomed and finally chosen to
grace the Great One's bed? Her position
must have been dictated by presenting her
lord with his first son. The sons that
followed, bred on a succession of con-

cubines, would only earn their mothers the position of Kadins, all subservient to the mother of the firstborn who, if her son survived and became ruler, would inevitably become the Queen Mother, only one step below the Sultan in the hierarchy of the Palace.

"You will play your king's song for me," the voice commanded and the accented English was liquid and sibilant.

Juliet bowed her head in assent and stared fixedly at the lute. Her rose-tipped fingers brushed the strings, and she began slowly but gained confidence as the notes came out as she had practiced. It was a slow sweet air, a compound of dignity and sadness, and in the playing of it, Juliet's mind wandered over the fresh greenness of an English spring, the scent of young wall-flowers beside the door of Mrs. Shepheard's kitchen, the burgeoning of honeysuckle and the sun with its golden fingers drawing up the curtain of early mist.

It wasn't until the Sultana murmured "You are sad for your country," did Juliet realize that she had played the song with such feeling that tears stood on her eyelashes and the emotion had been noted by the reclining lady.

Juliet smiled and brushed away the tears. "The Crown of Veiled Heads is very wise. It is true that I thought of my country as I played but I am not ungrateful for the kindness and courtesy offered me since arriving at the Palace."

"I, too, have my memories," the soft voice sighed. "Did they tell you I was from Sicily?"

"No, Sultana Valideh. A most beautiful country, I believe, although I have never seen it. May I say ..." she broke off, remembering that this was no ordinary conversation. Only speak when required, it had been impressed upon her.

"Why do you pause?"

"Forgive me, Sultana Valideh. It is not my place to make comment on anything without your permission."

"Then I give you permission. A thought half-expressed leaves one in bewilderment. Continue."

"You are most gracious, Sultana Valideh. I was about to say that you speak the English tongue with great fluency."

"That is so." The Queen Mother nodded. "English and French I learned as a child for there were many foreign travelers who came to the vineyards of my father." She was quiet for a few moments, her face soft and dreaming, as if she recalled a happy childhood.

"How many years do you have?" she asked abruptly.

"Sixteen, Sultana Valideh."

"I had borne my lord's son at that age," the Queen Mother said, and there was an edge of pride to her words. "Our union was blessed by Allah." She reached a plump hand to a tray of marzipan. "Play something else, a tune of liveliness, the music of dancers.''

Juliet obeyed. She had once been to a country fair with the Shepheard children and there a fiddler had played so briskly to the crowd that the young men and girls had jigged to his music. Her own rendering of his piece was not in the same class, the lute and violin being poles apart, but the Queen Mother seemed not to find it distasteful.

Juliet grew a little cramped in her cross-legged position but she dare not move until told. Relief came with the advent of a group of ladies who surrounded the reclining figure, seating themselves silently on cushions and regarding Juliet from dark expressionless eyes.

The Queen Mother spoke. "It is time to bathe and rest. Your music was pretty. Now I give you leave to retire."

Juliet rose slowly and tried to make her movements graceful. She bowed, arms across her breast. "I have been highly honored, Sultana Valideh." And she backed her way out of the presence.

It is time to bathe and rest. The words repeated themselves in Juliet's mind as she walked shakily along the short corridor. Relief that she had not done anything too stupid made her a little lightheaded. Bathe and rest. Her thoughts skittered wildly. Was it not restful enough to recline on cushions eating marzipan? What else was there for a Queen Mother or a Kadin to do? No longer did they need lessons in deport-

ment and allure to catch the eye of the
Great One. Their duty was fulfilled by the
bearing of sons.

She suddenly longed desperately for the
cool air of England, the fresh chill wind on
her face instead of the warm, perfumed atmosphere that hung everlastingly throughout the Palace. Country air or sea air, what
did it matter as long as she could breathe it.
Perhaps neither would ever be hers again.
This was her life and likely to remain so. A
guest they called her but what name would
it be when they realized the ransom was not
forthcoming. And what fate awaited her
when it was also found that her purity had
been defiled.

The small boy, Hyacinth, was squatting
on the grass in the shade of a giant
magnolia tree. He rose, bowing, and she
followed his small erect figure back the way
she had come. Khurrem had been waiting,
and at the sight of Juliet she came forward,
her dark eyes gleaming with curiosity. She
was followed by a cluster of brightly-garbed
maidens, all eager to share in Juliet's
exalted moments with the Queen Mother.
They waited, impatient for her words and
Khurrem's translation. Their questions
fluted and trilled about her, rising, soaring,
like the soft hum and sweep of bird wings.

"They have never been so honored as
you, Lady Juliet," explained Khurrem.
"And few will ever see the Sultana Valideh
unless they became Kadins and ennoble

their lives by bearing the Great One's
sons."

"What do they wish to know?"

Khurrem spread her hands. "But everything is of interest, my lady. Such visits are
not common and they would know every
detail, so they may emulate in all things so
supreme a person."

"I see," said Juliet. "Well, the Sultana
reclined on cushions of gold, and her gown
was of softest muslin of paler shades and
woven throughout with gold and silver
thread. Such jewels I have never seen in my
life."

Khurrem translated swiftly and the girls
nodded. Would they all, wondered Juliet in
amusement, become gold-clad tomorrow,
bearing cushions of gold satin wherever
they chanced?

She thought of the Queen Mother's
parting words. It is time to bathe and rest.
Her amusement turned to laughter. The
girls paused in their chatter and gazed at
her enquiringly. Would they not find it
humorous too, as their days were spent in
complete idleness? Rest from exhaustion
was an impossibility here.

She sensed rather than saw a figure
drawing close behind her. A particular
perfume identified that person for her and
she had no need to glance around. The Lady
Gabriella was within earshot and there
would be no amusement in her eyes if Juliet
made public her own. It might be looked

upon as a criticism of the Queen Mother and such things could not be tolerated.

"I found the Sultana Valideh most charming," she went on in a clear voice. "I could not have been received more kindly and with such graciousness had I searched the world over. An exquisite and beautiful lady who honored me by calling my unworthy lute playing pretty. It is an experience I shall treasure always." She glanced round innocently and met the gaze of Lady Gabriella. "I cannot express fully the great honor done to me. It will be a cherished memory," she finished gravely, trying to read the amber eyes in an effort to judge if she had overdone the complimentary words.

Lady Gabriella smiled, her eyes approving. No praise was too high, no words too grand, it seemed, to describe the mother of the Great One. The Mistress clapped her hands.

"It is time to bathe and rest," she declared and Juliet lowered her gaze glad that she had not discarded the half-veil on entering the harem gardens.

X

The Mistress of the Harem found Juliet in the summerhouse the day after her visit to the Queen Mother. Her amber gaze rested on Juliet and she smiled.

"Another great honor has been bestowed upon you, my lady." She drew from her sleeve a small square of gold silk. "The Sultana Valideh has sent you a token for the pleasure you gave her."

On her open palm lay a magnificent ruby ring set in diamonds. Juliet stared speechlessly at the blood-red stone. The gardens of the Palace faded. There was no sound of birds or the rustle of garment. She was alone in an icy world of silence, moonlight blurring the crimson through falling tears. It had all begun with a ruby ring—the ring her mother had hidden from her greedy, rapacious husband, the heirloom treasured over the years that had finally brought death to Lady Westover.

Juliet flung up a hand to shade her eyes. She felt sick and faint. The world came back suddenly. An amber gaze was on her and voices twittered in her ears as the girls gathered, staring in admiration at this most unusual gift bestowed by such a great lady. The birds called and swooped again. Lady Gabriella took the cold hand and slipped on the ring. It lay warm and heavy on Juliet's finger. She steadied her mind with an effort.

"How . . . how very kind of the Sultana Valideh," she managed through stiff lips. "Please convey to her my grateful thanks."

The Mistress nodded. "You are quite pale, my lady. This honor has overwhelmed you. It is rare for the Sultana Valideh to send gifts. She will be pleased to hear of your gratification."

Juliet bowed gravely and left the gardens to seek solitude and sanctuary in her apartments. She longed to tear off the ring and fling it away but the gift was well-meant. She must wear it or risk offending that powerful lady, the Crown of Veiled Heads.

Khurrem came to her in great excitement that night. The Lady Gabriella had announced a visit of some importance to be in the offing. An Emir and his entire court from the North were to pay a week-long visit to the Sultan.

"Already," said Khurrem, happily, "his highness has ordered the extra filling of the snow pits. Luckily, the caravan from the mainland with the dates, plums and prunes has been shipped, and a consignment of honey also. . ."

"Stop," said Juliet. "Did you say snow? How on earth . . . ?"

"It is quite easy, my lady. The snow is taken from the mountains and packed in felt sacks carried by mules to the sea coast. From there it is shipped to whomever wants it and is stored in special pits underground. Iced sherbet is most enjoyable, especially when flavored with amber or musk or water lilies. Honey or violet flavoring is more costly but the Sultan will not mind that to please his guests."

"Well," said Juliet, dryly, "I cannot imagine his concubines will be invited to the banquets, so why all the excitement?"

"The silk merchants are coming to show us their new cloths. The Mistress says everyone must wear something new and she is allowing us our own choice of color. What will be your fancy, my lady?"

Juliet stared at her. "I don't see how these two events are connected," she said slowly. "What have new clothes to do with the entertaining of the Emir by the Sultan?"

Khurrem sank onto her cushions and regarded Juliet gravely. "It is the custom, my lady, for the Sultan to offer entertainment other than food. If the Emir or one of his dignitaries signifies another desire, then it is granted him. He has only to state his preference and the girl is given to him as a gift. She will then enter his household and go with him when he leaves."

"And the Sultan can always replace her on the next slave market day," said Juliet caustically.

Khurrem spread her hands and shrugged. "If Lady Gabriella says go, one must go. The alternative is death!"

"And . . . and when is the Emir expected?"

"Next week, my lady, but the silk merchants come to this court tomorrow."

"Into the women's quarters?"

Khurrem laughed, her eyes bright. "But they are women, too. No man may steal his way into the harem for the eunuchs on the gate feel the merchant's bodies to be sure they possess no male features."

Juliet visualized those soft plump hands exploring thighs and breasts and restrained a shudder of revulsion. "How . . . how undignified!"

"The merchants expect it and how else can they bring in the wares? The eunuchs are thorough in their examinations. They would be flayed alive and their heads stuffed with straw if they let through a man by carelessness. And the man himself—he would spend many lifetimes in torment before his head topped a gate spike."

Juliet was appalled by Khurrem's serene expression and casual words, but, of course, she was of this faith too and saw nothing out of the ordinary in this way of dealing with wrongdoers. But Ross? Did he understand the penalty for attempting to communicate with her? He must, she realized, and yet he had spoken so calmly in the haremlik.

She considered all the avenues open to them. Whatever happened, Ross must not risk his life in a futile rescue attempt. She must extract a binding promise that he would leave the island at the first opportunity. Her own fate was as nothing compared with the safety of the man she loved. Slavery was her future anyway. Did it matter that it was in Zanzibar and not New South Wales?

For most of that night sleep eluded her. As dawn drew the earth into light with ribbons of pearl, she rose and dressed quietly. Leaving Khurrem curled into a ball like a honey-colored bear cub, she made her way to the fourth court. Only the gardeners were about as she mounted the kiosk steps. The lute lay where she had left it. She sank onto the satin cushions and rested it on her lap. The garden was quiet, free for the moment from twittering girls.

Only the birds called. Perhaps, Juliet mused, Ross could make his escape in the train of the Emir on his departure. So many slaves and attendants—who would notice an extra man amongst them? Ross was

dark and tanned. Arab dress and the beard
he intended growing—and it must by this
time be of a respectable density—would
allow him to mingle without comment. Yes,
she would put it to him the next time they
met. The next time? The words sounded
hollow in her own mind. Their meeting in
the haremlik had been weeks ago. What
chance had they of meeting again? She
rose, sighing, and returned to her
apartments as Khurrem came drowsily
awake.

It was the day of the first visit of the silk
merchants, a highlight in the lives of the
girls. They clustered like pampered
children, awaiting a special treat. Their
minds were childlike although their bodies
were well-versed in all womanly arts.
Khurrem, too, was caught up in the excitement.

"I pray to Allah that the Emir's nephew
will be in his following, my lady. Will he
remember me, do you think? He once
wanted to buy me."

Juliet looked into the glowing face of the
almond-eyed girl. "He will remember you.
How could he not? He will know of your
master's death and may, even now, be wondering what happened to that beautiful
Ethiopian girl he desired."

"He will not know that I am here."

"No, that's true, but surely all this . . ."
Juliet waved an arm towards the gate
where the first of the women merchants

was coming through, "must mean that you will be displayed to the visitors."

"Yes," Khurrem agreed. "After the banquet we are expected to serve fruit and sherbet, tempt their appetites with sweetmeats." She smiled. "Fleurette is hoping she will be asked to play the lute and the Sultan may order dancing."

Juliet looked about her, seeing a small group of girls listlessly fingering the rich materials now laid out. She nodded towards them. "Those girls looking at the brocades do not seem to share in the general excitement."

Khurrem followed her gaze. "Ah, but they will not be present. The Great One has ordained it."

"Not be present? Are they being punished for something?"

"No, they are being saved." Khurrem smiled at Juliet's puzzled expression. "It is simple, my lady. They have not yet gone down the Golden Road."

Realization brought the color to Juliet's face. "Oh, I see. His highness will not risk their contact with other men should they prove too desirable. Is that it?"

"Of course. By the rules of etiquette, he could not refuse." She shrugged, glancing about. "All others here have taken the Golden Road, save you and I, my lady, and I would not please him since I have been the concubine of another."

Juliet said nothing, remembering. She

too, had been the concubine of another. Concubine, lover, mistress, it was all the same. She tried not to think of the future when the Sultan ran out of patience at the non-arrival of the ransom. Perhaps death would be preferable to a return to the slave market when her lack of purity was discovered—as inevitably it must.

Lady Gabriella was beside her, smiling. "You do not choose your silk or satin, Lady Juliet."

"I, Lady?" Juliet stared. "But I am not a member of the household."

"Nevertheless, his highness is most generous and wishes every female here to indulge her taste. Will you not do so?"

"It would be an honor to please his highness, Lady." She looked into the fathomless amber eyes and her heartbeat quickened unaccountably. "I shall not be there when. . ."

"Oh, indeed not, Lady Juliet. It would not be proper for you are not of the faith. I, myself, observe the proceedings from behind a lattice screen. The girls are aware that I watch their deportment and behavior and know that any laxity on their part will be punished. You will join me behind the screen?"

The voice was soft and musical. A question or a veiled command? A polite invitation or a hint that Juliet herself might one day be required to kneel before a visiting dignitary and pander to his needs?

She managed a serene smile. "I would deem it a privilege, Lady Gabriella, and a most unique experience for one of my race."

"Then may I suggest the amber silk? My own gown will be bronze-colored and we shall blend into the golden screen drapes without being conspicuous."

"A pretty choice," Juliet murmured. "I have a fondness for the shade, myself."

Lady Gabriella smiled and drifted away. Khurrem came to Juliet's side. She had a length of violet silk in one hand, a turquoise brocade in the other. Her brows were drawn together in thought.

"My lady, I am torn between desire. Silk or brocade? Which shall I take?"

Juliet turned to her with relief, dismissing her own uneasy thoughts.

"The silk without a doubt. If the night is hot, the silk will cling to your body and show it to advantage—which I am sure you will want if the Emir's nephew is here. One look and he will be filled with desire. The brocade holds to its own shape, not yours. It will stand when you want to sit and prickle in the heat. But the color is pretty."

Khurrem nodded sagely. "There is much knowledge in you, my lady. It is plain to see that many highborn men have desired you at the court of your English King, yet your father has not given you to any. He sets a high price on you—a prince perhaps?"

Juliet laughed. "Dear Khurrem, I am not so highborn as to interest a prince but there was a price, I agree.''

And I paid it, she reflected. Am I any different from Khurrem who was sold into bondage by a father who lacked affection for his child? Different only in respect to the future, and somehow Khurrem's was brighter. Khurrem had no deception to practice for it was known she had belonged to another. She watched the girl return the turquoise brocade to the merchant.

The eunuchs began to move amongst the girls who hurried with their final selections. The merchants began to roll up silks and satins, wrapping the rolls in cotton cloths. They eyed the eunuchs warily, knowing their goodwill to be essential. A word of complaint to the Kislar Aga and their visits to the Palace would be stopped without reason given. It was the most profitable trade in the whole of Zanzibar and eagerly contested by all women merchants. Where else could one sell an abundance of costly fabric and receive most lavish payment? So many new girls to dress and so many occasions that demanded new gowns. Next week they were to come three times! The women, rolls on heads and under arms, gathered at the gate, scrutinized by the eunuchs and herded through, to pass along the other courts before reaching the main high gates where the guards released them into the city.

Juliet watched them go, envying them their freedom. Then she pushed the thought away. Had the Vizier not been in the slave market that day, she would indeed have remained the purchase of the camel trader. Her mind flitted briefly over Ross Jamieson. So long and never a sign from him. Was he still here? He had no obligation towards her, a mere convict girl. Why should he put himself in danger? But he had given her hope. Dear God, did he mean it? She turned blindly towards the summerhouse. It was dangerous to think such thoughts.

The week preceding the Emir's visit saw the Palace seamstresses hard at work, sitting cross-legged on Persian rugs in the gardens surrounded by slave girls, sewing the delicate fabrics into styles chosen mainly by the concubines with Lady Gabriella in command. Each girl strove to make her design more elegant and sensuous than her neighbor's and there were scenes of bickering when a particular feature was thought to have been copied. Appeals to Lady Gabriella were frequent and the Mistress of the Harem dealt strictly and uncompromisingly with them. New hairstyles abounded and new ways of applying cosmetics were tried. Each girl intended to be the most desirable of all when they were called to the entertainment.

Even Khurrem was as one with the girls, and Juliet could not resist a certain excitement as the day approached. From behind the latticed and curtained screen she and

Lady Gabriella would see all, the Sultan
and the Emir, the households of both, and
the beautiful girls in their rainbow silks and
satins. Laughter and the sound of male
voices were so unusual that Juliet could not
blame the girls for their excitement and
feverish preparations.

Khurrem stood before Juliet clad in the
violet silk, her hair dressed high and
threaded through with amethyst stars. Her
eyes, outlined by kohl, looked enormous.
Delicate tinting of cheeks and lips glowed
above a long, slender neck around which
hung a necklace of amethysts. Bracelets
and rings on fingers with lacquered nails
sparkled brightly, and to complete the
artistry, an aura of violet-scented oils.
"My lady?" queried Khurrem, her eyes
anxious. "I have never before had such
splendor. My old master was generous but
he had not such a treasure house as this to
choose from."
"You," said Juliet firmly, "are by far the
most beautiful girl in the whole Palace. See,
the silk is warming to you already. If that
young sheik is with his uncle tonight, he
cannot fail to agree with me."
"Beautiful is common here." Khurrem
shrugged away the word. "Would I bring
him to desire me for his own?"
Juliet smiled. "Since I am not a man, I
cannot answer that, but if he desired you
when you were unattainable how much

stronger his desire will be when he knows you are within his grasp. The pleasing of him is up to you, my dear Khurrem. No one can help you in that."

Khurrem nodded. "Pray Allah he is come with the Emir."

Lady Gabriella's voice was heard in the corridor. "It is time," muttered Khurrem and held open the door.

"Good luck," whispered Juliet, passing her closely.

Khurrem smiled doubtfully and shook her head. "It is all ordained by Allah, my lady."

"Then Allah be with you."

Dressed in her amber silk, Juliet was jeweled but not as splendidly as the girls for she had no part to play tonight. Lady Gabriella beckoned her.

"We shall take our places first." She looked round at the girls, trembling and excited. "Do me honor tonight, my children. Remember everything you have been taught. Do not shame my teaching by forward behavior. Be conscious all the time of the Great One's presence. Go now to the antechamber. You will be summoned."

She turned to Juliet, laying a cool, long-fingered hand on her arm. "Come, follow me."

Juliet followed the slender, swaying figure through the gardens and the third court, through gates guarded by enormous men, curved knives strapped to fine leather

belts about their patterned robes. Both she
and Lady Gabriella were veiled and walking
with eyes downcast. Juliet risked an upward glance. The guards were staring into
the distance as if the passing of two women
was inconsequential and less important
than the drifting flight of two songbirds.
Lady Gabriella turned in through a small
arched gateway between marble columns.
Another lawn, another fountain, bordered
flowers of every hue and perfume, brilliant
swooping birds, the air alive with song.

Not only birdsong, Juliet realized as her
heart began to beat a little faster. Voices—
men's voices—and the low rumble of
laughter. At the door of the building they
were challenged by giant Nubians, un-
sheathed scimitars glinting wickedly in the
late sunlight. Lady Gabriella spoke briefly
and they passed between the guards. A
pale-skinned youth with black eyes
escorted them along a short passage, his
slender figure swaying his robes with
almost as much elegance as the Mistress of
the Harem. No one spoke as the youth held
aside the gold brocade curtain. Lady
Gabriella's presence was an accustomed
occurrence, it seemed.

Juliet looked about the small room with
interest. Three walls were silk-draped, the
fourth a gilded latticework grill. Climbing
flowers twined up on both sides to meet together at the top. The air was heavy with
their perfume. Lady Gabriella pointed

silently to the heap of satin cushions and Juliet seated herself. Lady Gabriella sank onto another pile and Juliet noted the silk cord by the lady's hand.

They sat for what seemed a long time to Juliet, then the voices diminished and one pair of hands clapped. As if it were a signal, Lady Gabriella leaned forward and pulled gently on the silken cord. Filmy gauze beyond the latticework screen parted and the banqueting hall was revealed.

Juliet looked out and blinked. She imagined their position was somewhat like a theater box but appearing from the other side no more than flower-decked latticework. The walls of the banqueting hall were hung with carpets, the scenes so delicately woven that they seemed to live and breathe. From the exotic to the erotic, from hunting leopards through birds and flowers to the abandoned joys of the flesh were depicted in precise detail.

The brief twilight was gone and lamps illuminated the guests. Jewels flashed and robes became multicolored under the green and ruby-glassed lamps. The scent of spiced meats rose to them, along with fried oysters and pilafs with cucumber and rice. Forty or fifty courses were common, Juliet had heard, and maybe more on Sabbath Friday. No wonder the girls preferred to lie on cushions and eat from low silver tables.

Juliet heard the soft breathing of Lady Gabriella as she leaned closer to the lattice.

She removed her own gaze from the lounging, dark-faced men and followed the direction of Lady Gabriella's eyes. The girls were coming in. Soft-footed, moving like dancers, their painted faces and lithe bodies caused a stir amongst the men. Each girl carried a silver basket of fruit—melons, plums, dates, pears, the fruits of the world for a man as rich as the Sultan. She peered through the grill, searching out the violet silk figure. There she was—Khurrem, the beautiful Ethiopian.

Juliet watched her closely. The Emir's nephew—was he here? The vibrant body in the skin-hugging silk flowed like a gentle wave to the shore, seemingly idly but inexorably moving in one direction. Past the supine men she flowed, a fixed smile on her face, until a handsome Arab broke off his conversation and looked hard at her. He beckoned and Khurrem floated to his side. She knelt, head bent, arms extended in offering, the violet skirts billowing then settling about her. The Arab sat up and reached a hand to raise her face, Khurrem's chin cupped in his fingers. Had she made her landfall, Juliet wondered, and glanced sideways at Lady Gabriella.

The amber eyes were resting on the girl in violet silk. She had not missed that long sensuous glide. Juliet tried to read her expression but the Mistress of the Harem was long experienced in hiding her emotions. Her smile was faint as she looked at Juliet.

"A pity about your maidservant, my lady."

Juliet felt her heart flutter. Had Khurrem committed some sin in her approach to the young, blue-robed sheik? She raised her brow in simulated surprise.

"A pity, Lady Gabriella? In what way? Is she at fault somewhere?"

"In no way at all and that is the pity. I would have liked to offer her to the Great One, for she is quite ravishing, but. . ." She shrugged, spreading her elegant hands. "Another lord has known her. It is impossible."

Juliet let out her breath slowly in relief. She had become fond of Khurrem and wished the girl well.

"The honored guest she is attending seems well satisfied, Lady Gabriella. See how he shares his goblet of koshab with her. Who is he, do you know?" She waited for the reply and was also well satisfied.

"That is Sheik Abdul Aziz, a nephew of the Emir. It is said that his Excellency has more fondness for him than for his own son." Her gaze moved away and a slight frown marred her perfect features. "Fleurette attends Hamid, the noble one. See the magnificence of his robes and jewels. He outshines the Emir and almost rivals the Great One. It is unwise to do so but he is headstrong."

Juliet peered and found Fleurette kneeling close to a heavily-built man who reclined on his cushions, allowing Fleurette to feed him grapes. A handsome man but his expression was bored and petulant. His fingers moved over Fleurette's arms and shoulders, caressing but in perfunctory fashion. His gaze, Juliet noted, seemed more intent on the white-robed attendants in their hats of gold-embroidered red silk. She wondered, with a little shock, if his tastes lay in another direction.

Lady Gabriella clicked her tongue. "Such inattention shows a lack of manners. He should await the signal from the Great One with wellborn indifference."

Juliet looked at her curiously. "The signal? Is there some entertainment planned?"

Lady Gabriella shook her head. "He is impatient for hookah to be brought in."

Juliet felt a little out of her depths. Lady Gabriella saw her puzzlement and smiled. "The substance has various names but the Great One provides the finest quality of hashish for his guests. The substance is heated and its smoke passes through cooling water into the tube of the pipe stem."

"Ah yes, I see. The men of my country smoke pipes too, but they burn tobacco."

"Tobacco is forbidden here. Do your men also take the forbidden strong drink?"

Juliet nodded. She did not add that women took strong drink, too. She remembered the gin-sodden girls held in her Bristol prison, accused of riotous behavior, even assault, but she refrained from speaking of them.

"Where does the Great One sit?" she asked. "Can we see him from here?"

"It is difficult, for his throne is raised and beyond the main assembly under a tent of cloth of gold. Many attendants surround him—the Chamberlain and Grand Vizier, and the royal bodyguard, of course." She turned to look into Juliet's face. Her words, so evenly spoken, clamped an icy hand on Juliet's heart, freezing her into utter stillness.

"It is said by the Vizier that the French ship which carried your letter to England has now returned. No message has come from the lord, your father. The Vizier is puzzled and asks for explanation. What reason can he offer the Great One for this discourtesy?"

XI

Juliet stared blankly into the amber eyes, her wits scattering like falling petals. Dear God, she must think, gather her thoughts and give some reply to Lady Gabriella. But what? She had known all along that this must happen. Even had her father been rich, he would not have acknowledged her existance. Why should he? Zanzibar or New South Wales—what difference did it make as long as she was out of England and no threat to him.

She controlled her emotions with an effort, praying that her shock had been mistaken for astonishment.

"No message at all?" Her voice came out flat and even, surprising even herself. "I am at a loss for reason. Frankly, I am appalled. Are you sure the French captain understood the need to return with a message?"

"Quite sure. The matter was dealt with at
Consular level. The French are more
practical in these things than your own
countrymen." Lady Gabriella smiled. "A
private transaction between your father
and a minor French diplomat."

"Yes, I understand," Juliet said slowly.
It was cleverly done, without the
knowledge of the British Government. Had
she really been Lady Juliet Westover, the
highborn lady she pretended to be, and the
British diplomats had caught wind of it,
they would have demanded her return.
Perhaps the secrecy was in her favor. They
were still unaware that her passage on the
'Grace' was to end at a penal colony. She
felt calmer now and raised her gaze to Lady
Gabriella and spoke casually.

"My home is many hundreds of miles
from London and road travel is difficult at
this time." She shrugged lightly. "It takes
time to gather together a large amount of
money. My family coffers are not as full as
those of the Great One. An English gentleman counts his wealth in land, not jewels."

Lady Gabriella frowned. "You are saying
that land must be sold to gain the ransom
figure."

"Exactly." Juliet felt her confidence returning although she knew her delaying
tactics could only serve to put off the inevitable. "A gentleman respects his land
and returns his money to it, improving its
fertility and adding more stock, that is
cattle or crops."

Lady Gabriella nodded. "I will tell all this to the Vizier but he will wonder why a message to that effect was not brought by the French captain. Perhaps tomorrow, when the English ship calls. . ." She turned her attention to the lattice window.

Juliet stared down into the banqueting hall, barely seeing the activity below. It all seemed unreal and tawdry. The Great One with his vast wealth, his Palace, his richly dressed court and concubines—what need had he of ransom money? He was rich beyond measure but he had the power to demand more. In spite of the heat, Juliet felt cold. She was glad when Lady Gabriella rose and gestured her to follow.

Back in her apartments, Juliet stripped herself of the amber silk and laid the bracelets and rings to one side. Wrapping herself in a silk robe, she sank onto the cushions. How long would the Vizier wait? Should she confess all to Lady Gabriella in advance, reveal that she was no lady of rank and they could stop expecting the ransom money? What then? Reveal her lack of purity and promise to be a good little slave girl?

The Vizier's words on the beach came back to her and she shuddered. "The tongue or hand that strays from the path of righteousness may lawfully be struck away." She had lied; they had both lied, she and Ross, in word and deed for her hand had written the letter. The ganching spike

that pierces the body, the lingering torment
before death! Dear God, it would be that,
her mind said, and she turned her face into
the cushions. The Vizier was not a man to
lose face calmly. His revenge would be
terrible. And where was Ross who had
sworn she was unblemished? Had he
escaped and left her to her fate? No, no, she
would have heard had he left the island. She
sat up, trying to think clearly. He was still
in Zanzibar, a prisoner too, but with more
freedom than she had. There was no escape
from the harem. How could he have
thought there might be when the eunuchs
were always watching and beyond them,
the gates and the Janissaries.

A faint smile touched her face. It was all
in the lap of the gods or destined by Allah,
as Khurrem would have said. It all came to
the same thing in the end. Fate. Destiny.
What is to be will be. It was poor con-
solation when one considered the ganching
spike!

She raised her head as Khurrem herself
slipped into the room. Her wide almond-
shaped eyes were those of a sleepwalker
and she glided over the carpet as if on air.
Juliet had never seen such an expression of
rapture on any face in her life. Khurrem
stood quite still in the center of the room,
then sank to her knees, head resting on outstretched arms.

"Allah is good."

Juliet heard the low murmur of Arabic

words and her heart contracted painfully, a mingling of happiness for Khurrem and fear for herself. But she could not afford to show fear—not yet. She forced a smile as Khurrem twisted her lithe body into a cross-legged position and looked up.

"So," said Juliet. "Allah is good and Sheik Abdul Aziz remembers with affection, yes?"

Khurrem nodded. "I saw him instantly and kept my eyes on him, for had I met the gaze of another who beckoned, my duty would have compelled me to obey the summons. Did the Mistress make any comment?" Her gaze rested anxiously on Juliet.

"Only that the honored guest seemed well satisfied with your attentions."

Khurrem sighed happily. "He will ask the Great One for me. He has promised."

"You will go with him when he leaves?"

"If the Great One will allow me, yes." She hesitated. "But you, my lady? Will I have your release, too? I am here only because you wished it and the Vizier gave permission." Her smooth shoulders rose and fell. "Had you not honored me, I would have been some merchant's property. How can I leave you?"

Juliet thought of her own future. Perhaps there was little of it to consider. She said calmly. "You are released from me the moment your sheik obtains the Great One's permission. It is your destiny to be reunited with Abdul Aziz. I will not stand in the way of it. You will go with my blessing.''

Khurrem took Juliet's hand and pressed it to her forehead in homage. "Allah will aid you, my lady. He is good and all-seeing. How can it be otherwise? Our lives are ordained."

Juliet smiled but held silent. Ordained by Allah but directed by the Vizier and the Sultan. Did the slaves and eunuchs find comfort in knowing that their lives were ordained by Allah? Did they accept the pain and mutilation as destiny? Were the executioners, those deaf mutes with pierced eardrums and slit tongues, content in the belief that Allah had proscribed these roles for them?

She pushed aside the fearsome thoughts. There was still time and, please God, Khurrem would have left with her sheik before verdict was passed on her mistress.

The girls who assembled daily in the fourth court to greet the silk merchants were no longer the idle, gossiping group of before the visit. The Emir and his retinue had breathed new life into them. They still gossiped but the bored bickering had gone. Each girl was eager to share her experience with another, to remark on some feature of the sheiks and compare the flowery compliments. It was expected very soon that each dignitary would have made his first choice, having looked over the charms of the girls.

For most of the sheiks, it would be a pleasant but temporary diversion since they had, Juliet supposed, households of their own.

The younger men like Sheik Abdul Aziz, the beloved of Khurrem, might seek to buy the favored girl, one who had taken the Golden Road already and not conceived a son for the Sultan.

Three days of talk and feasting had gone by. Lady Gabriella was far too busy supervising the chosen girls as they were bathed, oiled, scented, and prepared for the summons, to invite Juliet to the secret room again. Juliet was relieved, remembering the cold chill that had gripped her when the Vizier was mentioned. She was content to sit in the garden kiosk and improve her handling of the lute. Fleurette was too involved in the activity to instruct her in the correct fingering. Juliet thought of the petulant face of the man she had seen being served by Fleurette. Would she be sent to him if he asked? Juliet glanced over at the girl. Her face was calmly beautiful, her expression serene. Were they simply gratified to be chosen, their bodies honored by these visiting sheiks? Since they were bred to subservience, to please a man or work for him, she supposed their minds contained no other thought, save to present themselves alluringly. Every man was a lord, automatically superior by virtue of manhood.

Juliet plucked idly at the lute strings and was so immersed in her own thoughts that only the sweet drift of perfume indicated the presence of the Mistress of the Harem. Lady Gabriella sank on the cushions beside her in a graceful, sweeping movement that reminded Juliet of the effortless settling of a butterfly on a petal.

Juliet felt her nerves tighten but she smiled at the Mistress. "You are to be congratulated, Lady Gabriella. The girls do credit to your teaching. The Emir's party can rarely have seen such a gathering of beauty. The Great One must be well pleased." She kept her tone soft with admiration. Could flattery of this powerful lady soften her attitude when the worst came to pass?

Lady Gabriella smiled. "All has gone well, so far. The Vizier reports the satisfaction of the Great One. He also reports the failure of his inquiry to the English ship which docked at dawn." She paused. "However, his highness is gracious and no decision will be made while the Palace entertains such important visitors." She rose and stood looking down at Juliet. "It is known that the Great One holds an English girl hostage. The Emir and his party have shown interest in you, for some have never known a girl of your race."

The lady's smile was a delicate thing, a mere relaxing of her features, but to the girl staring up, it was a sharp file drawn across taut nerves. Her mind emptied, save for a sense of premonition. Lady Gabriella's next words came as no shock.

"Since the Great One himself has never granted you audience, it was thought fitting by the Vizier that I should present you in person to the whole assembly after the evening meal tomorrow."

Juliet sat very still after the Mistress had moved away. Tomorrow was the fourth day of the Emir's visit. She was to be displayed to the sheiks. For what reason? Only one sprang to mind. The Vizier had decided her story was untrue and no ransom would come. The Great One was graciously revealing her to possible buyers. Already half-convinced of her worthlessness by the Vizier, he would play out the charade of still believing her of value, thus raising her price should anyone show interest. Polite reluctance on his part, a show of indecision to encourage the bids, then a gracious shrug and acceptance of the bargain. Far more profitable than waiting for a ransom that never came.

Juliet stared down at the hands clenched in her lap. Dear God, what else could it be? It was logical, and even she could think of no other reason for this summons to the banqueting hall.

Juliet's body slowly relaxed under the ministrations of the women of the baths. Lying on the marble couch, she closed her

eyes while they kneaded and scrubbed her
body. The flower-scented massage oils
soothed her skin and the Mistress of the
Baths was deft in her task of removing the
smallest hair. Fragrant steam clouded the
air as strong fingers dealt with the washing
and anointing of her hair until it gleamed as
dark and soft as sealskin. The usual stream
of cold rose-water brought reality back and
sent the blood surging through her veins.
Then, wrapped in large soft towels, she
rested on another couch. This time she
could not drift into sleep for the Mistress of
the Harem waited in her apartments to
prepare her for the coming ordeal.

"The amber silk," said Lady Gabriella.
"It has not been seen before and I will dress
your hair myself with golden thread." She
eyed Juliet critically. "Plain gold, I think.
Bracelets and neck collar with solid gold
band rings of engraved design. A golden
maiden for all to see." She smiled briefly.
"It will show the noble lords that the Great
One prizes you highly."

And why not, thought Juliet. A girl so
richly decked in a king's ransom of solid
gold was not to be bargained for lightly. It
was a warning, however unsubtle, that only
a price higher than the value of what she
was wearing could be considered seriously.
Was she thinking like the Vizier or was it all
in her imagination? She believed she was
right in her conjectures and this was to be
her punishment. There was no profit to be

had by putting her to death. But Ross—ah yes, how the Vizier would enjoy the slow destruction of his strong vital body. She closed her eyes briefly. It had not yet come to that.

She followed Lady Gabriella through a marble-pillared passage, not the way to the secret room but the route taken by the concubines. Soon, she would be paraded before the Sultan and the dark-visaged men of the court, the black-eyed arabs in the retinue of the Emir. They would see a pale-skinned girl, amber-gowned and so heavily encrusted with glistening ornaments that she might appear as a golden statue. The neck-collar and bracelets hung smooth and heavy, priceless in themselves but mere baubles in the vast wealth of the Sultan.

Lady Gabriella laid a hand on her arm as they halted in the antechamber. The perfume from Juliet's own well-oiled body rose about her as nervousness warmed her, but above that she detached a sweeter smell that dizzied her mind. She remembered the hookah pipes. Of course, the feasting was over. Those guests who preferred the mental esctasy to the physical were having their whims indulged.

"Remember," Lady Gabriella was saying, "that the Great One needs obeisance far deeper than the one I taught you for the Sultana Valideh, for he holds the thread of life in his hands. Though you are not of the concubines, it is wise to offer the courtesy as with your own king."

"I understand," said Juliet through stiff
lips. "What is expected of me after I have
made my obeisance to the Great One? Do I
return here?"

Lady Gabriella considered the question.
"If you are greeted in your own tongue, and
some of our visitors are well-traveled, it
would be a gracious gesture to speak a few
words, would you not agree?"

Juliet nodded slowly. "Yes, but they do
understand that I am not for their pleasure,
do they not?"

"They are quite aware of your position,
my dear," returned the Mistress smoothly.
"It is one which may only be changed by
the Great One in his infinite wisdom. Now,
follow me."

The double doors, inlaid with ivory and
mother-of-pearl swung open silently as the
Mistress nodded to the impassive guards.
The two women passed through into the
long banqueting hall. Heat flowed towards
them, bringing the same sweet scent of the
pipe smoke. The lamps threw garish color
onto the white-robed servants who hurried,
barefooted between silver tables and piles
of variegated cushions on which men
lounged. Beside each knelt a female figure.
The light shifted so rapidly that Juliet
could not distinguish their features. She
stood blinking for a moment, seeing a blur
of gold in the distance.

"Go!" hissed Lady Gabriella, giving her a

small push. "The Great One has seen you."

Juliet moved forward, remembering the slow rhythm and sway she had been taught. The length of the room seemed to multiply and the golden throne curtains retreat before her. As she advanced, the noise abated and heads turned to stare. She reached the throne in almost complete silence and looked into the face of the man who held her future in his hands. Then she remembered that a woman must not gaze boldly at a man and lowered her eyes as she performed a deep obeisance, her arms crossed over her breast. The face she had glimpsed was middle-aged and plump but the eyes had been points of dark burning fire, sharp eyes betraying an intelligence of mind that must surely see through her sham.

She rose, her eyes above the half-veil downcast modestly. Should she now turn and walk away? Obliquely, she noted the turn of the Sultan's head, his gesture, then a man detached himself from the rest and approached her. She tensed as that familiar, terrifying voice spoke.

"Lady Juliet Westover. You are still our guest it seems."

It was the Vizier and his eyes were as cold as his voice. "The lord, your father, has not seen fit to respond with speed on your behalf. His highness finds that strange, since he is a most loving and compassionate father himself."

Juliet drew in a breath and met the Vizier's eyes. "I am at a loss, Excellency. I can only suppose my father has met with some accident that prevents him replying immediately."

"Do they not have scribes in your country?"

Juliet sensed the hidden mockery in his voice, and despite her fear, a touch of coldness edged her own voice.

"Naturally one can obtain the services of a solicitor but they cannot be commanded to instant obedience as if they were slaves."

The Vizier stiffened visibly and Juliet wished she could recall those unwise words. He was already her enemy. Why must she make it worse by stupid retort?

His eyes narrowed on her. "Insolence comes more readily to the tongue of the lowborn, my lady, and I have only the word of the ship's captain as to your status." He smoothed his beard slowly, dark hooded eyes unblinking, like those of a sparrow hawk watching the movement of a field mouse. "True, he seemed to bear you no fondness if the terms in which he spoke were sincere. And yet he drew my attention to you when your purchase had been concluded with a trader of camels. A change of heart or mind? An intriguing question, my lady. One wonders why."

"Self-preservation, perhaps?" Juliet strove to keep her voice casual. "Since I was known to be in his cargo, questions would be asked."

"But not by the lord, your father, it seems. He is apprised of the situation and conditions for your release, yet no word has come. Another intriguing question."

"For which I have no answer unless you permit me to write another letter."

The Vizier smiled and gave her a brief bow. "Let us delay the consideration of such matters until later. Our noble guests must not be neglected. Did Lady Gabriella make that plain?" Without awaiting reply, he turned and mounted the steps of the Sultan's dais.

Juliet moved slowly away. Naturally, the Mistress of the Harem took her orders from the Vizier but couched them in softer terms. Her loyalty was total and Juliet could expect no help there. The Sultana Valideh? Did a mother count for anything under the absolute rule of her son? Unlikely. Without awareness of it, she shook her head as she wandered down the hall.

"The beautiful golden one shakes her head," came a soft, slurred voice. "Is she struck dumb by the splendor of chief's and despairs to find herself alone? Come, bird of paradise. I will honor you."

Juliet's eyes found the speaker. He lay on his pile of cushions, plump and sweating. Strong white teeth grinned from a face young but old in dissipation. One plump brown hand held the hookah mouthpiece, the other patted the cushion beside him. It was Hamid, the man Lady Gabriella had considered discourteous.

Fleurette knelt by his side. Juliet noted the slight bruising of her wrists and shoulders. She smiled at the girl but was unprepared for the frankly hostile stare. Was this man so important as to be worth ill-usage? Fleurette held a marzipan sweet to his lips but he brushed it aside, staring at Juliet. She smiled uncertainly, wishing herself away, but he beckoned imperiously.

"Come. I have knowledge of your speech. It would please me to honor you with my words." He waved dismissal to Fleurette, who rose. As she passed Juliet, her eyes were bright with anger. Juliet looked after her helplessly and moved nearer to Hamid. He patted the cushion again and she had no choice but to sink onto it gracefully.

Hamid scrutinized her face closely. Every breath he exhaled bore the sweet but sickly scent of the drug that slurred his speech.

Juliet turned her head a little, pretending to examine the contents of the fruit dish. Hamid belched, and Juliet was glad she had turned her head away to avoid the hot blast of his breath. It was considered good manners, she knew, an audible sign of appreciation after eating, but it was little comfort to the one who sat closest. She waited for him to speak.

"I am a man of culture and travel," he said. "From Constantinople to the Red Sea. I have been to Alexandria where the Nile flows into the ocean. I have sat at the feet of great men and my mind holds great knowledge."

He paused, seeming to wait for response. Juliet glanced sideways at him. "How . . . how very splendid. Did these great men teach you English?"

"Not they, but a white slave I bought from the Corsairs. A white man, but stupid."

"Why stupid?"

"Is it not stupid to spend five years over a task that could be completed in five weeks? I had to flog the fool daily for his slowness."

Juliet felt a moment of pity for the unknown tutor. Hamid's English was good but it was not a language that could be learned in five weeks. She suspected the slowness to be on his part, the flogging the result of impatience.

"He taught you well," she said cautiously. "Does he still serve you?"

Hamid smiled. "He was of no further use when I became excellent in the tongue. I had him garroted so that he could teach no other. What use is a slave who has outlived his usefulness?"

He took a piece of Turkish delight from the dish and thrust it into his mouth. "Eat. I give you permission."

Juliet obeyed, nibbling a corner of the square of sugared jelly. She felt Hamid's gaze move slowly over her and sat a little more upright, wishing the amber silk had not been cut to follow every line of her body. The heat of the room molded it closely to each curve.

Hamid took her free hand and began to fondle her fingers and stroke the back of her hand. His palm was damp and hot. He paused only to take in a mouthful of smoke from the long ivory stem.

Juliet felt her senses begin to swim. Hamid's body loomed large beside her, the odor of spiced food and perspiration strong on him, mingling with the scent of the smoke. She blinked rapidly and managed to focus her eyes on the archway where Lady Gabriella stood. Fleurette was beside her and both women seemed to stare in her direction. She tried to read their expressions. Fleurette's still hostile—and Lady Gabriella? Was she satified or angry that Juliet had taken Fleurette's place. Since Hamid had addressed her in English and she had been bidden to respond with graciousness, how could she be at fault? Perhaps she had stayed too long. Well, that could soon be remedied. She began to withdraw her hand from Hamid's.

"I have stayed too long in your excellent company," she said, smiling. "The Lady Gabriella has need of me."

He grasped her fingers tightly and she winched. "She is a mere woman. I am a great lord and command you to stay. Are we not promised entertainment of all exquisite natures? Why do you seek to draw away? No woman shall thwart my desire."

"I will send Fleurette to you for she longs to be at your side. . ."

Hamid spoke slurringly but his dark eyes fixed her with a fierce greedy look. "You are a white-skinned girl, very highborn and pure. You will be my favorite concubine and I lie with you first every night." His voice grew unsteady but the enlarged pupils of his staring eyes were frightening. Juliet pulled her hand free.

"I am not a concubine, nor a slave. You cannot buy me. I spoke with you from politeness. I am not for sale!" Her voice was low and vehement.

The smile was more of a sneer. "The Vizier has hinted and, by Allah, I mean to buy you!" He took a deep pull of the pipe and blew the smoke over her head. Her defiance seemed to excite him. "I will take you and beat you and take you again until only Allah is greater than I in your eyes. Your hands, with those white fingers, shall prepare my pipe whenever I command. You shall call me lord and master and beg to share my sweetest dreams of Paradise." He thrust the pipe stem towards her. Smoke curled from the end, a drifting cloud in her face.

Juliet never knew whether he intended forcing her to inhale the smoke but suddenly she felt sick with terror and drenched in perspiration. If she stayed a

moment longer her senses would leave her.
She had to get free, into the fresh night air
and away from this obscene threatening
creature. She struck out blindly in panic
and fell onto her knees. Her fingers caught
the ivory mouthpiece of the pipe. It was
jerked from Hamid's hand. Both the stem
and the water-filled jar shattered violently
on the marble floor.

Juliet, now on her feet, watched in sick
fascination as a runnel of water soaked its
way into an Oriental carpet. She was
vaguely aware that all sound had ceased
and she had become the focus of every eye.

XII

Figures closed about her. She turned, catching her foot on the leg of the silver table. It fell with a crash, showering Hamid with fruit and sweetmeats. His angry bellow rose and was drowned in the sudden babble of shouting, laughing voices. Dark eyes watched. Teeth flashed eerily in the lamplight. The air was charged with expectancy as if a baiting of some wild animal was about to begin. A scream rose in her throat, then her head jerked sideways as a blow on the cheek took away her breath.

The bearded face of the Vizier swam into view. His eyes were of black marble, his lips so compressed they were almost invisible. He spoke sharply in Arabic and Juliet saw Lady Gabriella, ashen-faced and trembling. The long tapering fingers took Juliet's arm, the nails biting painfully. Fleurette was there, now kneeling beside Hamid, smooth-

269

ing his brow with a rose-water scented
cloth.

Lady Gabriella was pulling her towards
the archway, hurrying, insistent. Juliet
moved willingly, anywhere to escape from
the eyes that followed her, contemptuous
and speculative. The concubine stood in
open horror but the men exchanged sly
grins, whispering God knew what lewdness
to each other. Her mind cleared in the
cooler air of the corridor and Juliet knew
quite well that as a marketable property,
her value had fallen. No highborn lady
could be guilty of such discourteous and
clumsy behavior. Whatever doubts the
Vizier had, her actions could only confirm
his suspicions that she had lied. Dear God,
what now? The slave market or the
executioner?

Lady Gabriella remained tight-lipped
until they were approaching the women's
quarters, then she stopped and pulled
Juliet round to face her. She was still pale
but her trembling had ceased. She drew in a
deep breath.

"I took great pains to instruct you in the
art of pleasing our guests. You repay me by
insult and conduct of the worst kind. You
have brought disgrace upon me in the eyes
of the Vizier and the Great One. What explanation can you offer?"

"The man, Hamid . . ." she began but
Lady Gabriella cut in.

"The man, Hamid, as you call him, is
Hamid the Noble One, a lord and only son

of the Emir."

Juliet felt her heart jerk painfully. "I didn't know that," she said in a whisper. Dear God, the Emir's son! She could not have chosen a worse man to insult. She rallied her wits and looked hard at the Mistress of the Harem. "Neither did I know of the plan to show me off as some creature to be bought. I learned that from your noble Hamid who was most explicit in describing how I should fare at his hands. I found his coarseness offensive. Am I to be blamed for trying to leave his side?"

Lady Gabriella stared at her. "A woman must wait until dismissed. It is forbidden to criticize a man. He is her superior in every way and she must accept."

Juliet sighed. "Indeed, it seems so in your world. I am deeply sorry if you consider that I have brought disgrace upon you. What can I do to make amends? I will offer my apologies to the Vizier and to the lord Hamid, if you wish it."

Lady Gabriella smiled faintly. "It is out of my hands—and yours, too. The decision has already been taken in the customary manner."

Juliet's throat tightened. "And what . . . what is the customary manner?"

"You will be given to the lord Hamid when he leaves. The Great One can do no less than deliver you to the man who claims insult. It is for him, then, to decide your punishment. There is no longer any question of payment as the Vizier hoped.

He is, therefore, very angry.''

"It is unjust!" Juliet exclaimed.

"The Great One is the fount of all wisdom and justice. What he decides cannot be questioned. He is the chosen of Allah and can do no wrong.'' They had reached the door of Juliet's apartment. "You will not be called into the banqueting hall again. Prepare yourself to depart from here in three days time. Until our visitors leave, Fleurette will serve the lord Hamid, for she knows how to soothe a man's anger. It is a skill you had best learn.''

She opened the door for Juliet to pass through, then closed it behind her. The soft hiss of her slippered feet faded away. Juliet sank on her cushions and thought of her bleak future. Hamid was a man to extract great pleasure, she guessed, in punishing a helpless victim like the poor tutor, garroted when Hamid considered himself proficient enough in English. The casual way he had ended a man's life. Could she endure? Would it not be better to put an end to her own life here in the harem? Three days. Surely enough time to find a quick and easy death—not the living death that Hamid promised.

Khurrem came in an hour later, looking pale and nervous. She regarded Juliet gravely from wide dark eyes.

Juliet tried to smile. "Are you allowed to consort with one who has fallen into disgrace?''

Khurrem's eyes filled with tears and she sank to her knees beside Juliet. "Oh, my lady, what can I say? There was much talk after you had gone. I begged my own lord to intercede but he can do nothing for he is only the Emir's nephew."

Juliet was touched by the girl's concern. "Dear Khurrem, there is nothing anyone can do. I am now the property of Hamid." She smiled wryly. "I hardly think I shall be a favored concubine." Tears pricked her eyes and she turned away. "Go to your couch, Khurrem, for Allah has smiled upon you. Be happy for my sake." She finished in a muffled voice and buried her face in the cushions.

Juliet woke before dawn, surprised that she had slept at all. The air was cool and she slipped into a robe and left the apartment. She could imagine that her shame had spread through the Palace. No girl would want to be seen speaking to her, except Khurrem, perhaps. She wandered towards the kiosk. The lute lay to one side and she picked it up, sinking onto the cushions, placing the lute in her lap. What point now in practicing on the instrument?

A voice spoke from above her head. She jumped and a lute string shrieked in protest under her jerking finger. A gardener glanced her way.

"Don't look up. Pretend to tune that damned thing and listen."

Juliet bowed her head, letting her unbound hair mask her face. She was trembling, her breath coming harshly.

"I've been here for hours," the voice continued evenly. "The grapes, unfortunately, are not ripe enough for Bacchanalian revels but I'd give a year's pay for a jar of sherbet manned by ice cubes. You don't happen to have about your person. . . . ?"

"It's all right, Ross. I'm in control now." He had gone on talking, she knew, to give her time to recover the shock. The voice, low and even, held no hint of strain, but the humorous tone he had adopted communicated itself to her and she felt his strength flowing down.

She straightened, tossing back her hair, and produced a couple of melodic chords. The gardener, she noted, had returned to his flower bed. It was the time of decision.

"Before you say anything, Ross, the answer is no."

There was a moment of silence. "No? What does that mean? I haven't told you my plan yet."

"Then don't."

"For God's sake, Juliet, are you saying you want to stay here?"

"I'm saying that I want your promise to leave Zanzibar as soon as you can. Steal a boat and get away. Forget about me. I should only add to your difficulty. You can do it on your own."

"Leaving you here to bear the brunt of my lies?"

"I cannot blame you for that for my own lies were by omission. Had the Vizier not believed your story that day in the slave market, I would have remained the property of that camel trader. At least I was saved that fate, for he was crude and stank of his trade."

"Listen to me, Juliet. . ."

"No, Ross, you listen to me. You are aware, I am sure, that the Sultan is entertaining grandly this week an Emir from Mogadishu with a large court of splendid nobles. Their state is far higher than that of a mere camel trader and any girl would be glad to exchange that fate for a life of luxury."

"What the devil are you getting at?" Ross demanded.

"I was permitted into the banqueting hall last night when they were being served by the girls. I intend to indicate to the Mistress of the Harem my willingness to be equal with them. The Emir's nephew desires to buy Khurrem, for he knew her once, and she is wildly happy at the prospect of leaving with him. Could I likewise interest a young sheik, he will suppose my lack of innocence to be due to the fact that the Sultan has honored me. I believe it is quite acceptable to. . ."

Ross's voice cut in, low and furious. "Will you stop your babbling, girl! This Palace has more tongues than a village gossip. I know exactly what happened last night, which is why I came here today. Dear God, do you suppose I want such a future for you on my conscience?"

"And do you suppose I want your death on mine?"

A vine stem cracked as Ross shifted his position. Juliet risked a quick glance upwards. A dark bearded face glared down. If it hadn't been for the blue eyes she could easily have taken him for an Arab.

"Your beard is magnificent," she said unsteadily. "A hint of chestnut but not out of the way."

"Proof that I once made the pilgrimage to Mecca," he snapped. "They dye them red after visiting the birthplace of Mohammed. Now, listen to me!"

"No."

"It's going to be a long day up here," Ross sighed. "I hope to God they water the vines."

The leaves shook and trembled, and a vine stem stirred, dislodging a shower of unripe grapes.

"Stop it, Ross, for pity's sake! The eunuch is looking. He'll call the guard. We shall both be stuffed with straw! Go away, please!"

"Not until you listen."

It was the implacable tone of authority and she recognized it. "Very well, I'll listen, but it's madness."

"And do exactly as I say? Give me your promise."

Juliet let out a long breath. "All right, I

promise. I'm sure the view will be entrancing from a spike on the gateway."

"When the silk merchants come today, look for a woman in a black burka. She brings her rolls in a horse-drawn cart. Admire particularly a length of scarlet satin. Have her unroll it in the kiosk. Inside you will find a similar black burka. You will leave the Palace as her assistant—a deaf mute."

"And feeble-minded with it!" Juliet said resignedly. "Can you trust her?"

"For a consideration—yes. I have promised her the jewels you'll be wearing so don't forget to put them all on!"

Juliet resisted the sudden urge to look up. "But they are only lent by Lady Gabriella."

"By courtesy of the Sultan. Don't worry. His coffers are full. I must go now before I'm missed."

"What do I do outside the gates—if I get that far?" she asked quickly.

"Get into the cart with the rolls. It has a green canopy. I'll be there."

There was a faint slithering sound, then a shadow moved into the sheltering palms, paused before melting into the shade of a plantain tree, then there was nothing.

After Ross had gone, Juliet sat very still on her cushions, thinking of the thing she had to do. It was dangerous but there was no alternative that Ross would accept. To back away now would put his life in peril.

To take the jewelry loaned by the Mistress seemed wrong but to appear unadorned would not command her to the eyes of the merchant woman. The rewards of duplicity must be worth the effort.

Later, Juliet dressed herself in the pearl-edged kaftan, filled her arms with solid gold bracelets and plaited her hair with loops of pearls. The blue dress she eyed sadly. It had no place in this scheme.

By the time she reached the fourth court, the merchants were already there. Velvet, brocades, satin and taffeta in every shade imaginable vied with the living blossoms and the fluttering girls in their bright silks. Rolls lay open on the shorn grass, burka-clad women pointing and gesticulating. Juliet watched for a moment, her gaze seeking the one in the black burka, then she moved forward, pausing by each group, admiring, smiling and fingering satin and velvet. She let her gaze wander over the stock of the woman in black. Her nerves jumped in sudden panic. There was no scarlet satin to be seen!

The woman had glanced at her, showing the professional smile of a saleswoman and held up for her inspection an ivory brocade worked with gold thread. Juliet found Khurrem beside her as the woman laid out an amber velvet and looked up questioningly.

Juliet shook her head. She noted wryly

that the other girls moved away at her approach showing sudden interest in the wares of another merchant. She moved in isolation. Khurrem, her arms full of yellow silk, glanced over her shoulder.

"The Kislar Aga is at the gate, my lady. The merchants must go soon. What color would please you? I will ask this woman if she has it."

Juliet noticed with growing alarm that the women were beginning to wrap their rolls in coarse protective cotton. The harem girls were clustered in groups comparing their choices.

Juliet took a deep breath. "I want scarlet satin," she said flatly.

Khurrem spoke to the woman who rose to her feet, smiling. She had been squatting on a small roll. Juliet felt her blood run boiling from her nerve ends, leaving her cold and damp with perspiration. In the roll was scarlet satin!

"You are pale, my lady." Khurrem's voice came anxiously and faintly, as if from a long distance.

Juliet steadied herself. "The sun is hot. Tell her to bring it to the kiosk." And she turned blindly away and sought the blurred outline of the summerhouse.

The cool mosaic was under her feet; the woman behind with the rolled silk was blocking the light. And Khurrem was there, too. Juliet dragged her thoughts together.

"Khurrem. Go and prepare a jug of

khoshab in our chamber. I am quite well
now. Wait for me there and I will join you
presently."

Khurrem obeyed from habit, and Juliet
looked at the woman. The merchant raised
her eyes from the gold bracelets on Juliet's
arms and turned, slipping a black burka
from the roll. In the shadows of the vines,
Juliet pulled it over her head and slipped
her arms into the wide sleeves. The
merchant had rewrapped the roll. It was
now in its protective covering. She thrust it
into Juliet's arms and they hurried over the
grass to collect the remaining rolls.

The merchant thrust her way to the head
of the line, dragging Juliet with her.
Clutching the roll to her chest, her eyes
fixed on the path, Juliet trotted clumsily in
the woman's shadow. As they passed the
Kislar Aga she heard his voice. He was
counting the number of merchants!

The women were escorted along by a
succession of eunuchs. Gates and courtyards unrolled behind them. She strained to
see the main gate. By now, the Kislar Aga
must surely have finished his count. And
reached a conclusion! One extra merchant
was on the way out! They'd never make it
before the alarm was raised. Hurry, hurry,
her mind screamed, but the pace never
varied. Then the tall gates loomed before
them. A faint sound, growing stronger, was
following rapidly. Voices, running footsteps, coming closer. Juliet was stumbling

over the hem of her burka, the roll of satin a
heavy weight in her arms. They were
through the gates but the Janissaries were
staring back into the court. Someone was
shouting. Juliet daren't turn round. All her
concentration was on finding the cart with
the green canopy.

It was there, drawn up by the wall, the
horse facing away from the palace. A tall
bearded man in a turban stood beside the
horse, looking towards the palace gates.

Juliet was halfway to the cart, the merchant beside her, when a hand fell on her
shoulder. The roll of cloth spun from her
arms as she was jerked back and fell solidly
at the yellow-booted feet of her captor. He
was shouting and the woman merchant was
pointing to her assistant's mouth and ears.
Juliet squinted up at him and let her jaw
hang lopsided. She crossed her eyes for
good measure. He recoiled slightly and his
fingers left her shoulder to fasten round the
haft of a scimitar. Allah protects imbeciles
and children, she thought wildly. Where
had she heard that?

Then the yard was filled with sound—the
high-pitched voices of the eunuchs, the
shouted order of a Janissary officer and the
loud complaining of the women merchants.
A sinewy hand clutched Juliet's wrist. A
quick twist and the gold bracelets were
gone, the woman herself melting into the
anonymity of the crowd.

Juliet located the green-canopied cart

again. Then, with bowed head she thrust
herself sideways and bored through the
milling crowd with scant regard for toes
and ribs. Using her elbows and fists indis-
criminately, she forced a passage round and
under the waving arms. Only a solid body
stopped her progress. Her clenched fist,
with all the force she could muster, took
him in the midriff.

"Christ!" The words came explosively. "I
might have known."

Her gaze flashed up into the bearded face.
She hadn't envisaged a turban. Her mouth
opened but there was no time to speak.
Ross had lifted her bodily and tossed her
without effort into the back of the cart. She
fell on her face onto a bed of rolled silks.
The cart creaked as Ross flung himself onto
the driving board. They began to move. The
sway and jerk as the horse was guided too
quickly round obstacles threw her from one
roll to another.

A voice let forth a stream of Arabic so
close that she flinched. The horse struggled
to break free from the hand that clutched
its bridle. Ross's voice rose, and from the
tone he was delivering a string of violent
invectives. A whip cracked but the horse
was still held captive.

A pistol shot exploded, its reverberation
so close that Juliet was stunned by the
sound. A sighing gurgle and the thud of a
heavy body brought her head up in panic.
The gun was in Ross's hand and a guard lay

dead. Then the horse reared and bolted, hurling her back onto the rolls.

The palace and the dead Janissary were left behind as the horse tore through the narrow alleys, scattering people and over-turning stalls. Juliet clung to the rolls of silk as she was buffeted about. Ross was swearing under his breath and trying to control the horse. In spite of it being a thin, raw-boned creature, it had a neat turn of speed, he admitted, but if they weren't to go hurtling off the jetty at the bottom of the hill, he must exert all his strength.

He risked a glance over his shoulder. Juliet was still there but the cart itself was in danger of disintegration. Several boards had been torn off in their headlong flight. How soon before the rotten woodwork parted company from the worm-eaten shafts? They spun crazily on down long, sloping streets and the smell of the sea grew stronger. The mad burst of speed slackened quite suddenly. Ross hauled in the reins and the horse answered at last. The bazaars had been left behind. The warehouse section reared ahead. He scanned the area swiftly. Some of the buildings looked derelict. As good a place as any, he judged, and the palace was far behind.

He brought the panting horse to a halt in the shadow of a tall wooden building. It seemed deserted. He climbed down past the heaving, sweat-soaked flanks of the animal.

"Juliet?"

Her head rose and the grey eyes stared dazedly. She came to her knees, rubbing her arms and elbows. "Where are we?"

"Somewhere safe, I hope. At least until the search gets under way." He lifted her down and, holding her by the shoulders, looked into her face. "Are you all right?"

She nodded but he saw the signs of strain round her eyes and judged her not far from collapse. He lifted out a goatskin and a small bag from the cart and laid them on the ground. The horse he led onto the dusty sun-filled road again and gave it a hard slap on the rump. It bucked indignantly and skittered off at a sharp trot down the road leading to the sea.

With the goatskin slung over his shoulder, the bag under his arm, he slipped an arm round Juliet's waist and led her into the empty, echoing building. He climbed with her to the highest point without relaxing his strong grip about her waist. Her unsteady breathing and stumbling pace warned him that she was nearing the end of her endurance.

They said nothing as they climbed. When he had satisfied himself that the tiny one-windowed room overlooking the harbor had a door that could be secured, only then did he relax his support of her. By that time she was very pale and sank onto the empty grain sacks with a sigh. Her eyes were grey sunken pools but her wavering smile convinced him of her spirit.

They shared bread and olives, washed down by water from the goatskin. "Rest now," he said, and the last thing she saw was Ross positioning himself by the grimy window, the pistol thrust in the sash of his tunic.

XIII

The sun was well down before Ross left
the window. From his vantage point he had
seen the stationary horse and cart led away
by Janissaries. The woman silk merchant
had been there too, locked in argument with
the soldiers. He watched her closely. She
didn't appear to be under arrest. No one
had seen them together and she hadn't
been near the cart when he had thrown
Juliet into it. A simple theft, she could
claim, and nothing to connect her with
either of them. One burka-clad woman was
much like another.

He frowned, considering the possibilities.
To betray them would only incriminate the
woman herself and she was too cunning to
do that. Had things gone as planned she
would have been amply rewarded for
holding her tongue. But now? In addition to
the Sultan's guards, were they to be hunted

by a vengeful woman? As the darkness
grew more intense, he relaxed. No one
would search at night. A watch set on the
boats in harbor would prevent an escape by
sea, and tomorrow a full scale search could
be implemented.

The grain sacks rustled and he turned to
see the dim outline of Juliet sitting erect
and rigid. "Ross!" The breath whispered
from her lips on a rising note.

"I'm here. It's all right," he said evenly
and crossed the room.

She sighed. "I thought you'd gone."

"Not yet." He sat on a sack a few paces
away but didn't attempt to touch her.
"How are you feeling?"

"Better." She noted his distance and
kept her hands on her lap. The last thing he
wanted at this moment, she supposed, was
a languishing woman in his arms. She had
been tempted to reach for him but the
slightly abstracted note in his voice had
warned her. The significance of his words
floated up. Not yet, he had said in answer to
her remark.

"You are going out?" she asked. "Tonight?" She couldn't see his expression in
the dark.

"Tomorrow the area will be swarming
with Janissaries and there'll be a price on
our heads. If we are to leave at all it must be
tonight."

Juliet locked her fingers together to stem
the relief she felt. He was not leaving her

.

alone, as she had feared.

"You needed rest." he went on. "I couldn't risk you fainting and drawing attention to us." His profile was clear in the fading light.

"I'm sorry," Juliet said in a subdued voice. "Those long courtyards and all those eunuchs watching . . . and then the uproar at the gates. . ."

The shadowy face turned towards her. "Forgive me. I'm not blaming you. I can guess what you went through, but we're only halfway home. I need you to be strong if we're to succeed. I'll explain it to you as we eat. Come, forget today and think of the next step. I'm only sorry I couldn't pay the merchant her due."

"The silk merchant?" Juliet smiled, feeling her strength revive. "She made sure of her payment at the gates by stripping four gold bracelets off my arm!"

"Did she now? Good. Payment enough, I think."

"Especially as two of them had emerald set clasps. They must be worth a fortune."

"Or freedom, which is more valuable." He reached for the goatskin and the remains of the bread and olives. "We'll take the goatskin and refill it from a street fountain. Pereira should have provisioned the dhow as we arranged."

"Who is Pereira? Is he going to help us?"

"Pereira's services go to the highest bidder." Ross said, dryly. "He's a renegade

Portuguese who found Mozambique a little
too hot for his health. He's a smuggler of
anything and everything."

"How could you meet him? Weren't you
guarded the whole time?"

Ross's voice carried amusement. "I got
to know my escort very well. They
introduced me to the delights of the town.
Mustafa liked hasish and Osman was
besotted with a dancing girl in a souk
bordello. I gave them my promise as an
English gentleman that I would not try to
escape while in their charge so, with only
one at a time to watch me, I was allowed to
mix with the bordello customers. That's
how I met Pereira. While Mustafa sat
dreaming of houris in Paradise, I was
arranging things with Pereira."

"Can you trust him?"

"Only until he gets a better offer. Do you
have any jewelry on you?"

"Yes, I still have pearls in my hair and a
pendant of Lady Gabriella's."

"Good. The Vizier missed the gold in my
money belt and I have promised that to
Pereira. A little more inducement won't
come amiss if he quibbles. As an added
persuasion I've got the gun."

Juliet thought of the dead Janissary.
"You would use it, wouldn't you?"

"If necessary, yes." His tone was short.
"I've no wish to enter Paradise piecemeal.
Put up your hood and veil. It's time to go."

Juliet followed Ross down the wooden

stairway. Outside, the town was quiet, only the faintest moonlight showing deserted streets. They stood in the shadows for some minutes, motionless and listening.

"Can you see well enough to follow me?" asked Ross.

"Yes. In your shadow, as the Koran decrees, my lord." Juliet returned softly.

"Good. It will look better that way if we are noticed," said Ross, and set off down the incline.

He moved swiftly and silently. Juliet trotted behind, peering through the eyepiece of the burka. Rather like a blinkered horse, she thought in a flash of amusement. What you can't see won't frighten you!

Ross was outpacing her but she daren't cry out. Nor dare she lose him in the warren of alleys. She trotted faster, the burka billowing in her wake. They were approaching the harbor area. There was music, a high shrilling sound of voice and stringed instrument. Lamps glowed in low windows and the night breeze gusted with strange smells.

A door opened suddenly, light falling on her black-clad figure. That quick instinctive glance had dazzled her eyes, and she couldn't see the alley any more. And Ross had vanished! A voice called, lewd and inviting, and she took to her heels. Blundering round a corner she felt herself caught in a grip of iron and dragged into the shadows. Her gasping breath was stilled by a hand clamped over her mouth.

"Don't scream or I'll be tempted to break your neck," a voice threatened in English and Juliet sagged in relief.

The hand was removed. "Why couldn't you stay close?" asked Ross.

"I'm doing my best," Juliet whispered indignantly. "You were going so fast."

"We have to catch the tide. Try to keep up," he said briefly and released her.

Juliet rubbed her wrist, muttering an uncomplimentary remark under her breath, but Ross had moved away and she scrambled after him. They skirted the harbor and turned out of an alleyway into a square. Juliet was so close that when Ross halted abruptly she found her face buried in his back.

"Quiet," he said unnecessarily, as she struggled for breath.

She peered round his shoulder and saw the reason for his stillness. Two Janissaries were seated on the stone edge of a fountain. They were talking and laughing, both drinking from the same flask.

"Damn," said Ross. "I can't fill the goatskin while they're there." He looked about him. "Wait here," he commanded, and merged into the darkness.

Juliet felt very vulnerable with her back to the wall. She could see the soldiers clearly but hoped that they were too engrossed to notice her in the shadows. A window slammed and she jumped. A soft footstep sent her pulses racing. She turned her head cautiously. Someone was coming, a goatskin over his shoulder. The Janissaries looked up. She glimpsed Ross and her eyes opened wide as he lurched towards her, his voice raised unsteadily in song.

One of the soldiers called something and was answered in Arabic. At the sound of the slurred voice they grinned and their remarks seemed of a derisory nature.

"Come," said Ross, and weaving and stumbling he dragged her into the mouth of an alley, tossing back a laughing comment to the lounging Janissaries.

"What did they say?" gasped Juliet.

"I'd rather not tell you."

"Why not?" She stared into his face as they passed a lighted window and saw his glinting smile and raised eyebrows. The blue eyes met hers for a fleeting second, and she understood.

"Oh!"

"Exactly. The nature of the conversation was highly indelicate so we'd best not run into them again or they'll hold me to my offer. It seemed wiser to act the drunk."

Instead of making directly to the harbor, Ross led her by the back streets to a spot further along the beach. The lights receded and soon they were walking on sand but keeping close to the sea. Several times Ross pulled her down into a sheltering sand dune while he listened and watched.

Juliet stared back to the harbor where

dhows and fishing boats clustered. She saw
Janissary uniforms and the spark of light
on weapons as men patrolled the docks.

"The tide is right to carry us down the
island coast and then we'll steer West for
Dar-es-Salaam," muttered Ross. "But
where the devil is Pereira?"

They waited in straining silence for what
seemed an hour, then the soft swish of oars
came to them. A faint outline darkened the
horizon and the splashing ceased. A boat
was idling offshore.

"Stay here," said Ross, and eased himself
slowly upright.

Juliet clung to the spindly tufts of grass
and kept her eyes on his receding figure. If
she lost him now she might just as well
walk into the sea, rather than face a
reception committee from the palace. The
sea breeze was making her eyes water and
the hiss of shifting sand made it difficult to
hear properly, but no sound of a struggle
came to her. It must be Pereira.

Ross materialized beside her with a sud-
denness that made her gasp. He picked up
the goatskin.

"Keep your head down and don't speak.
Pereira expects two passengers but he
doesn't know who you are. The price would
be higher if he did."

They reached the water and Ross waded
in to toss the goatskin into the stern of the
boat. He came back and lifted Juliet above
the water level and deposited her beside the

goatskin bag. Then he climbed in and took
the second pair of oars. He spoke to the
man behind him and two pair of oars
dipped. When they were clear of the shore,
Pereira ran up the sail and the oars were
made fast. A faint moonlight illuminated
the heavens.

Juliet peered cautiously through her
burka veil. The Portuguese was short and
strongly made. He wore a stained
European-style suit with a collarless shirt
and his beard almost met the matted hair
on his chest. His eyes kept turning to her
curiously as she crouched beside the goatskin bag.

"Who's the woman, Captain? I expected
another of your crew. There could be
trouble for me if you're stealing someone's
wife."

"Nothing for you to worry about, Pereira.
She's nobody's wife, just a girl I'm taking
along for female company. I won her in a
wager with a Janissary." He gave an ex-
pressive shrug. "If there's none of your
own kind about, you take the nearest one to
hand. She's a willing wench and the nights
get cold."

Pereira grinned. He understood this kind
of conversation. His expression was
salacious and Juliet lowered her gaze,
feeling his eyes run over her shadowed
body as if to gauge her attractions.

"Young, is she?" he asked.

"Young enough." said Ross.

"Does she speak English?"

Ross shrugged again, opening his eyes in surprise on the dark face. "I don't know. I never asked her."

Pereira chuckled. "Willing, you say? How about sharing her? I'll knock something off the price of your passage."

Ross gave him a cool look. "Ask me again when we reach the mainland. I think you should be concentrating on our direction at this moment. We seem to be nearer land than we were."

Pereira glanced over his shoulder. "It's all right. The current sweeps round the South of the island, but we'll set course West before long. You've got the gold?"

"Of course."

"How about settling with me now? We can come to some arrangement over the girl later."

"Why now? We shan't part company until we reach Dar-es-Salaam."

"I like to do business first. I only saw the gold in the bordello. How do I know you still have it?"

"I give you my word that I still have it in my belt. You must trust me, just as I have to trust you."

Pereira shifted his gaze to the sea. "There are sharks in these waters, Captain."

"I know." Ross rested his back on the side of the dhow, his arms outstretched on the woodwork. His attitude was relaxed but he was watching Pereira closely. The breeze

was fresh, but the Portuguese was
sweating. "Is that relevant to our conversation?" Ross asked gently.

Pereira shrugged. "I mention it only because unseaworthy boats can founder in
these waters."

"And is this one unseaworthy?"

"No, no, not at all, Captain. But if we
should chance on a reef and a catastrophe
occurred. . ." His shoulders hunched and he
spread one thick-fingered hand.

"You would like to make sure of your
payment first, yes?"

"I am a business man, Captain."

Ross brought his hands together and
leaned forward. "But not much of a sailor,
are you, Pereira? You should have corrected
your steering ten minutes ago by my
reckoning. We're out of the mainland
current and now heading into the island
again. This divergence draws us back to
Zanzibar. Are you just a poor sailor, or is
there a richer reward waiting?"

"You wrong me, Captain. On my
honor. . ." The Portuguese half-rose, his
expression outraged, but his dark eyes were
searching the coastline.

"I would sooner trust to the stars." Ross
said curtly. "You forget, I'm a sailor not a
soldier. I've had time to study these waters
and the heavens above, and I'll be damned
if we're going back to Zanzibar. Get out of
my way or I'll send you overboard."

Pereira gripped the tiller. "Sit down,

Captain. A miscalculation only. Give me
the gold now and I'll alter course."

"I'm coming for the tiller, Pereira, don't
try to stop me."

"I'm afraid I must, Captain." Pereira
reached behind him then jerked the tiller.
The boat heeled sharply.

Thrown off balance, Ross grabbed the
mast, swung himself round it, his head
down to avoid the sail, and came back to
face Pereira in a crouching position. In the
moment it took to free a loose rope from his
wrist, Juliet had caught the spark of steel
in the moonlight. In Pereira's free hand was a
long bladed knife and its point was aimed at
Ross's heart as he threw himself forward.
Juliet didn't know whether Ross had seen
the blade or not, but her reaction was instinctive. Heedless of the rocking boat she
came upright.

"Ross! Look out! He's got a knife!"

Ross checked abruptly, twisting himself
sideways beyond the range of the knife. He
was breathing fast and the blue eyes were
narrowed as he stared into the mocking
face of the Portuguese.

"So," said Pereira, "it is the English lady
you abduct. I doubted you would be such a
fool but his Excellency was convinced of it.
He will be most happy when I hand you
over. And when the Vizier is happy he is
generous to those who help him."

"And you get paid twice. I understand
now your impatience for my gold. It would

sadden your heart if the Vizier confiscated it. How much is he paying you?"

"More than you can afford, my friend."

"The lady is still wearing the harem jewels. They are worth a great deal."

Pereira smiled pityingly. "Harem jewels? What would I do with them? The Sultan has unpleasant ways of dealing with those who steal the treasures from his harem." His gaze turned to Juliet. "And especially unpleasant if the treasure is a girl he has not yet enjoyed." His gaze switched back to Ross. "And your fate will be that of all seducers, my friend. If the girl escapes the execution, she will be sold." His face broke into a sudden leer. "I might even put in a bid for her myself. On the other hand, I could make her part of my reward."

"Don't get too excited by the thought, my friend," said Ross quietly, and uncoiled his length in a low crouching leap at Pereira. Juliet gasped at the swiftness of his move. This time it was a perfectly controlled maneuver which brought Ross dangerously close to the knife. But with one arm pinning the man to his seat and the other clamped to Pereira's wrist, it was a trial of strength. Pereira was unable to rise but his knuckles whitened as he kept his grip on the knife haft, aiming blows at Ross with his free hand.

The small dhow dipped almost to the waterline, and Juliet had to clutch the sides

to avoid sliding over. The lack of rudder
control sent the boat heeling from side to
side, the sail catching every breeze and
sending them on a wildly spinning course.
Falling to her knees, Juliet began to crawl
forward. The sail was blocking her view.
She had to find out what was happening.

A muffled grunt of agony halted her. The
thud of a falling body shook the timber hull
and a white turban rolled towards her.

"Christ!" said Ross's voice almost in her
ear, and she froze with horror, seeing his upturned face on the planking. The light was
suddenly blocked out and the flash of a fast
descending dagger brought a scream to her
throat. Ross rolled and she heard the crack
of his head on the boat side. The fury of
Pereira's downward strike had brought him
to his knees. Ross was up first, and the two
bodies were locked in one solid silhouette
that swayed and staggered over the pitch-
ing deck.

Juliet knelt, clutching Ross's turban to
her chest. There was nothing she could do
but watch numbly as the struggle went on.
The two men were evenly matched, it
seemed. She could only pray that Ross succeeded in overpowering Pereira. The alternative was not to be borne. If Ross died,
her own self would die with him.

Out of the corner of her eye, she saw
something arc and fly towards her. She
flinched as it plunged on to the planks. A
soft thud and tinkle and she was staring

down at Pereira's dagger. She reached for it quickly, wrapping her fingers round the sticky haft. She almost dropped it as quickly when she realized the stickiness was blood. She looked up and at the same moment the planks shuddered under the weight of a collapsing body. There was a long mind-numbing silence, broken only by the sound of someone breathing deeply. Juliet held herself very still, the knife blade turned out.

The breathing eased and a voice spoke "Juliet?"

"Dear God!" Juliet said in a gasp. "Ross! Are you all right?"

"Bloody but unbowed!" he said on a note of grim humor.

"Is . . . is he dead?"

"No. Just sleeping it off. We lost the knife between us. Had to be fists."

"I've got the knife."

"You have? Good girl, we shall need it. Can you come nearer? I'm not quite up to crawling over to you." There was a faint trace of exhaustion in his voice.

Juliet made her way swiftly to where Ross sat, his hand on the tiller. Pereira was stretched out at his feet. Juliet averted her eyes and looked at Ross. She could see that his tunic was torn and stained, but in the dark it was impossible to distinguish dirt from blood.

"Are you hurt?" she asked.

"A cut or two, nothing vital," he answered, his eyes on the island. "But the boat's taking in water. Hadn't you noticed?"

Juliet looked down, realizing for the first time that her feet were wet. She gave a little laugh. "No, I hadn't. I thought it was the sea washing over every time the boat heeled."

"The planking is rotten, and we didn't improve it by our activities. It won't get us to the mainland so I'm putting in to the island."

"Back on Zanzibar? But the Vizier will be waiting."

"He'll be waiting for Pereira to put in at an agreed point. We shall send Pereira on without us, and he can make his own excuses to the Vizier. If he hadn't been so insistent on being paid I might have believed his navigation to be correct in these waters."

Pereira was beginning to stir when Ross found what he was looking for. Beyond the stretch of beach, fringed by reefs and islets, tall limestone cliffs drew themselves up in the interior. They ran roughly parallel to the beach from North to South. A range of these hills, he had learned, was separated by fairly deep valleys and ravines. The East coast was flat and barren, but the Western side was fertile. Good growing land obviously meant a higher population, and perhaps the clove plantations were on this part of the island too, but in a hilly verdant area it was possible to hide, he reasoned.

He steered the dhow into a tiny bay, then rose stiffly to his feet. For a moment the horizon swung crazily, making him feel lightheaded, then he took a deep, steadying breath. This was not the moment to faint. Neither was it the moment to grimace at the sharp pain in his chest. Pereira had done a pretty good job with his knife before being overpowered.

The boat nudged into land and Ross stepped into the shallows, guiding Juliet onto the sand. The goatskin seemed heavier as he passed it to her. It was a matter of moments only to search through Pereira's pockets. A small amount of money in the local currency, but more importantly, a tinder box came to light. He slipped both into his breeches pocket.

Three of the oars he tossed into the sea. With the remaining oar he smashed the tiller. Wedging the bladed end between boat and rudder attachment, he was able to splinter the connecting rod. That oar then followed the others and was lost to sight in the sea.

By the time he had finished Ross was breathing heavily and gripping the side of the dhow. Dancing lights blurred his vision, his head was throbbing, and the water swirling round his knees had turned to ice. He lowered his forehead to his hands and realized that he was drenched with perspiration, yet he was shivering with cold.

He was suddenly and quite violently sick.
When the spasm had passed he raised his
head and felt a shade better.

Pereira turned on his elbow, staring
about him with a dazed look. He pulled
himself into a sitting position and saw
Ross. There was fear in his eyes.

"I'm not going to kill you, Pereira,
though God knows you deserve it. I shall
leave that punishment to your good and
generous friend, the Vizier. The current, I
imagine, will take you to the precise spot
where the reception committee awaits.
Isn't that how you planned it?"

"He forced me into it, Captain. Before
God, I'm sorry! Trust me now and I will
take you to the mainland. I will not even
ask for payment. Is that not an expression
of my good will?"

"Pereira," said Ross patiently, "save
your breath. This boat would never reach
the mainland. It's over twenty miles away.
I suppose you thought this old bucket was
good enough to carry us a few miles down
the coast, so why waste money on a seaworthy craft? It might just stay afloat long
enough to reunite you with your friends.
Goodbye, Pereira."

Ross gave the boat a heave and it floated
free of land. The Portuguese scrambled for
the tiller, gazed for a moment in horror,
then turned a face dark with anguish on
Ross.

"This is inhuman, Captain. You are

sending me to my death!"

"I am merely returning the compliment."

"He will have me tortured! My blood will be on your hands."

"Then you'd better dive overboard and take your chances with the sharks."

"I can't swim!"

"How very unfortunate!" Ross's voice floated mockingly across the water.

Pereira's voice rose in anger. "How can you call yourself an English gentleman?"

"I never did. I am not an English gentleman, just a Scottish adventurer."

The fading voice threw back a string of oaths. "You will suffer for this. I will have my revenge."

Ross wasn't sure how long he had been standing there, gazing blankly over the dark sea. He came to himself with a shudder, and the pains in his body ached and stung as he turned wearily to the sandy beach. Juliet was standing watching him from wide eyes but he could not conceal the effort it took to walk the few yards towards her.

Her hands came out to steady him. "Sit down and take off your tunic." she said.

"We haven't time to rest," he tried to say, but his legs would no longer support him and he sank to his knees breathing harshly.

"This won't take long," she said, untying the long sash about his waist. "You're hurt and losing blood. Apart from leaving a trail any child could follow, you won't get far in your condition." Her fingers moved deftly, unfastening the tunic buttons. She fought back a gasp at the sight of his bared chest. The brown skin was crisscrossed by knife slashes, most of them fairly superficial, but one cut that ran from shoulder to breast was oozing blood in a steady stream. It was an ugly, jagged wound, and if the flow of blood wasn't stopped, Ross would bleed to death.

Juliet slipped out of the burka and removed her kaftan. The waistcoat followed, revealing the fresh white cotton blouse she had donned yesterday morning. Kneeling before Ross, naked from the waist up, she began to tear the cotton into strips, cutting the sewn edges with Pereira's knife.

Ross watched from hazy eyes, his lips smiling a little. Juliet gave him a sharp upward look. "I'm not doing this for entertainment value. It's the only way to save your life. Try to help by getting out of your tunic."

"Yes, my lady," Ross murmured and slid the tunic from his shoulders. The movement made him sweat but he clenched his teeth, watching Juliet make a thick pad out of the body of her blouse.

"Hold it over the wound," she said crisply, and with the long sleeves of the blouse torn into strips and knotted together, she had sufficient length to bind the bandage tightly in a diagonal fashion

round his neck and underarm. She eased
him back into the tunic, buttoning it
quickly over his shivering body, and with
the sash she devised a sling.

"Try not to use that arm," she advised.
"We must halt the bleeding."

When she had dressed herself, she slung
the goatskin bag over her shoulder and regarded him doubtfully. "Can you walk if I
help you?"

With a supreme effort he came to his feet,
swaying. Juliet slid her shoulder under his
good arm and smiled up at him. "Lead on,
Captain. We'll stay the night at the first
suitable shelter we come across. By the
way, do you still have the gun?"

"Tucked in the back of my breeches."

"I wonder why you didn't use it on
Pereira when he produced the knife?"

"I couldn't be sure how far we were from
his rendezvous. A shot would have alerted
the Vizier. With the corsairs on our tails we
wouldn't have stood a chance."

Juliet didn't make any more conversation. The effort of climbing was enough
for them both. The beach had given way to
the rise of cliffs and as they progressed the
ground became steeper, bushes and trees
thickening, so they had to turn and twist
many times to penetrate deeper.

Ross's breathing became labored but he
said nothing, his teeth clamped hard together. Juliet knew he must rest soon or
collapse. She glanced round desperately. It

seemed to be getting lighter but what was
that dark shape almost obscured by trailing
vine and wild plantain trees?

"Stop, Ross. I think there's a cave." She
slid her shoulder away and peered through
the foliage. Were there wild animals on
Zanzibar? She approached cautiously and
stared into the small opening. It smelt
unused and there was no sign of habitation.
The ground was a mass of small plants and
moss-like creepers and appeared to be dry,
set back under a rocky projection.

She returned to Ross. His eyes were
vague as she took his arm. "We're here. A
safe shelter." She held back the bush and
urged him through. He stumbled into the
cave and she could see that he was only
holding himself together by sheer will-
power. She dragged the goatskin up to him,
then arranged the bushes to cover the entrance.

She lay beside him and unstoppered the
bag. "Drink first and then sleep. Put the
gun between us with the knife."

"To repel all boarders." He grinned
weakly and put the mouth of the bag to his
lips. He drank deeply and the blood rushed
to his face. He made a choking sound and
drew in a rasping breath, his eyes wide with
shock.

"God in heaven!" he gasped, with a force
that startled her.

"What is it, Ross? Is the water bad?"

He shook his head and began to laugh

weakly. "It seems," he said in a strangled voice, "that my Arabic is not as good as I imagined. That's not water. It's pure, bloody arrack, a local version of firewater!"

He lay back on the moss and as she watched, his eyelids drooped, then his eyes closed. The strained look was smoothed from his face and his even breathing told her that he was already asleep. She replaced the bag stopper, smiling.

With the gun and knife between them, Juliet curled herself into the folds of the burka and let herself drift into sleep.

XIV

Juliet came slowly to full consciousness, her body relaxed and warm. Memory returned swiftly and she leaned up on one elbow to look anxiously at Ross. He was asleep but his breathing was shallow and troubled. The bones of his face were stark against the pallor of his skin, and his eye sockets were sunken. She saw the great patch of blood on his tunic and her fears rose. The bleeding from the chest wound had not stopped. She recalled it as being fairly high towards the shoulder. Nothing vital, he had said, and the absence of blood in his mouth and throat seemed to preclude a punctured lung. But if he wasn't to slowly bleed to death some effort must be made to stem the flow.

She laid a hand on his brow. There was a cold clamminess about it. Last night she had been too tired to do anything but sleep, yet the coolness of the air as she rose and moved to the cave entrance indicated a drop in temperature. It must have been colder during the night and, from the feel of Ross's skin, he had been affected by it.

Pushing back the hood of the burka, Juliet's fingers came into contact with the pearls looped in her hair. She untwined them swiftly. Each pearl had been held in a tiny pocket of gold thread, then joined to its neighbor by linking thread. The pearl itself was undamaged. With Pereira's knife she separated thread from pearl then sat looking down at her handful of pearls. Disguised in her burka, continuing to act the deaf mute, it was possible she could trade the pearls for food and water—a blanket even and a shirt for Ross. She wrapped them carefully in a strip of cloth left over from her blouse and tucked the knot into the waistband of her harem trousers.

Ross was stirring as she crawled into the cave again. He opened his eyes and stared at the rocks above him, then turned his head slowly as she approached.

"Ross, we must talk," she said urgently. "What do you know of this area? Will there be people, a market even? Are the plantations nearby?"

"You can't . . ." he began and tried to lift himself up. The effort brought the sweat pouring down his face and he lay back with a strangled groan. "God in heaven, I can hardly move." He began to shiver and

Juliet reached for the goatskin bag.

"Don't try to argue with me, Ross, for heaven's sake. You're in no condition to do anything. Drink some of this—what did you call it—arrack?"

"Fermented palm juice and guaranteed to remove the lining of your throat with one swig." He grinned weakly. "It also adds fire to the loins but one should be in the best of health to take advantage of that!"

"All it is required to do at the moment is to keep you warm until I get back. We daren't risk making a fire in daylight, so tell me what I want to know."

The arrack had brought a little color to Ross's face. "I believe," he said, "that as this is the fertile side of the island, all the agriculture will be here. Rice, sugar, maze, and of course the clove plantations. I can't let you go, Juliet, it's too dangerous. The plantation is manned by slaves. There'll be guards."

"And why should they be suspicious of just another robed female? The island is full of them, but I won't go near the plantation. All I want is a market."

"Tomorrow," he said. "I'll be better tomorrow. Leave it until then."

"But we've no food," she said gently. "Without food and warmth you cannot hope to feel better tomorrow."

"Juliet—please! Not today, they'll be searching. Too risky . . . get sticks . . . fire tonight . . . better   tomorrow.   Please.

Promise me!" His voice was fading but his eyes held hers with an intensity she found disturbing. He was terribly weak, she realized, and the effort of argument was taking what little strength the arrack had given him. The dark-rimmed eyes were losing their focus. She spoke quietly.

"I promise, Ross. I won't search for a market today, but give me the tinderbox."

His hand moved slowly. "Pocket. Can't . . . can't reach."

"Let me," she said as he lay back exhausted.

The tinderbox, together with Pereira's coins, slipped onto the moss. Ross's eyes closed as Juliet curled her fingers around the coins. Perhaps he would sleep a little, comforted by the promise she had given him. But it was a promise she had no intention of keeping. Another night of exposure, without food and with his wound untended, could well be his last. A fire would help but the cold ground combined with a thin, blood-soaked tunic was not enough.

"I'll gather sticks," she murmured, but there was no reply.

Pulling up the hood and veil of her burka, she backed out of the cave. Once outside she added the coins to the little bag of pearls then reached back for the knife. The sun was bright in her eyes as she peered through the protective bushes. No one was visible. The cave was not very high up the

cliff but the ground swept down and away
in a mass of greenery that grew sparser as
it receded. She couldn't hear the sea but
believed they had pushed inland from the
direction in which she was staring.

How did one set about seeking a market,
she wondered, gazing from side to side.
Which way must she go? She left the
shelter of the bushes and turned to look
behind. Limestone cliffs loomed high. The
valley behind might be cultivated but first
the ridge must be crossed. She eyed it
doubtfully. That trip must be deferred
while she explored this side of the range.
But first the firewood.

The hot weather had dried out many
small trees, and dead branches were
plentiful. Soon, she had acquired quite a
pile, stripped to a manageable size with the
knife. She staggered back to the cave and
dumped them behind the bush. It was hot
and she was perspiring. The burka was an
irritant but she daren't discard it. The
waistcoat and kaftan could be left behind in
the cave with the turban she had
unexpectedly clung to.

Ross was still asleep but his restlessness
and sweat-sheened face worried her. She
turned away. There was nothing she could
do for him at the moment. Even to bathe
his wound required water. As she thought
of water, her throat ached with dryness. A
stream? There had to be fresh water somewhere in these hills—a spring, a lake, or

something. Even though it was the hot
season and lakes might dry out, springs
didn't usually stop running, she reasoned,
or wells would be empty. There had never
been any lack of water in the palace.

She blew gustily through her veil and set
off, moving sideways and higher. Occasionally she notched a tree trunk to be sure she
returned the same way. The sun was overhead when she paused, gasping, and sank
to the ground, convinced that the journey
was a sheer waste of time. Lying flat on her
back she gazed up at the tree tops until her
breathing slowed. She became aware of the
wild life about her. The birds calling and
swooping above her head were beautiful.
Brilliantly plumaged, long-tailed tropical
birds were quite at home in these hills. A
small monkey swung by from branch to
branch and the grunt of a wild pig floated
through the air.

Now that she herself had stopped
moving, Juliet was aware of many sound
and smells—the heavy fragrance of
unknown blossoms, the stealthy movement of small animals and, in the distance, a soft tinkling sound, almost bell-
like. Was it some habitation, or did the
natives bell their sheep and goats? And
yet it was not quite like a bell. Rather
uneven and continuous—like water falling
over rocks!

She came upright in a movement Lady
Gabriella would have deplored, and listened

intently before trying to follow the sound. A small ridge lay ahead and as she breasted it cautiously the sound was clearer. And it was definitely the sound of water cascading down the rocks, she thought jubilantly. She was tempted to race towards it but held herself back. Someone might be there. The Vizier's men could well be scouring the island already. She lay on her stomach and wriggled her body slowly forward until she reached a small plantian tree.

Through its leaves she found herself staring at a foaming cleft in the rocky face of a hill. Gorgeous, wonderful, crystal-clear water was flinging its rainbow-colored spray high into the air before surging down into a small pool at the foot of the cliff. A few goats were grazing on the incline but nothing else stirred. There were no Janissaries stationed near the goats nor on the rocks. Her eyes turned yearningly to the water and she drew herself up and began to walk slowly forward. Nothing happened, no alarm was given, and the goats ignored her completely. She reached the pool and sank to her knees, throwing back the burka hood and veil. With cupped hands she drank and drank and the sweet water was better than any wine. She dipped her face into the pool and the water ran smooth as pure silk over her chin and neck.

But how to carry it back to the cave? Had anybody previously discarded a container? She scanned the area but saw nothing of

use. A few dried out coconut shells caught
her eye. Someone had lopped off the tops to
get to the milk, but the flesh inside the
green shells was brown and dry. Her eyes
rose. Coconuts nestled high in the trees but
the tall trunks were bare of footholds. Not
impossible to climb for young native boys,
she supposed, but she couldn't see herself
attempting it.

She was eyeing the goats when she heard
a sound that was hard to define. A sharp
click, then a green object splashed lightly
into the pool. The sliced top of a coconut
surfaced. Juliet swung round in alarm and
as the goats parted momentarily, she saw a
small boy squatting beyond them. His
shaggy black head was upturned as his
mouth received the stream of coconut milk
from the shell he had just decapitated.
Small black hands held it aloft. He wiped
the back of one hand across his mouth and
thumped away a goat with the other before
tossing the coconut aside.

Juliet sighed with relief, and the boy
turned his head. He stared at her solemnly
for a moment then he grinned, touching his
forehead and heart in an Arabic greeting.
Juliet answered his gesture and smiled,
rising and moving over to where he sat. He
grinned again, quite happy to show her how
it was done. Juliet had only seen the hard-
shelled hairy brown coconuts in England
but these were green and straight off the
tree. The expert way the boy sliced off the
top was intriguing. She watched carefully.

Food and drink all in one nut and the hollowed out shell could become a drinking vessel, but there was still the problem of water.

Accepting the coconut from him, she tilted back her head and drank. It was like sweet milk and quite delicious. She followed his example and wiped her mouth with the back of her hand. He said something in a language that wasn't quite Arabic. She decided she had better remain a mute so touched her lips, spreading her hands and shaking her head.

His large black eyes were sympathetic, she thought. Perhaps he was quite used to meeting afflicted people or those who had been punished by the Arabs for some sin. He was obviously a slave himself, an African child kidnapped and taught to herd goats for some master. She squatted beside him and pointed to the water, then opened her arms in a gathering motion and pointed behind her, shrugging. He stared in silence for a moment, then his face broke into a smile and he copied her movement. Juliet nodded and spread her hands, looking questioningly at him. He put his hand on a goatskin beside him. Juliet nodded again more vigorously, pointing from the goat-skin to herself, then behind.

The boy shook his head and Juliet swept a hand round to indicate the abundance of goats. She raised one finger, looking pleadingly at him. Pereira's money, she

remembered. Perhaps the boy would sell
her the goatskin. She brought out the
knotted rag and slid a few coins from it. She
had no idea of their value but the goatboy
would know. He looked at the coins as she
held them out, then reached for the
goatskin. As he turned, Juliet noticed the
rug he was sitting on. It had been woven of
goathair into a striped, patterned cloth. She
touched it, feeling the thickness. Would he
sell the rug, too? It was exactly what Ross
needed.

She put it to him in mime but again she
received a shake of the head. All of
Pereira's money she poured onto the grass
and sat back, looking at him. He stared at
the coins, then at her and she knew from his
expression that he was surprised by the
amount. As his hands reached out she
touched his shoulder. He glanced up and
she patted her mouth, running her hand
down her body to finish with a circular
movement over her stomach.

He shook his head, sadly this time, and
she realized that whatever food he had
brought was gone. She peered into the
small metal cooking pot he showed her. It
had contained rice, she noticed, but it was
scraped clean. She smiled and sat back,
then a thought crossed her mind. How
stupid not to have thought of it before.
Although battered and smoke-stained it
was still a cooking pot and she needed that
more urgently at this point than an offer of

the whole Imperial Treasury. She held up
the pot by the hooped handle, pointing to
the rug, the goatskin, and the pot. The boy
seemed surprised at her choice, but when
she pushed the coins towards him he
grinned and shrugged, accepting the exchange.

He was obliging enough to refill the goatskin bag from the pool and they parted with
smiles and bows. Juliet knew he was
watching her as she moved off, the bag on
one shoulder, the rug over the other, and
the freshly-scoured cooking pot slung over
her arm. She made for the shelter of the
bushes in an upward direction, only
changing her route when she was out of
sight.

She wondered if he would tell anyone of
their encounter. Suppose he was questioned
by the Vizier's men? With her dark hair and
her skin tanned from the voyage on the
'Grace' and dressed in the costume of a
Muslim woman, he had no reason to suppose her other than an Arab girl. A grey-
eyed Arab girl? Even that was possible on
this island of slaves and concubines.

She followed her own trail of notched tree
trunks slowly. Under the weight of the rug
and goatskin bag, her body was itching
with perspiration. How delightful it would
have been to strip off her clothes and
plunge naked into that pool! Was it a
favorite place with the goatboy? It was
more than likely, so she must content

herself with a wash from the water she was
carrying. But first she had to make Ross
comfortable and attend to his shoulder.
How had he fared in her absence, she wondered, trying to hurry herself along.

The sun had moved a long way since she
had set out. Night seemed to come quickly
in this part of the world, without the
gradual twilight common in England. Her
sandaled foot came into contact with
something hard that gave way and rolled
before her. A coconut lay at her feet. She
picked it up and dropped it into the cooking
pot. Well, it was something. And she hadn't
had to climb a tree to get it! The bread and
olives they had shared seemed a very long
time ago and she was conscious of feeling a
little light-headed with hunger.

As she approached the bushes concealing
the cave entrance, she saw something that
made her buckle at the knees. Her heart
gave a great leap then lurched erratically.
The rug and goatskin bag slid unheeded
onto the ground, the only sound to disturb
the evening air being the thump and rattle
of the cooking pot as it bounced over a rock.
She swayed, feeling the blood pound
through her temples. A pair of scuffed
leather boots protruded from behind a
bush!

Juliet forced herself on. Had Ross been
found and killed? Was she to discover his
lifeless body and be confronted by a waiting
Janissary? One of the boots drew back. She

gasped, then heard the click of a gun being cocked.

"Who is it?" a husky voice whispered.

"Ross!" Juliet breathed in a choking voice. "It's me."

"Advance—me—and be recognized." There was a forced humor in the weak voice, and Juliet advanced with a rush, pushing aside the bush with a shaking hand.

Ross was lying full length outside the cave, his head resting on a rock. Somehow he had managed to remove the tunic and this was pillowed under his head. The pistol he was grasping in both hands still had the barrel pointing towards her.

"Juliet?" He squinted up at her then sighed, laying the pistol on the ground. "Where the devil were you? I've been out of my mind with worry. You promised me. . ."

"I know, Ross, and I didn't find a market anywhere but I had to try." She knelt beside him and looked into the bone-white face. "Why did you leave the cave?"

"Too cold. The sun was warm. I managed to roll out and get this damned tunic off. It's stiff with blood. Better without it." The words seemed to tire him.

Juliet's gaze moved to the bandages. There was little unstained and the blood was still damp. He answered her unspoken thought.

"Opened it up again, I'm afraid. Only one thing to do. Cauterize."

Juliet's eyes widened and she stared at
him blankly. "Cauterize? You need a
doctor. . ."

"How the hell do you get a doctor? Surrender to the Vizier? You've still got the
knife, haven't you?" In the dark sunken
sockets, his eyes were a brilliant blue. There
was no sheen of perspiration on his skin
now, she realized in a heart-jolting moment.
It was stretched dry and taut over the
bones of his face. He was burning up with
fever! She had to do as he said. It was the
only way to stop the bleeding.

She nodded wordlessly and pushed
through the bushes towards the things she
had dropped. The rug she laid close by
Ross, then carried the goatskin bag
containing the arrack to him.

"I suggest you get good and drunk on
this," she said as his eyelids fluttered and
rose. "If I kill you in the attempt, you won't
know so much about it."

He grinned weakly. "Doctor Fernley
wouldn't approve of your bedside manner."

"Oh, God! I wish he were here now!"
Juliet said in a shaking voice and turned
away.

The thought of what she had to do sick-
ened her but Ross would die anyway if she
didn't try. It was his only chance of survival. She built the fire carefully, surrounding the small hollow with stones
before using the tinderbox on the sticks.
She set the water-filled cooking pot on the

flames and having found Ross's turban in a corner of the cave, set to work with the knife, unwinding the cotton to cut into bandages.

When the water was hot she carried it to where Ross lay. From scooped hands she let the water cascade over his chest, loosening the pad she had made with her blouse. Thankfully, it had not dried and stuck to his skin. She lifted it away with great care then forced her reluctant gaze on to the wound. In broad daylight and in sharp contrast to his white face, the cut stood out fiery red, a long jagged knife stroke that had been delivered with desperate intensity by Pereira. An ugly, twisting, red-lipped slash that still oozed sluggishly.

Juliet swallowed hard, clamping her teeth together to stop them from chattering. She gathered the bloodstained rags and returned to the fire where she thrust the knife blade into the flames. While it heated she watched Ross. He seemed to have consumed quite a quantity of the arrack and was lying with his eyes closed. Asleep or drunk he might still resist the scorching pain she was about to inflict on him.

She took a deep steadying breath, picked up the fresh bandages and pulled the knife from the flames. Crossing to him she stared down, considering, then knelt and laid her body across his hips, one hand gripping his good shoulder. Before she lost her resolve altogether, she laid the hot blade down the

length of the wound, held it for a second
then brought it away quickly.

But in that second Ross's body jerked
violently, almost throwing her off, but she
clung to him, using her strength to hold
him down. The sick, sweet smell of scorched
flesh was in her nostrils. Ross's arm flailed
and his knees came up. His fist took her on
the side of the head, almost knocking her
backwards.

"God damn you, Ross! Lie still!" she
screamed, tears and perspiration soaking
her face. The shudder that wracked him
jerked her own body too, and she gritted
her teeth on the surging sickness she could
barely contain.

Then he went limp, so completely and unexpectedly that her heart turned to ice in
her sweating body. The knotted muscles
under her hands flattened and he was
motionless. She moved back shakily. God in
heaven, she had killed him! Sinking back
onto her heels she took his wrist. At first
her slippery fingers could detect no pulse,
then she felt a faint reedy throbbing. A
gasp of relief shook her. Thank God! He
was alive!

With the tears pouring down her face, she
lifted the goatskin and ran a stream of
arrack across the flat angry wound on his
chest and shoulder. He jerked a little but
remained still. The lips of the wound had
been sealed. No fresh blood oozed out. She
worked quickly then, dipping the bandages

into the water and laying them over the wound. The last two strips she passed round his neck and under his arm, crisscrossing them over his chest to hold the pads in place.

As she finished, Ross stirred. He was still deathly pale and his body twitched convulsively. His eyelids rose and the blue eyes stared, hazed and unseeing.

Juliet grasped the rug. He would never be able to move into the cave tonight. She tucked one side under his body, urging him insistently until he finally understood what she wanted. His brow furrowed with the effort but she managed to drag the rug beneath his back and hips. Thank God it was large enough to wrap over his shuddering body. The thick woven goathair would withstand the chill of the night air and she tucked it firmly round his shoulders and close to his neck. He gave a long sigh and she knew that he had lapsed into unconsciousness again. She prayed it would merge into sleep.

Only then did she realize how bone tired she was. But there were still things to do. She made up the fire and put fresh water to boil. She cleansed the knife and sawed off the top of the coconut, pouring the milk into the cooking pot to warm with the water. She thought of the goatboy's dexterity but her hands were too clumsy tonight to risk the slashing knife.

Ross moaned, drawing her attention. His

head turned from side to side. Juliet
stumbled to her feet, lifting the pot from
the fire. Kneeling beside Ross she guided
his lips to the rim. He drank thirstily and
the hot liquid seemed to calm him. He sank
back and she tucked in the rug again.
Laying the empty pot aside she reached for
the arrack and took a mouthful. The fierce
spirit left her gasping but it warmed her
blood. She lay by the fire and drew up the
burka hood. There was nothing else she
could do for Ross and she was too tired to
worry about the Vizier's men finding them
in the open. If Allah willed it, she thought
hazily, then so be it. She fell asleep on that
thought.

Some hours later she woke. It was dark
and she stared at the sky wondering what
had disturbed her. The fire had died and she
realized she was achingly cold. A soft moan
floated on the night air and she forced her
stiff body to respond. There was barely
enough moonlight to direct her but she
crawled to Ross's side. He had thrown off
the rug that covered him and her reaching
fingers touched his burning hot flesh. He
would surely die of fever or exposure if he
didn't stay covered. There was only one
solution. She removed the burka and harem
trousers, standing naked and shivering in
the cold air, then lay beside Ross and pulled
the rug over them both. She clung grimly to
his body, resisting his efforts to push both
her and the rug away. His skin was like fire,

spreading heat through her. Her own cold
body must have eased him for he fell asleep
again and was still. She relaxed as warmth
crept round her and she too fell asleep, her
arm about his waist, her head tucked under
his chin.

When she woke again the sun was well
up. Light danced through the leaves of the
bushes, flickering over her face. She eased
herself cautiously away from Ross and slid
from the rug. He was still asleep and his
breathing was even. His flesh was cool to
her touch and the skin of his face not so
tightly drawn. A hint of color showed on his
cheeks. Juliet found herself crying sound-
lessly as she knelt beside him, her heart
aching with the joy that flowed through
her. He was going to live, thank God, he
was going to live! The bandages she had
used were unstained, the slow ooze of blood
had been stemmed.

Wiping away the tears she dressed in the
trousers and burka, tucking the cloth-
wrapped pearls into the waistband again.
Today, she really must find food. If Ross
was to regain his strength, he would need
more than coconut milk. She left him
sleeping and made her way through the
undergrowth in a different direction from
the one she had taken yesterday. There
were many tall coconut palms, their heads
above the bushes. A few coconuts had
ripened and fallen, and these she set aside.
Pushing through a broad, long-leafed bush,

she was delighted to find stems of coarse banana-like fruit and a wild orange tree caught her eye. Her spirits rose. They could live on fruit and coconut milk until she found the market. There had to be markets and villages along the coast. Fish, rice, goat meat—even the manioc Khurrem had mentioned. Her stomach churned at the thought, and she gathered the fruit in the folds of the burka and made her way back to the cave.

It seemed even hotter today—or was she weaker from lack of food? Ross's boots were a welcome sight! She gave a gasp of laughter and staggered light-headedly to his side, cascading the fruit to the ground. Before his eyes were fully open, Ross's reaction was swift. His hand was on the gun before she could take a breath. Then he saw her.

"Don't creep up like that," he said sharply. "I could have shot you."

Juliet sank to the ground pushing back the burka hood. She gazed at him stonily, then looked at the ground, her spirits dampened by the reception.

"If it be to your pleasure, effendi, I will attend you with cymbal and clarion, a mighty sounding of drums of a skyrocket to announce my arrival. The Vizier, I am convinced, would be highly delighted. He might even offer a word of thanks," she finished in a small voice.

Ross stared at the downbent head above

the sagging shoulders. He reached out a hand and lifted her chin. Unshed tears glittered in her eyes and he saw the dark shadows beneath. Her hair hung lankly, tendrils sticking damply to her cheeks. Hazy pictures flashed through his mind—Juliet with the red hot knife, sobbing and screaming at him as he fought her off, then the blessed relief of drenching cold, then sometime later a hot milky liquid poured down his parched throat. There couldn't have been much rest for her last night.

"Forgive me, Juliet," he said gently as she twisted her face away. "I was half asleep and you startled me. Was it hellish for you last night?"

She shrugged without replying.

"It must have been," he went on, "but you saved my life. Now it's my turn to do the providing."

"You can't. You're not strong enough yet," she said flatly, glancing up.

Ross saw the dark mark on her temple "My God! Did I give you that bruise?" He sounded so shocked that Juliet grinned suddenly.

"Oh, go to hell, Ross Jamieson! Have a banana and shut up!"

He grinned in return. "Insubordination? I shan't be at your mercy much longer, ma'am," he said mildly, but there was a glint in his eye. "Just remember that!"

Lying side by side in the shade of the bushes, Juliet felt ridiculously happy as they ate bananas and oranges, washed down by coconut milk. They must have slept a little for the sun was dimming when she finally stirred.

Ross opened his eyes. "Where are you going?"

"To start the fire," she said. "We shall have boiled coconut for supper—whatever that's like."

"I'll cut it out of the shells if you bring me the cooking pot. By the way, where did you get it? This rug, too."

"From a goatboy in the hills. I bought these and a goatskin of water with Pereira's money. And Ross, there's a pool and a waterfall up there. When you're stronger we'll go and bathe."

He laughed. "I'm beginning to smell like a goat myself. Can we spare water to wash in now?"

"Yes, we have plenty," Juliet said, placing the cooking pot beside him with the knife. "You can wash while I cook the coconut. Don't damage the shells. They're our only drinking cups."

The fire was burning well as Juliet placed the pot of milk and shredded coconut on the flames. She stirred it with a stick, eyeing it doubtfully. Perhaps it wouldn't be too bad. She rose as Ross called.

"Juliet? Will you help me off with my boots, please?"

Ross disappeared behind a bush to one side of the cave. She heard the sluicing of water and from the corner of her eye saw his breeches thrown out onto the goatskin rug. She kept her eyes firmly on the pot, wondering in amusement if he would stride out naked. Somehow that thought made her feel shy.

The contents of the pot were bubbling, the coconut soft, when he merged. She didn't look round as he returned to the rug but lifted off the pot, setting it on the ground to cool. She glanced at him then. The rug was folded decorously over his stomach, the breeches and boots lying beside him. He looked fresh and clean, his dark hair lying flat. The damp bandages were still in place.

She carried the pot over to him and divided the mixture between the two empty shells.

"How do you feel?" she asked.

"Wonderful. And do you know, this stuff isn't at all bad."

Juliet laughed. "Well, it's filling if nothing else. I'll try and do better tomorrow."

"We'll talk about that in the morning," he said, lying back and smiling up at her, "I'm too tired to argue tonight." His eyes closed and he was quiet.

Juliet rose and looked down at him. He was much better. Perhaps he would sleep right through the night, regaining his strength. She gave a sudden shiver. The air was cooler. If she washed by the fire she wouldn't get chilled.

She stripped off the burka and the trousers and tilted the goatskin bag over her head. The lukewarm water ran deliciously down her skin, washing away dust and perspiration. She set down the bag and smoothed the water over her skin, running her fingers through her hair and down her sides. The water streamed out of her long hair down her back, washing her legs and feet. Reaching for the trousers she began to towel her head.

The ghost of a laugh floated to her. "I like the cut of your jib, ma'am," a soft voice said and she swung round to see Ross leaning on one elbow, regarding her with open admiration.

"I . . . I thought you were asleep!" she gasped, blushing furiously.

"It's a long time since I saw you like that," he said. "Have you finished?"

"Yes, why?"

"Then come to bed. I've poured out a tot of arrack for each of us." He smiled under her questioning gaze. "But that's all I'm up to doing tonight so you're quite safe. Besides, I seem to recall you sharing my bed last night. The rug's quite big enough to cover us both. And if you stand out there much longer you'll catch your death, as my mother used to say."

Juliet laid down the harem trousers and walked over to the rug. She was conscious that he watched her but it didn't seem to matter anymore. Those nights on the 'Grace' came to her mind and it was with a sense of homecoming that she slid under the rug and into Ross's arms.

He kissed her gently, smoothing the damp hair from her brow. His fingers moved lightly over her breasts but no further. They both knew it was not the time for passion. Only their arms and shoulders were close as they sipped the arrack, and they were content to smile into each other's eyes without speaking.

When the coconut shells had been emptied, Juliet laid them aside and moved away from Ross. She was warm and clean and not hungry anymore. And the man she loved was beside her. What more could anyone ask? The stars dimmed and faded and Juliet drifted into sleep.

XV

Ross was the first to awaken. He opened
his eyes to a world he had barely noticed
during his fever. He felt well and strong.
The wound was just a dull ache. He flexed
his arm experimentally and there was no
sickening pain. It must be early, he
thought, for the day had a crisp bite to it.
He turned his gaze and saw the top of a
wildly disordered head close to his chest.
Leaning on his good shoulder he looked
down at Juliet. She was breathing softly,
her parted lips young and vulnerable. For
so small a girl she had a rare courage. Without her he could not have survived. He
owed her his life and must repay the debt
by getting her off this island. The method
of it was still unsolved, but at least they
were free.

"Wake up, woman," he said, kissing her
eyelids and cheeks until she stirred. The

slowly opening grey eyes looked at him
hazily, then she sat up in a swirl of hair and
warm golden body.

"What is it? Did you hear something?"

"No. But I've a sudden longing for your
enchanted pool and waterfall." His lazy
gaze followed the line of her slender throat
and rested on the young breasts. He ran
gentle fingers over them and she shivered
as the cool air tautened the nipples. The
blue eyes rose.

"I suggest we move camp, and what
better place than one with fresh water close
by?"

"But what if the goatboy is in the habit of
watering his flock there?"

"Why should he mind? He was not unfriendly to you, was he?"

"On the contrary, but he might hear of
the search for a man and woman. The Vizier
would pay well for the information. We
can't risk being betrayed."

"Then we'll find a shelter nearby and
visit the pool when the boy goes home."

"I like that better, and there are plenty of
coconuts up there."

Ross laughed. "Are you proposing to feed
me boiled coconut every night? I have the
feeling I could grow very tired of it."

Juliet smiled. "Until I find a market you
must be content with fruit and coconuts."

"Until *I* find a market," corrected Ross,
and as Juliet opened her mouth to protest,
he kissed her full on the lips. "Be quiet,

woman. I'm perfectly fit and don't require coddling anymore."

"Coddling!" Juliet gasped. "Is that what you call. . ."

She was silenced again by his lips. He held her down with surprising strength. "I'm better, do you hear? It's time I was back on the muster." He frowned ferociously. "There'll be no more creeping off to rendezvous with Arab goatboys."

"African," she corrected, undaunted by his frown.

"African?" He released her and drew up to rest in the crook of his arm. "I wonder," he went on thoughtfully, "if I know his dialect. In ten years of seafaring I picked up a fair bit from the ports of call. I'll offer to buy a goat from him and see if it works."

"And if he sells you one," said Juliet firmly, "don't ask me to prepare it for the pot."

"Of course he won't sell one," Ross said, grinning. "He's herding them for his master. Now, go and get dressed before I forget my encounter with Pereira."

They bundled everything, even the bloodstained tunic, into the rug. Ross spread the cold fire wide, kicking the stones away with the heel of his boot. He raked the flattened grass with a twigged stick until there was barely a sign that anyone had stayed there. Then, with the bundle slung on his good shoulder, he followed Juliet up the hillside. She smoothed earth over the notches she

had made in the tree trunks until they were
indistinguishable from the bark. In spite of
the problems still to come, she was quite
lighthearted. She was with Ross and he was
back to health. All other problems were sur-
mountable.

It had been wise to begin their journey
before the full heat of the sun bore down.
Today, the brazen orb seemed more
virulent, and despite the arched boughs
over their heads shielding them from the
fiercest rays, they were soon soaked and
gasping. Juliet glanced constantly at Ross
but the sweat-sheened skin of his face had
not lost color.

During a short period of rest, he glanced
frowning at the sky. "I think we shall soon
have more water than we need. The rainy
season starts in early April. We must find a
weatherproof shelter and stock up with
food."

"How long does it last?" she asked.

"Perhaps for weeks. I don't know, but we
must prepare for it."

They reached the ridge from which Juliet
had peered down over the pool. "Can you
hear the waterfall?" she asked, her eyes
glowing.

Ross nodded, smiling into the flushed
face by his shoulder. "I can hear the goats,
too, so it must wait for a while. Come on,
before we find the urge to dive into the pool
irresistible."

They backed off the ridge and circled the

area, searching for a deep cleft or cave in the limestone rock. Juliet pointed out one or two likely places but had her suggestions dismissed perfunctorily.

"Look higher," Ross said. "Too low on the ground and we shall be flooded when it rains."

Juliet sighed and padded behind him. "We're looking for a shelter, not a manor house."

He paused and looked over his shoulder, his blue eyes holding a glint of humor. "We may be here for years, who knows? Time enough to found a dynasty!"

"Years?" she echoed. "Oh, heavens!" Her voice trembled with laughter. "How many ways can one serve coconut, I wonder?"

But Ross had disappeared into the greenery. She scrambled after him and found him staring with great satisfaction into a waist high, deeply recessed cave.

"This is it," he said. "High enough off the ground and with a sloping projection to channel off the rain above." He tossed in the bundle, then turned and placed his hands on her waist, swinging her up and onto the rocky ledge of the entrance, before following her into the interior.

They shared the last of the bananas and water, lying on the goatskin rug. Ross glanced at their possessions. "Pity we lost my turban. It would have been useful."

"It was, but we didn't lose it. You're

wearing it as a bandage."

"I am?" He glanced down. "Well, I'm damned. I don't need the bandage now but it'll never make a turban again. I'll use the tunic sash instead." He picked up the bloodstained tunic. "Will this wash? I'll have to wear something for the market."

Juliet brought out the pearls. "These are from my hair and I still have the pearls sewn on the kaftan. I'm afraid all Pereira's money is gone."

"Never mind. We're rich enough with those and the gold in my belt. Stay here while I go and have a word with your goat-boy. He can tell me where the market is."

As he was talking he wound the black cotton sash round his head in a most professional manner. Under her interested gaze, he grinned. "Osman showed me how. Very useful fellow, Osman. Delighted in answering questions."

"Did you get the gun from him?"

"No. Only the infantry have guns. I did a deal with an Armenian in the bordello for that."

"You seem to have spent a great deal of your time in the bordello," Juliet couldn't resist saying.

"So I did. One picks up a great deal of information in low places."

"Not to mention attractive girls."

"True enough, and one of them was most obliging."

'I can imagine," said Juliet, looking down at her hands.

"I bought information on the structure of the palace from a girl who had been a servant there. She knew the layout of the gardens and the women's quarters. How else could I have known where to find you?"

Juliet looked up hesitantly. "Were they very beautiful? I mean the dancing girls, and . . . and the other . . . the one who . . . who obliged you?"

Ross glanced at her. "Reasonably attractive, if you've a mind to take a musk-drenched female and overlook the fact that everyone from Janissary to camel-trader has received the favor of her body." He paused, his gaze more intent. "But you're really asking me something else, aren't you?"

"I'm not asking. . ." she began, flushing.

"Not in words, but your eyes are. Good heavens, child, I was far too busy climbing that bloody kiosk roof night after night."

Juliet stared at him. "You mean you were there more than once?"

"Well, of course. And I was getting pretty desperate after I heard talk between the silk merchants of a visit to the palace. I bribed the woman outrageously but I never thought it would be so difficult getting a message to you. I knew of their summons before you did. I kept hoping you'd be alone but you never were."

"Until I took up the lute! That's why I went out early—to practice."

"Thank God you did. The woman was

scared and I knew she would never attempt it twice. It was one chance only. There wouldn't have been another."

Juliet clasped her arms round herself and leaned back in the shadows. She sat very still, watching Ross from misty eyes. He had been free to take a woman in the bordello but he had used that freedom to secure her release, weeks of captivity, but she believed him too fastidious to risk bedding a woman whose favors were openly marketed. She didn't flatter herself that his restraint had been for her sake, more the fact of there being no other choice. Even had she not loved him, she would have given herself gladly whenever he wished, as a small token of her gratitude for the dangers he had undergone in her interests.

With the tail of the turban hanging over his damaged shoulder, Ross dropped out of the cave. "Give me the tunic, will you? I'll wash it while I get to know your friend. Collect some sticks while I'm gone and plenty of fruit."

"Yes, master."

He gave a grin and disappeared into the bushes. Juliet restrained her first impulse to follow him. His wound was healing cleanly, his strength returning, and he would not thank her for following him about like an anxious nanny. She picked up the knife and slid from the cave, determined to follow his orders strictly.

Ross ambled down the incline to the pool

without glancing at the goatherd. A first survey had convinced him that the boy was alone. He squatted on his haunches at the pool's edge and drank before immersing the tunic. The thin cotton gave up its stain in favor of a rusty brown and he slapped it on the rocks as he had seen the women do with their garments. Another rinse, then he squeezed out the water and spread the tunic to dry on the grass. Only then did he glance round idly.

He met the interested gaze of the goatboy and gave him a greeting in Arabic. The boy grinned and returned it clumsily as if it were not familiar to his tongue. Ross moved his position a little closer and tried a few words of mainland dialect. The boy launched into a flow that was too fast for Ross to understand. He raised his hands in protest and the boy grinned and subsided.

Ross then scoured his memory for all the words he had gleaned from a number of dock workers at the 'Grace's' various points of call. They were mostly concerned with cargoes. He glanced at the goats for inspiration and a phrase floated into his mind. Fine goats, was it? He tried it out and the boy nodded vigorously and patted the nearest animal. A common question from sailors in unfamiliar ports was the direction to a market, usually to buy trinkets for their families.

His question had the boy pointing beyond the pool. It was enough. Ross rose and picked up the half-dried tunic, shrugging himself into it. He smiled and patted the boy on the shoulder before moving slowly away to skirt the pool.

The market was farther away than he imagined. It would be getting dark before he reached the cave again, but he was determined to carry as much back as he could. He came upon the market suddenly, beyond a bank of palms. For a moment he stood in the shade, surveying the scene carefully. It was small by comparison with the markets in the capital and unlikely to be frequented by Janissaries from the palace, unless the search for them had spread across the island.

He stepped forward and joined the buyers, ambling between squatting men and dark-clad women. There was a money changer to one side and Ross dawdled nearby, wondering if the man would accept gold or pearls. He noticed gold bangles being exchanged for money and decided to chance a few pearls. The transaction was completed without any surprise on the money changer's face and Ross had a stream of coins dropped into his hand.

Rice, meat, cheese, and large flat loaves were bought, together with another cooking pot. Onions, oil in small containers, vegetables and even coffee were on display. A long-handled woven basket was needed finally to carry his purchases and he wondered even then if he could manage to get

them all back to the cave. He glanced at the
handmade garments laid out and thought
of Juliet perspiring in the burka. They both
needed something cooler to wear, like these
thin striped cotton robes and flat leather
sandals. He added two outfits, roughly
gauged as to size, to his collection and gave
a final glance round.

The last time he had bought something
for Juliet, it had started with a hair ribbon.
A length of colorful plaited kid skin caught
his eye—ideal for that long black hair, together with a loose white cotton shirt to
replace the one she had torn up for
bandages. He stared ruefully at the basket.
It overflowed and he still had change from
the pearls, but it was enough and he needed
nothing heavier to strain his shoulder.

The journey back was uphill most of the
way, with few stretches of horizontal path,
those merely goat tracks pounded flat by
passing hooves. He rested several times
and the shadows grew longer after each
pause. The rope handles of the basket cut
into his shoulder and even with the pad he
had made from the turban, the load seemed
to gain in weight, but he could not risk
using his newly-healed shoulder. He found
himself staggering a little, his breathing
ragged and his mind floating emptily under
the dark sky with its pinpoints of twinkling
lights. He stopped, letting the basket slip
to the ground, and stared blankly at the
stars. They were darting and dancing,

blinding him with light as they chased each
other with silvery chimes across the
limitless expanse of black velvet sky. He
sank to the ground and drew up his legs,
clasping his arms round his knees. The
stars were too bright and he closed his eyes
and rested his chin on his knees. The
changing key of their song was not
unpleasant but rather soothing, he thought
vaguely, and his mind floated away on a sea
of soft laughter.

Juliet had spent the afternoon collecting
fruit and coconuts. These she had stored in
the back of the cave and she surveyed the
stock with satisfaction. She hoped Ross
would bring some change of diet from the
market but if he was unable to find it, they
would not starve. She smiled to herself.
Boiled coconut and banana? That might
not be too bad. She had made an attempt at
slicing off the top of a coconut and had been
quite successful. The milk from that,
together with a banana, was all the break
she allowed herself before setting out to
collect firewood. It seemed darker tonight.
Should she light a fire to direct Ross to the
cave or would it attract undesirable
attention? She decided to wait. He was sure
to be back before nightfall. For a long time
she sat at the cave entrance, watching the
sky darken. A small worry began to build
up inside her. Had Ross run into trouble?
Could the Vizier's men have come across

him in the market or on the hills?

She slid from the cave. It was too early to worry. There was still enough light for her to go to the pool and fill the water bag. The goatboy and his goats were gone. The water from the cleft splashed and tinkled down, rippling the clear pool and reflecting back the first stars in shimmering points of light. Juliet drew out the filled skin and carried it back to the cave, then busied herself building a fire ready for lighting. With nothing left to do, her worry loomed larger. It was quite dark now. But where was Ross? Setting aside the Vizier's men, he could have had an accident, a fall maybe? He might even now be lying injured somewhere in the darkness, perhaps unconscious. And if his wound had opened, he would bleed to death with no one to help him! But how could she search the whole area without even knowing which direction he had taken?

Oh, God, why hadn't she given in to her impulse to follow him? At least she would have known which way he had gone. No use sitting here like a frog on a lily pad, she decided, dropping to the ground. Returning to the pool she stood in thought for a moment. The market had to be downhill. No one would haul goods for sale very far. Near to the coast perhaps but not the way they had struggled that first night. Beyond the pool? If she took a wide-ranging zig-zag route she might discover a way to the

market. And the goatboy and his flock? Of
course they would have forged an
accustomed route for themselves and that
should be easy to follow. She set off hope-
fully, trying to keep to the goat track.

The path was well trampled but it veered
and turned back on itself as if the goats had
been in no hurry and the boy content to
follow their amblings. For all her careful
tracking, she could still hear the sound of
the waterfall in the distance. She wouldn't
get far at this rate.

And then she fell headlong over something that grunted! She screamed in shock
and flung out her arms to grasp the bushes
as she rolled over and over down the hillside. Branches tore at her burka and only
the solid trunk of a palm tree halted her pre-
cipitous descent. For a long moment she lay
winded, her eyes looking up into the sky,
then her wits recovered and she lay still,
listening.

What had it been? A wild pig? She rolled
cautiously over onto her stomach and
stared up the hill. Nothing stirred. The
silence was so intense she could hear her
own heart thudding inside her rib cage.
Then the faintest sound came to her—a soft
slithering movement. Her mind groped
wildly to identify it. A smaller creature
than a pig? A mongoose or—oh, God, not a
python! Khurrem had spoken once of
seeing a man crushed to death in the coils of a
huge snake. No, no, it couldn't be a python,
she decided. It had grunted!

A little encouraged, she slid her body sideways and pulled herself onto her knees. It had gone very quiet again and she had lost the goat track. She must find it afresh, skirting whatever it was she had fallen over. With extreme care she crawled up the hillside, casting about for the track. A hump of a rock was silhouetted against the sky and to that spot she gave a wide berth. The creature had obviously been sleeping nearby when she had stumbled over it. She looked up the hill, then gave a quick sideways glance at the rock as she drew parallel and a yard away. The breath left her abruptly and returned on a choking scream as the rock changed shape and spread over the space between them with alarming speed. Something descended on the back of her neck, driving her body flat to the ground.

"Don't move, I've got a gun!" a voice threatened.

The warning was unnecessary. Juliet, pinned to the ground, her mouth full of wiry grass, was incapable of movement. The weight on her neck lifted and fingers twined in her hair. She waited, anticipating the pain of being hauled up by her hair, but the fingers were suddenly withdrawn.

"Oh, God!" said a weak familiar voice, torn between laughter and astonishment. "I should have known. Who else would risk gallivanting about these hills in the middle of the night?"

Juliet, her shock turned to anger, spat

out grass and said acidly, "You, I suppose, are immune to these risks! What are you doing, lying out here in the cold?"

"Resting," he said calmly, "It was a long haul from the market."

Juliet sat back on her heels, peering down into the pale oval of his face. He lay on his stomach, his cheek resting on his folded arms. He was completely relaxed.

"Are you hurt?" she asked uncertainly.

"My pride is somewhat dented. I'm afraid I was a touch over-boastful as to my strength this morning. Very lowering to the ego, you know, but I shall revive presently."

"It's not far to the cave. You can hear the waterfall from here."

"So that's what it was. And I thought the stars had taken up bell-ringing."

"It seems to me," said Juliet firmly, "that you are becoming a trifle unbalanced. You're cold and weak and very likely hungry. Come back to the cave."

"Tomorrow."

"You can't stay out here all night. You'll die of exposure."

Ross's eyes closed. "Go away, woman," he murmured in a tired voice.

Juliet drew in a deep breath. "If you think I'm going back to the cave on my own, you're mistaken. It's cold and dark and there's no fire. I expect by now it's full of crawling things and if anything touched me I should scream. I won't go by myself and that's final!"

She stared hard into Ross's face and saw the ghost of a smile curve his lips. His eyes opened on her.

"You describe the perils attendant on our little pied-a-terre so eloquently that as a gentleman I feel moved to protect you from them. Trouble is, I can't move."

"That's because you've let yourself get too cold," Juliet remarked in a practical manner. "When you start moving you will feel warmer. Let me help you up."

Ross sighed. "I can see I'll have no peace if I continue to defy you. Very well, I'll make the attempt and discard the final shreds of my manly dignity. You may view me with pity or superiority, just as you wish."

"If you set your dignity above a hot fire and a warm rug, then you deserve to be left here all night. Even boiled coconut is better than nothing at all."

Ross drew himself to his feet slowly and stiffly and Juliet slid her shoulder under his arm. "Lean on me, I'm very strong."

"You're a tyrant too, my girl," he said, breathing hard. "But at the risk of incurring your displeasure, I must decline the boiled coconut tonight."

"Perhaps you're right," she said philosophically. "I'll heat some milk and there's plenty of arrack left. That might do you more good."

She stared up at him, wondering why he was laughing.

"You forget," he managed on a strangled

gasp, "that I was coming back from the market. Somewhere around here is a basket of food. What the devil did I do with it?"

"Oh, Ross, how marvelous! I'd forgotten about that. I'll come back for it when we reach the pool."

Urged on by Juliet, Ross managed to reach the flat ground by the pool. He sank onto a tree stump, his swimming head held firmly between his hands, his elbows on his knees. He was furiously angry at his own weakness but unable to do anything about it. When Juliet returned, dragging the bag behind her, she found his stillness and the sag of his shoulders alarming.

She knelt before him, waiting silently for him to recover. After a while he became aware of her presence and looked up, smiling ruefully. There was a little color in his cheeks but the lines of strain were apparent. He opened his arms and Juliet moved into his embrace, resting her cheek gently against his chest.

"I'm sorry," he murmured into her hair.

"For what?" she asked softly. "You found the market and brought back the food. We can rest now for a few days in our—what did you call it—our little temporary lodging?"

"You never were a servant, were you?" he said with seeming irrelevance, but she understood him.

"No. I had a governess who taught me French and mathematics, but neither accomplishment did me any good. It's all in the past now." She drew back. "I'll go and light the fire. Rest here a little longer."

"What about the crawling things?" He smiled up at her as she rose.

She gave a gurgle of laughter. "They never bothered me at home, but mind you, they could be much larger here. I'd have second thoughts about them then."

She merged into the bushes, pulling the bag behind her and Ross was alone with his thoughts. He sat for a long time staring over the water that now reflected the moon as well as the stars. For a man who had always enjoyed good health without giving it much thought, he felt the humiliation of weakness, the sheer inability to complete the task he had set himself. To let a girl half his size drag him up the hill and make off with the basket so cheerfully was galling.

His head had stopped swimming and he began to feel a little better. She was right, he acknowledged, to remind him that pride was no substitute for the comfort of a warm bed and food in his stomach. He managed a wry grin. Confound the chit. But what other girl in his long acquaintance with the opposite sex would have left the protection of the cave to come in search of him? There was no lack of courage in her. That, and a determination to make the best of every situation, were qualitites out of the common. Like her honesty and practicality. And yet she was wellborn. He was convinced of it now. What could have happened to place a young gentlewoman aboard a convict transport? He believed her father was alive. Surely a gentleman would have made the most strenuous efforts to prevent his daughter being exiled to New South Wales? No crime could be so enormous as to have a young girl of good family banished from her native land. But he remembered suddenly the barrier she had erected when he had questioned her about her father aboard the 'Grace.' A protection from grief? He remembered too the name she had inscribed on the ransom note that day in the haremlik.

Sir George Westover, Baronet had been written in a small neat script. At the time he had wondered why she had not declared him a lord or an earl. A minor title had not seemed to carry much importance. Unless, he reflected, she had despised the lie and written the truth. That would account for her breeding. Should he then have left her at the palace to await deliverance? Another memory stirred. She had written the letter at his insistence, knowing very well that Sir George was quite unable to respond with any degree of success. But knowing that, she had been reluctant to listen to his plan of escape, urging him to make the attempt alone. It didn't make sense. Unless she saw no greater future outside the palace than in it.

But he could not have gone without her.

Leave her to the wrath of the Vizier or the entertainment of a visiting Arab? His chest heaved suddenly and the pounding of his heart hammered home the truth to his brain. Unrealized and unadmitted until now, he knew beyond doubt that Juliet Westover had crept into his heart and mind. Whatever she was or had been was of no account. She was his body and soul for the rest of time. But he must be careful not to show it. He had taken her innocence on board the 'Grace' but she was her own person now and entitled to make her own choices.

He rose to his feet and stood for a moment until his dizziness passed. Bananas and water were not the diet required for trekking up and down hills, he admitted, but now they had food he could rest and regain his strength. He made his way slowly towards the cave, directed by the glow of the fire.

Juliet looked up from the pot she was watching. The flames gave her face a rosy sheen and her grey eyes sparkled. Her expression was radiant. She rose immediately as Ross stood blinking at her. Before he had the strength to voice any protest, she had helped him into the cave, and removed his boots and tunic.

"Take off your breeches and wrap yourself in the rug," she ordered, returning to the fire.

She was back in a few moments, carrying

a coconut shell brimming with hot milk and laced with a generous dash of arrack. Warmth streamed through Ross's body as he drained the shell. Juliet's face shimmered before him. She was offering him bread and cheese.

"I thought you would be asleep before I had cooked the rice and meat," she said, and her voice seemed to come from a long way off.

"Tomorrow," he muttered. "I'll eat tomorrow." And he was sound asleep.

Juliet sat by the fire eating bread and cheese and sipping her own drink. She felt inordinately happy. Ross had brought back more than she had expected and a quick survey of his injured shoulder, as she removed his tunic, showed that his wound was undamaged. All he needed now was rest.

She blinked sleepily into the fire, then laid aside her empty shell. She left the burka where it fell and climbed into the cave, sliding under the rug beside Ross. He didn't move as she tucked herself in, and she lay with her cheek on his strong warm back, her arm round his waist. Her eyes closed and the arrack she had added to her own milk sent her into a sleep as sound as his.

XVI

Juliet slid her body sinuously, and with as little movement as possible, down the length of the goathair rug. Ross was asleep and she didn't want to disturb him. Her heels encountered the rocky edge of the cave shelf and and she wriggled her ankles and calves free until her legs dangled over the rim. When her toes touched grass, she slid completely out of the rug and finished in a sitting position.

Lady Gabriella would be proud of you, she told herself, grinning inwardly. Except that her action had been in reverse, it was the traditional and strickly prescribed method of entering the Great One's bed. It was not for his companion of the night to join her lord in the usual way, but to insinuate herself with the utmost grace between the covers at the foot of the bed, starting at his feet and working her way

upwards until she lay beside him. And
what, Juliet wondered wryly, did the Sultan
really think as he waited and watched the
half-choked bundle come squirming up to
his side. He was probably so arrogant, she
decided, that an entry in any other manner
would result in the poor concubine being
swept off to the executioner.

She shivered and reached for her burka.
A similar fate might be forecast for any girl
found to be less than virgin. What a furor
that would create if the Sultan discovered
such a tarnished blossom in his bed! She
began to see that Ross had been right in
forcing her to accept his plan. Had she
stayed, the truth must eventually have
been revealed and in a palace of women and
eunuchs, where no man but the Sultan was
welcomed, there was no possibility of a girl
being deflowered by any other. By easy
reckoning it must therefore be assumed
that Juliet herself came by her carnal
knowledge before her admission to the
palace. And there was only one candidate
for the role of seducer. The man claiming to
have been entrusted with her care! Ross
had known this all along but had had no
way of knowing if their deception had been
discovered. Yet he had continued in
captivity, conscious that every day might
be his last. Was it possible that she really
meant something to him? It was a warming
thought.

She glanced at the sky. It was not as

bright as it had been and the air held a
humid quality. Perhaps the rainy season
was on its way. All their possessions,
meager as they were, must inevitably be
stored in the cave. To kindle a fire in the
interior was not practical, but the meat and
rice, she supposed, could be eaten cold
when cooked. What else had he brought
from the market? It had been too dark last
night to examine the contents of the basket
thoroughly. She spread the items on the
grass. A small Aladdin-type oil lamp,
onions, sweet potatoes, cooking oil—and
could that really be coffee? A dark, lumpy
substance in a twist of paper caught her
eye. What on earth was that? A tentative
taste convinced her that it was some kind of
coarse brown sugar. Jaggery, she believed
they called it.

The urge to drink coffee was too overpowering to resist. She built a little fire and
set the small cooking pot to boil while she
rinsed her hands and face, then set out the
bread and cheese on a plantain leaf. A pinch
of coffee dropped into the boiling water produced a delicious aroma and she quickly
beheaded a coconut to add milk, together
with some grains of the jaggery.

Ross opened his eyes on a bright-eyed,
tangle-haired creature kneeling beside him
on the goathair rug. She held a brimming
coconut shell towards him.

"Will my lord take coffee?" she asked,
her eyes dancing. "Hot chocolate in the

boudoir is a little outré, don't you think, for
an English gentleman? Oh, but I forget.
You're not an English gentleman, are you?
Just a Scottish adventurer."

Ross grinned, accepting the shell.
"Exactly so, my lady, which means I don't
play by any of the accepted rules of con-
vention. We Scots make up our own to fit
the occasion." He drank and remarked,
"You make a good cup of coffee. I grew
quite tired of the thick mud that passes for
coffee in this part of the world." He glanced
down. "Breakfast in bed, too. I'm overwhelmed. It was only a small gift."

"What was?"

His dark brows rose. "You mean you
haven't emptied the basket yet?"

"I found the food, then I was so taken by
the coffee I had to make some right away."

"I thought females set more store by new
clothes."

"I never had any—except those you
bought in Capetown." She dropped her
gaze and the dark hair concealed her
expression but Ross thought her cheeks
had colored. "Do you mean you bought
something for me in the market?" she
finished awkwardly.

"For us both," Ross said quickly. "A
couple of robes and some sandals but I
picked up a length of plaited kid skin which
you can cut to length for your hair or as a
belt if the robe is too long. Nothing of consequence really. Oh . . . and a sort of shirt to

replace the one you tore up for me." He kept his eyes on the bread and cheese, cursing his inept tongue for bringing back unpleasant memories to her.

He lay back on the rug, his gaze on the rocks above. In his most casual voice he said, "Perhaps we can indulge in the luxury of a bath tonight after the boy has gone. For myself, I shall be glad to get out of these boots and filthy clothes and wear something cooler."

"And I," offered Juliet with determined cheerfulness, "am getting pretty sick of this black burka."

She slid from the cave to add a few more sticks to the fire. The goat meat, thankfully, had been chopped into pieces already and she placed some in the larger cooking pot, together with a small amount of oil. When Ross came out of the cave she was slicing onions and potatoes. He disappeared into the bushes with the water bag, coming back later to stretch himself out in the shade, some distance away. He seemed to be none the worse for his market adventure, she decided, but a few days of food and rest would harm neither of them.

In the absence of plates and cutlery, they ate the stew with their fingers from plantain leaves. No meal had ever tasted so good, Ross declared, but he'd been a fool not to have thought of dishes and forks in the market. Juliet, overheated by the fire and the humidity, gave him a vague smile and climbed into the coolness of the cave to rest. She fell asleep almost immediately and didn't waken until the sun was going down.

Ross had spent the afternoon with the knife, trying to atone for his lack of tact by fashioning two spoons from a lopped-off tree branch. He regarded the results critically then began to smooth the wood with a stone until all the roughness had been worn away. Juliet came upon him unexpectedly and her delight pleased him.

"All sailors are whittlers at heart," he said, shrugging, but he was strangely touched by her appreciative comments. "It helps to pass the long hours on a voyage." He looked up, smiling into the face of the girl who had suddenly become so important to him. She asked for nothing but gave of her strength and spirit to the problem of survival for them both. He realized he was staring and looked down but Juliet still had her gaze on the spoons.

"I think I'll go to the pool," he said abruptly. "The boy should be gone by now." He rose and moved over to the basket, drawing out the larger robe and sandals. "These other things are yours." He turned without glancing at her.

Juliet regarded him, puzzled by the frown and the offhand manner. "Shall I come, too?" she asked in a subdued voice.

"No!" The answer was sharp. He glanced at her then. "I mean, it might not be safe. I'll check the area and find out how deep the water is."

"I can swim."

"That's not the point. It will be better to go separately."

"Do you think the Vizier's men might be about?"

"I doubt it. They'll not risk being stranded in these hills at night."

"Then what are you worried about? We can take the gun."

Ross gave her a hunted look and resorted to anger. "Good grief, girl, can't you understand that I want to take every precaution? Don't make it difficult by arguing."

"I'm sorry. Go alone if that's what you want. I didn't understand."

"It isn't that, its. . ." He paused, baffled, and started again. "It isn't that I don't want you to come. It's because we shall have to swim naked and . . . and dammit, girl, the pool's too small to preserve the decencies."

Juliet's eyes grew round as she stared at him. "Isn't it a little late to start thinking about my reputation? Especially as we are compelled to sleep under the same rug every night."

"I know, but there's nothing we can do about that in our present circumstances. I'll try to make things easier for you by keeping my distance."

Juliet gazed at him thoughtfully, unable to fathom this sudden change in him. His teasing remarks had led her to suppose that only physical weakness held him back from more loving embraces. Was it shameful to admit to herself that she had looked forward to renewing those passionate stations in life? If they found the freedom they sought, he would captain another ship while she had, inevitably, to continue her journey to the penal colony. At this point, she supposed, he must begin to untangle his life from hers. The sea had brought them together and the storm had driven them closer. But no longer storm-tossed lovers, just companions in adversity. Was that what he wanted?

She rose gracefully, as befitted a harem-trained female, and regarded him with dignity. "I will, of course, abide by any decision you choose to make, Captain Jamieson. I understand your feelings and will do my best to respect your privacy." She smiled with a desperate effort, praying that her lips would not tremble and reveal the desolation in her heart.

Ross took a deep breath and stared into the stiffly smiling face under the damp, curling hair. He didn't move but all his senses reached out to enfold the slim smiling girl into his arms. God in heaven, it was going to be a superhuman task to deny every clamoring impulse! He could only do it if she fully understood his reasons. He sensed that there was some hurt in her and knew that his approach had been clumsy.

"Juliet," he said on a determined note, "it is not my privacy I am concerned about but yours. You are a wellborn female—a lady.

On the 'Grace' you were the convict girl I forced into my bed. I can't undo that now but I can behave as a gentleman should and treat you with a courtesy that has been sadly lacking in my conduct so far. I . . . I realized last night that your father is indeed Sir George Westover and . . . and only lack of funds prevented your release. Forgive me for raising a painful subject but I fully intend to return you to him."

"But you forget, Captain, that I am still a convicted felon."

"And you forget, Miss Westover, that the 'Grace' went down with the loss of some convicts. As far as the authorities are concerned, your name will be listed amongst them, should I get back to send off my report. Only your father will know differently from your letter."

Juliet clasped her hands together. "I could start a new life," she said on a soft breath. "A different place and with a new name. Thank you, Captain."

He made a gesture of dismissal. "So you do see, don't you, that with a respectable future ahead of you, it would be ungallant of me to place your reputation in further jeopardy by compounding my errors, however much. . ." He caught back the words sharply.

Juliet looked down, veiling her eyes. "I see," she said. "It is my reputation you seek to preserve, not your own?"

"My own? Good God, I have none!" he

said with a laugh. "As a seaman perhaps,
but with no family to disgrace, I have gone
my own rackety way since a lad of fifteen. I
respect the Company and the men I sail
with but I live by my own code of conduct.
But Juliet . . ." he paused and she raised
her eyes to his. "You will not suffer by it, I
promise. I'll get you home and no one will
ever know of these adventures from me."

"Thank you," she said mildly and
watched him turn and leave her. The
desolation of her heart had eased with his
explanation and a small flame was growing
in its place. She couldn't yet tell him that
her father was the last person she wished to
see, but he had given her the hope of a new
life. She pondered his words for a moment,
her mind dwelling on the ones he had left
unsaid. However much . . . I want you?
Could the broken sentence have finished
that way? And more to the point—was she
prepared to accept being treated with
formal courtesy? It would be a novel
experience, she decided, but quite outside
anything she had ever known. The thought
of Ross Jamieson according her the awe-
some civility due to a lady made her laugh.

Her eyes were drawn to the basket. Only
Ross's suddenly discovered scruples
prevented her from taking that longed-for
swim. She pulled out the cotton robe and
sandals. Why should she be bound by his
scruples and denied the luxury he was enjoying at this very moment? It was quite

unfair. However cross he might be, she was determined to stay no longer in this filthy sweat-stained burka.

She moved up the path with caution, her heart beating a little uncomfortably. From the shelter of the bushes she peered down on the pool. And there was Ross, sleek as a seal, cutting through the clean water with long lazy strokes! She watched the strong brown arms rise and fall as he swam from one side of the pool to the other. How long had that taken? Time enough for her to enter the water while his back was turned? The burka and harem trousers dropped silently and she awaited her moment. He reached the near bank, swung about, and sliced idly away from her.

On silent feet she raced the few yards and slid quickly into the pool. In such clear water, she could see the pebbly rocks shelving away and she let herself sink, diving forward within inches of the bottom, to glide along the turquoise-green length with immense satisfaction. However angry Ross might be, her joy in this first swim could not be spoiled by a few harsh words.

A surge and flurry of water overhead brought her to the realization that she must surface and take another breath. Had he passed her by? The pool wasn't so large that she could hope to remain unobserved for long. She had begun to rise when her hair was grasped in a fierce clutch and she was drawn rapidly up, only to be thrust

down again. Her arms flailed wildly and she
brought up her knees, kicking out at whatever was holding her. Another moment and
she must expel her last breath and inhale
water. Her struggles to rise grew desperate,
her hands clawing at this barrier between
her and the air. Surely it wasn't Ross trying
to drown her! No, that was ridiculous!
Someone else must have entered the water
after her. The Vizier's men? Had they
waited and watched for just such a moment
when their quarry was naked and unarmed?

The thundering in her head made coherent thought impossible. In the second
that her breath finally escaped and bubbled
to the surface, her face was pulled clear of
the water. Her mouth opened and she drew
in a rasping breath that seared through her
lungs, making her gasp and cough in pain.

"God in heaven!" came an astonished
voice. "Juliet!"

She blinked the face into focus through
streaming eyes and looked on Ross.

"Is it necessary to half-drown me," she
spluttered through her coughing, "before
discovering that fact? I thought it was the
Vizier's man holding me under."

"And I thought you were one of them
which is why I kept you down. I'm sorry,
but what the devil are you doing here? I
told you to stay in camp."

"While you enjoy the delights of this
pool? As an equal partner in this venture I
see no reason why I should obey your

orders, Captain. I am not one of your crew."
She tossed back her hair and trod water,
eyeing him defiantly. "Does it matter that
we have no bathing clothes?"

"To me it does!" he returned, tight-
lipped, then spun about in a flurry of water
and struck out for the opposite bank.

Juliet watched the strong brown
shoulders rise and fall as they powered
furiously away. She smiled. How long
would his new resolve last in the confines of
this small pool as they passed and repassed
each other? She swam lazily towards the
waterfall and through the deliciously
drenching spray that spun away from the
cliffside. Her fingers met a small ledge
directly in its path and she found toeholds
to draw herself up clear of the foam.
Balancing precariously, half-blinded by the
force of the water in front, she executed a
dive into the pool, flashing through the
spray to enter the frothing water like a
rainbow-tailed comet.

Ross had glanced up at the moment she
dived. To his startled gaze, she resembled a
glittering mermaid, spinning out through
the waterfall in a long, graceful movement
before disappearing into the foaming water
at the base of the cliff. It was madness to
dive blindly, forced down by the power of
the streaming water! The pool was rock-
edged. Suppose she had been struck a
glancing blow by one of the rocks? He was
swimming strongly towards the spot where

she had vanished before he had finished the thought. He scanned the area. There was no sign of a surfacing head.

He took a deep breath and dived into the bubbling depths, reaching the bottom with rapid strokes. There was no trace of the crumpled figure he dreaded to find. He cast about in a futile effort until the need for air was urgent. As he surfaced, red-faced and desperate, he saw her.

She was floating calmly on her back, her arms rising and falling in gentle movement, completely unconcerned that her dive had been highly dangerous, and unaware, it seemed, of his own efforts on her behalf. His fear turned to anger. Confound the girl for putting him through that terrifying experience! With his teeth clamped together he drew in a harsh breath and struck out towards her in a fury of flying water.

Juliet heard him coming and let her eyes close. One could almost fall asleep on this softest of all beds, she mused, keeping herself afloat with the minimum of movement. She wasn't prepared for the angry voice that disturbed her peace.

"How could you be so harebrained? I never saw anything so reckless and stupid! Don't ever do that again, do you hear?"

She opened her eyes, amazed at the vehemance in his tone. "Of course I hear you. I should think everyone within five miles does too, but what are you talking about?" She stared into the blue eyes glaring down at her.

"That dive. That ridiculous, mad dive! Didn't you realize how dangerous it was, shooting through the falls like that?"

Juliet smiled. "I found it most exhilarating and I'm quite used to diving. Were you worried about me?" Through half-closed eyes she watched him, still smiling a little.

Ross suddenly became aware that he was too close to that naked, golden-cream body. The fading sun touched the water-sheened skin, turning it into peach colored satin and the long black hair floated wide in the pool. He knew he should draw back but somehow he lacked the power of movement.

Juliet lifted a hand and rested it on his shoulder. She let her body sink until she was upright, then turned to face him, placing both hands round his neck. The muscles tightened under her fingers as Ross strained away, trying to drag his wits together.

"It's getting cooler. We should go," he managed breathlessly, endeavouring to disengage himself.

"As you wish," she said, unclasping her hands. She rested them on his chest and let herself sink slowly down, her fingers drawing a trail down his body as she went.

As if her hands were red hot, Ross flinched away, then gasped as her touch reached his loins. It was Juliet who moved back, her chin just bobbing above the water. He saw the shimmer of her rising body as she floated away, then her face

turned to the sky and the exquisite golden
figure with proud pointed breasts drew
swiftly away.

The power of movement returned to
Ross, and in its wake rose a flame of desire.
Whether her touch had been accidental or
not, he knew that he wanted this girl with
an intensity so fierce that it was
frightening. How could they live and sleep
together with this longing inside him? His
own words rose to mock him but he must
accept the situation. It was her right as he
had pointed out. It was too late to change
his mind but what of all the long nights
ahead? He pushed the thought away. It
would be despicable to go back on his word.

He raised his head and stared. Damn the
girl! She was climbing into the waterfall
again! "Juliet!" he roared, but the rushing
water shut her off from all outside sound.

Ross flung himself forward, swimming as
strongly as he could towards the fall. As he
met the froth of water he looked up and saw
her outlined above his head. He yelled again
and waved his arms in a commanding
gesture, willing her to look down. When she
did, he thought he glimpsed a grin on her
face but it might have been a distortion by
the torrent. But this time she didn't dive as
he feared but leapt through the fall, feet
first. She entered the water directly in front
of him and as her legs flashed down, his
reaching arms caught her about the waist
and they plummetted to the bottom together.

Ross's feet touched the rocks first. He pushed upwards with Juliet clasped tightly in his arms. They surfaced, both gasping, and Juliet's arms were round his neck again and their bodies were locked in a close embrace. She raised a laughing face.

"I didn't dive, Captain, sir."

"What you did was almost as dangerous, you idiot child!" He couldn't help his grin of relief any more than he could resist her tempting lips. He bent his head to meet them and their entwined bodies sank to the bottom of the pool again. They rose, laughing, and Ross clasped Juliet to him and began to propel them, one-armed, to shallower water.

He stopped swimming when he was able to stand chest deep. "We should go," he said again.

"Soon," said Juliet and drew herself higher in his arms. Her breasts moved over his chest and her legs parted to encircle his thighs. Her skin was like sheerest silk. The blood pounded through Ross's temples as her softness pressed on him. His hands moved down her back and he felt the hardness build up in his loins. He fought against the rising passion but her legs held him fast and he was drowning in desire.

With sinuous movement, Juliet eased her body over his hips until she felt the rigid maleness of him, then her body opened like a flower and she took him into the heart of her tender flesh. She clung to him, her lips on his face and neck, as a throbbing ecstasy filled her being. After so long apart, she exulted in the joy of being united again with Ross. All those nights on the 'Grace' flowed back into her mind and she received his body with as much urgency as he gave it. In spite of his fierce love-making, Juliet found echoes of his consideration and tenderness from the 'Grace,' and he did not handle her roughly as a less sensitive man might have done.

Their first passion spent, they moved from the water and lay on the rough grass of the poolside. The haze-edged sun glowed sullenly down; the air was moistly still. Not a leaf stirred and the birds were silently winging to the shelter of the trees. But the two motionless figures below had eyes for nothing but each other.

Ross stroked the drops of water from her breasts, lowering his head to kiss the taut nipples. His fingers glided over her stomach, exploring each gentle curve of her body. His lips caressed her thighs and she gasped as his tongue parted the delicate folds of her skin, then he drew his body slowly up the length of hers and their coming together was a more leisurely affair without the fierce urgency of their first mating.

The sun was almost gone and their bodies were warm and dry when Juliet rolled over to look down on Ross as he lay relaxed on his back. His eyes were a brilliant blue, reflecting the last traces of daylight, and his dark hair was a mass of tangles to equal her own. He took her into his arms and drew her body close so that they lay heart to heart and thigh to thigh.

"We should go," he said lazily.

Juliet kissed him. "You keep saying that."

"I know," he said with a grin. "And I should have gone the first time I said it then all this wouldn't have happened."

"Are you sorry?"

"No, but it's a sad reflection of my conduct. I had resolved to treat you like a lady and not force you into response like I did on the 'Grace.' I can't forgive myself that."

Juliet grinned down at him. "Do I appear the reluctant maiden? I might have been on the 'Grace,' but now that you have taught me the delights of the flesh, I am reluctant only to forego them! Don't treat me like a lady, Ross. I couldn't bear it. That's why . . ." She stopped suddenly, and, to his amazement, a blush mantled her cheek.

"That's why what?" he demanded.

"That's why I seduced you in the pool," she said primly, lowering her gaze.

Ross stared at the downbent head, then he began to laugh, holding Juliet close to his shaking chest. "Well, I'm damned! I thought you were hanging on because you were out of your depth. You should have mentioned it. I wouldn't have fought so hard to resist my baser self!"

As he was speaking the sky turned black

and the clouds opened. Drenching rain
poured down, the cold drops stinging their
sun-warmed skin.

"We really should go now," Ross said,
still laughing, and Juliet scrambled to her
feet.

"My new clothes!" she exclaimed.
"They'll be ruined!" She was racing
towards the bushes before Ross was on his
feet.

He watched the slim, golden figure with
flying black hair merge into the haze of the
downpour. Then, still laughing, he snatched
up his own clothes and followed. The rain
was so heavy he could barely see ahead but
he came upon Juliet in a flurry of dripping
leaves and swung her into his arms together with the bundle she clutched. Half-
blinded by the rain and slapped by the long
flat leaves of the plantain trees, he
staggered erratically towards the cave and
Juliet, quivering with laughter, clung wetly
to his neck. He pushed through the
sheltering bush and rolled Juliet onto the
goathair rug, tossing their damp bundles
into the back of the cave before climbing in
to join her.

"Thank heavens you left the basket inside the cave," Ross said, eyeing the
cooking pot on the dead fire. "There must
be three inches of rain in that already." He
felt Juliet shiver beside him and reached for
the goatskin containing arrack. "Sorry I
can't make coffee but this will warm you."

He poured two measures into the hollowed-out shells.

"All our clothes are wet. What are we to wear?" Juliet wondered aloud.

Ross lifted his coconut shell and smiled over the rim. "I rather like you as you are." He was entranced to see her blush and try to hide it by lifting the coconut shell and draining it at one gulp. Her color deepened as the fiery liquid took the breath from her body and she gasped. He removed the shell from her limp fingers and, while she fought for air, he took her in his arms and pulled the rug over them both.

With the arrack boiling through her chilled body, Juliet melted into Ross's embrace, her head under his chin, her arm round his waist. The rug was warm and the heat of his body drove the chill away. She pressed against him, her skin taking fire from his. The tropical storm roared by unheeded as they lay drowsy and content. They must have slept a little, lulled by the pounding rain, and Juliet woke to find Ross kneeling beside her with bread and cheese. She sat up, accepting the food gratefully.

The darkness outside the cave was intense and the wind still shrieked, lashing the trees and bushes into a mad frenzy. The oil lamp Ross had lighted glowed from a small ledge of rock above.

"What a pity the rains have come," she said. "We only had one swim."

"Perhaps we can amuse ourselves in

other ways while we're confined to the cave," Ross said solemnly. "After all you did combine swimming with another activity which I am too much of a gentleman to mention! But whenever you feel inclined to seduce me again, I will offer no . . . no shy resistance!"

Juliet saw his lips clamp hard together as he struggled desperately to hold back the laughter that bubbled up inside him. She flung her leaf-plate, crumbs and all, into his face and launched herself after it.

"You . . . you beast!" she gasped, fighting her own laughter. "You're making excuses now. I don't believe for a minute you could have kept up your high-flown resolve of treating me like a lady!" She rolled over him, pulling his hair as he lay helpless with laughter. "You were ready enough to take me when I came to you."

He grasped her wrists, holding them wide, so that she lay spread-eagled over his body.

"Very true," he admitted, smiling. "I was full of desire and you were so irresistible. I cursed myself for a fool ten times over. I meant the words when I said them, but your coming to the pool overturned my mind and I couldn't see you without wanting you."

Juliet relaxed her muscles and let her body go limp. She moved her hips over his, feeling the silken hair against her skin. Her gaze rose impishly to Ross's face and she saw his eyes widen as his hands released her wrists and moved down to her shoulders.

"Would you deprive a man of initiative?" he said, his voice husky with laughter. In one quick move he had rolled her over and was now the one above. "Leave me my pride, girl. Allow me to be the seducer of unwary maidens!"

There was no more talk as his lips met hers firmly. They sank together into a sea of timelessness, only their senses answering the desire between them. The storm faded into the background and the oil lamp flickered and finally went out as passion mounted and ebbed until the pale strands of dawn began creeping from the hilltops.

The weak sun crept into the cave and fell on the two tangle-haired bodies fast asleep under the goatskin rug. The rain had ceased and birds were beginning to emerge with a shaking of feathers. The smell of drying earth rose as the sun strengthened, but from inside the cave there was no movement. All passion lay drowned in sleep.

XVII

The sky still held an ominous greyness when Ross left the cave next morning. He moved beyond the sheltering bushes into a clear span of ground and raised his gaze heavenward. The dark brows were drawn together in thought. The rainy season was almost upon them. It could rain for weeks on end and they would be marooned in these hills, all tracks to the village impassable, unless one chose to battle through mud that could be knee-high if the rains were of the torrential kind he had experienced in Ceylon and the islands of the Far East.

It was madness to delay any longer. Far better to seek a hiding place at sea level, even if it brought them nearer to the Palace. He sat on a rock, pondering the possibilities. The Sultan's army, scouring the low-lying ground, the harbor and the small villages that dotted the coastline, had found no trace of them. The hills were the obvious alternative and presumably the search was on already. Luck didn't last forever so it was only sensible to make for the place that had been searched before. It would be searched again, naturally, but perhaps only cursorily, while the main body of Jannissaries quartered the long ridge of hills above. Not an enviable task, especially with the rains coming, but their obedience to the Sultan would keep them there.

Horses, he thought suddenly—or rather those sure-footed shaggy ponies he had once sighted going by hill routes to gather fruit and coconuts from the higher slopes. Two ponies to carry them swiftly to the coast. To travel by horseback was to have an advantage over any chance meeting with searchers on foot. Where did one purchase them? And would that purchase cause comment that might reach the ears of the Sultan? Steal them? That might be easier and less suspect. A man with a shaky knowledge of the language and art of bargaining, was sure to be noteworthy. That was it, then. Ponies it should be, and acquired by stealth.

Juliet, watching him from the bushes, saw his nod of satisfaction. She was setting out the fruit and flat loaves of bread when he returned.

"The sky is not promising," she remarked. "We must keep everything under cover."

Ross nodded. "It is time we left these hills before the pools overflow and the tracks sink into morasses of mud."

"And go where?"

"The only sensible thing to do is to make for lower ground while we are still able."

"It's logical," Juliet agreed. "But dangerous, surely?"

"I know, but we are too far from the harbor. We might stay here for months, or until the Jannissaries stumble over us. Down there, we have a chance at some ship. We might steal a seaworthy fishing boat and sail to the mainland. If we delay any longer, the seas will be too rough and we must wait until next year. Can we hope to stay undiscovered until then?"

"All right, Ross. I'll start to pack the things we shall need. How many days will it take to walk? Do you know how far it is?"

"I wasn't proposing to walk. We need mounts." He drank from his coconut shell and smiled at her. "Begin your preparations by all means. I shall go down to the village and ... er ... obtain a couple of ponies."

Juliet looked at him silently, trying not to show the alarm she felt. Of course it was sensible to move away from a place that might have them marooned for weeks under the slashing rain and filling springs that lay above. In spite of the inconstancy of their lives, the fear of discovery and the Vizier's vengeance, it had been an idyllic time. Companionship by day and the bliss of Ross's lovemaking by night. But this was not his life. He was a free man and must re-enter the world of other free men. Neither was it her life but freedom did not beckon to her so insistently.

Ross stood up. Juliet's gaze rose with him. He was staring across the landscape with an air of abstraction. It was as if he had already left this place and their life here was just an episode to be viewed with fondness at some odd moment in the future. It was fanciful, she knew, for they were a long way from safety but the tall, dark, bearded man before her had the face of a stranger. Or perhaps it was the face of the man in the tricorne hat who had stared down on the figure of the convict girl lying half-conscious on the deck of the 'Grace.'

Juliet rose, her eyes on the dark face. "Ross . . ." she began and then her throat closed. Why risk stealing ponies and raising a hue and cry? It might be quicker but infinitely more dangerous and give another party reason to hunt them. Knee-deep or neck-deep in mud, what did it matter as long as they were together?

Ross was looking at her. "Take care," she said and her voice came out as steadily as if she was warning him only of some prickly vegetation beyond a hand of plantain fruit.

"Aye, aye, ma'am," Ross grinned, and the blue glitter of his eyes made her glad that her sentiments had been unvoiced. He wound the sash turban about his head. "I should be back before dark, with one pony at least.''

He bent and dropped a kiss on her cheek. It was a brief gesture of thoughtfulness for she knew his mind was already intent on carrying out his plan. Inside his pocket lay the pearls from Juliet's hair. Surely enough to buy two ponies honestly if he came upon a horse trader making his way to the capital. He discarded the idea immediately. Horse traders were merchants and merchants lived by gossip. A stranger buying two ponies? Who would not prick up his ears in view of the Vizier's reward? The situation therefore reduced one to dishonesty.

As Ross skirted the pool and began to descend the hill, he glanced at the sky. The sun looked down, drawing moisture from the air and the rich smell of earth with it. But at this time of year the sun was capricious. Any second she could turn her face away and send the rains whipping down with the sharpness of needles, cold and shredding to the warm skin. It must be now, before the season hit its peak and the rocky springs surged down to drench the land. The waters of the pool had been still, with the faintly glacial aspect one found in colder climes. Soon, that would be full to overflowing and the goatboy must find his grazing elsewhere.

The village lay before him, cooking fire smoke rising in upright columns. Little

wind even here on the seashore, and the sea
rolled in lazy swells to retreat without the
flurry and tossing of foam-edged ripples.
Very soon, he thought, and quickened his
steps. Reaching the low flat walk where the
merchants displayed their goods, he fell
into a slow amble, passing around and
between stalls and patches of ground where
fruit and coconuts made pyramids on the
sand. A donkey or two eyed him
dispassionately, blinking flies from their
long lashes, twitching tails about their
flanks.

He wandered through the village, his
spirits flagging. Hadn't anyone a good,
stout pony? Even the donkeys were
securely attached to the shafts of carts and
within easy vision of their owners. From
one end of the market to the other he
strolled, his path erratic. Not a confounded
pony to be seen! He became aware that his
aimless wanderings were focusing eyes
upon him. Had he not passed this same
stall three times? The woman ladling fried
meat from a large oily pan set on a bed of
charcoal had lost her first welcoming smile.
She now regarded him with some suspicion.
Dammit, he would have to buy something!
He glanced at the basket by her side. Flat
loaves of bread, to go with the spicy meat,
he supposed.

Peering down into the pan, he thought he
recognized mutton. He gave the woman a
curt nod, as if he had been making com-

parisons with her fellow meat fryers and concluding that her own was worthy of his purchase. With folded arms and haughty expression, he remained immobile until she had sliced two loaves, heaping the meat sandwich-fashion and presenting them to him, the warmth held in by a folded plantain leaf. He dropped the coins she asked into her greasy palm and carried the food to a scatter of boulders beyond the stall. He sat down, and conscious that the woman glanced his way once or twice, felt impelled to show interest in her fried mutton. He chewed slowly, letting his gaze wander the landscape in gloomy contemplation.

A furtive stir on the sand behind brought his head round sharply. No Jannissary with flashing scimitar, as he had half-expected, looked down on him but a young boy in a ragged tunic. Ross's first impression was of the boy's incredible thinness. There was little flesh on his arms and legs and their joints looked large by comparison. His wide black eyes were fixed on the food in Ross's hand, then he glanced briefly into the dark, bearded face and retreated a few paces to squat on the sand. Like a hungry dog that has been cuffed for approaching its master too eagerly, the boy sat mute and still with that same expectation of finding a dropped morsel when the way had been cleared.

Ross raised his hand and crooked a finger. "Come," he said in Arabic.

The boy looked at him but didn't move.
Ross repeated the word but still the boy
remained squatting. Had he been duped too
often to accept the word at its face value,
thought Ross? Poor devil, he looked half-
starved. Ross, himself, was not particularly
hungry so he wrapped up the remaining
bread and meat into the plantain leaf and
wedged it in a corner of the rock. He rose
and stretched. Glancing at the boy, he
waved a hand towards the spot, then
walked away without looking round.
Another circuit of the market with as much
success as the last, and he returned to the
boulder. Both boy and leaf-wrapped food
were gone as he had expected. He stretched
again. What a wasted journey this had
been. The village was too small, too far
from any route into Zanzibar. Maybe he
should move down the coast and seek a
larger village. Could he do that and get
back to the cave before dark?

He thought of the night Juliet had come
down the hill in search of him. He smiled to
himself. Better get back and let her know of
his failure in this village and his plan to
look further afield. If it grew dark and he
was not back, she might take it into her
head to come looking.

If he hadn't been thinking of Juliet, he
might have noticed some newcomers strag-
gling into the market at the opposite end
from where he stood. He moved past the
stalls again, making his way back in the

direction he had come. Along the beach where the sand dipped and the rocky outcrop began, he must turn into the trees out of sight of the market. He ducked under a tent awning and saw three men by the fresh-water stall. They looked tired and the sweat on their faces streaked the dust. As he drew level, the tallest man glanced over his shoulder and paused in the act of raising a beaker to his lips. His eyes met those of Ross and recognition flared in the dark eyes. The shock to them both was mutual.

Mustafa, his guard of those many long weeks in Zanzibar! Mustafa, the one with the fancy for the hashish that swept him into dreams of Paradise with the houris! Recognition between them was so instant and shocking, that both men remained motionless as if carved from the Italian marble of the statuary in the Sultan's gardens.

The metal beaker fell from Mustafa's fingers. He spat out the mouthful of water, his chest expanding as he drew in a harsh breath. His mouth opened but before a word of warning roared out, Ross had moved, driving a clenched fist deep into Mustafa's midriff, his wrist burying itself in the soft paunch. The sound became a gurgle, Mustafa's eyes bulging as he fought for breath. His companions looked round, observed their comrade's suffused and agonized face, then their eyes narrowed on the tall bearded man by his side.

Ross pushed Mustafa towards them with
an air of distaste and strode away. He
walked swiftly but knew that Mustafa
would have recovered his breath before he
made the trees. Let him reach those and he
might have a chance of escape. Three Jannissaries, however hot and tired, were un-
equal odds. He had barely reached the
dipping sand when the voices rose in con-
fused babble and the sound of running feet
thudded the sand behind. The voice of
Mustafa, hoarse and furious, was strident.
Ross broke into a run. They knew who he
was now. It was not a time to retire with
dignity.

He flung himself over the rocks and leapt
for the sheltering trees. The path snaked
ahead. Pursuit was too close for there to be
any sense in keeping to it. He thrust into
the bushes, fighting through the heavy-
stemmed vines blocking his way. His mind
began to work, calculating his chances. Not
good at all but he would not lead them up to
the cave. Double back to the market and
hope that his pace would outstrip them,
tired as they were. From the far side of the
village, he could strike again into the trees
and force a path diagonally to meet the
track that would lead him to the pool.

Twisting and turning, he drove an erratic
path through tree and bush, but all the time
he heard his pursuers shouting and guiding
each other. They were too determined and
too fearful of the Vizier to allow themselves

to be shaken off, and Ross admitted to himself that he was far from leaving them behind.

He paused once to regain his breath. He listened. Mustafa's voice, he knew. One other answered him constantly, the same voice each time. One other? But there had been three men together at the water stall, all dusty and all dressed in the familiar uniform. Two figures were moving, one on a level with him and one on higher ground. He saw them intermittently, the bob of their turbans through the leaves. Where was the third man?

Ross looked round. Nothing seemed to stir in this direction but the absence of the third man worried him. Had they considered that he might double back and the third man lay in wait for just that eventuality? Higher then, not back to the market. He began to climb, silently and with caution. Could he but reach the higher ground, then the searchers might pass harmlessly beneath him.

He turned aside from a thorn bush and glanced down. The village lay below and the glinting sea beyond. Smoke still rose and the business of the market went on. Ross struck upwards again. The voice of Mustafa sounded alarmingly close. Was he rising too in an attempt to cut off the higher ground? One above and one on a level but where was that other? Like a cornered fox they were driving him westward. If the third man was higher still, he could do nothing but run level with the sea and hope to outpace them. Zanzibar was to the East and the farther away they got from it would mean that reinforcements were less likely.

His boot struck a rock, sending it hurling down the incline. Damn! He was dropping too near the shoreline and the sound must have given his position away. He ducked under a low tree and took a tangent that might lead him between his followers. The bushes were sparse but a prone man. . . The thought was never finished. A tree seemed to rise above him, a tree that flung out a heavy branch to take him on the side of the head. A flashing arc of silver dazzled his eyes and he blinked and ducked as the light thrust down. A hissing breath of wind fanned his cheek. Vaguely he heard voices shouting and the bewildering dazzle was still, but the tree came nearer with a whining rush of sound. Darkness fell swiftly and all feeling was gone save the pain and the impression of falling for a great distance with no world below to catch his twisting body.

XVIII

Ross came to consciousness very slowly. At first he resented it for awareness carried pain. His head throbbed as if he had fallen down a companionway and landed on it. Was that it? He was not alarmed by the thought. Every seaman alive at one time or another had lost his footing in the lee of a gale or the lurch of a ship. But thought increased the pain and he lay still, hoping to slip into unconsciousness again. He didn't and the thoughts started afresh. It was very quiet and there was a darkness on his eyelids. It must be night time. A rustle as someone moved and spat warned him that he was not alone. Nothing moved beneath him. He was not then on a ship. He stayed motionless. He could really do little else with the throbbing in his head. Memory returned slowly. There had been a tree with thick cudgel-like branches. No, not

branches, but a man with a cudgel. And a
scimitar, he remembered. Had he not
ducked, his head would not now be throbbing. Perhaps a throb was preferable to de-
capitation. What had stopped the man
wielding the scimitar, the man disguised as
a tree? Mustafa's shout, of course. The
Vizier would be highly displeased if only a
dead body was delivered to him. The Vizier
himself wished to plan the death, that torment of a thousand lifetimes as he had
promised.

Meanwhile Ross lay still, his back on the
sand, his mind drifting in and out of awareness. Only a fool would rush towards that
goal, he thought, hazily. Let the Vizier wait
until he felt better!

He awoke again to a whispered conversation. Mustafa was speaking and Ross's
wits were a great deal clearer. The throbbing had become a dull ache and he was
able to comprehend the odd word. Mustafa
was worried. His voice was touched with
anxiety. What if the infidel died in their
care? Abdul had struck the blow but his Excellency would blame them equally. He,
Mustafa, was not eager to yield himself to
the ganching spike, therefore, Abdul must
go swiftly to the town and in the greatest
secrecy bring back a physician. And let it
not be one who had business in the Palace.
There was such a man, residing for con-
venience near the bordello, and he was discreet. Their murmuring voices faded, and

the sound of boots on the pebbly ground receded.

Ross waited, listening. He could still hear the sea but the market noise was gone. Only in the distance could he hear faint voices, the bark of a dog and the bleat of a goat. He allowed his eyes to open slowly. He looked up into darkness but it was not nighttime as he had supposed. There was a roof above him, one made of poles lashed together with tough vines. Without moving his head, he slanted a look sideways. Upright poles of wood, narrowly placed and also lashed with vine. So, he was in some kind of cage. The corners were held to the ground by stakes of iron, driven deep into solid bedrock. A kind of wicket gate was set in one side. A chain secured it.

How long had he been unconscious? The sun was still shining but the shadows stretched themselves across the sand as if twilight was approaching. He must have been senseless long enough for them to carry him here and long enough for Mustafa to become anxious. The sand between his fingers held a chill. He moved them experimentally. Thank God they hadn't bound him, though how he was to escape without a knife, he had no idea. The vine lashings looked old and tough.

A whisper of sound drifted over his head. "Effendi?"

Ross lay still. A trick to test the depth of his unconsciousness?

The voice was very young, Ross decided, and the formal words were strangely accented. He rolled his head in the speaker's direction. A small dark face with an African cast of feature looked in upon him gravely.

"My health has been better," Ross said, with a faint grin.

The boy nodded and passed a metal cup through the bars. "Arrack, Effendi. I steal from pigs." He jerked his head sideways and the cynical expression sat oddly on his young face, but the eyes held a mature shrewdness.

Ross accepted the arrack gratefully. The liquid fire set his head throbbing but gave him the strength to roll over on his stomach and face the boy.

"What is this place?"

"Arabs build many cages over island. Put in people to wait punishment. You not village man, Effendi. Why soldiers put in Arab man?"

"I'm not an Arab man. I am from England."

"Ah. Then you do bad things to Arabs. That is good." There was a wealth of satisfaction in the words.

Ross smiled. "They do bad things to me first. My ship was wrecked and they took myself and my lady captive. We are trying to escape from Zanzibar."

The boy's eyes gleamed. "Then I help you." He reached back into his belt and produced a broad-bladed knife. "I cut where vines are old and dry. Jannissaries too lazy to mend. I know bad places." He began to saw at the lashings. His thin arms and sinewy hands moved softly and with precision.

Ross watched the intent face under the shaggy head. "Why do you help me?"

The boy shrugged but went on sawing. "You give me food. Jannissary only kick. I am not dog, Effendi. One day I go my father's home. All eat there. Much money in sea, my father say."

The lashing parted with a dry snap, as sharp as a pistol shot. Ross, now on his elbows, stared down the darkening beach to the village. The boy caught his glance and grinned. He looked very young at that moment.

"No hear, Effendi. They frighten you die so one drink much arrack and the other sleep deep with many smiles."

Ross managed to grin in return. "Mustafa, no doubt, who dreams of his houris in Paradise."

The boy moved to the next vine strap.

"What does your father mean by much money in the sea?" Ross asked.

"My father tell of shell with pearl inside. Many lie on sea bed. Arabs come then and catch my father. He work on plantation but they beat him too much. Now he is sick old man. One day we go back to island of my father."

The second lashing snapped. Ross rose dizzily to his knees.

"Effendi may come through other side now. I hold back poles."

Ross crawled and squeezed himself through the opening. He collapsed, panting on the sand outside. The boy lowered the poles carefully and stood, looking down on Ross.

"Where Effendi go now?"

"Up the hill with as much canvas as I can muster," Ross gasped and his head began pounding again. He forced himself to his feet. He swayed only a little.

The boy watched him gravely. "Effendi lean on me. Just for little while," he added, seeing Ross's dark frown.

"You're a good fellow," said Ross and took the boy's shoulder. "I'm cursing myself for feeling so weak-kneed but I will thank you most heartily for your help as far as the trees."

The cooler air with its freshening breeze took the muzziness from Ross's head. In the shadow of the trees, he halted, removing his arm from about the boy's shoulders. From his pocket he drew a handful of pearls. "You speak of pearls, my friend. Did your father ever see the like of these?"

The boy stared with wide eyes at the pearls revealed on Ross's palm.

"You wish money for them, Effendi? I know man who . . ."

"Good. Then take them to your man and get much money. Buy yourself a fine boat and sail with your father to his island. I give you thanks for my deliverance. Now go with God and may your landfall be all you desire."

The boy knelt and pressed his forehead on the back of Ross's hand. "Effendi is most good man," he said huskily, then rose, gave Ross a smile of supreme joy and melted silently into the darkening background.

Ross sighed and stared up the hill, then set himself the task of reaching the cave before it was fully dark. And before Juliet decided he had been away too long and must therefore stand in dire need of rescue. It was even more important now for them to leave the cave. Although the whole island of Zanzibar was ridged north to south with hills, the fact that Mustafa had seen him in that particular village, indicated the nearness of their hiding place. In spite of the rains, that encounter must give the search added impetus, especially in the minds of Mustafa and his comrades when they discovered the empty cage. The urgency with which they must renew their search, so that no one should ever know they had had the infidel then lost him, would be uppermost in their thoughts, Ross assumed.

He found himself on the track leading to the pool. He wasn't quite sure how he'd got

there, some instinct perhaps, but he would
follow it while no one pursued. Only the
return of Abdul to rouse them from their
drugged and drunken stupor would reveal
the loss of their prisoner.

Bushes tugged sharply or wetly at his
shoulders and legs as he forced himself on.
His movements were jerky but he con-
centrated doggedly on the narrow track
though it danced oddly before his eyes. The
dips and hollows tempted him to turn aside
and rest for a while but he drove himself on.
Juliet was there on the hill above the pool.
She must not leave the safety of that cave.
Therefore, he must reach the cave before
she left it.

He was sweating now and the ache in his
head distorted his vision. Trees stood in his
way on the track. Or was it three tracks?
He couldn't remember three but strangely
they all ran parallel up the hill so one of
them had to be right. He came upon the
pool quite suddenly. For a moment he
stood looking at that flat black water. He
swayed slightly and a shiny disc of pale
gold seemed to float out from the edge
of the pool where it had appeared to cling
precariously. He pondered on this for a
while then the pale gold became a deeper
hue and his mind recognized it for the
moon's reflection. He took a few steps forward.

A dark figure rose from a sitting position.
God in heaven, not now after all those years

of struggling upwards! He would not be taken again. Anger and frustration tore through him. His blood was on fire. Damnation to his enemies. He was a Jamieson of Arbroath! No Jamieson ever went down without a fight. He launched himself at the figure, roaring defiance in a mixture of every language he knew.

Juliet stared in amazement as Ross lurched forward, his voice an almost incoherent jumble of words. The spirit of Jamieson of Arbroath met in mortal combat with his enemy, but the body of Jamieson failed the spirit. No imprecation was strong enough to command the body's obedience. The legs wavered, the knees buckled, and with arms outflung to catch the throat of his enemy, Ross Jamieson went down in a sprawling heap on the wet grass at Juliet's feet.

She knelt beside him. "Ross. Are you all right? What is it?"

"God save the king," Ross muttered fiercely, his fingers clawing the grass as he tried to rise. "And to hell with the Sultan."

"Yes, of course," said Juliet.

"And a pox on the Vizier and all his diabolical works."

"Yes, indeed. Especially on his diabolical works."

The soft, female voice seemed to penetrate Ross's stupified mind. He raised his head slightly and peered into the shadowed face, rimmed by golden light. "Who is it?"

The light danced about the head, glittered and spun, gaining intensity all the time.

"It's Juliet, Ross."

He blinked. "Juliet? Why are you wearing a crown?"

Juliet gazed into the strained face worriedly. He looked exhausted. What had happened? Was that a bruise on his temple? She spoke lightly.

"I will remove it if you think it too fine for a commoner." She moved her position, guessing that Ross was staring into the face of the moon. "In a moment we will go to the cave. I have a stew of meat and onions already cooked."

Mention of the cave steadied Ross's thoughts. "Yes, the cave. We must leave at dawn before they come."

"Who, Ross?"

"Mustafa and Abdul and the other fellow. They were in the village."

"They saw you?"

Ross was struggling awkwardly to his feet. "Caught me, too," he gasped.

Juliet slid her shoulder under his arm. "Tell me in the cave while you eat and rest."

It was a staggering journey to the safety of the cave and Juliet would not allow Ross to talk until he had eaten and was stretched out on the goathair rug. He was here and nothing else mattered. The long hours of waiting and the anxiety as darkness drew near had given her a mental exhaustion that only his return had lifted. She knelt beside him, watching the color come back to his face, the lines of strain easing. The tiny flame from the oil lamp fell on his face and the life and light came back into his eyes.

"I made a friend without knowing it," he explained. "A young African boy, son of a slave who had outworked his usefulness, poor devil. I gave the lad food and he used his knife to free me from the cage in return."

Juliet's eyes widened. "They put you in a cage?"

Ross nodded. "The usual thing, I'm told, for wrongdoers, according to my young friend. I gave him a handful of your pearls to buy a boat. He dreams of taking his father back to their island." He yawned, his eyelids drooping. "God give them a fair wind." His eyes closed and as Juliet watched he fell asleep.

She smiled and reached to extinguish the lamp. Slipping off her burka, she lay down beside him, her mind easy. Her body relaxed against his and she, too, fell into a deep sleep. The rain began again lashing at the trees but the world outside was alien and went unheeded.

High above on the hillside, a man crept from another cave and squatted in the sun, gazing down. Below him lay a pool, newly-filled and glinting brightly in the morning

light. He watched a goatboy bring up his
herd, then his gaze scanned the surrounding area. There was no sign of life apart
from the darting birds. He scratched his
bearded chin and settled his damp turban
more securely. Last night when he had
sought shelter from the rain, he was
convinced he had seen a tiny glow
somewhere in the undergrowth below. But
with the coming of day he saw no
habitation, only endless trees and bushes.
Had it just been such another as the
goatboy, seeking a temporay shelter? Or
could his search for the man and woman
really be at an end?

The sun was stronger now, throwing out
more heat, and the steaming ground gave
up its rich earthy smell. He narrowed his
eyes, his gaze suddenly intent. Something
was moving down there amongst the trees.
A small figure, clad in a striped robe, was
passing from tree to tree, bending now and
then as if collecting firewood but pausing
occasionally to look about as if fearful of
being observed.

In one fleetingly glimpsed clear view, he
saw the fall of dark hair. A woman! A
peasant woman, gathering sticks to
prepare a fire for her family's early meal?
There was no sound of childish voices but
she was unlikely to be alone. There could
well be a husband. He watched and
wondered. She was a long way from the
village and somehow she hadn't the gait of

a peasant woman. Was it possible she was the woman he sought? And if she was, her companion must be close by. He rose and began a cautious descent, his bare feet making no sound on the moist earth. From habit he used every tree and bush as cover, moving as silently as a hunting leopard.

Juliet ascended the hillside, delighted to find so many fallen branches. A few more and she could return to the cave and build a fire. She was ravenously hungry and the sooner the rice and meat were cooked, the better. Straightening her back, she turned to retrace her path. Coffee would be welcome at this hour. She smiled as she thought of Ross, still buried in slumber under the goathair rug. He had wakened once and drawn her into the circle of his arms. She doubted there would be any ill effects from his brief captivity.

What was that? Her smile faded and she stared at a bank of trees. Had there been a flicker of white? She backed away, retreating into the shelter of a bush. An animal or—oh, God, not discovery by the Vizier's men! She had begun to believe that their paradise would extend forever but it was ridiculous to suppose they had been forgotten. The Vizier was not a man to overlook the insult of being deceived. Their fate would be the harder for it.

As she stared, a figure moved into her view. Dark, liquid eyes looked straight into hers. Above the beard, the mouth split into

a wide smile, teeth flashing. Juliet recoiled
from the triumphant grin, her bundle of
sticks showering down as she fumbled for
the knife. The haft turned in her sweating
palm and dropped tinkling into the scattered pile. She fell to her knees, searching
blindly, unable to tear her gaze from the
grinning face. The knife was gone—oh,
God, help me find it—her mind pleaded.

The man came nearer, his hands outstretched before him. He said something
but Juliet's mind was trapped in terror and
the words didn't register. The grubby white
turban loomed over her crouching figure
and her control broke.

A scream tore from her throat. High,
wild, like a creature in mortal pain, she
screamed again and again. Birds rose in
alarm and the hills flung back the echoes of
total terror.

XIX

Ross heard the scream as he shrugged the cotton robe over his head. It was a cry of extremity and his blood chilled at the sound, then roared through his body in a great surge of heat. He snatched up the gun and hurled himself towards the source of that heart-stopping cry. Heedless of stones and sharp twigs scoring the skin of his bare feet, he thrust through the bushes, ducking the low branches, his eyes searching.

"Juliet!" he roared in an agony of fear. "For God's sake, where are you?"

A thin wail answered him and he plunged towards the sound, flailing the great leaves aside and leaping the fallen trees. He landed on the edge of a clearing and saw her crouched, arms upraised to shield her face. His second glance took in the man staring down, a look of bewilderment on his face.

"Stand back!" shouted Ross and raised the gun, aiming it at the man's chest. At the sund of a gun being cocked, the man's head swiveled and he started back, his dark face full of alarm. His arms spread in a gesture of entreaty and to Ross's amazement, he sank to his knees.

"Captain sahib, please not to shoot. I meant no hearm to memsahib."

Ross stared into the black, frightened eyes. "Who the hell are you?"

"Captain sahib, it is I, Joseph, your servant."

Ross moved to Juliet and drew her to her feet, supporting her with his free arm. She clung to him, trembling and pale. "What happened?" he asked.

"I . . . I saw him through the trees. He seemed to be following me. I took him for one of the Vizier's men, then I dropped the knife and I couldn't find it."

"Did he touch you?"

"No . . . no, he just came towards me, grinning, as if he was happy to catch me alone. I was so frightened, I screamed. Is he an Arab?"

"No, memsahib. I am Joseph Garcia from Goa. "Please believe me!"

"You're certainly from the Indian continent," Ross said. "But that information could have been easily come by from any of the convicts that survived. You don't look like Joseph Garcia!"

"No, Captain. We not looking same as

before. You wearing no beard either on ship. Not much good food here for man having no money. Must steal in dark. Get thin." He turned his gaze to Juliet. "I cook nice food on 'Grace,' memsahib. You very pretty in blue dress captain buy in Capetown."

"Oh, Ross, I think it really is Joseph."

"I'm inclined to agree with you. Starvation changes people's looks drastically, but I can't help wondering how the devil he came to be on Zanzibar when the ship sank off Mafia Island."

"Joseph can tell us later. We are all hungry so let's eat first."

Joseph gave her a grateful look and, with Ross's nod of permission, helped Juliet gather the sticks together. Although he was practically convinced of the man's sincerity, Ross kept a firm grip on the gun. It could still be a trap with Joseph as bait to flush them out of hiding and into the arms of the Vizier. As they walked back to the cave, Ross kept a sharp lookout and watched the Indian carefully in case he made some signal.

But Joseph was only too eager to help. He took over the fire building and arranged a canopy of wide leaves between the cave entrance and the bushes so that the smoke rose and diffused, adding only a slight haze to the atmosphere. While the rice and meat cooked in one pot, Juliet made coffee in the other.

"Was it Abu Kasim who arranged your passage here, Joseph?" asked Ross, casually. "He is a generous man to his friends, I'm told. Where did you meet him?"

Joseph looked blank. "I am not knowing this gentleman, Captain sahib."

"But everyone on Zanzibar knows him. Next to his highness, he is the most powerful man in the capital."

"I am not being in Zanzibar Town, sir. I hide in country. Very much questions be asked by Arab peoples. I join slave men sometime for little food when guards don't look but fisherman very good to me."

Juliet watched Ross with a puzzled frown. "Who is this Abu Kasim, Ross?"

"His Excellency, the Vizier, my dear. I wondered if he had taken Joseph into his service. After all, he can identify us better than anyone."

They both stared at the Indian.

"Surely Joseph would never betray us to the Vizier!" exclaimed Juliet. "That would be sending us to certain death."

"But the rewards are great. Think of Pereira."

Joseph looked from one to the other with bewilderment on his face. "I not understanding your words, Captain sahib. I speak only to African peoples who must work for Arabs. They tell me of much searching for white man and lady by soldiers. I wonder who is running away.

Later there is talk of ship's captain and I pray to Holy Mother that it will be my own captain sahib."

"But that doesn't explain your presence on this island."

"No, Captain sahib, so I go back to starting. When boats come after 'Grace' hit rocks, I go to fetch ropes for people to climb down. Memsahib see me go to rope locker. Then, lot of noise and water come in. I cannot open door again so I break window. There is much fighting and people fall in sea. I am very frightened to see sharks so I climb to rocks on island. Then our ship sink and pirates go away. I think maybe they take all sahibs for no one is left. All night I hide, my heart full of sadness, then I walk and walk. I come to village where all men live by fishing. They let me stay because I am dark like them and I help with the boats."

Juliet spooned rice and meat onto three plantain leaves. Joseph accepted his share gratefully and they ate in silence until the leaves were emptied.

"Go on, Joseph," Ross said, but there was more friendliness in his tone.

"I ask the fisherman if they go to mainland but all are afraid of being taken as slaves. They fish only between Mafia and east side of Zanzibar. We meet other fishermen from this island and they say the Great One has come to his palace with many slaves from the market in Dar-es-

Salaam. My mind wonders if captain sahib
and his officers have been brought to
Zanzibar and I ask my brothers to sail near
the coast so that I can swim ashore. I living
long time near harbor and listen to men
talking. There is much excitement for they
say a white lady has been stolen from
Sultan's household by man who kill guard.
In their speaking of ship's captain, I think
of you for no other ship has foundered in
these waters since the 'Grace.'

"So you came in search of us?"

"Yes, Captain sahib. I want to go home to
my wife in Goa. She will think I am dead
when they tell her the ship is lost. I am not
liking this island at all."

Ross smiled. "We're not exactly enjoying
it either." His glance rested fleetingly on
Juliet and his smile deepened. "Oh, it has
its moments to be sure, but I don't care to
spend the rest of my life with the Vizier
breathing down my neck. The devil of it,
Joseph, is how to get off this cursed
island."

"Steal a boat, Captain sahib?"

"And have the corsair fleet catch us
before we're halfway to anywhere?"

"Ross," said Juliet, "do you remember
that French ship, the one they sent my
letter on? If trading vessels call here, we
might be able to arrange a passage
aboard."

"I don't think their trade with the Sultan
would flourish if they were known to have

assisted in the escape of wanted criminals,"
Ross pointed out. "You forget—I killed a
Janissary."

"Well then, could we smuggle ourselves
aboard?"

"I imagine the Vizier will be alert to such
an attempt and extra soldiers will be posted
around the harbor whenever a ship comes
in. They might even have the power to
search a ship before allowing it to leave.
And whatever nationality the ship is, the
captain would be powerless to prevent us
being hauled off. Even if it were a British
vessel."

"So we spend the rest of our lives here?"
Juliet asked gloomily.

"Unless we can think of something
they'll never suspect." Ross regarded the
Goanese thoughtfully. "If a British ship
puts in, then Joseph has the best chance of
mingling with her crew. He can go aboard
with them and the guards won't stop him.
After all, the Vizier doesn't know he exists.
How about that, Joseph? You'd be halfway
home to your wife."

"No, Captain sahib!" Joseph said firmly.
"Not deserting you and memsahib for a
saving of me."

"But you must, Joseph. Captain
Jamieson is right. Nobody is searching for
you." Juliet urged but the Goanese shook
his head. She looked at him helplessly.
"You could mention us to the captain if it
would ease your mind, but not until you're

safe and miles out to sea. Why, Joseph, what is it . . . ?" She faltered to a halt as she saw tears in the man's eyes.

"Memsahib, Captain sahib, you both talking of my go home on English ship. You not thinking of you! Much shame on Joseph for leaving sahib and lady to being die. No facing left! How looking at Company sahibs?" In his agitation, Joseph's precarious grasp of the English language was deserting him and Ross leaned forward to pat him on the shoulder.

"All right, Joseph. We won't insist on it, at least not yet, but if we are captured you must remain out of sight, then do your best to escape. You understand?"

"Yes, Captain sahib." He rose to his feet and salaamed. "Now I am going back to harbor. Maybe learn of English ship come one day then captain sahib make clever plan. We all go home captain sahib think good." He beamed down at them for a moment.

"Wait, Joseph." Ross crawled into the cave and returned with a handful of gold coins. "You'll need money for food and accommodation. Don't take any chances and come back here if you have any trouble. There's room for three."

"Thank you, sahib, but I stay in little cave on hill. Can see the waterfall from there and lot of country. Anybody come, I tell you quick." He salaamed again and left, soft-footed.

"I'm so glad Joseph survived," Juliet said. "I grew very fond of him on the ship. I hope he can get back to Goa."

"So do I, but even if I order him to board a British ship I've no way of watching him do it. He's a stubborn fellow when it comes to loyalty."

Juliet smiled. "Then captain sahib better think good plan or Joseph's confidence in you will be sadly dented."

Instead of returning her smile, Ross drew up his knees and sat with his chin resting on his folded arms. "Do you know," he murmured into space, "I keep coming back to something you said to Joseph."

"What was that?"

"About mentioning us to the captain after they'd sailed."

"Does it help? I only said it to make him more willing to agree."

"Yes, I know, but supposing Joseph could take a written message to the captain. They'll all have heard about the loss of the 'Grace' but if I could write and sign a letter, the British authorities will know there were survivors. A request through diplomatic channels might persuade the Sultan to clemency. At least for you and the convicts."

Juliet thought of the girls at Bagamayo. "I can't speak for the men," she said, "but I doubt the girls who were sold with me would thank you. They were quite content to go with the Arabs who bought them.

And who knows where they are now? It
would only be exchanging one kind of
captivity for another in a penal colony, even
if their owners would give them up."

The blue eyes stared towards her. "That
problem can be left to the authorities. I am
more concerned that you escape the Vizier.
When your father produces your letter, the
authorities must acknowledge your presence here, and as a lady of rank. . ."

"I am also a criminal." Juliet reminded
him flatly. "I can expect no extra effort to
be made on my behalf."

"Oh, hell!" said Ross, dropping his head
onto his knees again. "I'd forgotten that."

"I'd rather take my chances here than go
back to England in chains," Juliet said
miserably.

Ross moved to sit beside her. He
gathered her into his arms and spoke softly
into her hair. "We'll both take our chances,
but we must get off this island first. We'll
sort out the other problems later. Now,
what can we use for ink?"

"Ink? You're going to write a letter
then?"

"It's the only way, but don't worry—I
won't mention your name. We'll just be two
survivors from the 'Grace.'"

"We have no paper to write on. No pen,
for that matter."

Ross lifted her chin and kissed her.
"Where's your ingenuity, girl? A strip of
my tunic, a pointed stick and the juice of

berries—if we can find some black ones!"

"I've seen dark berries around but I've left them in case they were poisonous."

"Good. I'll go and collect some. Don't clean out the rice pot. We'll need something to thicken the juice."

He was gone before Juliet could ask what he planned to write. No females, other than convicts, had boarded the 'Grace' in Bristol. How then could he hope to keep her identity secret? It was stupid of her to imagine the past could be hidden, even if they succeeded in leaving the island. But whatever her own future, Ross had to be saved from the Vizier's vengeance. If there was a chance of freedom she must force him to take it. Only death lay in store for him here. As for herself, did it really matter if she was sent to the slave market again? Having known Ross's body, they could never take that from her, however she was used.

When Ross returned she greeted him calmly, resigned to her fate but unwilling to mar his optimism by expressing doubts about the scheme. During the afternoon it began to rain again. Juliet removed her robe and lay wrapped in the rug, watching Ross write his message in the light of the oil lamp. He laid it down carefully to dry, then glanced over at her.

"Shall I read it to you?"

Juliet shook her head. "No. Whatever you've decided I'll help in any way I can."

Her voice trembled a little and she held out her arms to him, already feeling the pain of their parting and wanting the comfort of his embrace for as long as he was allowed her.

Ross tossed aside his robe and joined her, holding her body tightly against his. "Don't be afraid, Juliet," he said gently, misunderstanding her emotion. "Joseph will take the message to the captain and we'll find some way to get you aboard even without waiting for the Sultan's deliberations." He smiled into her eyes. "We could always stain your skin and dress you as a lascar seaman! You're small enough to pass muster and I know you'd be brave enough to try."

"And how would that help you? Do you expect Joseph and I to sail away without you? I can be as stubborn as he is. No, Captain sahib, we go together or not at all, just like Joseph says."

Ross sighed. "I never had such an insubordinate crew in my life."

Juliet slid her arms round his neck. "You probably never seduced one either!"

A smile curved Ross's lips. "You can be sure of that. We never carried females before. And talking of seduction. . ."

The sky turned black outside and the rain gathered in intensity, concealing the cave entrance with a heavy downpour. Behind the curtain of water Ross and Juliet were oblivious of everything but each other. A different storm raged through them both—a storm of desire that rose and paused and rose again, carrying them along on a torrent of passion that engulfed their minds, leaving only the senses alive to respond to the touch of mouth and body.

Neither could remember falling asleep but they woke to the dawn and lay smiling at one another. Ross rolled over onto his stomach and regarded her gravely.

"Are you hungry?"

Juliet couldn't hold back a gurgle of laughter. "Starving! I wonder why?"

Ross grinned. "They do say that love-making makes one hungry. I'm ravenous myself but after the loving feast you served me during the night, I hardly liked to mention the fact before you admitted it yourself, in case you accused me of too much concern for my stomach."

"We haven't much left. Cheese and bread perhaps."

"I'll avoid the market until after I've seen Joseph."

They slipped on their robes and ate the bread and cheese, drinking a little arrack until they could start the fire and brew coffee.

Joseph came back in the afternoon. To Juliet's delight he had brought food. Several large pilafs stuffed with cooked chicken and each wrapped in muslin, cooked rice, and a twist of highly colored

sweets which he presented to Juliet with a
bow.

"My wife, she liking these very much,
memsahib, I thinking you also."

"Oh, Joseph, how kind of you. Thank you
very much."

"I use Captain Sahib's gold," he said with
a little smile, "so he be buying really."

"Well done, anyway," said Ross. "What
have you learned at the harbor? Tell us
while we eat."

"I am thinking is good news, Captain
sahib. They packing many sacks of spice
for ship to take in two days expecting. I
talk to men. They say maybe it is ship from
India, come to carry spice to land of white
Sultan, long way over water. What you
thinking, Captain sahib?"

"I'm thinking, Joseph, that maybe they
talk of King William, our own monarch.
And if that is correct, then without a doubt
it must be a British ship, and certain to be
an East Indiaman. A Company ship,
Joseph. What could be better? The captain
is bound to believe your story when you
give him the letter I've written. I only hope
your friends at the harbor are correct in
their information. Two days, you say? With
a day to load her that could mean she'll
leave on the evening tide, three days from
now." He glanced at Juliet. "I think we had
better move camp nearer to the capital.
We'll set off in the morning. Join us here,
Joseph, will you?"

"Yes, Captain sahib. I take you to safe place near harbor then I am coming back with things I hearing." He rose to go but Ross halted him.

"Let me give you the letter for the captain. It's best that you have it now in case we get separated. If it is a Company ship you must deliver it into his hands personally, Joseph. Don't allow anyone else to take it from you."

"No, Captain sahib. But I not staying on ship. I coming back to you and memsahib."

"It would be very foolish of you to do that. If you're safely on board you should stay there."

"But captain of ship maybe sending message. I must be coming back then for telling you." He beamed at them both benignly.

Ross sighed and shook his head. "Was ever a man plagued by two such reluctant escapers. I doubt if the captain will give you a message but I'm sure you'll bring me one just the same."

"Captain, sahib?" queried Joseph, his face a study of innocence. "I not understanding."

"I wouldn't take my oath on it, lad, but have it your own way. Here's the letter. It's written on cloth so tuck it into your turban."

"Yes, Captain. Quite safe now. I go to my cave and coming back tomorrow."

The rain began again before it was dark.

Juliet sat at the cave mouth watching the
sheet of water take away all visibility. This
was their last night together in the hills, the
last time she and Ross could shut out the
world and belong only to each other. Where
would they be tomorrow? In some harbor
shanty with Joseph? Not daring to venture
abroad for fear of being seen by the Janissaries?

It had to end sometime, she told herself.
What man of Ross's stamp would be content to live in hiding day after day, even
with a girl who gave herself so gladly to him
and satisfied his senses. A true man needed
more than that. He needed an aim, a purpose of life, and Ross's aim was to get back
to his job of commanding a ship. There was
no place for her in his future and the sooner
she accepted that fact the better. What use
had he for a convict girl, a runaway concubine, the penniless daughter of a
drunkard? A man of looks and charm could
expect to be feted by the best society when
he returned as a hero.

"Do you realize," a soft voice said in her
ear, "that this is our last night of en-
chantment? In a way I shall be sorry to
leave our little paradise but there is a whole
future out there. We must grasp the chance
of living it."

Juliet turned to him, smiling. "Yes, of
course we must move on. It would be silly
to imagine the Vizier has given up his
search but at least we have been lucky

enough to escape from his clutches so far."

"Without you I could have been dead twice over. That merits undying gratitude."

"I don't want your gratitude, Ross. I want to see you safely off this island. You have more to lose than any of us if the Vizier finds this place."

"I intend that we all get off the island, whether on this ship or the next."

That night Ross's lovemaking held an extra tenderness, as if it must last them both for a long time. His touch was so gentle that Juliet's heart seemed to weep within her, but she hid the desolation and answered him with equal tenderness. There was no laughter between them, no fierce urgency, just the knowledge that tomorrow lay waiting, as yet unseen but with the hand of fate poised above to record their progress.

They woke before it was really light and breakfasted off cold rice and bananas. Ross gathered together his boots and breeches, tunic and sash. He smiled down at Juliet. "I'll wash and dress at the pool. There'll be enough water left in the goatskin for you. Back to the harem clothes and the burka, I'm afraid. We'll be safer traveling that way." He hesitated as he picked up the gun and looked at her. "If you would prefer the pool . . . ?"

"No," Juliet said quickly. "I'd rather not

go there again."

She watched his tall figure duck through
the bushes and then began her own preparations. She didn't want to look on the
cold, early morning water of that deserted
pool. The image she clung to was of a
sparkling, sun-kissed enchanted place,
where a man and a girl laughed and loved
and loved again. She drew on the cotton
shirt Ross had brought from the market,
secured the harem trousers in place and
donned the kaftan and jewels given to her
by the Lady Gabriella. The stronger market
sandals she wore, stowing the flimsy pair in
the now empty basket along with the
striped robe. Her hair was a tangled mess
but with a sprinkling of water and a drag
through with her fingers, she was able to tie
it back with the kidskin plait. Lamp,
cooking pots and spoons went into the
basket. If Ross carried the rug she could
manage the basket easily after Ross had
added his own robe. She looked round the
cave, smiling a little. Not much of a house
moving and easily accomplished.

Outside the cave, she sat on a stump of
tree waiting for Ross's return. It was quiet
and peaceful but she laid the knife nearby,
determined not to lose it as she had done
when Joseph appeared so unexpectedly.
Ross seemed to have been gone a long time.
Had he met Joseph on his way down? Were
they discussing their new hiding place?

The bushes beyond the cave entrance

rustled and she heard the sound of a booted step. That must be Ross now. But why was he forcing the bushes instead of ducking under them and leaving them undisturbed? It must be Ross—it had to be Ross—and yet her mind chilled with doubt. Joseph? No, Joseph would not be so clumsy; he had moved too stealthily the morning they met. Her hand went out to grasp the knife hilt. She felt the grass under her fingers but nothing else. The knife was gone! How could it have gone? She had laid it so carefully to hand.

She half rose from the tree stump, the beginning of panic rising from the pit of her stomach. The knife! She had to find the knife, it was not Ross. The move she had begun was never completed for an arm encircled her waist, dragging her down again onto the stump. As her mouth opened to scream, a hand, foul-smelling and greasy, clapped itself over her lips. But the sound was still in front of her! Two of them?

The bushes parted and into her view stepped a short, thick-set figure. Above the beard, the swarthy face glistened with sweat. The European-style suit he wore was even dirtier than when they had met before. Pereira, the renegade Portuguese, Juliet realized with horror. The last time she had seen him was in the boat Ross had pushed out to sea, rudderless and oarless. She remembered his oaths and threats of vengeance. But who was holding her? Of

428   RELUCTANT RAPTURE

course, it had to be an Arab, a Janissary
guard. Pereira must have made his peace
with the Vizier in return for a promise to
hunt them down.

Pereira swaggered forward and looked
down, a smile of satisfaction curving his
thick lips. He fanned his face with a soiled
and tattered panama hat.

"So, English lady, we meet again and I,
Angelo Pereira, have the upper hand. Now
you will answer all my questions with truth
or many bad things will happen to you." He
looked past Juliet and spoke a few words in
Arabic.

The hand left her mouth and Juliet took a
deep breath and spat viciously onto the
ground, then glared up at Pereira. She was
tempted to scream, but that would prove
she was not alone. If she spoke loudly
enough, that in itself must be a warning to
Ross.

"Do not scream, lady," warned Pereira,
"or Selim will cut your throat. But only a
little, you understand. I have no wish for
you to be dead."

Juliet felt the cold blade of the knife rest
lightly on her neck and repressed a
shudder. With an air of unconcern, she said,
"Screaming would avail me nothing. No one
will come to my aid."

"The English captain. Where is he?"

Juliet shrugged. "Wherever it was we
saw you last, I suppose. He bled to death on
the beach so I left him. I had no wish to be

accused of killing him. A girl must look after herself in this world."

"You're lying. I don't believe a word of it."

"Why should you care anyway? You wanted him dead, didn't you?"

"But the Vizier wants him alive and I have promised to deliver him."

"Or maybe bad things happen to you?" mocked Juliet and was startled to see Pereira's face suffuse with blood.

"When I failed him that night, he had me whipped! Me, Angelo Pereira, a Portuguese citizen! Someone will pay for that indignity with his head. Until I see the English captain looking down from the gate spike, my honor will remain unsatisfied."

"Your honor!" exclaimed Juliet, her voice rising with derision. "What honor is that, pray, accepting payment from both sides and breaking your word when it suits you? Do you expect me to believe your only reward is to have the satisfaction of delivering a man to his enemy? Forgive me if I find that argument less than convincing!"

"Oh, no, my dear lady, I have some other reward." He grinned, showing stained teeth. "I am to have you! There is no place for a harlot in the palace but I am not so particular as his highness. The Vizier only wants the Englishman. You are beneath his notice so he gives you to me when I hand over the man."

He turned his head listening, and Juliet

heard it too. She drew in her breath but the
scream was never aired. A cloth was thrust
between her teeth and knotted behind, then
the Arab's fingers closed round the kidskin
binding of her hair and jerked back her
head roughly. The flat of the knife turned
and she felt the sharp edge pricking her
skin. A hard knee ground into the small of
her back and from that uncomfortable
position she could do no more than emit a
strangled gurgle.

Ross ducked into the clearing, completely
unaware of the ambush. He stopped
abruptly as his gaze fell on Juliet, held fast
in the grip of a turbaned Arab. The gun he
had raised in a reflex action was no use. He
couldn't fire without risking Juliet's life.
His hand closed fiercely on the gun butt as
the Arab grinned and made a sawing movement. A trickle of blood ran down the
golden length of her forced-back throat.

"Welcome, Captain," a soft voice spoke
from the depths of a bush behind him. "I
would strongly advise against pulling the
trigger if you point that thing at me. Selim
will assuredly complete the task of cutting
the throat of your woman." Pereira was beyond Ross's view. "Drop the gun, Captain.
I have one also and it is aimed at your back.
You dare not shoot Selim without
endangering the girl and if we shoot each
other, then Selim might delay their
departure in favor of other plans. You
understand me, Captain? The Visier knows

she cannot be virgin, so what difference will Selim's attentions make?"

"God damn you, Pereira! Tell your friend to take that bloody knife from her throat!"

"The gun first, Captain."

Ross had no choice but to obey, and he dropped the gun reluctantly.

The Arab released Juliet's hair as Pereira spoke to him but he still held her as a shield against his body. She was struggling to speak but the gag muffled her words.

"Move forward, Captain, and sit down." Pereira slid from the bushes and picked up the gun. "This is a happy day for me. Both of you at once. The Vizier will be pleased."

Ross frowned at him. "Why should the Vizier need the girl if he knows she is no longer suitable for the harem? Set her free and I will go willingly with you. You have my word on it."

"The word of an English gentleman? I don't make that mistake twice, Captain."

"Let her go and you can put me in bloody chains if you want. How could I escape from the two of you?"

"My orders are to take you both, Captain. What becomes of the girl later is in the hands of his Excellency. Maybe I could put in a good word for her—providing you give me no trouble on the journey. The Vizier will be too happy to receive you to bother much with the girl. It will undoubtedly be the slave market for her." He stroked his beard thoughtfully. "The life of a palace servant might be preferable but it would cost much in bribes." He gazed down at Ross. "You still have the gold you once promised me, Captain?"

"Yes, I still have it. Would that guarantee her a place in the palace?"

"Assuredly, Captain. I will pledge my word in return for your own, plus the gold."

"Very well. I have no choice but to trust you."

Ross looked at Juliet who was shaking her head vigorously. Her eyes were glowing with fury as she glared at Pereira, and her face was red with the effort of trying to speak. Behind her the Arab was tying her wrists together. He then rose and approached Ross. With Pereira pointing two guns at him, Ross could do nothing but allow his own wrists to be secured.

Why was Juliet being so vehement, he wondered. There was no other way of ensuring her safety other than by trusting Pereira, although the man had little to commend him. He was a liar and a cheat but with the handing over of himself, there might be a grain of decency left in the man towards a European woman. That and the gold were all he could rely on. Thank God he had given the message to Joseph already. The Goanese must now see that the only alternative was to get himself on board the English ship alone.

"Why don't you remove the lady's gag, Pereira?" Ross asked, frowning. "It seems unnecessary now that you have me fast."

"Remove it, Captain? And permit the wench to hurl more abuse at me? She'd best stay silent or I may regret my generous offer. Come, it is time to move. We have a long way to go."

XX

"How far is it to the capital, Pereira?" asked Ross, without moving his position.

The Portuguese shrugged. "Ten ... twelve miles, maybe."

"Are your horses below?"

Pereira's laugh was harsh. "You think the Vizier permits me horses? He gives me one guard only. When I complain he says it is for the sinner to repent in hardship and humility. So, Captain, we walk! We should get there tonight."

"Are you suggesting the lady must travel on foot for over ten miles in the heat of the day? That's impossible!"

Pereira shrugged. "Maybe we rest sometime. It is of little consequence."

"I disagree. We need water. I intended filling the goatskin bag."

The Arab picked up the bag from the cave shelf and flourished it at Ross,

grinning. There was a sound of swirling
liquid and Pereira smiled unpleasantly.

"You play for time, Captain. There is sufficient in the bag for your journey."

Ross recognized the arrack container.
"We need water for the journey, Pereira,
fresh water. That's something I brought
from Zanzibar a week ago. It's no use to us
now. Taste it if you don't believe me."

Pereira frowned and spoke sharply to the
Arab who unstoppered the bag and sniffed
the contents. He wrinkled his nose. "Bad
water," he said, but Ross caught the
sudden gleam in his eye before his glance
slid to Pereira.

"Taste it, man!" growled the Portuguese,
then snarled something in Arabic.

Selim took a long swig and wiped his
mouth with the back of his hand. He stared
sullenly at Pereira. "Bad water," he repeated and spat on the ground within an
inch of Pereira's foot.

The Portuguese quivered with rage and
his complexion turned a dull red. "Insolent
dog!" he roared. "Brainless half-wit! If the
water's bad, get some more. Don't stand
there like an idiot. No wonder the Vizier
gave you to me. He knew you'd be less than
useless!"

"There's fresh water in that direction."
Ross jerked his head over his shoulder and
moved his position close to Juliet. He wondered if he could encourage the animosity
between their captors. That shouldn't be

difficult with Selim already resenting Pereira's attitude—but how would it help them? Both men were afraid of the all-powerful Vizier. Still, it was worth a try, if only to witness Pereira's discomfort.

He watched thoughtfully as the Arab tucked the knife in his sash and moved out of the clearing. If he hadn't told Pereira of the bag's true content it could well be that he was partial to arrack himself and intended to empty the bag out of Pereira's sight.

Ross settled his shoulders against the cave rocks and regarded Pereira who squatted uncomfortably, holding a gun in each hand. The man was nervous, Ross decided. His suit was already wringing wet. Could he add a little more tension to the Portuguese?

"You really shouldn't have done that, Pereira," he observed idly.

The man jumped. "Done what?"

"Forced poor Selim to drink that arrack. You know the Koran forbids strong drink. He might decide you have put his immortal soul in danger."

"Arrack? Who cares?" snapped Pereira. "He does what I tell him to do."

"For the moment, yes, but if your orders conflict with his beliefs, you're likely to come a poor second to Allah. And you did call him a dog! If I were you, Pereira, I'd watch my back when Selim's around. He has the knife and you know how silently an

Arab can move. Would the Vizier mourn
you? I doubt it, as long as Selim delivers us
to him."

"Hold your tongue or I'll put a bullet in
you."

Ross laughed. "I don't think so. The
Vizier is reserving such pleasures for himself, and they won't include a simple
shooting."

While they waited for Selim's return,
Ross considered their situation. Joseph had
been due to meet them here and Joseph was
late. That could only mean he had
approached the cave with his newly-learned
caution and was now in possession of the
facts. There was nothing he could do
against two armed men but Ross suspected
that Joseph would follow until all hope was
gone. Only then would he board a British
ship. Well, at least the Company, and later
the authorities, would know of the fate of
the 'Grace' and her crew. Lost at sea was no
epitaph for a ship's captain.

The sun's heat grew stronger and Ross
eased his shoulders against the rocks. He
glanced at Juliet. The thought of losing her
now was a dull ache. The sooner they killed
him the better. He could not envisage a life
without this girl who had given him so
much, but his last act must be to see that
she came to no harm through knowing him.
And could he really trust Pereira? But what
alternative was there?

"Can't you take that damned gag off the

lady?'' he asked irritably.

"I'll take it off when I'm ready to," Pereira said with a sneer. "I thought you liked your women to be silent, Captain. That's what you said to me once."

Ross shrugged and said no more, but as the sun steadily ascended, he began to wonder about Selim's absence. Had there been enough arrack left to render the man senseless? Was he curled up under a bush, lost to the world in dreams of Paradise? He schooled his face to blankness as Pereira began to fidget and sweat even more.

The Portuguese rose and eyed Ross malevolently. "Where the hell is that swine?"

Ross returned the look blandly and shrugged. "Filling the goatskin, I suppose. Unless, of course . . . well, no, he wouldn't do that. . ." he broke off, grinning.

"Unless what?" grated Pereira.

"Unless he decided to empty it first . . . into himself! Perhaps he succumbed to the desire to taste forbidden fruit, though he is a follower of the Prophet. However, you know him best for he always does as you tell him. Isn't that so? Would he dare disobey your orders?"

Pereira's expression changed from anger to suspicion and then to a look of apprehension. Ross watched the play of emotions, guessing at Pereira's thoughts. If Selim were dead drunk there could be no moving off immediately—no moving, in fact, until the Arab had recovered. With the

onset of the afternoon rains, combined with
the early fall of night, the hills must still
surround them when darkness came. With
no food and water and two prisoners to
guard, Pereira needed Selim.

"Come," said Pereira abruptly, gesturing
with the guns. "We will go to this pool. If
what you say is true, I will have the man
whipped when we meet the Vizier."

Ross sighed and pushed himself to his
feet. "His Excellency might wonder that
you allowed your subordinate to indulge in
such sinful pleasures. However, I am sure
you'll be able to convince him that no blame
can be attached to you." He smiled into the
uneasy face of the Portuguese and was rewarded by a savage thrust of the gun to his
ribs.

"Go!" Pereira snarled.

"Ladies first," Ross said mildly and
shouldered Pereira aside to allow Juliet to
pass before him.

The Portuguese took a hasty step backwards, his color deepening. "No tricks,
Captain, or you'll be sorry."

"You have the armaments, Pereira. What
could I possibly do?"

"Move, damn you!"

With Juliet leading they made their way
up the incline, ducking under the bushes,
hampered by their bound hands. In the distance they heard the bleating of goats and a
young voice raised in song.

"The goatherd is coming," Ross said conversationally. "Best get Selim out of there before he's seen."

They moved to the crest of the incline and looked down over the pool. Selim was there, lying on his stomach, his head resting in the water. The goatskin bag was floating free.

"Asleep?" queried Ross, then as they drew nearer he saw the blood on the rocks above Selim's head.

Pereira drew in a jerky breath and plunged forward. The Arab's face was completely immersed and the area of water around his head was stained with pink. Pereira rolled him over and they saw the blood-stained temple.

"He's dead!" Pereira muttered, his face shocked.

"Poor devil," said Ross. "He must have fallen and knocked himself out trying to fill the waterbag. Drowned by the look of it."

"Drowned?" Pereira stared at the floating goatskin. "He drank the arrack, damn him. I might have known! Stupid, useless fool!" He rose to his feet and aimed a savage kick at the body. The dead Arab slid forward, floating face down in the pool, his arms outstretched.

Ross heard Juliet's muffled gasp of horror at the grotesque sight. He turned swiftly and barred her view, moving as close as he could. She rested her face on his chest. "Don't look, darling," he whispered. "Pereira's so mad with rage and fear, he's disgusting. The poor devil didn't deserve that."

Pereira came up swiftly. "Go. We travel now. Quickly."

Ross looked around to see the first goats appear over the far ridge. With Pereira's gun prodding his back, they retraced their steps to the cave.

"Down the hill," ordered Pereira.

"Without water?"

"No time for that. I want to be out of the hills before nightfall."

There was nothing to do but obey the urging of the gun. Pereira was jumpy and his eyes were never still. For a city man, the hills and undergrowth held unseen menace and Ross could understand his nervousness. Even so, they were unlikely to cover the ten or twelve miles before the rains came. These limestone cliffs held many caves and he supposed even Pereira must need rest and shelter.

Was Joseph following, he wondered, as time passed and they were still fighting their way through bushes? It wasn't easy without the use of their hands and on the narrow track. Ross deliberately held back, allowing Juliet to make the pace, in spite of the oaths and buffeting he received from the man behind.

The torrential rain began on time and the heavens darkened with the fury of it. The path turned to mud and before long they were all fighting for breath, sliding half-blinded down the hillside. Helpless to protect their faces from the flailing leaves, Ross and Juliet ran the gauntlet of wind-lashed bushes that clung and slapped, drenching them fresh each time they struggled through. Juliet's sandals skidded in the mud, and without the support of her arms she staggered and fell full length onto the path, bringing Ross to a slithering halt, bearing back hard on the Portuguese.

"For God's sake, Pereira," he yelled into the wind, "find a shelter. We can't go on in this weather." He was down on his knees beside Juliet as he spoke.

It was too dark to see her face clearly but he guessed she had been dazed by the fall for she lay still, her cheek in the mud, her breathing labored. He looked up at Pereira, his eyes brilliant points of light in his angry face.

"This is madness. We shall all break our necks before we've done five miles. The rain will ease later. We must wait until then."

Pereira waved his gun. "Go on. I order you to."

Ross stood up. "Don't be a fool, man. She can't go on any further without a rest. She'll have to be carried and I can't do that with my hands tied."

"Stand away," ordered Pereira and went down on one knee beside Juliet. "Get up! I give you an order."

Juliet's eyelids fluttered and her eyes opened slowly. She blinked into the rain and Ross saw the rubbed marks of the gag on her cheeks. His anger rose.

"And while you're down there, Pereira, you can remove that damned gag from her mouth. Breathing is hard enough without that."

Pereira looked up to see Ross towering over him. The gun barrel swiveled.

"Get back."

"My hands may be tied but my legs aren't," Ross said menacingly. "If you don't remove that gag, I'll boot you down the entire bloody hillside!"

Pereira stared at him for a moment, then hauled Juliet into a sitting position. With her body between them he felt for the knot in the cloth and removed the gag, tossing it aside. He rose, glaring at Ross.

"There! I do this favor because I am a human man. Now we move on."

"Not yet. There is a rock face down the track a little. If there's an opening, Lady Juliet will rest. Pick her up and follow me." Without waiting for an answer, Ross pushed through the bushes.

Pereira's mouth opened and closed in frustration. He was tempted to empty his gun into the receding back but fear of the consequences held him back. The Vizier would have him flayed if all he could deliver was a dead man. He growled in his throat and dragged Juliet to her feet, pushing her in front of him as he strove to keep the tall figure in sight.

When Ross stopped, they were close

behind. He nodded to a flat ledge down into
the rock. "Help the lady up there, Pereira.
There's enough overhang to keep the worst
of the rain off all of us for a time. It should
ease off in an hour or two."

"Don't give me orders," snarled Pereira,
with the desperate anger of a weak man.
"Why should I help her?"

"Because I can't, you fool!" snapped
Ross. "If my hands were free I wouldn't let
you come within a mile of her. The longer
she rests, the sooner we'll set off again.
Haven't you any sense?"

As Pereira glowered in indecision, Juliet
spoke. "Don't bother. I can manage by myself. I would as soon he didn't touch me."
She wriggled herself onto the ledge, grim-
acing at the pain in her bruised shoulder.
"Thank you, Ross, for getting that filthy
rag out of my mouth." Should she reveal
Pereira's duplicity over the gagging, she
wondered? But common sense held her
silent. Ross didn't need the bitter
knowledge that his willing surrender had
brought about no change in Pereira's plans
for her future.

Ross saw her brave smile in the gloom
and, on an impulse, bent to kiss her gently,
feeling the swollen lips under his own.

"Stand away," ordered Pereira, trying to
regain his authority.

"Go to hell!" Ross said and turned his
back on the Portuguese.

Pereira simmered in silence for the next

hour, occupying his mind with thoughts of
what the Vizier had in mind for this insolent Englishman. But more pleasurable
by far were his own erotic plans for the girl.
Why hadn't she told the captain, when the
gag had been removed, that her future was
not to be in the palace but as the woman of
Pereira? The thought nagged at him like a
aching tooth. Why did she hold the knowledge to herself? He would have expected
her to reveal their conversation at the first
opportunity. Why hadn't she? The answer
was so simple he almost laughed aloud. The
captain's gold, of course! It would be no use
to the captain where he was going. The girl
obviously felt entitled to her share but was
loathe to shatter the captain's high opinion
of her character. Let the captain go happily
to his fate, secure in the knowledge that he
had bargained for her safety, and then it
would be a different story. With the gold in
his own possession, he would be invested
with all the qualities of the Englishman! She
would come readily enough to him then!

"Shall we move on?" said a bored voice in
his ear, and he jumped, coming sharply
back to reality. "The rain's almost stopped
and the sky is clearer."

Pereira scrambled to his feet, hiding his
grin. The poor misguided fool was in a
hurry to meet his fate. Did he expect to see
the girl safely in the palace before he kept
his appointment with the Vizier?

With Juliet once more in the lead, they

struggled on down the hillside. With the slackening of the rain, they could see better, but Ross was in no hurry to leave the sheltering trees and kept the pace deliberately slow. If they reached sea level by dawn, he must contrive they pause before moving into the open where they might be observed by other searching parties. There had to be some way he could leave Juliet behind. In spite of Pereira's assurances in return for the gold, the man might seek to make extra profit by consigning Juliet to the slave market anyway. For some reason Pereira had lost his first edginess and no longer thrust the gun barrel into Ross's back as he had done constantly before they rested. What, Ross wondered, had brought about this subtle change in the man? There was an air of smugness he distrusted.

He stared at the sky, noting the first stars and trying to gauge the miles they had traveled. Perhaps not as many as they seemed but he hoped Joseph was somewhere behind, guided by their noisy progress. He could trust Joseph to get Juliet aboard a British ship in some disguise or other, if it were possible to divert Pereira's attentions and allow the party to be split. Ross thought of the knife Selim had tucked in his sash. He couldn't recall seeing it on the body when Pereira had rolled him over, and Pereira didn't have it. Was it at the bottom of the pool? Or was it now the possession of Joseph? And if Joseph were following . . . ! He took a deep breath. Was it wise to feel more hopeful? Joseph had survived so far by his wits but he was a gentle man and his Catholic upbringing would inhibit him taking a life—even Pereira's.

They rested once more and this time it was Pereira who fell to his knees. Ross watched him sardonically as he waved the guns, indicating his permission for them to sit. By his gasping and wheezing, Ross guessed that the Portuguese had never taken so much exercise in his life. Juliet seemed to have recovered from her fall and she smiled at Ross as they sat with their backs to the trees. Her clothes were soaked and the rain had partially washed the mud from her face, but she was pale and her hair hung wetly round her cheeks. Ross found to his surprise that these observations were possible in the light of early dawn. He stared upwards to where the moon had paled and the stars were no longer visible, and realized they had walked all night.

It grew lighter as they moved on, and the warmth of the rising sun took the clamminess from their clothes. The ground flattened out and the bushes thinned. Trees were getting fewer and the earth became mixed with pebby sand. Only a few limestone rocks were left of the hills. With a few hundred yards to go before emerging

within sight of the sea, Ross knew that
their only chance was to remain under cover
on the hillside.

He glanced over his shoulder at Pereira.
The man's face was practically puce and he
was sweating heavily, his feet stumbling
and catching at rocks.

"Better stop for a rest, Pereira," said Ross.
"You're on the verge of a heart attack."

Pereira's voice came wheezily. "Move on,
we're not stopping." He jabbed the gun
barrel viciously into Ross's back.

Ross sidestepped quickly to avoid the
thrust and his boot caught in a looped tree
root. He staggered, off balance. The boot
held, then released itself so rapidly that
Ross had no chance to right himself. His
body twisted and he spun away from the
tree to fall heavily onto a ridge of limestone.
Without the use of his hands to break his
fall, his forehead met the rock with stunning force.

Juliet heard his groan and swung round,
her face full of alarm. "Ross!" she screamed
and ran back towards him, falling to her
knees. Her eyes went to Pereira. "What
happened? Did you knock him down?" Her
gaze was fiercely accusing.

"I didn't touch him! The fool fell over a
root. Get up, both of you. Now!"

"He can't. He's unconscious. "Oh, God,
look at the blood on his head!"

Pereira peered down suspiciously. "It's a

trick. Get up man!" He aimed a kick at
Ross's leg but there was no reaction. He
stared with impotent fury, his chest
heaving. There was no doubt the captain
was genuinely unconscious. All they could
do was wait until he came round. He wiped
his sticky face with the back of his hand
and gestured to the girl to come away.
"Leave him alone. Take the chance of a rest
in the shade." He indicated a clump of
bushes. "Sit there where I can watch you
both. We've come so far and I don't intend
losing either of you."

Juliet sank down thankfully on the
sparse grass and leaned her back against
the thick stem of the bush. With her hands
tied she could do nothing for Ross even had
they water and cloths. She closed her eyes
against the sun and listened to the sound of
the sea in the distance. After that nightmare journey through the hills in the wind
and rain, it was pleasant to sit relaxed, with
the sun drying out the once beautiful harem
garments. Lady Gabriella would lift her
hands in horror if she saw the mud-streaked
kaftan and wrinkled satin trousers. Her
mind drifted a little in the peace of the
morning with only the birds and the sound
of the sea to be heard.

But there was something else, her tired
mind acknowledged—a shifting sound, a
trickle of falling pebbles and the labored
breathing of a heavy body. Her eyelids
flickered reluctantly and she opened her

eyes, blinking. Pereira was closer than he had been. He was beside her now, his thick lips parted in what she supposed was a smile. She came fully awake, pushing herself away from the bush.

"Don't be alarmed, my little dove," he said. "It is only Angelo, your future master and lover. Until the clumsy fool recovers his senses we can't move on, but we can use this time alone to get better acquainted." He put a hand to her cheek and she flinched away. "A little sore where you fell, is it? When we reach my house I will soothe your entire body with the most fragrant oils. With my own hands I will draw your sweetness forth and make you glad to be Pereira's woman."

Juliet threw herself back as far as she could go. "Leave me alone," she gasped. "You promised Captain Jamieson. . ."

Pereira laughed. "How else could I persuade him to drop his gun? But you were wise not to speak of my original plan when you had the chance last night. I am more attractive with the captain's gold, isn't that so? We are two of a kind, my dear. We shall deal very well together. Let the fool keep his illusions. Play your part with a touching farewell, then we will take his gold and laugh at his simplemindedness. But enough of words. I can't wait to look on my reward."

He laid aside the gun and, to Juliet's horror, began to pull aside her kaftan. She

jerked away and in her haste lost the
support of the bush, falling back onto the
grass. He took her action for encouragement and began unfastening her shirt,
smiling down into her face.

"I knew you'd be willing," he grunted,
then his groping fingers were inside and
moving over her skin.

She brought up her knees but his legs
were heavier and he pinned her down, half
covering her body. With her shirt opened
wide, Pereira gazed down on her bared
breasts. He bent his head and a sick feeling
of total revulsion welled up in Juliet. The
thought of those gross lips on her breasts
brought a tearing scream to her throat. She
arched her back, trying to roll away from
the weight bearing down on her spine and
bound wrists.

"No, no! My back ... you're hurting
me ... cut me loose, for God's sake!"

"And have you rake my face in your
passion? Ah, no, little one. All I want is a
taste of your body. Later, you can fight and
claw me if that is your way of loving, but
now there is not enough time to show me
your harem tricks." He took her by the
shoulders and tried to cover her mouth with
his, but her threshing head made the
contact impossible. "Damn you, wench,
stop wriggling!" he roared in exasperation.

"Captain sahib, wake up! Wake up for
sake of Holy Mother and memsahib!"

From the depths of nothingness, Ross's mind registered a disturbance. His ear was assailed by a murmur that went on and on, and the constant vibrating of his shoulder sent the pain rocketing to his head. His mind rose slowly and reluctantly, the voice drawing him upwards with the urgency of its tone. There was no avoiding the insistent pull of his senses, and his own mind caught the infection of panic. Through the mist of pain and fear he fought his way to the surface. The words began to make sense.

"Wake up, wake up, please Captain sahib! Memsahib having too much struggling. Other sahib very bad man. I cutting you free, sahib. Be hurrying, please, for Joseph not liking to take life, but memsahib good lady and pray Holy Mother to forgive Joseph Garcia."

Ross opened his eyes on the distraught face of Joseph. His head still throbbed but his wits were coming alive, and he felt the blood begin circulating through his numbed wrists. With Joseph's help he struggled to his feet, gasping as the sun struck his eyelids. His stare was hazy for a moment, then his eyes focused on the two struggling figures. He saw Pereira's hand rise, and the slap as it descended on Juliet's face drove all weakness from Ross's body. He forgot his throbbing head and flung himself with a roar of rage across the intervening space.

Pereira's head turned and his jaw sagged.

The man he had left bound and unconscious was hurtling towards him, his free hands bunched into fists and an expression on his bloodstained face that sent the blood flying from Pereira's own. He rolled away from Juliet and flung himself in panic upon the gun.

Ross saw the fingers close round the butt and threw himself full length at Pereira, reaching for the wrist. They closed with a thump of bodies and rolled down the incline. Pereira had the advantage of weight and lack of injury, but Ross clung grimly to the gun arm, evading the butting head and vicious knee. It was a fight to the death and they both knew it. Terror lent Pereira strength and he struck out with his free hand at the gashed forehead. He had the satisfaction of hearing his opponent's gasp of pain and the grip on his wrist slackened. He bore down in triumph until the gun barrel was between their bodies, then his finger sought the trigger. His hand bunched as he brought the barrel round.

Ross felt the rigid knuckles turn on his chest. He shifted his grip over Pereira's fingers and exerted the utmost pressure he could manage. But Pereira had no thought to delay. He pulled the trigger as Ross gave his last desperate heave to twist the barrel.

The explosion was stunning. Birds rose crying and wheeled out to sea. The acrid smell of cordite hung on the air. Pereira sank down, and Ross, still grasping the gun hand, sank down with him, his legs collapsing beneath him. There was a moment of utter, mind-numbing silence, then Ross unclasped his hand. Pereira fell backwards, the blood seeping from his chest. There was blood on Ross's tunic and he gazed at it blankly, his mind emptied by the explosion. He was on his knees, motionless, when the outside world moved in with a rush of wings and the whisper of footsteps on sand. He turned his head vaguely towards the sound. Juliet, her kaftan flying, was stumbling unsteadily down the beach, her grey eyes enormous in her pinched face. The first to reach him was Joseph. He squatted before Ross, his dark skin greytinged.

"Captain sahib, you are hurt? There is much blood."

Ross moved his body experimentally. "No, Joseph, I don't think so. It must be Pereira's blood. Is he dead?"

"He is being very dead, sahib."

"Better keep the memsahib away, then. Dead men aren't very pretty."

"She not taking notice of me, sahib. She coming see you not dead also."

Ross grinned weakly at the Indian. "I'll be damned if I ever met anyone like her!" He looked up as Juliet came to a halt, to stare down in breathless silence. "It's all right," he said quickly. "Pereira's blood, not mine." He rose stiffly and put his arms round her. "Did the bastard hurt you?"

She shook her head. "He didn't have the time for what he intended. He lied to you, Ross, about getting me into the palace. I was to be his reward for capturing you. I couldn't tell you then because of the gag, and later there seemed no point."

"God damn the bastard! I hope he rots in hell!" He stared over her head at the body and felt a surge of savage joy at the killing.

Pereira lay with his eyes closed, his lips drawn back in a rigid grin of triumph. His hand still clutched the gun. An unlikely suicide, Ross supposed, and one he doubted the Vizier would believe. He turned Juliet away gently and bent, reaching into Pereira's pocket for the gun he had surrendered. Joseph helped him drag the body to the shelter of a bush.

"We must be leaving this place, sahib," Joseph said. "Much walking to do to be catching ship."

"You're right, Joseph. By the way, how did you come by the knife? I thought it was in the pool."

"Yes, sahib, I take it from there. I am seeing peoples come to cave and wondering what I shall be doing. I see Arab come to pool and drink long time from goatskin bag, then he go to be filling from pool. He seems most dizzy and fall down, hitting head on rocks. Then he lie down for bathing bump on head. He putting face in water and I go to be helping keep face there. He not liking too much but after little time he not minding anymore. I hear someone coming so I go to hiding. I see you and memsahib and this very bad other sahib with gun, so I follow."

"Thank God you did, Joseph. You saved our lives."

"Thank you, Joseph. We should have been lost without you," Juliet said, smiling warmly at him.

"But still long way to catching ship, sahib and memsahib."

"Right again, my friend. We'd best be moving."

It was a slow procession that moved through the hillside. They kept within the protection of the trees as far as possible. Joseph ranged ahead, guiding them on the track he had used himself between the harbor and the cave. He collected a few oranges and bananas on the way, and these helped to quench the pangs of hunger and thirst. By the time they glimpsed Zanzibar in the distance, the afternoon was well-advanced.

Joseph turned. "I not thinking harbor safe, Captain sahib, so we go to village down coast some little way. Indian fishing man live nearby and he watch out for you if you give him gold piece. He not liking Arab peoples too much so you be waiting safe while I go to see if ship coming yesterday."

The sun was down when Joseph, moving like one of the shadows now stretching over the village, lef them and returned a few minutes later with his Indian friend.

"Gupta has nice fish curry for you, sahib,
while you wait. He say that ship in harbor
is English one so I go quickly to speak to
captain and tell him of these bad things. I
have message safe in my turban, sahib, and
soon I will come back to be fetching you."

Gupta led them into his hut and served
them food. He spoke no English, but
beamed on them as they ate his curry and
accepted large mugs of thick, sweet coffee.
He acknowledged their thanks and Ross's
gold coin with equal pleasure, then
gestured to the sleeping mat in the corner.
But Ross was too restless to sleep although
his bones ached intolerably and the wound
on his forehead stung. He tried to persuade
Juliet to rest but she refused.

"If I close my eyes now I shall sleep for a
week," she said. "I'd rather be on the beach
where I can see the lights of the harbor.
Let's go outside, Ross. If anyone comes I
don't want to be caught in here."

Gupta's hut was far enough from the
village for them to be unobserved as they
walked on the sand, their eyes constantly
turning to the harbor. Ross noted the tide
flowing southerly and supposed the captain
of the ship must be aware of it too, unless
he planned to extend his stay. Had Joseph
got aboard or had he been turned away?
Whichever the case he should be returning
soon. Had it been wise to let him go alone?
But a six foot tall Englishman in a

bloodstained tunic would have created too
much interest, especially if the Vizier had
his Janissaries still guarding the foreign
ships.

The moon was rising and there was still
no sign of Joseph. There had been time for
him to get there and back. Had the Vizier
caught him or had a ship's officer dismissed
his plea for an interview with the captain?
He paced the sands, frowning.

Juliet gasped suddenly. "Ross, look!"

He wheeled round and followed her gaze
to the harbor. A light blossomed on the
main mast of a ship, and in its glow he could
see the breeze catch the aft canvas and
spread it wide. The ship was standing off,
preparing to sail. Her anchor must be
slipped. She was putting out to sea!
Zanzibar had the only dock for a trading
vessel. There was no other on the island.
What in God's name had happened?

He watched in disbelief as the ship
showed more canvas, then the tide took her
and she glided down the coast. The breeze
flung back her pennon, and the moon
identified her as an East Indiaman. Her
stern lantern glowed, dimmed and faded as
if a curtain had dropped. Then she was
gone, lost in the velvet backness of night.

XXI

Juliet slid her hand into Ross's and leaned her head on his shoulder.

"This isn't what you expected, is it, Ross? What did you say in your message?"

Ross turned a slightly dazed look at her. "I can't understand what in hell happened. I explained the presence of three survivors of the 'Grace,' the captain, his wife, and the third one being the bearer of the note. I asked his help to rescue us. I left the rest to the man's own ingenuity. I can only imagine the message didn't get through or Joseph wasn't able to convince him."

"I wonder where Joseph is now? The harbor looks quiet. Perhaps he was aboard."

"And perhaps they handed him over to the Janissaries as a runaway slave." Ross said bitterly. "I wonder if Gupta can lend me a burnoose of sorts? You'll be quite safe with Joseph's friend until . . ."

"Ross Jamieson!" interrupted Juliet
forcibly. "If you think I'm staying with
Gupta while you go to the harbor, then I
may tell you that nothing is further from
my mind! If you go, I go. I refuse to be left
here, wondering what is happening!"

She turned away and began to walk down
the beach. Ross followed, taking her arm
and leading her towards Gupta's thatched
hut.

"Be reasonable, Juliet. . ."

"I am reasonable. You can't make me
stay. I am not your wife to order about,
whatever you pretended in your message.
If you are taken, then I shall surrender
myself to the Vizier, but I need to know
what   is   happening.   Don't   you
understand?"

Ross pulled her round and enclosed her in
his arms. He was smiling. "I understand
you're a stubborn wench, and wife or not,
you'll never take orders from any man if it
doesn't suit you." He raised his gaze suddenly. "What the devil was that?"

"What is it, Ross?"

"I thought I saw a light out to sea. It's
gone now but we'd best get under cover."
He looked round. "Those dunes. Get down
behind them. It might be a corsair boat
heading into Zanzibar."

They raced over the sand and flung themselves behind a hillock of spindly grass.
Across the quiet waters, Ross's ear caught

the muted sound of oars. Lying so low on the ground he noted a clear distinction between sea and sky. Something was marring the straight horizon, something small and fairly low in the water. It had no mast and whatever it was moved cautiously and without lights. His first thought was of the Vizier, learning their position from a brutal interrogation of Joseph, sending out his corsairs to trap them stealthily.

He could see the boat now with four men bent to the oars. A fifth, dark and turbaned, looked out from the prow. They were turning, making for the beach. Only Gupta's dwelling, somewhere behind them, showed a dim light. The turbaned man gestured towards it, and the boat swung, running up onto the beach. The hull grated on the shingle and the man scrambled over the side followed by a second who held the painter wrapped round his hand.

Ross eased the gun from his tunic. The turbaned man made a wide sweep, approaching Gupta's home silently. He disappeared inside. A few minutes later he reappeared to stare about the beach. The four men in the boat remained silent as the man began casting about, moving barefoot over the sand. A soft whisper floated on the night air.

"Captain sahib. Pleasing to come much quickly for Joseph. Do not be hiding long time for ship having trouble to wait. Current much strong for holding anchor."

Juliet gave a muffled gasp, her white face turning to Ross. She saw his teeth flash in a grin then he was on his feet, pulling her with him.

"Joseph! No Arab on this benighted island could speak so fetchingly and with the tongue of angels. For Joseph we come much quickly and with the greatest of pleasing."

They crossed the strip of sand at a run and the seaman holding the painter came to attention. "Captain and Mrs. Jamieson, sir? Captain Daly of the 'Alice' sends compliments and requests your attendance on board."

"Accepted with gratitude, lad. Lead on."

The seaman grinned and looked curiously at the small figure in the bedraggled harem trousers and stained kaftan. Juliet smiled at him as he helped her into the rowing boat.

"Thank you. I may look like a refugee from the harem but I assure you that I am quite as English as you are. You sound like a Devon man to my Somerset ears."

"Yes, ma'am. That I am and proud of it though Somerset be a nice place too," he assured her earnestly, settling her on the side plank with extreme tenderness.

Bedraggled she might be, thought Ross with amusement, but all four seamen were saluting her with the respect due to a lady, and it had nothing to do with their supposition that she was a captain's wife.

The journey back to the ship was accomplished more easily with the tide in their favor. Juliet stared over the water, waiting for the bulk of the 'Alice' to come into sight. The bobbing of the small boat was giving rise to a distinct feeling of nausea in the pit of her stomach and her head was throbbing, but she must not disgrace herself by being sick, she resolved.

The tall side of the ship loomed suddenly before them. Juliet stared up and saw the swinging rope ladder. She cast a glance at Ross and he saw the sick horror in her eyes.

"Hold her first, boys," he said quickly. "My wife has never boarded a ship this way before. I'll follow as a cradle in case her hands slip."

"Yes, sir." The seaman hung onto the ladder, making it as rigid as possible as Juliet forced herself to grip the rope.

Ross kept his feet one rung below but his hands gripped the side ropes just beneath hers. With his entire body cradling hers, they moved up slowly. It seemed an endless journey to Juliet and her body ached with tension but knowing Ross was preventing her falling gave her the strength to reach the top where hands drew her over the rail. She found herself supported by strong arms as her knees began to buckle.

Ross landed on deck, and the chest she was leaning on rumbled into sound. "Good grief, Jamieson! If I hadn't known you were coming I should have taken you for one of those corsair fellows with your beard and all. Your wife's about all in by the look of her."

"We've had a rough passage, Daly, but thank God it's over now. I'll take her to a cabin."

"Everything's ready. Follow me."

"I'm all right," Juliet said faintly. "Just a touch seasick from the boat."

"Nevertheless I'll carry you," said Ross and swung her into his arms. "A good night's sleep and you'll feel better."

"You sound like Doctor Fernley. I'm so glad he went ashore in Mozambique. They would surely have killed him."

"I imagine the good doctor is back in Capetown by this time. At least half the crew survived those murdering corsairs, I'm happy to say."

Captain Daly flung open a cabin door. "Only single cabins, Ross. We don't cater for married couples. I never knew you were married for that matter, but you can tell me of your adventures over dinner."

Ross sat Juliet on the bunk. "Married in Capetown, Tom. I took Juliet on what was supposed to be a round trip to Mozambique but the storm carried us north and we hit a reef off the islands." He straightened up, smiling. "I hope you can provide me with a uniform. Then I'll consign this outfit to the blessed deep."

Captain Daly grinned. "I can kit you out but not your lady wife. Your cabin's next door. I'll send a spare uniform along. We're pretty much the same size."

"Thanks, Tom. I'll join you later."

"Hot water in the cubicle, ma'am, and if you've no objection to wearing a nightshirt of mine, I'll have Ross bring one in."

"Thank you, Captain Daly. I should be most obliged."

The captain bowed and left them alone. Juliet smiled up at Ross.

"Safe and on our way to Capetown. We'll have to concoct a story to account for your presence there. Tom Daly is bound to ask how we met. The 'Alice' left Bristol for China shortly before the 'Grace' and he knows I wasn't married then."

"I suppose I could have been staying with friends in Capetown when your ship put in."

"There's a Mrs. Martell, widow of an old captain of mine, who made her home in Capetown. I usually call on her when I'm in port. She'd be the very person you might be visiting—her great niece, Miss Juliet Martell, a young lady I swept off her feet and married in a matter of days." He grinned down at her. "Would that do?"

Juliet laughed. "Very well, I should think, to satisfy Captain Daly, but if I were Miss Juliet Martell, I should certainly sue for divorce after such a disastrous honeymoon trip! Are you sure Captain Daly doesn't know your Mrs. Martell?"

"Quite sure. Captain Martell died when I

was about eighteen. That's seven years ago and I know Daly never sailed with him. By the way, how old are you? I never thought to ask."

Juliet considered. "If this is April, I rather think I'm seventeen."

"Seventeen? So young. I can see Tom Daly making capital of my sweeping off a seventeen year old after only a short acquaintance."

"I dare say you'll be able to bear his teasing until we reach Capetown. After that, it won't matter. Now, I think I'll take that bath and wash Zanzibar away for good."

Ross nodded. "Me, too. I'll drop in with the nightshirt and bring you a tray of supper."

As Juliet soaped her hair, she was reminded of the first time she had taken a bath on the 'Grace.' So long ago—and yet she was as much in the same predicament regarding her clothes. She couldn't possibly wear the harem garments again until she had washed them.

She was on her knees rinsing the clothes with the towel knotted under her arms when there was a knock at the door.

"Juliet? It's Ross," And he came in to find her as he had once done before. As their eyes met, they were both remembering the first time, but there was no anger in his face nor fear in hers.

"Your servant, ma'am," Ross said, smiling. "Though I would adorn thee in cloth of gold and the plumes of herons, I bear only Tom Daly's second best nightshirt. Unfortunately, he has no orders to put into Mozambique so your shopping must wait until we reach Capetown.''

Juliet rose, smiling, and indicated the pendant and bracelets of Lady Gabriella. "I should think those might cover a new wardrobe for the destitute Miss Juliet Martell.''

Ross laid down the tray he was carrying and tossed the nightshirt on the bunk. "Don't you want to keep those? I can buy you whatever you require. I owe you a very great debt and would like to begin repaying it in every way I can.''

"I appreciate your concern but there is not the slightest need to feel that you owe me anything. As long as I am thought to be dead, I can return to England and begin a new life. I will keep up this charade until we reach Capetown, then we may part as friends. As you said yourself, I have a respectable future ahead of me and with that jewelry and the pearls off the kaftan, I shall be comfortably placed when I reach England.'' She kept her smile in place as she regarded his changed appearance. "May I say that you look very much more like a sea captain than you did when we came aboard.''

She eyed the clean-shaven face and well-brushed hair with a steadiness she was far from feeling. The uniform set him apart from the Ross she had known and loved so dearly, but she must begin to put that part of her life behind her, however hard it would be. He was not responsible for anything that had happened to her. She had to make it plain that she expected nothing once they reached Capetown. Her past could be hidden from strangers but not from the man who had taken delivery of a consignment of convicts, bound for exile. That fact must always stand between them.

The blue eyes regarded her somberly for a moment. "We shall reach Capetown in about a week. Meanwhile, eat your supper and get to bed. Give me those wet clothes and I'll have the captain's steward dry and press them for morning. Goodnight, Mrs. Jamieson." He smiled slightly and left the cabin.

Juliet did as she was told and slept soundly until midmorning the next day. A tap on the door heralded Joseph, bearing a breakfast tray and her newly pressed clothes.

"Good morning, memsahib. It is very good day, yes?" He beamed on her happily.

"A most splendid day, Joseph, and one I never thought to see." Juliet tossed back her hair and sat up, smiling at him. He was wearing fresh clothes and he, too, had shaved off his beard. "I had no time to thank you last night but your appearance on that beach filled me with great happiness. Did you find it difficult to board the ship?"

"No, memsahib. I meeting other Goanese

boys and they take me aboard. Captain Daly sahib is knowing my captain sahib and he say too much risk to fetching you in harbor so he pretending to leave, then putting out lights and lowering boat. I hoping you stay with Gupta or I not knowing what to do. But you coming nearby so all is being very good. I looking after you, memsahib, till we coming Capetown, then captain sahib say he let me go on next Company ship to Goa. I thinking maybe I stay there long time. Captain sahib is giving me much gold."

Juliet laughed. "You can buy your wife a whole stall of sweets then, Joseph, to make up for your absence."

He bobbed his head, grinning, and brought out a large bone comb from his pocket. "Captain Daly sahib says to be giving you this, memsahib, and this also." He searched in another pocket and produced a toothbrush and a tin of tooth powder. He laid them on the chest of drawers and bowed himself out.

Juliet swung her legs out of the bunk and stood up. Her stomach seemed to do a somersault and she clutched the bunk, her head swimming. There was a feeling of nausea in her throat and she staggered into the cubicle to bathe her suddenly hot brow. She knelt beside the tin bath, her arms on the rim, until the feeling passed. Surely she couldn't still be feeling seasick? Of course not! How stupid, she told herself, not to have considered the natural outcome of all those nights of passion with Ross. A girl who gave herself so gladly to a man had only herself to blame if she became pregnant. And without a doubt, she was with child. She laid her cheek on her arms, pondering on her predicament. Ross mustn't know. That much was certain. Neither could she revert to being Miss Martell on her journey back to England. In the absence of a husband, she could only assume the identity of a suddenly bereaved young wife, returning to her homeland to bear the posthumous child of a husband struck down in young manhood by accident or tropical disease. She raised her head. The 'Alice' was on her way to England. She could stay on board. But here she was Mrs. Jamieson. It would be thought very odd for a newly married couple to part in Capetown at the end of their honeymoon. It would be better to disembark and take a later ship on which no one knew her as Mrs. Jamieson. But if there was a long delay her pregnancy might well become obvious and a passage refused. She shook her head and sighed, rising slowly to wash and dress. Capetown was a week away. Time enough to work out some plan.

Ross tapped on her door as she was combing her hair. "Would you like to take a stroll on deck?" he asked. "It's not too hot at this hour."

"Won't I look a little strange to the officers dressed like this?"

"They all know you lost your entire ward-robe when the 'Grace' went down so they are quite prepared to see an exotic Mrs. Jamieson on my arm." As Juliet hesitated he went on. "It would look even stranger if my wife refused to walk with me on deck. Come, let's play out the game until we reach Capetown. I only ask that you keep up the appearance of married bliss for both our sakes. I will not intrude on your privacy. You have my word on it."

Juliet bent her head to pick up the kid-skin plait and to hide the pain she felt at his words. He had accepted the release she offered last night but was prepared to play his part in the masquerade until the necessity was over. She tied back her hair and turned to him, a bright smile on her face.

"After so long in the harem, I feel I should veil myself in the presence of men."

Ross smiled. "You would disappoint them. They look forward to meeting you and the outfit is really most fetching. They'll find you enchanting."

As I do, he thought, and gritted his teeth to stop the words coming out. Enchanting, lovable—and so very desirable, but deter-minded to put the past behind her. A re-spectable future, she had said, reminding him of his own words. Did that future include a solid, respectable husband, a man to whom Juliet's past was a closed book? Was that what she wanted? To sever all links with the 'Grace' and himself? To wipe clean the slate of her life?

Over the next few days Ross found it increasingly hard to keep his temper as the officers of the 'Alice' made plain their admiration for Juliet. Only respect for her supposed status kept their attentions within bounds. Leaning on the deck rail, Ross found himself unable to join in the talk and laughter, but watched sourly as Juliet captivated them all. Dammit, he thought in sudden alarm, what if she were to prefer one of them? He turned abruptly and stared out to sea. Another man holding that silken body in his arms? Another man sharing the joy and humor of Juliet? Another man adoring her body as he had adored her under the goathair rug, or lapped in the sparkling water of the pool in the hills of Zanzibar?

"Stop glowering, Ross," came the amused voice of Captain Daly. "Let my men enjoy the delightful company of your wife while they've the chance. Not one of them will step out of line—you can be sure of that. Come to my day cabin and join me in a tot of something. Besides, I want you to read your own obituary!"

"My what?" Ross's brows shot up.

Captain Daly laughed. "Knew that would make you sit up. I've just come across it myself." As they descended to his cabin, he went on, "I had the paper from the captain of a Company ship. I'd just put in from

China and he was on his way here. It's a few months old but it reports the loss of the 'Grace' up the Mozambique Channel." He indicated the newspaper as they entered the cabin. "Not every man lives to read his own obituary." He chuckled and poured out two tots of rum.

Ross accepted the drink and read the account of his death. He looked up at the captain. "I lost some good men there, Tom, not to mention a bunch of convicts they ordered me to carry."

Captain Daly nodded. "I know how you feel, Ross, but it's one of the chances we take when we sign on." He drained his glass. "I'm due on the bridge. No need to go. Relax and get yourself up to date with the world." He grinned down at Ross. "Don't worry. I'll keep an eye on that captivating wife of yours."

Ross leaned back in the leather chair and crossed his long legs, determined to put Juliet out of his mind and concentrate on the newspaper. He read every word doggedly until he reached the obituary page again, but it might have been written in Chinese for all the impact it made. He was about to cast it aside when a name at the foot of the obituary column sprang out at him. Westover!

He scanned the brief paragraph. "Sir George Westover, Baronet and Justice of the Peace who lost his life in a fire which completely gutted Westover House in the county of Somerset, was buried today."

Ross sat back, stunned. God in heaven! Juliet would be distraught! Now that she was free to return to her father, he was dead and her home destroyed! She would have to be told and the only person to do it was himself. He left Captain Daly's cabin with the newspaper tucked under his arm and a determination to break the news gently. The sun had lost its radiance and the shadows grown long over the decks before he tapped on Juliet's door.

Juliet had been staring pensively out of her porthole for a long time since returning to her cabin. She had seen Captain Daly take Ross away and he had gone without a backward glance. Although the sun still shone and the officers of the 'Alice' continued their pleasantries, the day had grown dark and desolate for her. Ross seemed content to withdraw into the background, to watch impassively, his expression so reminiscent of those first months on the 'Grace' when his regard was cold and distant. During these last few days they had lost the laughter and companionship they shared on the island. It was inevitable, she supposed. They were back in the real world and Ross had to think of his career.

Without moving from the porthole, she gave him permission to enter, glancing over her shoulder as he closed the cabin door. He leaned against it without speaking and the blue eyes regarded her gravely. She looked

at the newspaper in his hand and forced her
lips to smile.

"Have you come to tell me that England is
at war and I cannot return home?"

He shook his head without returning her
smile. "No, we are not at war, but I have
some equally bad news to tell you ... very
much worse, in fact, from your personal
standpoint."

Her fingers curled tightly over the rim of
the open porthole. "My personal standpoint?" she asked faintly. "In the newspaper?"

"I'm sorry, Juliet. I don't know how to
tell you kindly. It concerns your father. I'm
afraid he died in a fire at your home, and the
house was burnt to the ground."

The grey eyes stared into his for a dazed
moment. "My father is dead?" She turned
her head away and stared unseeingly over
the ocean.

Ross took a step forward. He had the
urge to hold her close, comfort her in the
grief she must be feeling, but the rigid set
of her shoulders held him back.

"I'm sorry, Juliet. I had to tell you. I
couldn't let you sail on to England without
knowing of your loss of a beloved
father. . ."

He was unprepared for her reaction as
she swung round abruptly. Her face was
full of anger and her wide eyes glittered
with contempt.

"Beloved father!" she said harshly. "I

hated him! From the moment I was born he despised me because I was a girl. He treated my mother so brutally that she went in fear of her life. He drank and gambled away every penny we had until we lived worse than the poorest farm laborer. For what he did to my mother and me, I could never forgive him. I'm glad he's dead, do you hear?" She stumbled to the bunk and flung herself onto it, the tears streaming down her face. She raised her head once to glare at Ross. "You've done your duty, Captain Jamieson. Now you may go away and be glad you're not really tied to such an unfilial creature!"

Instead of obeying, Ross knelt by the bunk and took Juliet's hands in his. "My dear, sweet girl, I am tied to you more securely than if we'd been joined in church." The blue eyes rested on her face intently. "Would you care to make it legal?"

Juliet regarded him suspiciously. "You don't have to do the noble thing and make an honest woman of me. The situation has not changed. I can still go to England."

"I know, my darling, but I'd much rather you married me in Capetown."

"There is no need to feel sorry for me. . ." Juliet began huskily.

"I don't. I love you most desperately, as I found out on the island. I can see no future happiness without you. Will you marry me, Juliet . . . if only to discard the name of the man you hate?"

"But you can't . . . you shouldn't . . . I'm still a felon. . ." she protested, striving to stem the tide of love sweeping over her.

"God in heaven!" exploded Ross. "I don't give a damn for your background, but I know you didn't kill your mother whatever the court said."

"You told me you didn't read those papers," she whispered.

"I didn't, but I'm not a fool, child. The guard who brought you to the ship mentioned a very young girl who had been convicted of killing her mother. You've just become seventeen as you told me when we boarded the 'Alice.' From what you've said of your father, I imagine his violence was responsible for your mother's death and he lied to the court out of dislike for you and fear for his own neck. Isn't that right?"

"Exactly right, but. . ."

"Can you put our time on the island right out of your mind? Tell me now that you can dismiss our love completely and I will leave you in peace to create your own future."

"I could never forget that," she said softly and withdrew a hand to draw it gently down his cheek. "Never! But I can't let you sacrifice. . ."

Ross recaptured the hand. "Mrs. Jamieson," he said, with ominous calm, "if you won't say you'll take me within thirty seconds, I shall be tempted to force the issue in my own way. I adore you madly, my darling, and unless you want me to fall into a state of complete idiocy, I must beg you to tell me what you intend."

Juliet looked into the brilliant blue gaze and a smile began to grow in the dove-grey eyes. She rose, sliding her arms about his neck, and her warm breath brushed his cheek as she melted against his body.

"You once mentioned founding a dynasty," she murmured.

His arms closed about her waist. "Nothing would please my grandfather more. He's laird of a fine estate in Arbroath and the rift between us has long since been healed. Shall we begat a brude of Jamiesons to continue the line, my love?" His voice was full of gentle amusement.

"We have already made a start in that direction," Juliet said, softly.

The blue eyes stared down into hers. "And you were going to sail out of my life without telling me?"

"If you hadn't wanted me . . . yes."

Ross arms tightened. "Then for the sake of our dynasty, the sooner I get you bound hand and foot, my headstrong angel, the happier I shall be." And his lips came down firmly on hers.

The crack of billowing canvas came to them. Ross lifted his head, glancing out of the open porthole.

"We'll soon be in Capetown. The wind has changed."

"Indeed it has," Juliet murmured, drawing a hand down the hard tanned cheek. "A fair wind into the future."